Pip Fioretti lives in Sydney, and enjoys hiking, books, friends and family. *Bone Lands* is her first crime novel.

BONE LANDS

PIP FIORETTI

affirm
press

For Max

Aboriginal and Torres Strait Islander people are advised that this book contains references to historical events that may be distressing.

affirm press

First published by Affirm Press in 2024
Bunurong/Boon Wurrung Country
28 Thistlethwaite Street
South Melbourne, VIC 3205
affirmpress.com.au

Affirm Press is located on the unceded land of the Bunurong/Boon Wurrung peoples of the Kulin Nation. Affirm Press pays respect to their Elders past and present.

10 9 8 7 6 5 4 3 2 1

 A catalogue record for this book is available from the National Library of Australia

ISBN: 9781922992864 (paperback)

Cover design by Luke Causby/Blue Cork © Affirm Press
Cover images by Inge, Leah-Anne Thompson, Ben and Mieszko9 via Adobe Stock
Typeset in Garamond Premier Pro by J&M Typesetting
Proudly printed and bound in Australia by McPherson's Printing Group

MIX
Paper | Supporting responsible forestry
FSC® C001695

'Your sheep that were wont to be so meek and tame, and so small eaters,
now, as I hear say, be become so great devourers and so wild, that they
eat up, and swallow down the very men themselves.'

Sir Thomas More, *Utopia*, 1516

July 1911
Darling Shire, New South Wales

1

Few men out this way need an excuse to drink, or to fight, for that matter. But celebrations were scarce, so when the new king, George V, was crowned, coronation balls and dances appeared like flies around a corpse. I'd fought for Georgie's old grandma, Vicky, in South Africa. Oh yes, I had a long relationship with our kings and queens, always drinking their health and singing about how long they might reign for and killing their enemies and drinking and singing some more. But tonight, my job, as a mounted trooper, was to keep the peace.

I was sent to police the coronation dance held in Larne, three hours north of my post in Calpa. The Larne trooper, Parry, and I put a stop to the odd fracas, threw some drunks in the lock-up and hung about on horseback looking suitably grim, coat collars up, faces in shadow, horses breathing out plumes of steam. Every man jack in that dance hall who came out for a piss at the edge of the light was guilty, and we'd find ways of proving it if they so much as turned a bleary eye our way.

By midnight, the new king was christened and his people staggered out of the hall, stained with piss and splatter, and trying to recall how they got here and why. Soaked in rum, reeking of carbolic and hot shearer's armpit – a stench so ingrained you'd have to chip it off with a chisel – some fell in the dirt and some on each other. I'd been in that state myself more than I care to admit and found nary a laugh in it, just tar-black shame, some of which still held fast to the inner walls of my skull.

Finally, the last of them set off and the words 'God Save the King', accompanied by screeches of laughter, faded into the silence. Cleaning the hall wasn't our job so we just locked up and grunted at each other. Parry set off to patrol the road north and I set off for Kitty's house on the edge of town to try my luck. She tossed me out an hour later. The punt man was still up, albeit in a filthy mood, but he took me across to the west of the river and I set off on the long ride south.

Silent forks of lightning flashed in the west. Rain was coming in, driving the dust before it. It would be a long ride before I reached my bed but I didn't mind all that much, sleep being a difficult pastime for me. My horse, Dancer, picked his way along the rutted road. I lounged in the saddle, pulled my oilskin closer as the rain hit, fat drops pelting down, then settling into a steady downpour. Soon my boots were full of water, my feet numb. Dancer was fed up, ears back, plodding along with his head down, sticky mud cleaving to his hooves. Water rushed along a ditch at the side of the road, rain hitting the parched ground loud as a train.

Out of habit I took notice of the fenceline, looking for breaks. Through the rain I noticed a whole section down, sagging wires and a fencepost uprooted. It looked fairly recent. No dead roos tangled in the wire. What could have been fresh wheel tracks led across the fenceline, over the sagging wire and up a low rise. No stock around, just saltbush and the odd clump of mulga.

I saw the cart on top of the rise, no horse in the traces. No people. The rain continued its steady pace. I dismounted, took my rifle out of its holster, stomach clenched tight, and walked over to what looked like a pile of wet washing.

A young woman, sprawled on the ground, her skirts torn and her legs twisted. Rain fell on her face, washing the blood away and leaving a mask of jagged bone, tendon and muscle. I felt for a pulse and then lurched away and vomited, glad no one was with me. I'd seen death many times as a soldier, but I'd never seen a woman so brutally bashed. Still shaking, I turned back to her, fairly certain I knew who she was, but the state of her face left some hope I was wrong.

With the cloud cover the night was dark, and in the back of the cart I found a lantern. I took it out and crouched under the cart, trying to get a match to strike, hand shaking. Once it was lit I straightened up, then walked over to another crumpled pile and held the lantern aloft, the raindrops glittering as they smacked into the body of a girl, a blanket tangled around her feet.

I squatted beside her. She was facedown in the mud, her hair loose and flowing in the rivulets like shining seaweed. There was a small hole in her back which had to be a bullet wound. I couldn't tell if she'd been raped and I didn't want to go looking. I checked her pulse. People sometimes take a while to die, but she was gone. Her skin was as cold as the mud she lay in.

Lantern shadows danced like spirits of the unshriven dead. Back at the cart I found a young man slumped by the rear wheel, the side of his head caved in, his hands in his lap, water and blood dripping from his face. I recognised him, and fought off the urge to throw up again. It was James Kirkbride, and the girls were his two younger sisters, Nessie and Grace.

God in his wasteland of a heaven – who would kill these three?

Rain hammered my face, trailed down my back, dripped from my hat. I wiped my eyes, blinked as my mind galloped around in useless circles. Three dead. Two females and a male. Three in the morning. I needed a doctor, I needed a tracker, more troopers. I needed a slug of whisky. I heard a noise and swung around, ready to shoot.

Nothing.

Thunder rumbled in the clouds above. There were four Kirkbride siblings – another sister, Flora. I searched, frantically pushing aside scrub, holding the lantern aloft, shouting her name, my words drowned by the rain. If she was here I couldn't find her, but I couldn't keep looking. Complete the mission first – that was a rule the soldier lived by, and it was still deeply embedded in my brain, despite frequent flushing with alcohol.

I checked my watch – ten past three – put the lantern back in the cart, went back to Dancer and mounted up. He didn't have much left in him but I set him at as fast a gallop as could be managed in the wet. I needed to raise the alarm, get telegrams off to Bourke, find the doctor and get back to the scene of the crime as fast as I could.

The rain kept up, a relentless drumbeat. I remembered the ripple and snap of the Union Jack over our camp. The Butcher's Apron, as it was known. The call to violence, the thrill of it. Until it was done unto you. The Boer who attacked me cut my face in two with a bayonet, from hairline to jaw, then went at my chest, my arms, anything he could get at, scything my flesh like wheat.

I was fighting because I was young and foolish. He was fighting for his land. That's why he went for my face, I reckon. But it wasn't even his land – it belonged to the Zulu. I was an Australian, fighting to take it back from the Boer and give it to the British, after the Zulu had been knocked out of the game. Make of that what you will.

~

I galloped the twelve miles into Calpa like the devil was on my tail, dragged the postmaster from his bed and watched him falter as I dictated the telegram to my boss in Bourke. I couldn't officially name the dead, not yet, so I just said 'bodies'. Next I woke the town doctor, Joe Pryor. I saddled a fresh horse, Felix, threw a blanket over the exhausted Dancer, then set off back up the road to the dead.

I heard a shout and looked over my shoulder. A dark-hooded figure on a black horse riding at me, on its way to the apocalypse. Dr Pryor, huddled under an oilskin.

'How far?' he shouted.

'An hour.'

By the time we got there the rain had stopped, the sky cleared, the cold winter night closed in, crickets clicking in the darkness. My uniform stuck to me, clammy and cold. The three bodies lay there in the mud, exactly as I'd left them, pitiful and full of reproach.

Joe, holding a lantern, walked from corpse to corpse, breath misting, his boots squelching in the mud. 'You know who they are,' he said, glancing up at me.

'James, Nessie and Grace Kirkbride.'

'Who the hell would do this?'

'Just declare them dead so I can cover them.'

'Should have sent for Reverend Hickson too, because by God there's been some evil done here.'

'He can wait. Start with Nessie. If you can.'

The black, silty mud dragged at our boots, and we floundered about, destroying evidence, but there was no help for it. The rain had already washed away so much of what would have been useful. The chatter of birds and the glow on the horizon signalled dawn, and we were still waiting for somebody, anybody, to come and assist. I checked my watch – nearly seven – and made a note of it. Joe sat wearily on a log and lit a cigarette.

I had to know if Flora was lying out here, dead or dying. I headed off into the patchy scrub, silently begging a God I had no time for to spare her and take me instead. My shouts raised no answer.

I heard Joe call out and froze. *He's found her.* If I stayed by this mulga long enough, the universe would right itself and Flora would come to me, pushing through the saltbush, a smile in her eyes, some broken bird cupped in her hands.

I hurried back, heart in my mouth. 'Flora?'

'No. Just … yeah, it's eerie out here.'

The men who'd done this were long gone, but I was armed and he wasn't. He held out a lit cigarette and I took it, inhaling a lungful of smoke with relief. As I sat beside him I noticed a circular, dirt-covered sliver in the mud. You don't see perfect circles in nature that often. Picked it up, wiped it on my breeches. A coin, thruppence.

'It's like the Breelong massacre,' Joe said.

'It's usually white raping black, not the other way round,' I said, sticking the coin in my pocket.

'True, but it happens. Were they at the dance in Larne?'

'I didn't see them.'

'Why the hell were they on this road? I would have thought they'd go to the ball in Cobar?'

Robert Kirkbride, their father, owned the biggest station in the districts, and was rich and influential, so his four children were like local royalty. Attending a stockmen's dance was unheard of for such a family. Joe was right: the Coronation Ball in Cobar was where they should have been. Cobar was a fairly wealthy mining town to the east, and you didn't get there travelling the western road along the Darling.

A couple of wallabies, raindrops on their fur sparkling in the light, watched us from a distance then slowly hopped away. Rabbits ran about. The sun glinted on puddles of water, steam rose off the wet horses, water dripped from the leopardwood. Three people dead on my watch –

except I hadn't been on watch. I'd been fucking the Larne schoolteacher.

'Can you tell what time they died?' I asked.

'Hard to say … maybe seven or eight hours ago.'

'Around midnight, then?'

'Or a bit earlier. Impossible to get an accurate time of death, unless you have a witness.'

We sat smoking in silence. I slipped my hand under the oilskin and inside my shirt. The tangle of knotted and raised scar tissue covered my chest from armpit to midline. In idle moments, my fingers always sought this gristly map, plucking and rubbing, tracing each welt from one end to another, as if still unable to grasp what had happened.

Joe got to his feet. 'Someone's coming.'

2

Birds fell silent. Rabbits disappeared, the sound of the hoofbeats, two horses maybe, louder. I took my pistol out of its holster. Sergeant Ernest Martin and Constable Mick Lonergan cantered over the rise.

'Hawkins,' Martin said, with a brisk nod. 'Telegram said you had some bodies.'

'Informally identified as James, Nessie and Grace Kirkbride, sir.'

The sergeant's mouth fell open and he looked past me to the cart on the rise. 'Was it an accident? Cart overturn?'

Martin, a knobbly man in his forties with a brain too small for even the mounted troopers, lifted the sheet from Nessie, saw her face and replaced it quickly, swallowing hard, and then looked at the other two. Lonergan had his rifle in his hands, scanning the scrub. The ferrous stench of blood filled the air. The horses whickered softly, nosing the ground.

My heart was pounding so hard I expected it to punch through my chest any moment. 'I'll get a couple of the trackers up here,' I said, appalled at the shakiness of my voice. 'They might be able to find something.'

Martin blinked, an unlit cigarette in his fingers. 'It's like Breelong.'

The Breelong massacre happened near Dubbo in 1900. Two women and three children, axed to death by a black tracker called Jimmy Governor. I'd been in South Africa at the time but the story had come up often during my training. People in the bush didn't forget events like that.

'The bodies will have to go to Cobar,' Joe said. 'They'll have to bring the coronial surgeon from Dubbo, so he'll need to be notified. Better talk to the Kirkbrides fast, before word travels. They're in Cobar too, for the ball.'

Martin nodded. Kept nodding, because if he stopped he'd have to do something, poor bastard. Telling parents their child was dead was a hell of a job, but telling them three of their children were dead, killed by some person or persons unknown – well, I actually felt some sympathy for him. But we couldn't stand around waiting for him to fire the starter's pistol. People had been murdered and we needed to crank up the great mechanism that turned the wheels of justice.

'Lonergan, go to Calpa, fast,' I said. 'Telegram Trooper Hardy in Cobar asking him to find Mr and Mrs Kirkbride and saying Sergeant Martin is on his way to speak to them. Tell him to organise a doctor too. And to check the whereabouts of Miss Flora Kirkbride. Urgently.'

'A doctor?' Martin said.

'Mrs Kirkbride might need sedating.'

Once he was back on his horse, Martin got a grip on himself. 'You wait for the ambulance van, Hawkins. There should be some troopers with them. Get them to guard the scene until relieved, then find the trackers and set them on this. And make sure they're not armed.' Then he set off through the mud.

Joe looked over at me, eyebrows raised.

'I wouldn't go looking for the bastards who did this without a gun,' I said. 'Why should the black trackers?'

'You weren't here when Breelong happened. The Mawbey women were just the first victims – Governor and his brother went on killing. People are going to be jumpy as cats when this gets out.'

He was right. It wouldn't take long for accusations to start flying. It was the blacks, it was Queenslanders, it was monstrous, and everyone was going to be killed in their beds. We resumed smoking, one fag after another, hands shaking. Cockatoos screeched and carried on above us. Sunlight shining on the puddled water.

I should have been there to save them. The shame almost took my breath away, like a punch to the guts. Police the roads and keep travellers safe, that was my job when in uniform. If I hadn't taken my uniform off to slip into Kitty's bed, I'd have been there to protect the Kirkbrides. Or I'd be dead alongside them, and at this moment, that looked to be the better option.

Finally the ambulance van came trundling down the road, accompanied by a several troopers. Once everything was loaded, Joe, white-faced and shaky, rode after the van. I put the troopers on watch and left them to it.

~

Chilled to the marrow, hungry and exhausted after being up all night, I rode back to Calpa feeling like a beaten old dog, eyes gritty, filled with a sense that I'd passed through a terrible dream. The sight of the whitewashed stone police station, with its ramshackle stable and yards, raised my spirits. Sleep or write a report first? The place would be swarming with police wanting details at any tick of the clock, so that settled it.

I'd been derelict in my duty and people had died. That was a detail hard to get past.

In the business part of the police station there was a chest-high bench, where the incident book was kept and all paperwork was laboriously carried out. Behind the bench and below the side window was my desk, where I composed reports no one read, then there were shelves of files no one looked in. Out the back to the right was the lock-up and armoury, and to the left was the door to the private quarters.

I stabled Felix and went in the back door, through the laundry to the kitchen and the station proper, sat at the desk and found a fresh sheet of paper, and put my head in my hands. Then I went back out across the muddy yard to the stable, buried my face in Dancer's warm neck and wept.

~

I must have fallen asleep on the straw because that was where I woke several hours later, stiff and aching, the stable cat curled up on my chest and the scent of fresh horse shit prodding me to wakefulness. Sleeping in a damp uniform on the cold floor of a filthy stable was only marginally better than sleeping in a ditch, and I cursed myself for a fool.

Aching and filthy, I trudged back across the yard and let myself in through the laundry door. I found a half-full whisky bottle behind the mangle, took a few gulps and felt the liquid course through me, soothing and numbing.

Trooper Lonergan was in the second narrow bedroom making a dog's breakfast of his bed. If he was here then it was real. The Kirkbride siblings were dead, and it was not some horrific dream. Lonergan was currently stationed at Bourke, a trooper for about two years. At twenty-one, he was ten years younger than me, although he looked about fifteen. Swarthy black Irish, of medium build, noted for being a capable horseman but dragged his feet on paperwork. Typical for a mounted trooper – we were catch and coerce, not thinkers, you could say. Give us a herd of camel to cull and we were off, merrily riding and shooting and to hell with your apostrophes.

I did not want Lonergan here, did not need him here. I'd run this one-man station for three years and, apart from the trackers, never needed any help from anyone. I certainly didn't want him in my private quarters, watching me drink, touching my books, messing up my woodheap and leaving his filthy footprints on my clean floors.

'Corcoran's posted me here, sir,' he said, giving me a wary glance. 'I'm to run the station while you escort the detectives from Sydney. Sir.'

'Run my station?'

'Yes, sir.'

'What detectives?'

15

'Here's the orders, sir,' he said, passing me a couple of telegrams.

The first telegram said that Mr and Mrs Kirkbride and Flora had been found safe in Cobar. Tears welled up and I quickly turned away, shamed by how easily they came these days. The second telegram confirmed what Lonergan said. Detectives from Sydney were on their way.

~

While I'd been conked out in the stable, Mrs Schreiber had made breakfast and left it in the kitchen. A pan full of her best sausages, all fried up and sitting in their own grease. I cut a hunk of bread, wrapped it around a sausage and put a pot of coffee on, then reheated the remaining sausages. Lonergan, sniffing the air like a dingo, waited by the door.

'They do a reasonable breakfast at the Royal,' I mumbled through a mouthful of sausage.

'How come you get a cook, sir?' he said, venturing closer.

'I pay for her, that's how. Share her with Dr Pryor.'

'Is she German, sir?'

'Related to the kaiser. So watch yourself. And don't make extra work for her.'

Lonergan scuttled away and I inhaled several more sausages. Mrs Schreiber, a heavy, big-boned woman, was a miner's widow from Cobar who'd raised ten kids and run a boarding house. She was so used to hard work, she told me, that she wouldn't know what to do with herself if she stopped. She called me Herr Kapitän, as that had been my rank in the army – being a German, she had more respect for that than the mounted

16

troopers. She made rice pudding with poached quince when she was in a good mood. When she wasn't, I got jelly with nothing. So it paid to keep her happy.

I drank another coffee, closing my eyes as it went down. Flora was safe. I felt better with a full belly, and I went to my room and stripped off, hurling the damp shirt and breeches at a chair and hanging up the tunic to dry, again giving silent thanks for Mrs Schreiber and her domestic skills. The navy wool tunic and its brass buttons took a beating out here, but the army discipline of immaculate turnout was deeply ingrained in me.

I splashed my face with warm water and looked in the mirror. Hair and beard the colour of dried grass, red-rimmed eyes gritty with lack of sleep, dark circles under them like empty waterholes. And the scar, running from the top of my forehead across my nose and cheek and ending at my jaw. My heavy beard hid some of it, but it remained a confronting sight, even to me.

A Chinese bloke I met at the Sofala gold diggings sold me a jar of ointment that he swore would make the scar better. Smelled like cat piss but I rubbed it on religiously. I turned my head this way and that, examining the scar from all angles. Fading to white now, the scar looked like someone had penned a line across my face, marking me absent.

~

Mounted trooper stations functioned in remote areas as government administration outposts as well as being the coercive arm of the law. The bushranger days were nearly over so manhunts were rare. We tracked down sheep and horse thieves, maybe an escaped prisoner here and there, locked up the drunk and disorderly, issued permits and licences, hauled in mad bastards from out bush for the Master of Lunacy, registered guns, rounded up truants, ran pests out of town, conducted inspections under the *Diseases in Sheep Act* and a hundred other government functions. I'd done them all, and much of the time did them with Wilson Garnet, the senior black tracker. But we'd never had to look for men who could kill like they'd killed the Kirkbrides.

I rode downriver to Wilson's camp. Puddles of water glittered in the sunlight. Ducks swarmed the river, squabbling and taking advantage of the rainwater. Wilson was a Barkandji man, a police tracker like his father had been. He was at his campsite by the river, what they called the Barka, along with the rest of his mob. Their land stretched north and south along the river to Wilcannia. Legend had it the Barkandji tribes were ferocious defenders of their land. Now it was Kirkbride land. They only lived there and not on the reserves because they were useful to Robert Kirkbride as a source of cheap labour. Wool growers were not given to sentiment.

The scrappy camp under the redgums, corrugated-iron huts with bark roofs, was full of dogs and kids who ran alongside my horse as I rode in, laughing, teasing. Mud stuck to everything, the women's skirts and the kids' legs. Woodsmoke wafted around. Women tended fires, baking damper, tea boiling in the coals. A couple of them had slabs of wallaby meat, bloody and bright, fur singed away, cooking in the coals. The smell of it stirred a mighty hunger that even sausages and coffee could not touch.

I found Wilson sitting by a fire with a mug of tea. The kids made a racket and Wilson looked up and saw me.

'Hey, boss. Thought you be sleeping off the new king.'

'No chance of that. I was too busy watching everyone else on the scoot up at Larne.' I gazed around at the camp; it was business as usual with no tension in the air. 'Been an incident out on the Larne Road. Looks like ...'

It was hard to say it. Murder. Three people murdered. It would make the newspapers in Sydney and Melbourne. All over Australia, probably.

'Three of the Kirkbride children murdered on the western Larne Road. We need you up there.'

His face gave nothing away. 'Breelong massacre again, eh, boss?'

'Except it's not. Unless you ...'

He shook his head and threw the remains of his tea at the fire.

Most of Wilson's sons worked for Kirkbride as stockmen, and the women from the camp worked as laundry maids or domestics. He had relations all over the place. If there was anything to know, he would know it.

He found Frosty, his eldest, who was learning tracking. We went back to the station, where they saddled the spare horses. I issued them with rifles and sidearms, and we rode back up to the scene.

'Look for anything that might ... ah, just look for anything.' They knew what to do. I was finding it hard to put two thoughts in a straight line.

The Garnets examined the ground, then roamed around, pointing, conferring, slowly walking. The air was thick with the low buzz of flies. I stared at the bloodstained mud, churned up by Nessie's struggles.

Last time I saw Nessie, she'd been laughing with Flora on the homestead verandah. The four siblings were like puppies from the same litter: warm, familiar, inseparable. Now only Flora was left. The jaws of hell had opened, she was falling towards the flames and I'd let it happen.

I dragged my gaze away from the mud, and in the bright daylight noticed what could be a large bloodstain on the wooden boards of the cart tray. I made a sketch of it and noted the time. I also noted the absence of the horse that'd pulled the cart. Wilson and Frosty joined me and I tucked my notebook away.

'How many men, d'you reckon?' I asked.

Wilson shrugged. The scene was a hell of a mess. 'Have to keep looking.'

'All right, I'll leave you both to it. I'll be back at the station. If you see anyone suspicious, do not approach – report back quickly. Weapons to the ready at all times.'

Sergeant Martin could go fuck himself.

I made a note of the order and watched them return to the eastern edge of the clearing and vanish into the saltbush.

3

The Darling River is fed from smaller rivers in south-west Queensland, which in turn are fed by rainfall in the far north gulf country. These smaller rivers, like the Culgoa and the Barwon, cross the border into New South Wales around Brewarrina and converge into the Darling River. The river snakes its way past Bourke, a big transport town with wharves along the river and pubs full of paddle-steamer crews, bullockies, drovers and the usuals, and down south-west for two hundred miles through the Western Division to Wilcannia, and from there it goes to Menindee and joins the Murray. It's a wide river, busy with paddle-steamers taking wool to Adelaide for the sales, copper ingots from Cobar, supplies, passengers and more. There are two main towns on the river between Bourke and Wilcannia: Larne on the eastern bank, and around thirty-six miles south of Larne you have Calpa, on the western bank.

The Paroo River, also coming from headwaters in Queensland, runs parallel to the Darling only further west, although it's sometimes without water. It's the land between the two rivers that gives the best grazing, and some of the biggest wool outfits are situated there. The stock routes follow the river and that's how my town, Calpa, got started, as a summer stock crossing for drovers coming up from the south and heading west across to the Paroo. The paddle-steamers stopped there, too, if they had a reason.

Away from the river, stark plains stretched to the horizon on all sides, plains on which a man could die and never be found. As a trooper in a remote area, I had to be as vigilant about my own survival as well as that of others. Cobar was the nearest town to the east, about a five-hour ride, and to the west – well, there was dust, heat and the odd bore with a clanking windmill pumping up bugger-all.

The Calpa pub, the beating heart of the district, catered to the drovers and the permanent staff on the local sheep stations, the itinerant workers who flooded the place during the shearing, and the swaggies, hawkers, vagrants and assorted odd bods who lived on the riverbanks. There was a store which sold most things needed out here, a post office with a telegraph machine, my police station, a doctor's surgery and that was it. Quiet as the grave, usually, except for a few smack-ups now and then.

As I rode back into town, I noticed people milling about outside the police station. Everyone knew of the murders. Word travelled fast out here, and there were few dams to hold it back. People were talking, crying, stunned or just staring, looking for certainty, looking for ways to make themselves safe from this unseen threat. I rode silently through the clamour, sorted my horse out and then went inside.

A large, framed lithograph of Queen Victoria hung on the wall of the police station. Spotted with fly shit and now two monarchs out of date. I needed to do something about that.

I had hoped that an order would have come through setting out where and when. It would have to come via the telegraph office because I couldn't wait days for the mail coach delivery, which was how we usually communicated with Bourke. But there was nothing.

I pinned a bulletin to the police station noticeboard outside saying investigations were underway. They weren't. That the trackers were onto leads. I didn't know. That the situation was under control. It wasn't. But giving an impression of knowing what the hell you were doing was nine-tenths of leadership. The other tenth was luck.

~

I dropped into the chair at my desk, lit a fag with a shaky hand, found a piece of paper, chewed on a pencil and looked out at the muddy street. A sulphur-crested cockatoo gnawed at the telegraph pole outside, as if he'd seen me and thought, *yeah, good idea.*

The front door opened. It was Thomas Fletcher from Gowrie Station. Tom was a couple of years younger than me, a big fellow, built like a front-row forward. I got up from my desk and walked around the bench towards him.

'Is it true? Is Nessie dead?' he yelled.

Kev, the postmaster, had just entered the station. He took one look at Tom and slapped a telegram on the counter. I quickly signed for it and he scuttled out.

'Tom, maybe—'

'Is she?' he shouted.

'Yes, she is. She was killed with Grace and James out on the road to—'

'I have to see her.'

'The bodies are in Cobar, and I doubt you'll be able to—'

Before I could finish stammering, Tom raised his fist and slammed it into my face. I was hurled onto my back, slid along the floor and thudded into the wall. He loomed over me, panting, almost out of his mind. I judged it was best to stay put on the floor.

'You're under arrest, mister.'

Tom looked over his shoulder. Between his legs I saw Lonergan, standing in the open doorway, aiming a rifle in our direction, eyes wide with fear.

'It's all right,' I mumbled, hand to my throbbing face.

'Punching a mounted trooper? Are you out of your bloody mind?' Lonergan cried.

'To hell with both of you,' Tom shouted and marched out, shoving Lonergan's rifle to one side. I climbed to my feet and staggered over to the chair.

'You just going to let him walk out?'

'Settle down, he's just found out his girl's been murdered.'

Lonergan lowered his rifle and looked out the open door and down the street after Tom.

'He's not fit to be roaming Cobar looking for her body,' I said. 'Do you know Gowrie Station? Head north on the western river road and you'll find the turnoff about five miles out of town with a sign that says Gowrie

Station. Follow that road and you'll come to the homestead. Hurry there and tell his father, Will Fletcher. He might be able to send men to head him off or something.'

Lonergan nodded and went back outside to his horse. Cobar was a five-hour ride to the east from here, and Tom might just have run out of fury by the time he got there. He needed help, no matter what state he'd get to. And there was no way on God's earth Tom should see Nessie's body.

Tom Fletcher could land a serious punch, and my head throbbed. I wetted a cloth and put it against my eye to bring down the swelling. No ice out here – not in the Coolgardie safes that served the police station, anyway. With my good eye, I read the telegram Kev brought over. 'Detectives from Sydney coming STOP keep populace calm STOP no further action until instructed STOP.'

Kev was in and out of the station all afternoon. He was an older bloke, balding, thin and weathered, with a face like a gumnut. Had a Chinese wife, and I reckon that's why he was out here – easier all round. They grew red geraniums in a line of old kerosene tins outside the post office. Civic gardens, Kev called them.

'They caught them yet?' he said, coming in with another telegram.

'Yep, they're in Bourke now being sentenced,' I said, ripping open the envelope. He looked at me expectantly. It was an order to set trackers on the scene.

'They sending reinforcements?'

'Nope, we're not under attack. It's just a duplicate of a previous order. The populace can rest easy.'

'Can you tell me who they were at least?'

'James, Nessie and Grace Kirkbride, but I don't know any more than that. It's not official, so keep it to yourself.'

Kev blinked several times. 'They sure?'

'I found them.'

'Oh, Jesus, Jesus Christ,' he whispered, tears suddenly welling up in his rheumy eyes. 'But they were just babies. You found them?'

I nodded.

'Oh, Gus, mate,' he murmured.

I knew Kev was no stranger to hardship. I looked down at the paper in my hand, trying to keep a grip on myself.

'People keep tramping into the post office asking for news,' he said eventually, wiping tears from his cheeks. 'If you could issue regular official bulletins and pin them up outside, I'd be obliged. There's mud all around the place and I'm the one who cleans up.'

'I'll do that right away, Kev. But don't breathe a word as to who it is – not yet.'

~

At dusk I walked a few doors up to Joe's. Joe Pryor had worked in Calpa about a year longer than me, and as single men who liked a drink or three, we struck up a friendship. Joe, in his late thirties and unmarried, wore his dark hair longish, like a Victorian poet, and combined this with a luxurious military moustache and a penchant for black suits, even at the height of summer. From a legal family, he'd been educated at Melbourne Grammar and trained as a doctor at the University of Melbourne. What was this son of the establishment doing out here in the Never-Never? I think he pondered this question many times, often while deep in his cups. But we all had our reasons. No good asking, because then you'd have to reveal your own.

I found him in his backyard, staring at a row of brown-spotted cabbage, shirt sleeves up, leaning on a shovel. The chooks in their run stopped their muttering. His old dog hauled himself up out of the last of the sunlight and waddled over to say hello.

'All damaged by rabbits last night,' he said, nodding at the cabbage. 'I'd promised them to Mrs Schreiber for pickling.'

I held up a bottle of whisky. Joe dropped the shovel and we went inside to the kitchen. Everything was in order, which gave me a sense of comfort. A jam jar full of crepe myrtle sat on the whitewashed table, while a colander of potatoes, still crusted with black dirt, rested on a draining board. A mutton stew simmering on the stove filled the air with the scent of countless humble Australian kitchens, places where murder was only a story in a newspaper, soon to disappear under potato peelings.

We drank and he stared at his glass. I refilled it. We smoked, kept drinking.

'Walk into a door, eh?'

'Tom Fletcher.'

'Why?'

'Needed to punch something,' I said with a shrug.

'Poor bastard.'

There was a small iron crank handle on the table alongside a thick screw, an iron disc with holes in it and other bits and pieces.

'What's this?'

'Broken meat grinder. Mrs Schreiber wants me to fix it.'

I stubbed out my cigarette and tried fitting the pieces together. 'The circular blade goes in here.'

'Yeah, but there's nothing to hold it.'

A fly buzzed around the window above the sink. I poured some more whisky, considered the grinder pieces. Footsteps. We looked up. Lonergan slammed the screen door open, panting. 'Dr Pryor, you're needed at the Kirkbrides', urgently. Miss Flora.'

'Is she all right? What happened?' Joe asked, leaping up.

'Tried to drown herself in the river.'

'Alive?'

'Only just.'

Joe raced off to get his bag. I gulped my whisky, felt the burn of it, and took a few more swallows to kill the bees swarming through my veins. Ran back to the station to saddle Dancer.

～

There was smoke haze above the men's quarters at Inveraray Station. The dusk air was bitterly cold already, settling over the land like dread. Birds screeched and bickered as they settled into their perches for the night, an undertone to their racket, like they'd all gone mad and were fighting over some terrifying vision only they could see.

Joe shrank into his coat, stunned by the sudden rift in the world. The windows of the homestead glowed in the dusky gloom, lamps burning

28

to guide the spirits of Nessie, James and Grace home. Except they never would. I was relieved to dismount, plant my feet on the ground and toss the reins to the Kirkbride stable boy.

Joe was taken straight to Flora. I wanted to go with him but the maid took me to Robert Kirkbride's study. A large clock above the fireplace ticked, counting off the minutes that his children no longer lived. The fire crackled and hissed. A painted portrait hung above the mantel, a Kirkbride patriarch no doubt, all muttonchop whiskers and stone eyes. From somewhere in the house came the sound of a woman wailing, high and eerie, repeated with her every breath.

Robert Kirkbride was a tall, lean man with sparse, greying hair. His face had a hard cast to it, like a Greek mask, the eyes black and hollow. He wasn't a man to be trifled with and had more influence in the Western Division than was proper, to my way of thinking. But tonight, slumped in his chair, wearing rumpled pyjamas, he looked beaten. I've seen parents react to the death of their child – even had to deliver the awful news once or twice. They land on the reality of their child's death like a plum falling on granite. The mess could never be stuffed back inside the skin and made to look whole.

Reverend Hickson sat beside him, a hand on Kirkbride's shoulder, a copy of the Bible in his ample lap, flesh bulging above his dog collar. Hickson was the Church of England minister from Cobar. A sanctimonious prick who gloried in tragedy, he sniffed me out when I first arrived in the district – six-foot-four worth of trouble with a thirst for strong drink and a chip on my shoulder so big I could barely stand upright. After several encounters, Hickson gave me a wide berth.

'Mr Kirkbride,' I said. 'I am sorry to intrude on your grief, but—'

'How could Flora do this to us?' he murmured. 'How could she, after ...'

'I'm going to have to speak to McIntosh and anyone else who was witness.'

'I don't want this to get out. People will talk about her.'

It seemed the least of his worries. Flora had every reason to do what she did, and I'd challenge anyone who called her feeble-minded, or a disgrace, or guilty of an insult to God. If Hickson was peddling that line, I'd have words with him.

I left them, and as I was halfway down the corridor the Reverend called me back, a wary look in his eye.

'Constable, Mr Kirkbride wished me to ask you not to formally report this incident. It is a crime, I know, and God will view it as such, but let's leave it to Him to deal with.'

'I hope you aren't saying that to Miss Flora?'

'I minister to my congregation as I see fit, and you police as you see fit.'

'I police as the law instructs me to, Reverend.' *Bloody halfwit.*

'Mr Kirkbride is concerned that if this gets out, it will ruin her chances of making a good marriage.'

I must have failed in keeping up the dispassionate look all troopers strive for, because the Reverend raised his eyebrows.

'He has done you a great many favours,' he reminded me.

'Tell him I won't report it.'

But I still needed to know what happened.

4

Outside the night was frigid, arid air cold as a tomb. I pulled my great coat closer, scarf tighter, as I walked across to the stockmen's quarters to find the Inveraray overseer, Jock McIntosh, hardworking mainstay of this property. He and a couple of other men were quietly drinking in their mess. Normally alcohol wouldn't have been tolerated on the property, but nobody cared at this point. Grog was all we had. A small fire burnt in the hearth, giving comfort if not heat. I sensed there'd been little conversation.

'Can you tell me what happened, what you saw?' I asked, after I'd closed the door.

'They'd only been back from Cobar a half-hour,' McIntosh said. 'The Reverend was with Mr and Mrs Kirkbride, and Miss Kirkbride must have slipped away when no one was looking.'

'Who saw her in the river?'

McIntosh looked over at a stockman I'd seen around the place, a quiet, lanky fellow who was smoking like his life depended on it. 'Walsh?'

Walsh looked up with a start. 'Yeah, I was by the river, saw her float past, thought it was a cow at first. Couldn't believe it because there's no cows round here. Then I saw it was a girl. I shouted, thought she was dead, then Mac came over and we waded in and pulled her out. She was coughing and carrying on but just like in a daze.'

I scribbled this all down, got the names of the men who helped, the time and Flora's state.

'She gunna be all right?'

'The doctor is with her now.'

'She'd cut her hair off,' McIntosh said. 'Hacked at it with shears.'

I looked up at him. McIntosh was a cool-headed Scot, but his voice broke as he spoke.

Another fellow murmured, 'It's like they've been cursed.'

'Shut your yap,' McIntosh snarled.

He could shut them up, but it was what everyone was saying. The Kirkbrides are cursed, being punished. But if Kirkbride was being punished, I knew it would be by another human. God didn't go around punishing people or helping them. His indifference was supreme, like a neglectful parent. He was off at the front bar, drinking Himself senseless to blot out the folly of what He'd made, a squalling, destructive infant He could not raise to adulthood.

~

Joe joined me and we rode home, starlight illuminating the road, the howling call of wild dogs away in the darkness, the barked response from station dogs. The side of my face that had connected with Tom's fist throbbed like a beating heart.

'Will Flora be all right?'

'She'll have to be monitored for pneumonia after nearly drowning.'

'But her mind?'

'I'm not one of those doctors. I sedated her so she can get some sleep.'

'Pouring that opium muck down her throat will make it worse.'

'I'm her doctor and I have administered laudanum.'

I knew better than to argue with Joe on this. He wielded his stethoscope like a truncheon, always having the last word. We continued in silence. I'd spent a lot of time in a military convalescent home in Cape Town, recovering from my injuries, swilling morphine as if the hospital bought it in bulk and needed to get rid of it. It numbed the pain but didn't do anything for my mind, and it took a dogged perseverance to get free of its clutches.

The doctors in Cape Town told me I had neurasthenia and should pull myself together and be a man. Same thing my father said to me. He spent his life holding himself upright in the face of endless deaths and he expected his son to do the same.

But to my way of thinking, there was endurance and stoicism, and then there was something else. The mind was cleaved, leaving one division to its own terrible devices, even if the rest of the company was marching in formation.

As we neared town, I saw a group of men outside the police station. Joe kept going, I dismounted and the men looked at me expectantly. Senior men from the district, owners of the big outfits, their managers and overseers, holding lanterns, low voices, long shadows on the muddy road.

Doug Forsythe, owner of Tindaree Station, stepped forward. 'Gus, I know you're busy, but we need some answers.'

As if I had answers. Over Forsythe's shoulder and through the police station window I saw Lonergan at the counter, staring uselessly back at me.

'Bob Kirkbride said James was taking his sisters to the ball in Cobar,' Forsythe said. 'How the hell did they end up on the Larne to Calpa road, then?'

The men looked to me.

'We don't know at this stage,' I said.

'It can't be right,' he replied. 'Jimmy wouldn't go to a workers' dance, much less take his sisters to one. Mrs Kirkbride wouldn't have it. Because this is the sort of thing that happens.'

'The detectives from Sydney, they'll go through all of this.'

Forsythe gave me a sceptical look. All of them did. Capable and well-respected wool men, they'd cleared and improved a wasteland, grown wool on it that contributed to nearly fifty per cent of the national clip, fought off drought and pestilence, and no shiny-arsed detective was going to come out here and sort out local matters, murder included.

'We have to do it their way, Mr Forsythe. And it's not going to be quick, or pleasant.'

'We should go after them now,' Jim Crowther, the Tindaree overseer, said. 'We have enough men.'

'Sorry, instructions are to wait.'

'Ah, that's wrong,' cried Henry Peyton, the overseer from Gowrie Station. 'They'll be on their way to Queensland, and if we go tonight we might overtake them.'

'Go where? Up the east bank or the west? Over to the Paroo? Maybe they shot off to White Cliffs or down to Wilcannia? We can't go chasing hunches.'

'Surely Bob Kirkbride wants them caught as quickly as possible?'

The trouble was, I agreed. We needed to put pressure on the killers and quickly, let them feel the fiery breath of vengeance coming at them, hooves pounding, steel flashing. Then they'd panic, make the wrong call and we'd pounce, get their necks between our teeth and shake the bastards until their teeth rattled.

'If Sydney thought a manhunt now was the right way, they'd have ordered it. But they haven't, so we wait and go by the book, gentlemen. No vigilantism will be tolerated. Anyway, it's crutching time – which one of you can spare a dozen men for a manhunt?'

That silenced them.

'Check all your staff,' I added. 'Warn them everyone will be questioned and not to jack up about it. Word has gone up and down the river and there will be reinforcements. Everyone has to pull together, keep their wits about them and stay calm.'

I barged into the front office to check on Lonergan. 'Wilson turn up?'

'Nope.'

I snatched a completed form from the top of the wrong tray and slammed it in the right tray. 'This is a fucking firearms licence application, not a liquor licensing application.'

I straightened the blotter, checked under the counter to make sure Lonergan hadn't mucked the rest of the forms around, opened the incident ledger and ran my eye down the night's events. I picked up the firearm licence application again and read it this time.

'Thompson wants a pistol. Did he say why?'

'Ah, no? Was I supposed to ask?'

'What is it you do in Bourke again?' I slammed it down again. 'And get that tea mug out of here.'

'Yes, sir,' Lonergan said, blinking rapidly, holding a telegram envelope out to me. 'An order came in. I left it for you. Sir.'

'Here,' I said, shoving it back at him. 'Stick it in the right tray this time.' Then I stalked out and put myself to bed.

~

I woke with a shout, drenched in sweat, heart frantic. I scrabbled for a match on the nightstand, dropping them in the choking darkness, finally striking lucky and with a shaking hand holding the flame to the candle, still panting from terror. A soft, golden light bathed the room, throwing shadows on the wall. I propped myself up with a couple of pillows and lay there, taking deep breaths and hoping Lonergan hadn't woken.

My nights were often punctuated with such events. The extensive scarring on my chest and under my arm puckered and pinched, waking me to the illusion that the bayonet was slicing my flesh again. Laudanum brought on sedation, but nothing stopped the dreams, so I left it alone.

If I was alone, I could manage. With another man in the next room, I just didn't know.

5

I was fully awake before dawn, dressed, found a lantern, turned the wick up, lit it and blew out the candle. I worked the woodstove, bringing the coals back to life, fed it some more kindling, then went through to the station, re-read my report and added some details I considered useful. Until Wilson got back it was hard to know what to do or where to look, but time was slipping away.

I looked out the window as if that would magically make Wilson and Frosty appear, then remembered the order that came through last night, snatched it up and read. An inmate at the Kenmore Lunatic Asylum in Goulburn had hidden from his nurse and done a runner. He'd been seen in Cobar, gave troopers the slip and was last seen heading west on foot. His parents, the Jongs, owned a run near Curranyalpa. It wasn't known if they still lived there but that was where he was likely headed.

A routine job. These poor blokes made a beeline for the empty spaces, where they just let it rip. He was probably carrying no water, and if he was on foot between here and Cobar he may never be seen again. Heat, thirst or death by misadventure, usually at the hands of some sadistic prick who enjoyed baiting the mad, getting a few laughs from their distress.

I checked my watch, tucked it in my tunic pocket, saddled up and cantered up the western road to Gowrie Station, the second-largest station in the district, which shared a border with Inveraray. Because of the brilliance of the stars, it was never really dark in the open out here, and the soil, the scrub, the river, all were bathed in an icy, ethereal light. I rode up the long drive to the homestead, passing the laundries where white sheets hung on lines like ghosts who'd finished for the night. The lights were on in the stockmen's quarters and the homestead, the smell of frying bacon thick in the air.

I tethered my horse, went up the steps to the homestead and knocked. Will Fletcher came to the door. He was as big as his son, with a hard set to his mouth, a reserved and stoic man from a past era, a bit like my father. Firm believers in progress, empire and the sanctity of grazing.

'Sorry to disturb you, Mr Fletcher.'

'Have you come to arrest him?'

'For what?'

He nodded at my eye.

'No, just to see how he is.'

Mr Fletcher relaxed slightly, stepped out onto the verandah, closing the door behind him, and gathered himself. He shook his head, compressing his mouth until it disappeared.

'He's with his mother.' He paused for a long moment, staring at the dark shadows under the peppercorn tree. 'She gives him some comfort.'

'Detectives will be here soon, coming from Sydney. The investigation isn't going to be easy for anyone, but let me emphasise that striking a detective or a trooper, regardless of the situation, won't be tolerated. Stay with him when he's questioned, if you can.'

He nodded. 'Any news yet?'

'No, but you might want to call in your boundary riders and doggers.'

'I'll not be calling off the doggers just before lambing.'

'Fair enough, I know how busy the district is right now.'

He nodded. 'How are the Kirkbrides managing?'

Kirkbride grey-faced, Mrs Kirkbride wailing, Flora floating in the river, arms outstretched, dead leaves swirling around her slender body, giving herself up to oblivion as her wet skirts dragged her down.

Fletcher nodded at my wordless answer and disappeared back into the gloom of the homestead. I couldn't picture Tom with his mother as I had never met Mrs Fletcher. She was an invalid who rarely left her room, let alone the homestead. And as I'd never known my own mother, I was unfamiliar with the sort of comfort mothers could provide. But if ever there was a man in need of comfort, it was Tom Fletcher.

~

On my return to the police station I felt a stab of irritation at the sight of Lonergan, his black hair parted in the middle of his round skull, his hairy black brows like caterpillars. I shook some coffee beans into the

40

small wooden grinder and turned the handle, the sound of the grinding beans drowning out some stupid question of his. Found the coffee pot, spooned the ground coffee into the funnel, filled the base with water, replaced the funnel, screwed the top on and placed it on the stovetop. Lonergan watched the entire time. When I was finished, he handed me an unopened order, which I tore open and read aloud.

'Attend Bourke Station, stay overnight, then escort the detectives and equipment back to Calpa.'

Lonergan nodded. 'That's you, right, sir? Not me?'

I placed the sugar bowl and a cup on the table. What was I to do with this gormless trooper?

'As it's addressed to me, I think we'll assume it's for me.'

'Yes, sir.'

'Log it immediately, so it's not misplaced. While I'm in Bourke, you keep an eye and an ear out for this escapee from Kenmore Asylum—'

'What escapee, sir?' he said, eyes widening in alarm.

'Check the order logbook, see if it's been actioned, follow up if it hasn't, note your movements, note dates, times, when you had a drink of water, what you had for dinner, when you had a piss ... Are you listening, Trooper?'

'Yes, sir.'

'Do your rounds, but make sure you're armed and alert at all times. Ask Wally at the Royal if you need assistance. And write it all up.'

'Yes, sir.'

'And get it right,' I added with a scowl. Couldn't help myself. My incident book was a thing of beauty, and to have some coal cracker scrawling his half-formed thoughts on its clean white expanse pained me.

41

It was a six-hour ride upriver to Bourke. In summer it was a bastard of a ride, one I preferred to do at night if I had a choice. The thing to do was carry a tin of Josephson's Australian Ointment. Buckskin breeches were made so you didn't chafe, but six or more hours in the saddle on a hot day and everything chafed, from balls to brain. The glare was blinding but our official hat was a jaunty pillbox affair, which would be just the thing for a Parisian gendarme but was ridiculous out here. I shoved it in a saddlebag and wore a cabbage-tree hat like every other man in the bush.

The sun was on its way across a vast blue sky, a westerly wind blowing. I noticed a shape ahead in the distance, moving slowly. Dancer stopped at the sight of it. He didn't like things that moved, nor did he like things that didn't move. So there we were, his ears pricked forward, completely still, every muscle tensed and ready to flee.

'How'd you get into the police force, mate?' I said, stroking his neck. 'Bribed someone, eh?'

I urged him forward, but horses often sense things long before humans and I thought of the Kenmore escapee. But it was a rabbit shooter, dragging a heavily laden cart with racks and racks of dead rabbits hanging in the breeze. The stench from his load turned my stomach.

I stopped and he stopped, leaves and dust skittering around us. 'Headed back to Bourke?'

'Yeah, been on Booroondara Downs,' he said.

'Go to the dance in Larne on Saturday night?'

'Nope, nothing to wear. All me ball gowns are dirty.'

'Seen anything or anyone odd around?'

His weathered face split in a smile. 'Nah, mate, no more than usual. Who you looking for?'

I debated telling him, but men like this one, who got around the district, drank here and there, roamed the scrub, saw things.

'Three people murdered on the western Larne to Calpa road Saturday night. Two women and a man, siblings.'

His eyes widened. 'Who? They from around here?'

'Three of Robert Kirkbride's children. Keep your eyes and ears peeled for anything at all that strikes you as odd.'

'Jesus fucking Christ,' he murmured. 'My wife and kids, we're on the edge of town.'

'Tell 'em to keep an eye out, keep their wits about them. Superintendent Corcoran will be issuing a statement later today.'

'A statement, yeah, that'll protect them,' he said, then flicked his reins. 'Gotta get back. Thanks for the tip, Officer.'

I took out my notebook, noted down the time of the encounter and the nature of his business, tucked it away again and rode on. Inexplicably, my eyes filled with tears, which slipped down my cheeks, then vanished like rain in a waterhole.

On reflection, it was probably the smell of death that got to me. Dead rabbits drying in the sun. They shouldn't have been here. Everyone knew that, except the nong who thought shooting rabbits would be amusing. An Englishman, of course. Now, we Australians thought of ourselves as English, but the English didn't think of us like that. I learned that one quickly when I arrived in Cape Town. We were colonials, the Queen's Colonial Forces, and we'd do as we were told by our betters.

Back in 1899, when the call went around Australia for soldiers to fight the Boer War, what they wanted were bushmen, men who could ride and shoot. Because of the rabbit plague there were men like that in spades in Australia, including me, as I'd spent my school holidays galloping about shooting rabbits with mates, pretending we were picking off Mahdists for General Gordon.

I knew the British officers in South Africa thought Australians were good fighters, but when the uncomfortable questions were asked back in England, we were just a pack of troublemaking, knuckle-dragging ruffians good for executing. That we were good fighters was down to the rabbit plague, or that was my theory. Were we ruffians? That depended on the orders from our betters.

~

Hot, dusty, dry and hot, Bourke started as a fort and evolved into a transport town. Paddle-steamers, camel trains, bullockies, stock routes and the railroad all came to Bourke and fanned out from there. Hence there were a lot of thirsty men, the requisite pubs to service them and the troopers to watch over them. It had a couple of fine buildings, but the police station wasn't one of them.

Bourke was a posting men tried to get away from as soon as they arrived. But some liked it out here – Sergeant Martin for one. He was in the hallway when I arrived and pulled me aside.

'Hawkins, if you ever show insubordination again, I will have you dismissed, do you understand? And then you can fuck off back to wherever you came from.'

I stared at him for a moment, uncertain as to which moment of insubordination he was referring to.

'Don't come all wide-eyed and innocent with me,' he hissed. 'I give orders, you follow them. I am a sergeant, you are not.'

'Sir.'

'And get a haircut.'

Maybe Martin was referring to the crime scene, although it could have been just about any time we set eyes on each other. I didn't care much either way. I followed him into the briefing room, where our boss, Superintendent Jim Corcoran, stood in front of a gang of troopers. My mind snapped to attention as I took a place at the back.

'The detectives are arriving tomorrow morning,' Corcoran said. 'They'll be leading the investigation, not us, and they have asked that nobody give any details of the crime to anyone. Everyone got that? Not your mother or your mate or the man who cuts your hair. Complete silence on the matter. Senior Constable Hawkins will escort the detectives wherever they need to go but everyone has their part to play. Wait for orders, do your patrols carefully and thoroughly, and be on the lookout. I've issued a statement for the local papers, just to get them out of my hair. Do we speak to journalists?'

His question hung in the air. We dared not answer.

'No, we do not,' he continued. 'If you find them in a mess, get them out of it, but keep your mouth shut. Be on the alert at all times. If anything strikes you as odd, unfamiliar, let Bourke know and we'll pass it on to the detectives. Right, dismissed.'

Dismissal couldn't come soon enough for me. The room was crammed with troopers, all reeking of that distinctive soldier odour, unwashed body encased in wool and finished with a good helping of dust, dirt, grease and poor teeth. In confined spaces, it sent me spinning back to South Africa, the mission briefings, the ice in my stomach, the fear that there was a bunch of treacherous japie commandoes crouched behind the superintendent's desk.

I turned to follow the other troopers out but Corcoran called me back.

Jim Corcoran was in his fifties, tall and broad-shouldered, sporting an impressive moustache like a factory broom. He'd lost half an ear to a bushranger's bullet back in the day, and like a massive old fighting dog he commanded respect. He'd been a legendary shot, known for his relentless pursuit of bushrangers. If Big Jim Corcoran was on your tail, you might as well give up. Now he ran the district, scrabbling for funds and resources. That his population was the smallest in the state meant he had stiff competition. He kept a goldfish in a bowl on his desk, liked to stare at it. Word was he named the fish after his dead wife, and could be heard singing to it late in the afternoons. That sort of bullshit thrived out here.

'How the hell did you get that black eye?' he said.

'Thomas Fletcher. I confirmed to him that Miss Nessie Kirkbride was dead. He was upset. I've warned him not to do it again, but I see no useful purpose in charging him, sir.'

He grunted. 'If he punches a detective, he'll be sorry.'

'He knows.'

He sat back and lit a cigarette, inhaled deeply and said, 'Parry reckons you left Larne after the hall was locked up at midnight, but according to your report you didn't get to the scene of the crime until three. Should have taken you two hours at most. What were you doing?'

I knew this would come up. Nothing Corcoran could say would make me feel worse than I already did.

'I visited a friend and left Larne an hour later.'

'You visited a friend for an hour while on duty?'

A clock on the mantelpiece ticked steadily. Out in the street, wagons and carts rolled by, the clatter echoing off the buildings. Corcoran ashed his cigarette, glared at his goldfish.

'I'd like to offer my resignation, sir.'

'I won't accept it. Or not yet. We need every man right now. But it has been noted.'

Corcoran picked up his pen again, paused then slammed it down, pulled out a bottle of whisky, splashed some in a couple of tumblers and handed one to me.

'Sit down,' he sighed. 'These bastards in Sydney know bugger-all of the conditions out here. They may as well send a ballet company.'

'Two detectives are going to be flat out questioning everyone,' I said. 'District's full of crutching teams too.'

He downed his whisky and poured more. 'I know. But it's the usual story, do more with less and make the government look good while we're at it. And Robert Kirkbride has friends in high places, which makes it

47

difficult for everyone. I've secured six more troopers, but God knows where I'll billet them. Calpa can barely support the population it's got.'

'Tents, that'll do for a while. Meals and wash up at the Royal, horses can stay in the station paddock, if they send blankets and decent fodder. No grazing out there.'

'Good, you can be in charge of that,' he said with a grateful sigh. 'Now, before these dicks get here, I want to make it clear that you are escorting them, not directing their investigation or influencing them in any way.'

'But I found the bodies and have good overall knowledge of the district.'

'That's why you're escorting them. But this is one for the detectives. We assist, not influence.'

'Why would I try to influence them?'

'Because you're a damn know-it-all, Hawkins. And don't let your sympathies stop you doing your job. The blacks have hundreds of reasons to want to smash our faces in and rape our women. Countermanding Martin's order to disarm the trackers was wrong.'

'You send a black tracker, or any trooper, out unarmed to catch a murderer and he's not going to do his job properly, and why the hell should he? You've just made it clear his life is not important.'

'Martin gave you an order,' Corcoran said. 'Nobody's forgotten Jimmy Governor was a black tracker. People see trackers with weapons, they'll be terrified. I will query Sydney, and until I hear otherwise you will disarm them.'

'Wilson Garnet said they were terrified and not letting the women out without—'

'Garnets are station blacks, not all of them are.'

I said nothing. Wilson and Frosty were out there now and I wasn't going to track them down and take back their guns just because the brass in Sydney said so. I know, obeying orders without question is the God all soldiers worship, heads bowed, hands on hearts. It took moral discipline to do so, and if the order was stupid or dangerous or both, the greater the call on discipline. But I wasn't a soldier anymore.

Corcoran gave me a dark look. 'I'll find out. Don't think I won't.'

'Sir.'

'See the quartermaster in the morning before we go to meet the detectives. Get supplies for the six troopers sorted.'

'Charge it to Mounted Police or Detective Branch?'

'To us,' he said with a weary look. 'The bare minimum, understand? They can shoot a roo if they need more food.'

I wandered off to find a room for the night, puzzling over how Corcoran and Martin knew I'd armed the trackers contrary to orders.

6

A piece of chalk hit me in the face. The Latin master barked, 'You, Hawkins – *Dulce et decorum est pro patria mori* – who said it and why?'

I pawed my face, opened my eyes. The chalk was a chunk of rust from the tin ceiling of the hotel room. As I dressed, wincing as the scars pulled at my flesh, the well-worn phrase echoed, but nobody ever said, *Dulce et decorum est pro patria debilitari*. No, to be maimed for one's country was another matter entirely, just endless pain, knifing me if I turned this way or that, reached or raised my arm, breathed or held my breath, slept or lay awake. It wears a man down, to be in constant pain.

After a solid breakfast I went to the railway station, where I found Corcoran standing on the platform trying to read a copy of the *Western Herald* in the wind – a westerly, worse luck, which was bringing great rolling clouds of dust that settled on horses, walls, uniforms, hair, tongue, throat, eyes and mind. Corcoran shut the paper, almost mangling it in his frustration.

'Anything in the papers today, sir?'

'Headlines. Three dead after the Larne dance.'

'Names?'

'They wouldn't dare.'

'This isn't going to be like Breelong, sir. They knew who the killers were, had witnesses, it was just a matter of time before they got him.'

'It may come as a surprise to you, Hawkins, but I'm well aware of the difficulties.'

'Sir.'

Porters stood about waiting with their trolleys, peering down the tracks leading east. Soon the train pulled into the station with a great squealing of wheels, steam and coal smoke billowing everywhere. The two detectives were not hard to pick, both wearing city suits, their pallor standing out among the weathered locals like quartz in the dirt. They looked through the plumes of smoke and dust with disbelief.

Detective Inspector John Denning, a thin, dour Geordie in his fifties, eyes as hard as goat's knees. And Detective First Class Arthur Baines, a beat cop in a cheap suit, younger, stocky, fag-stained fingers, looking over the station with a mix of surprise and contempt.

'No,' Denning said, when Corcoran asked him if he'd been out here before.

'Never been west of Petersham,' Baines said with a nervous laugh. 'You got blacks out here?'

Corcoran and I exchanged a quick glance. Had they not been briefed, or did Bourke just get two of Sydney's finest?

'We've got a two-seater buggy, and quiet, steady horses,' Corcoran said. 'Senior Constable Hawkins here will escort you where you need to go. He knows the district, knows the people. We have all the equipment you need packed and ready to go, and a stenographer and typist who will be based in the Royal Hotel in Calpa.

'Distances are the defining factor in this district, as you may well understand,' he continued. 'We do not use telephones as they are not secure, but we rely heavily on the mail coaches and the telegram service and the integrity and quality of our troopers at each station. We have six junior troopers, who will be at your command to take statements and any other duties as you see fit. If you need more manpower, we'll find it for you.'

Denning listened while looking me up and down. I looked him up and down, hackles rising. Men staring at my face had copped my fist in theirs over the years, and I wasn't beyond hitting a senior officer, given enough provocation.

~

The six troopers waited patiently out the back. They were all young blokes, no more than eighteen or nineteen, and green as week-old mutton, but they jumped to attention and seemed keen to get going.

A cart full of supplies, including a typewriter, sat waiting. A bloke with a large moustache, a bowler hat and tight suit introduced himself as Mr Terrence Fraser, the typist and stenographer. He'd been seconded from the local magistrate's court and looked supremely disinterested in the whole affair. Then there were two carts, each with a towering load of hay and feed for the horses, driven by two local men, and four spare horses tied along behind the second cart.

The riverfront wharves were busy with four paddle-steamers loading or unloading, the water levels high enough for the traffic. The punt man loaded the forage wagons one at a time and took them across. Baines, fag in hand, watched the bustle on the nearby banks.

'Like bloody Circular Quay,' he said. 'You know Sydney?'

'Did my training at Moore Park.'

'Know your way around a horse, then.'

I gave him a sideways look. 'I'm a mounted trooper, mate – be a bloody shame if I didn't.'

'Yeah, right,' he said, distracted.

We could scarce hear each other over the grind of the engine pulling the punt cable, men shouting instructions as they slid the bales of wool down the levee banks of the river to be loaded onto barges, dogs barking, horses neighing. But Baines was a talker.

'You got the telephone at your station?'

'No, not secure. We use telegrams and the mail coach.' Was he not listening?

'So nobody's got a telephone in Calpa?'

'The big stations have them, but only to communicate with staff in distant parts of their property. Can't make calls to Sydney, if that's what you're hoping.'

He nodded, scratched himself, looked uncertain. We were a long way from Phillip Street.

Once the fodder carts were across on the punt, the cart with Mr Fraser went over, then the six troopers and their horses, then me and the spare horses, and finally the buggy with the detectives. I sorted them all on the other side with the troopers bringing up the rear, each leading a spare horse. It had taken an hour and a half to get everyone across and we had a six-hour ride to Calpa, probably seven, following the river road south as it clung to the curves and bends.

At the halfway mark we stopped. Horses were unharnessed, fed, watered and re-harnessed. While this was going on, Denning consulted his notes. Baines, squinting in the harsh light, looked around at the vast plains around us and back at the comforting milky brown water of the Darling. Mr Fraser smoked and read his newspaper. The fodder men leant against their carts and had a yarn about the business.

'We going to stop in Larne for a drink?' Baines said, looking at a map.

'Not if you want to get to Calpa at midnight. Larne is on the east bank, so we'd have to cross over on the punt again, then cross back.'

'Because Calpa is on the west bank, right?'

I nodded.

Baines shook his head as if he couldn't believe the poor planning that resulted in the two towns being on opposite sides of the river. 'It is going to be tough covering these distances,' he said.

'Not so bad when we get to Calpa. Crime scene is twelve miles north of the town, the Inveraray homestead about nine, and most residents are within a twenty-mile radius. Larne is thirty-six miles away, a three-hour ride.'

'Three hours?' he murmured. 'Bloody hell.'

We set off again, riding south with a harsh westerly coming at us. The

54

landscape didn't change and it was slow going. Nothing happened quickly out here: the distances, the climate, the way it slowed a man down on the inside to the point where days folded in on themselves. Yesterday became today and then tomorrow and yesterday again. Country like this turned a man's mind to such notions.

~

On arrival, I showed the detectives to the Calpa Royal Hotel. Wally Mansell, the publican, was happy to have three of his four rooms taken over. The government always paid its bills, so it was a win for him. I took the horses down to the police station paddock and turned them loose to get acquainted, then instructed the troopers on where to pitch their tents, where to eat and wash, and warning them off any alcohol.

The prospect of wrangling this bunch of boys, lured from labouring by the promise of money and manhunts, irritated me. All these people rudely crashing in on my solitude, my habits and routines. I didn't want or need any of them. Idiots, the lot of them.

At the station I took a bottle of beer from the meat safe out back, flipped the lid and drank. Inside, I found Lonergan on hands and knees, arse in the air.

'What are you doing, Trooper?'

'A mouse, sir. I lived the through the '04 mouse plague and it's not anything you want to experience. Sir.'

'This is my station and my fucking mouse, and I'll deal with it.'

'I can patch this hole, sir, quick—'

I stared.

'Yes, sir.'

On my way out I caught a glimpse of him rolling his eyes and shaking his head, took a step back and got right in his hairy paddy face. 'You better stay out of my sight while you're here, Trooper.'

'Sir.'

~

I left the detectives for a couple of hours to orient themselves, then strolled over to invite them for a drink, as was the welcoming custom in these parts. Baines was resting but Denning came out. The Royal Hotel, the only pub in town, was a place for stockmen and shearers to drink their wages and blow off steam. As the only cop, it was out of respect for them that I mostly stayed away unless there was trouble. A police trooper in a full pub is about as welcome as a dog at a game of skittles.

Wally, the publican, had a huge belly – all that beer had to go somewhere – and a head of thick white hair. He told me that one day, just after the 1890 floods, he woke up and his hair had turned white overnight. Reckoned he looked distinguished now, that he might even be taken for being part of the squattocracy, a notion that always set the pub rocking with laughter. Sir Wally of Pisspot Hall. He liked Rowland's Macassar Oil and slathered it on his white hair like dripping on a joint of lamb. I'd met a lot of publicans along the way and old Wal was one of the best.

Denning gazed around Wally's pub as if the place were a personal insult to him. The long wooden bar scarred with fag burns, the small range of cheap rum and whisky bottles on the shelf, the rickety stools, the pockmarked dartboard, the old photographs of the Calpa XI in their whites, the smell of beer and carbolic, Wally's old kelpie cross who growled at everyone, all of it humble and workaday. We took an unsteady table in the corner and Wally brought over a couple of beers.

'You served in the second Boer War, so I'm told,' Denning said, as he wiped the froth from his upper lip. 'I served in the first. Rifleman in the Gordon Highlanders.'

'The Gay Gordons. Thought you were a Geordie.'

'After the war. Grew up in Aberdeen,' he said.

'No trace of the Scot left in your accent.'

'And you?'

'New South Wales Mounted Rifles.'

'Under British command?'

'Attached to British units but commanded by our own officers.'

Denning looked over the rim of his glass and gave a derisive snort. 'Like the ones they executed for shooting prisoners. Couple of badly trained lieutenants, weren't they?'

'Not as badly trained as the soldiers they executed for cowardice after the Battle of Majuba Hill. I recollect they were Gordon Highlanders – maybe you knew them?'

Denning put his glass down slowly, placing it with precision on the coaster.

'Britain's biggest defeat, soldiers turned and ran and the rest were picked off by Dutch farm boys, so I heard,' I said. 'Damn fine shots, too. Offered to give your fellows instruction in musketry, apparently. General

57

Colley was a procrastinator, or so we were instructed in officer training. Act decisively, dislocate and disrupt, not sit on your hands and hope. Now, your average Boer—'

I was just warming up when Denning excused himself.

~

Later, as I fell into bed, I noticed, on top of the small bedside cabinet, a silver coin. The thruppence from the crime scene. A small hole had been drilled right where old Vicky's crown perched. Dated 1893, with the usual Latin incantation inscribed around the edge. But the back of the coin had been smoothed and replaced with an engraving of two initials, A and E entwined. Debasing the Queen's coin was an offence, but these love tokens were common.

Mrs Schreiber must have found it in my breeches. By rights, this was evidence, given where it was found. But I decided to hang onto it. Denning could go to hell.

~

Next morning, up early as usual, I quickly dressed and went through to the station to hunt down the errors Lonergan had made over the last two days. Couldn't find them, but that didn't mean they weren't there. I compiled a list of chores I expected him to do while I was out with the detectives, as well as a map of my beat, which I expected him to ride, not in a daze but on the lookout for disorder or the unusual. I had no faith in him and ignored him when he appeared.

The detectives were waiting outside the hotel, Denning consulting his notes. Baines smoked and gazed around, still wearing a look of city incredulity at finding himself out here.

'Not much of a town, is it?' Denning said.

'It services the local population well enough, sir.'

'Why do they have a senior constable stationed here? Waste of a salary. You should be in a bigger town.'

'I'm waiting to be reassigned, sir.'

'We'd be better off with the other trooper.'

'With respect, sir, I have been stationed here for several years. I know the people and they may feel more comfortable having a familiar face nearby when you question them.'

'We're not here to make them feel comfortable – the opposite, in fact. You will escort and advise on local conditions. You will not question any witnesses, interrupt or otherwise try to influence the investigation.'

'Sir, I found the bodies and have some ideas on—'

'I am not interested in your ideas. You will escort and protect.'

I mounted up and ordered the troopers to do likewise. If Denning wanted to spit his wee dummy, then so be it. The bush has its fair share of grumpy old bastards – more than its fair share, probably. Hardship doesn't grow pretty flowers. Inspector John Denning should feel right at home.

I led the way back to the scene of the murders along the muddy, rutted road. The troopers on watch, on rotation from Bourke, sagged with relief to see us, until I shot them a hard look that caused them to straighten up again. Police talk shop whenever they're together and stories of lazy, undisciplined mounted troopers could spread back to Sydney like a bad cold. Not that I cared much unless I was officer in charge. Then I did.

The Kirkbrides' cart was gone. Baines walked beside the wheel ruts and back again, then consulted his notes. The westerly from yesterday had blown itself out. Above us, a wedge-tailed eagle rode the updrafts. He was lucky to be alive, given it was coming into lambing season. Eagles loved newborn lambs as much as farmers hated eagles.

'Oi, Hawkins,' Baines said. 'What do you reckon happened?'

'They were coming from the north-east, travelling to their homestead, and someone's waylaid them and forced them up here. The fence has been pushed down and they've driven the cart over it.'

Baines pushed his hat back, swiped at the flies. 'Any other horse tracks found around here?'

'We won't know until the trackers return.'

'Killers were waiting for them,' Baines said, looking around with a grim face. 'Knew they were headed down this road and waited for them. Two things – it was personal or it was opportunism gone wrong.'

'Gone wrong?'

'Yeah, man wants what they have, they won't give it to him. His bloods up, it's not going as he planned it. He lashes out and then it's on, he runs amok. But he didn't start out that way. The sort of blokes that rob opportunistically are rarely masters of self-control.'

Denning joined us. 'Miss Nessie's face, that's personal. They had a gun, and we can see that they weren't afraid to fire it, so why beat the other two to death?'

Baines stared at the blood on the drying mud, smoking, frowning. A breeze stirred the coolabahs. A couple of ravens watched us, big, coal-black birds with a cry like an ancient lament.

'Was Nessie a flirt? Liked to lead men on, that sort of thing?' Denning asked.

'Not at all.'

'The younger one?'

'She's – she was – a child.'

'What about James Kirkbride?'

'He did not lead men on.'

Denning gave me a sour look. Jimmy Kirkbride cut a swathe through the female population of the district with a playful smile and one thing on his mind. But Detective Denning could dig that nugget up himself.

'What do you know about Robert Kirkbride?' he asked.

'One of the biggest landholders in the Western Division, with runs both north and south of here, and further east too. But Inveraray is the jewel in the crown, the one his grandfather founded.'

'Sheep, not cattle, right?' Baines asked.

'Sheep, yes. They run about a hundred thousand, and they're expanding now the worst of the drought is over. I know Jimmy wants – or wanted – to run another hundred thousand. He reckoned the land could take it if they did it right.'

'Jimmy's death's going to hit the business hard then, not just the family?'

I nodded. 'Their reputation is as a solid venture. These big stations run on British investment. Couldn't be done without it. But give 'em a nasty scare and the shareholders will pull out and put their money into Malay rubber, Indian cotton, Canadian wheat, wherever there's a profit to be made.'

'Anyone you know with a grudge against Kirkbride?' Denning asked.

'He's a rich man and getting richer with every clip. Success breeds enemies, but I personally wouldn't know about his business dealings.'

'*Cui bono*,' Baines said. 'That's what you look for.'

'Who benefits?'

'Yeah, because there's always someone.'

7

Next stop was the Kirkbride homestead. We heard the sheep before we saw them, a deafening rumble of bleats and hooves walking along the road. Kelpies, those small, pale-eyed demons, worked with the drovers to guide the mob, keeping them walking, keeping them relaxed so they'd be easier to handle in the yards.

Baines and Denning stared at the sheep, squinting and waving at the flies.

'Shearing time,' Denning said. 'In the middle of winter?'

'They're crutching the ewes – almost as busy.'

'What the hell is crutching? Sounds bloody painful,' Baines said.

'Shearing the belly, legs and crutch of the ewe before lambing. Keeps their arses clean and allows lambs to get at the udders more easily. All of these ewes, or most of them, are ready to drop a lamb or two.'

'They been moving the sheep around for a while?'

'Yep.'

'Going to make it hard for your trackers,' Baines said, arms folded, shaking his head.

'It will. But crutching has to be done before lambing, like Lent has to be done before Easter.'

Baines nudged a clump of tussock grass with his shoe. 'This what they eat?'

'If you're looking for green paddocks you won't find them out here,' I said. 'They aren't your superfine merinos. These are hardier, grow coarser wool, eat native grasses, what's left of them, saltbush, anything they can. Drovers move them around to feed, leaving some land for regrowth, 'specially after winter rain. Put the sheep back on to feed on the new growth and keep doing it.'

The mob finally moved on, leaving us choking in their dust. I stationed my six troopers along the driveway and told them to stay mounted while we continued up to the homestead.

Inveraray was built from stone and back from the river on the red dirt. Build on the black dirt and when the floods come you're in trouble. It was a large house with additions over the generations, partly up on stumps and with a wide verandah at the front, which looked east to the redgums and coolabah along the riverbanks. Two date palms, planted back in the 1850s, stood sentinel at the front of the house.

To the north of the house lay extensive vegetable gardens, worked by blacks and Chinese, watered by a mule-powered whim that extracted water from the river. Nearby were the stables, the stock and station workers' quarters, wheelwright, blacksmith, carpenters' shops, dairy, round yards and various pens. There had been a small school but that was closed as Kirkbride did not employ married men. Too expensive. Not far away were the four enormous sheds for the shearing, and far beyond that the tallow burner, the end of the line. It was a small village that revolved around the sheep, laid out like all the other big stations in the area.

I dismounted and a black kid of about fifteen came over and led our horses away. Baines stared, while Denning looked astonished.

'Haven't seen an Aboriginal before?' I snapped.

No answer. Of course they had – there were blacks in Sydney, and they would have come across them down in the Rocks or at La Perouse or elsewhere. Different to the ones out bush, though.

The native maid let us in and we were taken to the back verandah, which faced west towards the Paroo and the low, purple hills. Robert Kirkbride sat staring into the middle distance, still pale and shaky. Kirkbride's abiding passions were his legacy and seeing other men go to the wall, particularly those in the same industry. He never thought it would be him – but we don't, do we? The shock of this attack on his realm had aged him overnight, but he rallied to shake hands and call for tea.

'Tell us about your children,' Denning said in a respectful tone, those pale eyes missing nothing. 'Starting with James.'

Kirkbride caught his breath, like he'd been punched in the guts. He shut his eyes, spoke quickly in a monotone, pausing now and then. 'James was twenty-six. He boarded at King's. Went on to study science at the University. I didn't think he needed to but it's what he wanted. Then he came back and settled into helping me run the place. It would have been his one day.'

'A sweetheart?'

65

'No one special.' Kirkbride looked down at his hands and slowly shook his head.

'His sisters?'

'Loved the girls, always looked out for them.'

'Did they go away to school?'

'No, they did not. A girl needs to grow up in her own home, not be raised by strangers for a world she'll play no part in.'

Denning nodded sympathetically. 'Did they have a governess?'

'They did, and Grace ... we were looking for a new governess.'

'Why did the old one leave?'

'To get married.'

I'd been half-listening, my mind on Flora. But Kirkbride's last comment puzzled me. Wasn't what I'd heard.

'And the girls' ages were?' Denning asked.

'Flora is twenty-two, Nessie ... was twenty-one, and Grace was our little surprise, she had just turned thirteen the week before ...'

'Nessie have a sweetheart?'

'Thomas Fletcher from Gowrie Station. He'd asked me for her hand and was going to propose at the Coronation Ball.'

Kirkbride raised a hand to his eyes. Flies buzzed around the tea tray, desperate to get at the fruitcake under the domed wire food cover. Sheep bleated in the distance.

'What was Nessie like?'

'She was a joy,' Kirkbride said, swallowing hard. 'All of them rode, attended church, district picnics and dances. They were fine young people, the best a father could ask for.'

'We have the contents from the cart,' Denning said. 'Oilskins, a lantern, some blankets and a rifle. Is there anything else they would have been carrying? Any of their belongings missing?'

'Is that why my children were killed? For a ballgown and a fob watch?'

'I'll need a list, as soon as possible. Gowns, jewellery, suit, wallet, anything at all they would have had with them.'

Kirkbride nodded, then got up and walked to the end of the verandah to compose himself.

'You reckon Nessie didn't tease blokes, right?' Baines asked me, in a low voice.

'No, not at all,' I said. 'Men noticed her – men around here notice any female. But nobody would touch Nessie Kirkbride. Apart from her father being one of the biggest employers in the district, her sweetheart, Thomas Fletcher, is a big lad.'

'Is he the jealous type?'

'What man isn't jealous?' I said. 'But bashing his beloved to death because she smiled at another bloke – nah, not likely.'

'He punched you.'

'His blood was up, that's all.'

'You're happy with that?'

'It's not the punch out here, it's the context in which it's thrown. It's the local *lingua franca* – you have to listen in.'

Baines blinked a few times. 'A punch is a punch.'

Kirkbride returned and sat in his wicker chair. Baines and I swapped a glance of mutual incomprehension.

'Is that all today?' Kirkbride said.

'Is there anything in your life, in your business, your marriage, your past, that may have caused someone to hold a grudge against you?' Denning asked, softening his voice.

A wall came up behind Kirkbride's eyes and his jaw tightened. To my untrained mind it seemed like a blunt question with no chance of a useful answer. People don't want to dig up their dishonesty, their faithlessness, their meanness of spirit or tell a copper they've been less than a good Christian.

'No. Nothing.'

'May we speak to Mrs and Miss Kirkbride?'

Kirkbride looked at me, as if I could do something. 'What for? I've told you everything. And no, you may not, they are extremely fragile, and both are under sedation.'

'From the way I read these maps, Mr Kirkbride,' Baines said, 'you don't get to Cobar via the Calpa to Larne road. So why were they on that road?'

Kirkbride rubbed his face with his hands, blinked and stared into the distance.

Baines and Denning looked at each other. 'We need to speak to the servants who were here that day and evening,' Denning said.

'Yes, of course, I'll arrange it.' Kirkbride got up and went inside.

Baines reached over, lifted the fly cover and took a piece of cake, flexed his shoulders and sighed. 'Going to be a long investigation.'

Kirkbride returned and stood at the railing, looking out over the flat lands to the distant hills. The maid took Denning and Baines to the kitchen to speak to the staff. I waited for a moment, hoping to find out how Flora was.

'The markets will react to this, the share price will drop,' Kirkbride said to himself. 'I've seen it happen before. This could be the end of Inveraray.'

'McIntosh will keep it ticking over.'

'Damn these policemen. We're the victims here, and they dare to ask questions about our private lives? The insolence, the sheer impertinence of it ...'

Kirkbride and I had once been friends, and as he stared into the distance, arms dangling by his side, I felt a wave of pity for him. A loss of such magnitude, the brutality of it ... well, it seemed a miracle to me that he was still capable of standing upright.

'When you find the culprits, I want them dealt with immediately,' Kirkbride said, swinging around to look at me. 'Finish it. Lethal force, you understand?'

To hell with pity. The hide of Kirkbride, issuing orders to me like I was his personal bloody henchman. That wasn't how it worked in the traps. We didn't put on the uniform and then kill whoever we, or others, deemed guilty. Well, most of us didn't – I couldn't vouch for those bastards in Queensland. But Kirkbride was ordering me, not the uniform, and I struggled to put such an insult down to grief.

I left him on the back verandah and walked down the hallway to the blaze of light at the end, the long Persian runner muffling the sound of my boots, the grandfather clock steadily ticking. I knew the house from better days, and which room Flora shared with Nessie. I paused outside her door, wanting to kick it in, see if she was safe. Kirkbride appeared at the end of the hallway. We exchanged a look. I walked out into the fierce light of the day.

The detectives were off with the homestead staff so I sat and waited, letting the memories come. I first met Mrs Kirkbride and her daughters when I was invited to afternoon tea at the Inveraray homestead not long after I took the posting. Jimmy was the first Kirkbride to approach me as he remembered me from school, although I was much older. No doubt he told his parents I'd been an army officer and as such was fit to be entertained, because they sure as eggs would not be pouring tea into porcelain cups for a common or garden mounted trooper.

I'd entered the homestead drawing room with my heart racing and still remember every detail. The room was large, with a shaft of sunlight falling on an upright piano in one corner. It smelled of beeswax furniture polish, sweet and soothing, mingled with the homely smell of fresh scones and strawberry jam. The three Kirkbride sisters, seated on a crimson couch, were dressed in white, with white ribbons in their glossy dark-brown hair. They had creamy skin and mischievous smiles, like nymphs living in a charnel house and totally oblivious to it.

Grace was a child and Nessie a very pretty girl, but it was Flora, the older sister, who I was struck by. Her features, while unremarkable on their own, combined to give her an expression of such intelligence and candour it was hard not to stare. The three girls looked as if they had no idea what cruelty, bitterness, anger or melancholy felt like. I remembered that day so clearly, it was hard to believe half the people in that drawing room were now dead.

~

Denning and Baines returned eventually to their buggy. I mounted up and set off along the drive behind them, relieved to be looking at the wide blue of the sky, the scraggy saltbush, anything but other people's pain.

'Augustus.'

I turned in the saddle, brought my horse to a halt. It was Flora, running towards me, black skirts flapping like crow's wings. I jumped down and she stopped a few feet away, panting, her lovely face distorted by pain, her dark hair chopped and ragged like a street urchin.

'Who killed them?' she cried, holding her skirts in clenched hands.

'I don't know.'

'Why didn't you stop them? Isn't your job to stop people being murdered? What use are you if you can't protect us? None, that's what you are – utterly useless.'

She screamed the last two words. It was clear she was not under sedation.

'I wish it was you dead, not them,' she flung at me. 'I hate you, I hate you.'

She stared at me, panting, then the breeze picked up and a dog back at the homestead barked. She turned and ran, not towards the homestead but away towards the river. I caught up with her, grabbed her arm, yanked her close and pinned her arms. We were both panting, and she howled and kicked. McIntosh sprinted towards us from the yards, shouting.

'Thanks, Gus,' he panted, pulling her away from me. 'I'll take her. Don't know how she got out.'

Flora struggled against him like a wild animal, screaming incoherently as he dragged her along the road. More men came running to help. I couldn't bear it and turned away, tears threatening.

Denning watched with interest and jotted something in his notebook. My horse was down by the river in the shade, tail swishing at the flies. He eyed me with weary resignation, as if it were my fault the Kirkbrides were dead.

Flora was right. It was my job to save them and I hadn't, and it was an excellent reason to wish me dead. I wished it too.

8

As we rode closer to Calpa, I could smell my supper on the breeze, the familiar aroma of mutton stew. Seeing Flora in such distress had taken my appetite away, although I knew from long experience that I had to eat, as hunger brought out the worst in me.

Lonergan was in the laundry, washing his hands, and gave me a cautious glance, as well he might.

'Did you see the black trackers out the other day when you went to Gowrie Station?' I asked.

He blinked several times and cast his eyes heavenwards, looking for the right answer. 'Um, yeah? I think I did.'

'You think.'

'I did, sir.'

'And did you see that they were armed?'

'Yes, sir.'

Cunning little toss-rag. Put here to keep an eye on me.

'And you wired this observation to Bourke?'

'Yes, sir. Because I thought the blacks were to be disarmed. Sergeant Martin said so.'

'But you weren't there when he issued that order.'

'No, sir. But Trooper McNamara said Sergeant Martin had logged the order and he'd seen it.'

'Is Trooper McNamara your commanding officer?'

'No, sir. You are, sir.'

'Then why did you not query me first?'

'Ah ... because—'

'Because I have a reputation as being the maddest trooper in the Bourke Division, which includes Walgett and Wanaaring and therefore is some fucking achievement, right?'

'Ah, yes, sir.'

A brave answer, I'd give the hairy little bogtrotter that.

'I could be howling at the moon, Trooper, but I am still your senior officer, and if you wish to query my orders you come to me. Now, go and muck out the stables.'

'But it's dark, sir.'

I pointed at a lantern. He picked it up and went out the back. I saw the lantern light bobbing around while he looked for the pitchfork. With him out of the way I could have my supper in peace, and I filled my plate with the mashed potato and mutton stew that had been left for me on the stovetop. There was also a pie dish covered with a chipped old plate. I lifted it and saw rice pudding, smelled the warm milk and nutmeg.

While I forked potato and stew into my mouth, my thoughts returned to Flora, her screams of rage, her headlong rush back to the river to extinguish herself. I put my fork down with a shaking hand, a lump in my throat no food could get past.

In my room, I opened the drawer of the battered old bedside cabinet and took out a thick wad of letters tied with a white ribbon – one of Flora's which she'd given to me. These were her letters to me, carefully hoarded. I re-read them often, to bring her close and to remind myself of the man she saw in me, a man I sometimes barely recognised.

~

Not long after I went to tea at the Kirkbrides' there was a church picnic down by the river. On the day of the picnic, hessian sacks of grain were taken down to the river's edge and laid out for people to sit on. Men lit fires and boiled up billies, women spread rugs and everyone laughed and chattered. Kids threw balls or found sticks to wave about. Beer and lemonade bottles sat in the river shallows keeping cool; men cooked mutton chops on an old ploughshare, the familiar sizzle of mutton fat bringing in the flies and the hunger. Reverend Hickson, in his dog collar and black coat, said grace and everyone fell on the plates of potato salad, damper and meat.

If anyone anywhere wanted to destroy such a peaceful, harmless, idyllic scene, they'd see me, clean uniform, shiny boots, astride the mighty Dancer, looking humourless and longing for a mutton chop. Eventually, having assessed the threat to the picnickers as probably next to zero, I dismounted and had a cool lemonade, brought to me by Nessie Kirkbride.

'Would you like something to eat?' she asked.

'I can get it myself, but thank you,' I said just as Grace came racing up, almost bowling Nessie over in her excitement. A flock of vivid green budgerigars flew over just at that moment, and we all looked up as they swooped and looped in unison.

'Come on, there's going to be games and I need you to help,' Grace said, tugging at her sister.

Grace and Nessie left me to my lemonade and I watched as they melted back into the group. Grace was a long-legged, coltish child, her dark hair brushed back from her face and caught up with an enormous white ribbon. The two little boys from Tindaree, the Forsythe kids, followed her everywhere, as she did seem to know how to get amusements happening.

I downed a few chops and some damper, and went and stood by the fire to have a smoke and a cup of tea. Grace sprang up and brought me a plate with some cake on it.

'Dundee cake,' she said. 'It's very good.'

'Your favourite?' I asked, taking the plate.

'All cake is my favourite,' she said. 'The sweeter the better.'

'Where's your sister Flora got to?'

'Oh, she's wandered off somewhere, roaming about the place. Mother doesn't like it but she won't stop.'

I looked around but couldn't see her anywhere.

'Shall I go and find her?' she asked.

'No, then there'll be two of you roaming the bush,' I said. 'I'd better find her.'

'She'll be on the riverbank,' Grace said, skipping away. 'Tell her to hurry as we're having an egg-and-spoon race soon.'

The riverbank to the south, heading back towards town, was covered in rocks and slime, so I wandered along to the north, not far, just to see where she was. I kept walking, enjoying the cool breeze from the water, the ducks waddling away and jumping into the river as I passed, small finches skimming the surface.

Around the bend I came across her. She'd taken her hat, shoes and stockings off and had her skirts bunched high up as she waded in the water, her white, shapely legs glowing in the sunlight, her dark hair swept up, her graceful neck on display. She was softly singing to herself as she waded about, the water glittering around her thighs. Then she saw me.

'I'm sorry, Miss Kirkbride, I noticed you missing and—'

She waded out of the water and dropped her skirts. 'What do you want, Trooper Hawkins?'

'To see if you were safe, that's all.'

'Did my mother send you?'

'No, I—'

'This is my backyard and always has been. I'm perfectly able to enjoy it safely.'

'I'm sure you are, but there are snakes, and look, could you just come back to the picnic? It would make my job easier.'

She hesitated, then said, 'Turn away and I'll finish getting dressed.'

I turned away as instructed, but it was hard to turn away from that picture of her wading in the river. She joined me, keeping a respectable distance.

'Don't tell my mother, please, or anyone.'

'I won't.'

She had her hat in her hand and stopped to pin it back on. 'I find groups of people difficult ... We do lead very quiet lives out here.'

'But you are with your siblings every day.'

'You don't have to make an effort with siblings, but you do with strangers. Even people I've known all my life are still strangers.' She paused and added, 'You know what I'm talking about.'

'I do,' I nodded, glancing at her.

In that moment our gaze met and she smiled, a slow, sensual movement of her shining lips that made me catch my breath.

Grace came trotting along the stony bank, the big bow in her hair flopping. 'Come on, Flora, you're going to miss the three-legged race. You missed the egg-and-spoon race, and you always win that.'

Flora ran off with Grace, the two of them holding hands, laughing together, and my world shifted on its axis.

~

I put the letters away after carefully retying Flora's ribbon around them. Shovelled in the remains of my supper and prepared for the evening's duty.

We returned to Inveraray to conduct interviews with the men who'd been working that day. The road to Inveraray was also the road to Tindaree Station and eventually Larne. The Tindaree homestead wasn't on the river, being set further to the west. Along their fenceline were thick stands of remnant scrub. We plodded past, listening to the creak of saddle leather, the rattle of the sulky wheels and the cries of wild dogs somewhere out in the dark.

A shot rang out through the stillness.

'Jesus,' Baines cried, instinctively ducking down. 'What the hell?'

Then a volley of gunshot and a man shouted. I reached for my rifle. The detectives were unarmed. More shots rang out. They were getting closer.

'What do we do?' Baines shouted.

I fired my rifle into the air, so the shooters would know someone was here.

'Make ready,' I yelled at the troopers, who were breaking position and skittering about. A second later, a huge kangaroo bounded onto the road, hit the side of the cart, staggered and took off towards Calpa. My heart was thumping like his must have been.

I fired into the air again and shouted, 'Police, lower your weapons!' A bullet whistled past. Those fuckers. I wheeled my horse around to go in the direction of the shots. The troopers, like a bunch of ducklings, cantered behind me. I hadn't given the order, so what the hell were they doing?

'Hawkins,' Denning yelled after me. 'Inveraray, now!'

'Fall in, now,' I shouted at my troopers. I expected Denning enjoyed that little display of poor discipline.

Further along we stopped. There was no more gunfire, just the sounds of three men panting, and the jostle of six lads on horseback, the rush of the river and crickets.

'Bloody hell,' Baines said, white as a dish of milk. 'They could have shot us by mistake.'

I nursed my rifle across the saddle as we rode along, keeping an eye on the scrub to our left. We reached the turnoff for Inveraray and rode up towards the glow on the horizon, the light from a dozen or more kerosene lanterns. Smoke rose from chimneys in the homestead and the men's quarters, the acrid aroma mixing with the scent of the roast mutton they'd had for supper.

McIntosh came out and Denning and Baines told him how they wanted it to work and got down to it. Men left the quarters in pairs, and after the interviews straggled back inside.

I took my troopers off to the side, quietly gave them an emphatic reminder about the importance of waiting for my order, and then sent them off to take instruction from Baines. I lit a cigarette, leant against the rails of a horse yard and watched the stars until McIntosh came over.

'Your doggers out tonight?' I asked.

'Out every night this time of year – why?'

'Didn't you hear shots earlier? Too close to the road to be safe.'

'Nope, didn't hear a thing,' he said and lit up a fag. 'These coppers won't get much from my men. They're all good lads, hardworking, respectful.'

'They're after witnesses. Anyone who saw or heard anything at all that can help build a timeline.'

Denning appeared and asked me to go up to the house and get the list of valuables James and the girls had with them in the cart. I ground my cigarette out and started for the homestead, I climbed the stairs to the verandah and knocked. The maid answered and I told her what I'd come for. She ran off and several minutes later returned with a sealed envelope – and Joe Pryor carrying his black bag.

'Gus – what brings you up here?'

'Escorting the detectives. You?'

'Flora Kirkbride. She's very unwell. She's just about destroyed her bedroom, cut the bedding to ribbons, screams at her parents if they come near her. I've never seen anything like it.'

She blamed me, of course she did. I'm sure a lot of other people did too.

'Look, you better wait and ride back with us,' I said. 'Been a disturbance on the road tonight.'

'What happened?'

'Could be roo shooters getting a bit out of hand, but somebody's not being careful where they shoot.'

We took a seat on a bench on the verandah and waited. Did a lot of waiting in this job. A bit like the army, days of crushing boredom and then fifteen minutes of terror, then it was back to writing up requisitions for soap.

~

Back in town I went and had a beer at the Royal with the detectives. With Baines, anyway – Denning went to his room. There were a few locals, drinking and playing darts. A fire dancing in the grate, Wally's grumpy kelpie stretched out in front of it, growling at men who got too close.

'Denning a good boss?' I asked, as Wally served us a couple of beers, his oily white hair glistening in the lamplight.

'Never met him before. I'm from the Detective Branch in Phillip Street and he's a detective from the Head Station at Arncliffe. All of two words from him on the train to Bourke, yes and no.'

'Been inspector for long?'

'Couple of years, so I hear. He was a copper in England before he come out here. Solves most of the street murders he works on.'

'Which would be the same as in the bush, I'd imagine – drink, fight, fall over, kill the other bloke on your way down.'

'Pretty much,' Baines laughed.

'What did you find out from the men on Inveraray?'

'A few of the blokes reckon they saw James at the dance in Larne. Said they couldn't help noticing the boss's son at a dance for the workers. Here's what I reckon: killers see a rich man's son and heir and decide he's gotta have something on him worth stealing, so he's marked. And they waited for him.'

'Maybe,' I stubbed out my cigarette. 'But attacking the boss's son, risking him identifying you and then losing your job and being branded a troublemaker is not something the men out here would do. They look rough but they aren't stupid.'

'Then they weren't locals,' he said. 'Blow-ins, maybe, looking for easy pickings.'

'More likely, yes. Lot of them about when the crutching's on.'

'Why were the Kirkbrides at a workers' dance? Tell me that.'

'The girls were seen there too?' I asked.

'Nope, nobody saw them. So where were they? Doesn't make sense.' Baines took a long pull on his beer and looked around. 'Is Kirkbride liked in the district? Got a temper, mistreat his staff? Had affairs? Got another man's wife knocked up?'

I shrugged. 'Not that I've heard of.'

Baines smiled. 'I bet there's plenty of that goes on out here, nothing else to do.'

'Nothing but fencing, mustering, dipping, clipping, shearing, branding, feeding, fixing, castrating—'

'Yeah, all right. But while you're virtuously tucked up under your police regulation blanket dreaming of becoming a better cop, Robert Kirkbride could be having a taste of someone else's missus and got caught out.'

'Not my business. If they were going at it like rabbits in a public place, I'd have to do something. Once they shut that front door, mate, it's not a police matter.'

'What sorta crimes you got out this way?' Baines asked.

'Public drunkenness, failure to renew a firearms licence, threatening or abusive language, aggravated assault, vagrancy, escape from custody, desertion of wives and children, and stock theft. Stock theft is a very big problem.'

'How do you steal a herd of sheep?'

'Just take 'em. These are big stations spreading for hundreds of miles. Kirkbride has boundary riders, same as Gowrie and Tindaree, but the smaller outfits don't have the money to do that. You need money to grow wool. If you succeed at pinching another man's stock, you make a tidy profit to put back into your own business.'

'Is that something Kirkbride would do?'

'Wouldn't like to speculate. But he's got no reason to pinch other men's sheep.'

'Mate, some men don't need a reason.'

9

Tindaree, the third-largest property in the district, was flat out when we rolled up the next day, a cavalcade of self-important stickybeaks demanding their time and attention. The racket coming from the sheds was so loud we had to shout to be heard. If Denning expected them to down tools because Detectives From Sydney were waiting, he had another think coming.

The pregnant ewes waiting to be crutched were crammed into pens, panting and pressing against each other, and then suddenly one of their tormenters would appear, grab them by the shoulders and drag them into the inferno, shear their arses and hind legs, the steam engine grinding and stuttering as it powered two dozen pairs of clippers.

Relieved of half its wool, the ewe would be shoved out into another pen, where it would wait for its mob mates and then be put through a race into a larger pen and taken off to the lambing paddock. The wool went the other way, once it was off the beast. It was picked over, classed and ended up in the scouring shed, another hot, deafening netherworld, where all the burrs, dags and muck were washed from the wool.

From there it went into another massive shed, where men worked the wool presses and boys swept the loose wool, endlessly, all day. Then the final shed, where the bales were stacked and set to wait while the boss sorted the transport.

This entire performance went for days and days, like a factory. Food was shovelled into the men every few hours and they staggered to their quarters at night, dropping like stones into their bunks. The murders had hit the district hard but this was wool country, and even if the Lord came down in a blaze of glory for His Second Coming, He'd be made to wait until the ewes had tidy arses.

Any staff who could be spared from duties had been gathered and interviewed. We'd come back tonight to question those who couldn't be spared. I left the troopers to it and found the owner, Doug Forsythe, hanging over a post-and-rail fence, clipboard in his hand, watching the shorn ewes emerge from the shed.

'I'm busy, Gus, can't you see?' he snapped as he kept his eye on the sheep pelting down the ramp, legs splayed, eyes wild.

'Last night we were passing the turnoff to Tindaree when there was a whole lot of shooting. A roo bounded into us and nobody appeared. There are a lot of people in and about the area right now, city people, here because of the murders. You have to tell your men to be careful.'

'You sure it was my men?'

'On your property.'

He frowned. 'That don't mean it was my blokes.'

'Look, just tell them to be extra careful. I don't want to ship a dead detective back to the city and explain how it happened.'

'Yeah, rightio,' he said, his eyes on the slithering ewes.

I left him to it, but I was uneasy, and not just because of the Kirkbride murders. Every man in this district was working his arse off getting the crutching done and was too buggered to do much of anything else until it was over. Too buggered to murder, too buggered to shoot roos – and all of them, to a man, knew that if you were out shooting and you heard gunshot from another direction, you'd stop and investigate, or wait at the very least. It wasn't just bush etiquette, it was survival. To ignore those customs suggested some very dangerous or stupid men were around. Or blow-ins who didn't give a toss.

~

Friday morning rolled around and I woke to the sound of Lonergan heaving his guts up. That was what happened if you ate at the Royal, I knew from experience. Wilson and Frosty Garnet were still out scouting for tracks, leaving us stuck with the dreary work of interviews.

I escorted the detectives and troopers up to Larne for the day, the site of the notorious dance, and was on the alert for any gunshot. I wanted a word with those shooters from the other night, to see their licences, to see if I could find a way to get them out of the district – or at the very least read the riot act to them. Both Baines and Denning wanted to speak with them in regard to the Kirkbride killings.

'They could have shot Grace by mistake, right?' Baines said, still shaken by the shooting. 'Gone to investigate, James is angry and goes to shoot them so they smash his head in and do Nessie to shut her up. Like I said, blokes what do stupid, random things don't have a lot of self-control. Nessie's screaming, James is shouting, bang, dead, all three of them.'

~

Larne was a furuncle in the groin of the Darling, a three-hour ride north of Calpa, a place where drinking was the main occupation and the citizens nursed a chronic case of brown bottle flu. Paddle-steamers from Bourke forged their way through floating rafts of empty beer bottles and the odd rotting sheep carcass, then tied up at the Larne wharf to take on copper ingots and bales of wool. The pub and store serviced the local populations and the seasonal influx, and they had a school, a post office – built of brick, no less – a civic hall and a one-man police station. Trooper Parry, a grimy, saturnine man with pockmarked cheeks and cauliflower ears, nominally under my command, was not up to scratch, but he was here and that was the main thing.

The Larne hotel, also called the Royal, was timber and whitewashed stone with a verandah and an old and gnarled peppercorn tree out front. I took Denning and Baines in, introduced them to the publican and his staff, all who looked mildly incredulous at the prospect of being interviewed by a clutch of shavelings whose tongues protruded with the effort of writing and thinking at the same time.

I listened for a few minutes, then excused myself and rode out towards Curranyalpa. I needed to follow up on the Kenmore escapee, as Lonergan was dragging his feet and Trooper Parry was staring at a wall somewhere. Always good to find these fellas before they baptised themselves in the river and never surfaced.

~

Curranyalpa was no more than a bore with a name, on land scarred with eroded gullies, rabbit tracks and sun-bleached bones. This had to be some stringybark settler's land, somebody who'd sunk his life into a job too big for him. A clanking rusty windmill signalled the bore, vanes turning slowly, the ground around the trough cut to buggery by sheep, packed tight by all those sharp, cloven hooves.

A dog came hurtling out of nowhere, sending my horse into a flurry. I grabbed my rifle, aimed at the dog and was about to shoot when I heard a man cursing. The dog stopped, wagged his tail and ran back. He was just young and keen to say hello.

A tall, thin man appeared in a stained shirt and suspenders holding up filthy trousers three times too big for him. His battered felt hat had an emu feather on it, ruffling in the breeze, and he raised his hand to me while carrying a lowered rifle in the other.

'Senior Constable Augustus Hawkins, Calpa,' I called.

'Morning to you, Constable,' he said, and I realised he was a she. 'What brings you out here?'

'I'm looking for the Jongs – they live around here?'

'I'm Mrs Anne Jong, you got lucky,' she said with a smile.

Sadly, I was about to wipe the smile off her face. 'You run sheep out here?'

'Oh,' she said, looking around. 'Tried our hand at it but it's not for the likes of us. Need money to make money. I shoot rabbits, roos, dogs, goats, emus, whatever they'll pay me for, and I sell the skins. Feathers too. Big trade in emu feathers. English women can't get enough of them.'

'I'll bet they can't. Do you have a son called Albert Jong?'

Her shoulders slumped. 'Got out again, has he?'

'Done this before?'

She nodded. 'You better come to the house. It's not far.'

Their house was a tiny stone cottage with a corrugated-iron roof, ticking in the sunshine. An old Chinese man sat inside at a scrubbed table. He got to his feet, slowly and painfully, as I entered, and we shook hands. Mrs Jong placed a yellowing cloth on the table. It was decorated with neatly embroidered bunches of grapes.

'Our Dulcie made this,' Mr Jong said proudly, smoothing his gnarled hand over the cloth.

An embroidered mantel scarf hung over the neat, small fireplace, embroidered pennants with tassels.

'And did she make that too?' I asked.

He beamed proudly. 'She's very accomplished.'

'Indeed, you must be very proud.'

Mrs Jong laid out what was no doubt her best tea set, chipped white with sprigs of pink flowers, then she placed a plate of shortbread on the table.

'I use emu fat,' she said. 'No butter to be had out here. Plenty of sugar in it but – eat up.'

'Tell me about Albert,' I said, slipping the shortbread into my pocket.

'None of our others were like it,' Mr Jong said, hoeing into the emu-fat shortbread. 'Six children, one bad 'un, five come good. Not our Bertie. Poor lad.'

'He's coming this way, or so the reports say.'

They exchanged frightened glances. 'Set the place on fire last time, with us inside. Howling about demons,' Mr Jong said, tears welling up in his old eyes.

'Can you go and stay with one of your children until we find him? Might be easier on you.'

The old woman nodded, took her husband's hand.

'We got two sons in Cobar working the mines, one daughter in Wilcannia – that's our Dulcie,' Mrs Jong said proudly. 'The other two lads are shearers. They're always on the road, and when they're not they come here and help out. They're good boys, saving for their own land. We'll go to Wilcannia, see our grandchildren, eh, Eddie? Take your mind off Albert.'

Mr Jong nodded, dabbed at his tears. 'Dulcie has had troubles of her own, Constable. She's got three daughters, and a more mischievous bunch you couldn't find. There's the youngest, Molly, then the middle girl, Belinda, and the eldest is Rose.'

I nodded, drank my tea. These two probably never saw another person from one day to the next, and I was happy to sit and listen.

'They all go to school now. For a while they didn't because they was in Menindee. Well, Dulcie married a shearer, Howie Blackwood – he runs

90

his own team so he's doing well, can't afford to miss a job neither. But they had to move to Wilcannia.'

'Menindee's a long way from Wilcannia.'

'Howie's got family in Wilcannia, who can help Dulcie with the girls while he's on the job. Rose has been a handful ever since ...'

'That's enough now, Eddie,' the old woman said sternly. 'Thank you for coming out to warn us, Constable.'

I thanked Mr Jong, who was lost in thoughts of his granddaughter.

'Do you have a way of getting to Wilcannia?' I asked Mrs Jong as we walked over to my horse.

'Horse and cart, we load her up. Slow going but no hurry.'

'Get onto a road and away from the bush as quickly as you can, even if you have to go round about. If you see him, or think he's near, let us know in Larne or Calpa. And keep your rifle handy.'

'Not going to shoot my own son.'

'You might have to.'

'He doesn't know what he's doing,' she said. 'He can't stop, he's sick in his head.'

'Knowing that isn't going to protect you if he's of a mind to do harm.'

'Oh, it's the sane that do the harm, and they get away with it. Men who think they're educated when they're nothing but beasts beneath their fine clothes.'

Had to agree with that. I left her looking back at her tidy little cottage, probably wondering how she could pack it all into a wagon and get away before the storm arrived.

I rode back to Larne across the dusty plain, strewn with the bones of

91

dead animals and pockmarked with rabbit holes. I'd heard that during the Federation Drought ten thousand sheep being driven to the Darling dropped dead while only five miles east of Larne. Just couldn't make it to the river, which was dry anyway. And they were a fraction of the deaths.

Last century it was believed that rain followed the plough, so we pushed further and further into the west, hungry for land, telling ourselves God was a grazier and He'd approve of our taming the wilderness. Now, I watched the weather as a soldier was trained to do, but predict it? No, no more than a few days ahead, and even then there was no certainty. The idea that clearing vegetation would bring a celestial blessing as rainfall had to be one of the higher peaks in the endless mountain range of human folly.

~

Back in Larne, while I waited for the detectives and troopers, I lit a fag and leant against the post, took out my notebook and jotted down the details of the Jongs. I noticed several city types emerge from the hotel, blinking and looking around. One of them spotted me and introduced himself as somebody or other, journalist from a big-city paper. I shook his hand, curious, as I'd never met a journalist. A couple of the others sauntered over.

'I can't speak about the murders,' I said. 'Nor anything else. Ask the detectives.'

'Were you the trooper who found them? How did they die? Were they alive when you got there?'

92

I reached into my pocket and pulled out the emu-fat shortbread. 'Here you go, mate.'

That slowed him down for a moment, then he gathered his wits and carried on hurling questions at me like stones. I was about to lose my temper when Baines came out, lit a fag and told them to clear off.

'Just ignore them, mate. We give a scrap here and there, keep 'em happy, just doing their job. They can be handy, they get the word out, then people remember things, come forward.'

'Most of the people out here don't or can't read,' I said. 'And Kirkbride's worried about what they'll write about the family.'

'He's got deep pockets – the papers will tiptoe around him.'

'Did you find out anything new?'

'Barmaid reckons you've got the morals of an alleycat.'

'Polly said that?'

'She did, mate,' he said, with a grin. 'Forgot the flowers, did you?'

'You interviewed them about me?'

'Nah, you just bobbed up in the conversation, like.'

I brooded over Polly's observations. A bit harsh, I thought, a bit uncalled for.

Once all six troopers were finished interviewing, we reorganised and made our way north upriver, as far as the junction of the Warrego and the Darling. We visited people who lived alone or in ragged families, in shacks, hovels, humpies, tents and under trees. We interviewed cockies on small holdings, swaggies, bushmen doing odd jobs, people living on catfish, kangaroo, white flour, tea and hope, and all were as likely to go dancing in the new king as pay for dancing lessons. It was a complete waste of our time.

None of the local employers had wanted a dance in the middle of crutching, and it was damn inconvenient of the King to get himself crowned at such a time. Why couldn't there be a few words said at a Sunday church service, some employers asked, and be done with it? Most bush dances went all night so the next day would be a write-off. Paying the crutchers' wages while station staff lolled about with hangovers was not going to happen, so it was agreed that the dance would go ahead but end at midnight. After all, the Coronation Ball in Cobar was on for the toffs, and were we not all the King's subjects?

10

After a day pestering the population, I led the parade back to Calpa. The breeze wafted a stench our way. I knew what it was, didn't even have to look. A dead sheep caught in a snag and happily macerating until some poor bugger fished it out. The unspoken rule was that whoever lived closest to it had the chore. I hoped it was Kev this time, but when I let my horse go into the home yard by the river, I knew it was my problem.

Denning went to complain to himself in his room at the hotel, but I took Baines through to the police station kitchen and pulled some beer bottles from the meat safe. We sat at the table to drink, lighting up two fags and washing the dust down with a soothing ale.

'What's Africa like, then?' Baines asked. 'Seen any of those darkie women dancing around naked in what God gave 'em? Now, I'd like to see that, I would.'

'As an officer, my job was to keep my men away from fraternising with the locals.'

'The army has licensed places, don't they? For men to go to, like, make sure they don't get the pox. That's what I heard.'

'In India they do. The British army in Bombay have whole streets of brothels just for the military.'

'And in South Africa?'

'It's a ... let's just say it's a nastier trade, unlicensed and more akin to slavery.'

'Blimey,' Baines said. 'And the Australian soldiers, did they ...'

'A man spends weeks at the front killing, waiting to be killed, what's he expected to do afterwards? Saucy postcards and a hand shandy?'

'Yeah, right enough,' he said and finished his beer. 'How those statements coming on?'

'I'll hand them over to Mr Fraser tomorrow.'

I had very good reasons to be the one who found the killers, instead of Baines and Denning, and on the pretext of checking legibility, I took the troopers' notebooks at the end of each day and went through them, making notes, jotting down times and finding inconsistencies, marking them for future questioning.

The young troopers were inexperienced and were not going to press a man twice their age and tough as whitleather, especially if he made it clear he didn't want to answer questions, so I don't know how reliable the statements were. But Baines and Denning weren't worried. In fact, I had the sense they were simply going through the motions.

That night I woke to shouts and pounding on the station door, my heart just about leaping out of my chest.

Somebody was dead. More bodies. Don't let it be Flora.

I stumbled through to the station, opened the door and found a kid of about fifteen, eyes wide, hair dishevelled, panting.

'You're to come quick to Gowrie, and the doctor too. There's been trouble.'

That could mean anything. He ran off to rouse Joe and I pulled my uniform on, shook Lonergan awake and told him that until I got back he was to be ready for anything.

It was around one o'clock. Joe caught up with me and we hurried in stunned silence through the black night, memories of riding together to the Kirkbride bodies following us like spectres. At least we weren't heading to Inveraray.

The night was bitter and still, our breath pluming and a light frost already on the ground. Lights were on in the Gowrie homestead and in the stockmen's quarters. The overseer, Henry Peyton, met us, lantern raised, brows furrowed, shock etched deep in every line of his weathered face.

'Doctor, you'll be needed in there,' he said, nodding towards the stockmen's quarters. 'And, Constable, you'd better see Mr Fletcher up at the house.'

'What's happened?'

'A fight.'

My footsteps crunched over the frosty gravel. I entered the open door of the homestead, nobody there to greet me, so I just made my way to the sound of male voices. A woman was crying in a room off the hallway.

I found the door to the drawing room and opened it. A carriage clock on the mantelpiece ticked loudly. The dark polished furniture gleamed in the lamplight, the piano covered with a lace cloth, couches and chairs all clustered around the fireplace in a cosy circle. An open whisky bottle, the smell of camphor and cold ash. Tom Fletcher and his father Will standing in front of the dead fire. They looked over in surprise when I walked in.

'Who called you out?' Will Fletcher said, his craggy face pale.

'A young lad from here woke me and Dr Pryor.'

Father and son exchanged a look. Joe Pryor burst in, looking harried. 'Michael Pearson just passed away.'

Tom gave a strangled cry. Will Fletcher planted his hand firmly on his son's shoulder, squeezing hard.

I took out my notebook, trying to spur my mind into action. 'What happened?'

'Pearson made a few ill-considered remarks about Nessie Kirkbride,' Will said, while Tom stared at the ashes in the fireplace, tears rolling silently down his blotchy face.

'And?'

'Tom gave him a smack because that sort of talk won't be tolerated on this property.'

I remembered Tom giving me a smack the day after the murders. Not an experience I'd care to repeat.

'Pearson's dead. Must have been more than a smack,' I said, looking up from my notebook. 'I'll have to charge Tom.'

98

'Do it, I don't care,' Tom said.

'Hush,' Will snapped. 'You take my boy and not one family in the district will cooperate with you on your damned Kirkbride investigation.'

'It's not my investigation,' I said. 'It's the law.'

'You leave my son here, with me.'

'I'll have to take him into custody now and he'll go up to Bourke tomorrow and appear before a magistrate in Bourke.'

'You're going to put him in the lock-up?' Will shouted. 'No, I won't have it. Pearson was a nasty piece of work and lazy to boot. Just like him to stir up trouble.'

'This is murder, Mr Fletcher,' Joe said. 'Pearson's character is irrelevant.'

'Thank you, Dr Pryor,' I said. 'Would you care to wait outside?'

Shaking his head, Joe retreated.

'What are you charging him with?'

'Manslaughter at this stage, and if I don't charge him, Mr Fletcher,' I said, when we were alone, 'no working man in the district will cooperate with the Kirkbride investigation, or any investigation in the future, including the one into what happened out there between Pearson and your son. Could be Tom was acting in self-defence – we don't know yet.'

He looked at me, then saw what I was getting at. Appease Dr Pryor and sort it out later.

~

I wasn't going to handcuff Tom, even though Joe wanted me to. He was waiting for me outside on the homestead verandah.

99

'Look at the men,' Joe said, nodding towards the crowd on the verandah of the men's quarters. 'They must see justice being done, for the sake of good relations in the community. They sent for us – Fletcher didn't.'

'I'll sort it out,' I said, buttoning up my coat.

'I was in the men's quarters, Gus, I heard what they were saying about Tom, about bosses and workers. You don't read the papers, you think Europe is far away, but ideas travel.'

'Listen, mate, before you build the barricades, tell me: did you find out what Pearson said to Tom Fletcher?'

'No, I don't know. But I do know that to the men it appeared as an unprovoked attack on Pearson by Tom.'

I fetched Tom, and after he'd mounted up I cuffed him so everyone could see what I was doing, then we rode off. Once we were out of sight, I took the cuffs off. Justice was an abstract noun, and therefore as rubbery as you wanted it to be, especially out here.

~

'Pearson said Nessie got what she deserved,' Tom said, half an hour along the road. 'I gave him what he deserved and I'm not sorry I killed him.'

'Fair enough, but don't say things like that to me,' I said as we plodded along in the darkness. 'Judge will go easier if you show remorse.'

'The hell with that,' Tom cried. 'Why don't you just let me go? I'll head west, wait it out somewhere.'

'Spend the rest of your life on the run? Nope, the smarter choice would be to plead gross provocation and good character on your part.'

'Pearson said she was just a cunt on two legs like every other woman, said she got what she deserved for thinking she was too good for the likes of the working man.'

'There you go, gross provocation.'

The chorus of crickets and frogs along the dark river suddenly fell silent. I looked around, pulse rising. Nobody behind us, or not that I could see. Took my rifle out, mindful of unknown killers on the loose, madmen and careless roo shooters. And of the swirling animosity that had blown into the district from nowhere.

'Maybe the bastard killed her,' Tom said, oblivious to everything but his brooding pain.

'Could have. We'll look into it.'

I was thankful to see the lights of the police station looming in the distance. Lonergan was in full battle dress, armed and tense.

'At ease, Trooper, you can go back to bed. All sorted.'

He sagged with a mix of disappointment and relief. Tom went into the lock-up calmly. I gave him a slug of whisky and an extra blanket. He sat still and silent in the cell, looking up when I reappeared with a cup of tea for him. As far as I knew, he wasn't aware of what had been done to Nessie, or how she was killed. If he had been aware, I reckon he'd have done more damage before now, either to himself or someone else.

Tears suddenly appeared on his cheeks. 'I don't care what happens now, I just want to see her.'

Maybe the whisky wasn't such a good idea.

'Better give me your belt.'

He looked up, surprised, but gave it to me. Sometimes the darkness creeps up fast and you can't outrun it by thinking. I didn't want to wake to a sight like that. I dragged my armchair from the kitchen around the corner and into the small hall and parked it in front of his cell, covered myself with a blanket and tried to doze, hoping I'd wake if he tried anything. I don't know how long passed before I heard him speak.

'Gus.'

'Mmm?'

'What was she doing on that road in the first place? Why were they there?'

'Don't know.' I pulled the blanket up closer to my chin and sighed. 'Jimmy probably had some dollymop at the dance and took his sisters along to hide behind.'

'Mmm.'

'But why did Nessie agree to go with him? She knew I was going to be at the ball – she knew I was waiting for her ... Gus?' He banged the enamel tea mug against the bars, startling me out of my comfortable doze.

I straightened up a little with a groan. 'I don't know. Mr Kirkbride said they were going to the ball, leaving later because Grace wasn't well. He has no idea why they were on the Larne Road.'

'Kirkbride's a prick.'

Moonlight streamed in through the high-barred window in his cell. I took out my watch and checked the time. Three forty. I found the bottle of whisky, poured a splash into a pannikin and handed it through the bars to him, gulped from the bottle and sat down again, hoping the alcohol would make him sleepy. But it made me sleepy, him talkative.

'I want to talk to Nessie, I ... just need to see her one last time, tell her how much she means to me.'

'She knew.'

'We wanted to marry but Kirkbride said no. Then Father spoke to him and Kirkbride came around. He fixed a time in Bourke with his lawyers, who came out from Sydney, to discuss what he'd settle on Nessie. We were so happy that he'd finally agreed, even Mother said she'd attend the wedding, and she never goes anywhere.

'We go to the lawyers,' he continued. 'And we're sitting at this big shiny table and Kirkbride gets to his feet, pulls a handful of dirt out of his pocket and throws it on the table. Says, "That's all you'll get of my land." He'd organised it all just to humiliate us. Wasn't going to settle a penny on Nessie.

'I'd marry her with nothing but the clothes she was wearing, but Father said to hell with Kirkbride, marriage was off and I was to find someone else. Nessie thought it was me, that I didn't love her anymore. I couldn't tell her it was her father being a bastard. He was never going to allow us to marry, never. He was going to pick Nessie's husband and I wasn't in the running.'

I straightened up as Tom spoke. Everyone knew Tom and Nessie would marry. Everyone except Bob Kirkbride, it seemed.

'Kirkbride told me you were going to propose at the ball.'

'I just told you, he's a lying prick. When Nessie didn't turn up I thought it was because she was upset with me. I was desperate to talk to her, waiting and waiting ... and all the while she ...'

His face was in shadow, just his massive arms and chest illuminated.

Outside, a rabbit screamed as it died. A god-awful sound. The wild dogs hunted them down. Rabbits must have haunted sleep, all of them waking to the sound of their friend's death.

I picked up the whisky bottle, splashed some more in his pannikin and took a slug myself. Thought of how I'd failed to protect Nessie and Grace, Jimmy too.

Tom's big shoulders began to shake, his tears falling hard, then he raised his face, opened his mouth and howled again and again. I couldn't stand it another moment. Went out the back into the yard.

I could still hear him wailing for her, and I thought of Flora, how I'd failed her. I lit a cigarette, my hands shaking, tears suddenly coursing down my cheeks. Then I dropped my fag, went into the stable and buried my face in Felix's neck. I could barely hear Tom out here.

I stayed with the horses until I thought Tom had cried himself to sleep, then went and roused poor old Kev and sent an urgent wire to Bourke for an escort.

~

As expected, I was woken by Will Fletcher barging into the station before dawn, banging doors, calling out. Lonergan, half-dressed, hurried out and fell over me in my chair, kicked the empty whisky bottle spinning into the wall and fell against the station door. Tom, still alive, sat up, the blanket dropping to the floor.

I unlocked the cell and let him out. His father hugged him and I left them, washed my face, put on a fresh shirt, applied some ointment to my scar, rubbing it back and forth, trying to organise my sleep-deprived mind.

'Mrs Schreiber will be here soon, she'll do breakfast for you, Tom,' I said, entering the kitchen, working the coals and feeding kindling into the stove.

'What are you going to charge him with?' Will Fletcher said.

'Manslaughter.'

'I don't want those detectives on my property, y'hear?' Will said, trembling. 'I'll horsewhip them if they so much as walk past.'

'It won't be them. I'll take the statements. Lonergan, that means you will have to escort the detectives today.'

'But ... but, sir, I—'

I shut him down with a raised eyebrow. A day with Denning, Baines and the boys was an assignment nobody wanted, but this business with Tom Fletcher had to be done properly.

'I wired for an escort last night,' I said. 'So they'll take him back to Bourke.'

'Not in a van, I won't have it,' Fletcher bellowed.

'Please, Mr Fletcher, calm down. An armed escort, a trooper, will ride with Tom to Bourke. You can go with him if you like, organise bail. But both Lonergan and I have duties here.'

He looked at Tom, who was lost in his own misery and didn't seem to care what happened to him.

To my surprise, Trooper Parry from Larne turned up.

'I'm to take him as far as Larne,' he told me, 'then a Bourke trooper will take him from there. Short on horses at the moment.'

Not unheard of. I watched the two Fletcher men mount up and set off upriver with Parry. Inside, Lonergan was at the armoury, staring at the weapons like he was in a flower shop choosing the prettiest bunch for his girl. I couldn't stand it and went back outside for a moment to calm my nerves.

Wally appeared out the front of the pub, combed his hair back and slipped the comb into his shirt pocket, then lumbered over to say good morning, his dog trailing behind.

'What's goin' on, Gus? Why the Fletchers heading to Bourke?'

'Incident up at Gowrie last night. Tom Fletcher punched a bloke, killed him with one hit.'

Wally rubbed his enormous belly with a sigh. 'Gowrie is bloody cursed. Always bloody something happening on that bloody property.'

'Like what?'

'Will's father, old Bill Fletcher, died in the Federation Drought, just dropped dead in his paddocks. Bloody ravens ate half of him by the time he was found.'

'Were you here then?'

'I was. Like being in hell. Dead and dying stock, roos, birds, people starving. The bloody land blowin' away. But we've come back out of it, always do.'

'What else has happened on Gowrie? I asked.

'Overseer before Peyton cut his own bloody throat.'

'Jesus, why?'

'Drought got to people. Lotta death, lotta hardship. Hundreds of thousands of bloody sheep, just dropped dead. Roos, cattle, birds, you name it. Still haven't cleared the bones away.'

'And?'

'Mrs Fletcher broke her back, year before you came. Can't get out of bed now.'

'While riding?'

He laughed long and loud, big belly jiggling. 'You could say that, mate. She was having an affair with Bob Kirkbride, meeting out bush in secret. Didn't you know that?'

'Why would anyone tell me?'

Wally shrugged. 'Nuthin' else to do but talk about other people out here. Not like we have a music hall and moving pictures.'

'An affair with Bob Kirkbride, of all people,' I said, shaking my head at the recall of the man's tyrannical ways.

'Yeah, you and I wouldn't want to play a game of nug-a-nug with Kirkbride, but the ladies used to like him. He'd joke and carry on, lively up a dance or picnic, something Will Fletcher never done. But after the accident Kirkbride changed. Everything did.'

'Mrs Fletcher and Kirkbride were out riding together when she came off?'

'Yeah,' he said, giving a great sigh. 'A sad business. You'd never see a more handsome woman than Hester Fletcher, born to the saddle, could shoot, dance all night, run the homestead, always organising picnics and cricket games ... Yeah, she brought life to this place, I tell you.'

'Reckon Will Fletcher could have gone looking for vengeance?' I asked.

Wally turned and gaped at me like I'd lost my mind. 'Kill Kirkbride's kids for tupping his wife? Will's a good Christian man, turns the other cheek and sends the account to Heaven.'

Yet there were only so many times a man could turn his cheek before he gets jack of it. Kirkbride was ploughing Fletcher's wife, and then refused to let Fletcher's son marry his daughter? Insult piled on injury, by which time I'd be well up for a retaliatory strike.

'Virtue in suffering, mate,' Wally said, as if he heard my thoughts. 'That's what the nuns told us kids when they whipped us.'

He whistled to his dog and went back inside the pub. Baines and Denning appeared, Lonergan and the troopers assembled and off they went. I suspect Denning was relieved I was not on escort. I know I was.

Back inside, I pulled down the files for 1907, flipped through the reports until I came to the Hester Fletcher accident. Harry Greenleaf had been the trooper in attendance. Killed himself not long after, poor bastard.

I thought of Tom Fletcher's tale of Kirkbride's cruelty in the lawyer's office and wondered if Tom had told the detectives about it. I doubted it – no man wants to relate his humiliations to a stranger, particularly a fish-eyed, clammy-skinned prick like Denning. And Kirkbride had declared to the detectives that Tom intended to propose at the Coronation Ball, so he wasn't telling the truth either. Had Will Fletcher told the detectives Kirkbride had been at his wife? Again, how many men would admit that they could not keep their wife in order?

I leant back, put my feet up on the desk and lit a fag, watched the smoke rise. It was my duty to pass all this information on. But I decided to do some discreet digging first. I knew that while Will Fletcher could take a one-two punch, Tom could not, or would not. I had to be careful.

11

I rode up to Gowrie Station and saw a rough coffin lying on the back of a dray outside the homestead. I presumed Pearson was inside. The driver climbed up to his seat, picked up the reins. The body was headed to Bourke, and by the time it got there it would be on the nose.

Henry Peyton, the overseer, had rounded up half a dozen blokes who looked a bit resentful as they waited for me under a peppercorn tree. All of them were familiar, just ordinary men, hard workers, liked a laugh, born to the wool districts. One at a time, I took them over to the mess and we took a seat at one of the tables while the cook cleaned up around us.

'Name?'

'Clarence Hooker. I live on Gowrie and was born on the tenth of May, 1881, in Bourke.'

'What happened last night between Tom Fletcher and Michael Pearson?'

'We was having supper and sitting just over there,' he said, nodding at a long table beside a window. 'Just talking, bullshitting, you know what it's like. Girls came up, as they usually do, and we got to talking about who was the prettiest in the district, who we'd like to have connections with, just bullshit we've slung a million times. Beavins reckons Nessie Kirkbride had been the best-looking in the district, but now that fell to Sally Gilmour.'

'Who's she?'

'Mrs Fletcher's nurse. She don't go out much, but when you get a glimpse of her, you won't forget in a hurry. Yeah, then Pearson said Sally was a stuck-up bitch and that Nessie was too. Reckoned she got what she deserved. Women should know their place and shit like that. When he started on we just drifted away.'

'How did Tom Fletcher find out what he said?'

'Somebody musta told him. Wasn't me. Later we was over at our quarters, just having a smoke on the verandah before going to bed, and Tom Fletcher comes barrelling across from the house, walks straight up to Pearson and punches him. Just slam, in the face, one punch but a hell of a lot of power in it. Pearson goes down, bangs his head, eyeballs rolling around, all crazy. Fletcher walks away, back to the homestead.

'He'd done some damage all right. Pearson wasn't coming to and Beavins said it wasn't right, that Pearson had been minding his own business and had no warning. He and Maroney went to Mr Peyton about it and Peyton went up to house and that was it, nothing happened. Some of the fellas said that wasn't right, Pearson was still out to it, so they sent a rouseabout for you and the doctor.'

'You went to the dance with Pearson?' I asked.

'Yeah, and I don't know nothing about the Kirkbride killings.'

'Rightio. Send Beavins in, thanks,' I said, putting my pencil down and stretching my arms.

'Where's Tom Fletcher now?' Hooker asked as he got to his feet.

'On his way to Bourke under escort.'

'Pearson never said it to his face. He was a mean bastard but he wouldn't do that.'

'Who do you think repeated it to Tom Fletcher?'

'Has to be Beavins.'

'But Beavins was Pearson's mate. Why would he want his friend in trouble?'

''Cause he hates Tom Fletcher. Most of the fellas do. His father's all right, but when Tom takes over, if he ever does, we'll walk off.'

I'd never heard this before. 'Why do they hate him?'

''Cause he's a greenskin ... like you, like Jimmy Kirkbride was. Sons of rich men who have it easy, who think they know better than the working man. Everything falls into their lap easy like, and then they tell us what to do and take our women while we're busy working.'

'Tom Fletcher has been courting Nessie Kirkbride for years, not out tomcatting.'

Hooker stabbed the tabletop with a callused finger. 'I know for a fact he's been with Polly Jennings.'

'Every man in the district has been with Polly, so that's neither here nor there.'

Hooker gave a thin smile. 'Jimmy Kirkbride got what was coming to

111

him. Better watch out the same doesn't happen to you.'

'You threatening me, Mr Hooker?'

'Never.'

Beavins was next. He was a handsome fellow with a fulsome moustache, strong arms and a look in his eyes that said he'd be tough to bring to heel. I asked him why he repeated the insult about Nessie Kirkbride to her sweetheart. He looked down at his hands, glanced over at the door, a half-smile on his face, shuffled his feet.

'Pearson would be alive if you'd kept your trap shut.'

'Pearson would be alive if Fletcher had had the guts to give him fair warning. Pearson liked a scrap and he'd have done all right too.'

'Would have lost his job,' I said as I scribbled my notes.

'For punching the boss's son, yeah, too right he would, whether or not the boss's son deserved it.'

I looked up. 'Why did Tom Fletcher deserve it?'

'Not saying he did.' He was breathing heavily now, swallowing, his mouth dry.

'Why'd you tell him? Poor man just lost his girl and you go and repeat some foul comment about her that helps no one.'

Beavins said nothing, looked at the door. Someone was using a meat cleaver out the back, thumping it down like a guillotine, again and again.

'Did you see Nessie or Grace Kirkbride at the dance in Larne?'

'No, I already told those dicks I didn't see them,' he snapped. 'Saw Jimmy Kirkbride with his tongue halfway down the throat of Sally Gilmour, but.'

I noted that down.

'Gonna charge me?'

'Can you think of a reason why I should?'

He sneered and I let him go. I interviewed the two others, who each corroborated the version of the king hit to Pearson's head, with no warning. Maroney was furious about it. Said it was cowardly, called it murder and muttered that Tom Fletcher would not be welcome back on Gowrie.

'Given it's his home, that's going to be a little hard to get around,' I said.

'He'll be going to gaol if all is right with the world.'

He probably wouldn't go to gaol, but I said nothing. I was a greenskin, no matter how mucky and drunk I got, but what surprised me even more was all this workers versus bosses talk. Maybe Joe was onto something. Shearers could be a handful and weren't shy about asking for what they considered was theirs. Back in the '90s they had the woolgrowers by the short and curlies. But in 1907 all station hands had a twenty per cent wage rise and a cap on hours, and now Fisher was a Labor prime minister, they were fed and housed – what more did they want? Didn't want to see a greenskin kissing a girl they considered theirs, by the sounds of it. Well, that was the way of the world, and they could shut their eyes if they didn't like it. Out here it was every man for himself.

But I made a note of it.

~

On my way back to Calpa, I saw a small figure ahead of me, scrawny and unsteady, hand on a tree trunk holding himself up.

'You right, mate?' I asked.

Long, scraggly white beard, trousers mere shreds of fabric, held up by a bit of twine around his waist, one eye missing, just a sunken mess where his eyeball should have been. He carried a blanket roll on his back with a dented billy hanging from it.

'Good morning, Officer,' he nodded. 'Could do with a drink, if you have spare?'

I dismounted and unstrapped my waterbag and filled his billy. 'You don't want to be out here without water.' He drank noisily and I poured some more. 'Where you headed?'

'Calpa,' he said, wiping water from his beard.

'Not far now. But you won't last long if you don't get yourself a waterbag or two, won't be anything but bones in the dust.'

'God will provide, you see. He sent you along when my need was great.'

I couldn't say I felt the hand of God shoving me along, but no point arguing with a God botherer. I took his name and the address of his next of kin. Just in case.

'Thank you, Officer. You see? His Spirit is working through you, even in these dark days.'

'Why are they dark, Mr Doolan?' I said, strapping my waterbag back onto the saddle.

'Evil stalks the land.'

Normally, I took no notice of this sort of talk. Some swaggies were mad as cut snakes, some were liars, but they had a kind of bush network. News travelled quickly, and they knew things we were just waking up to.

'Evil gets around, mate,' I said, mounting my horse. 'What have you heard?'

'Children murdered, not far from here. Heard about it in Cobar, from a fella that reckons he knows who did it.'

I whipped out my notebook. 'This fella, did he have a name? Distinguishing marks, anything like that?'

'I wanted to pray with him for these children, but he said they were blacks and not worth his prayers. The Lord will avenge these poor souls but we must pray for them, I said, as the Lord instructs us to, the prayer of the righteous man has great power and the Lord will—'

'Where did these children die?'

'Wilga Downs, east of Cobar. He said a squatter drowned them in the Wilga Creek, caught them stealing yabbies, so he drowned them. My acquaintance was putting in a fence and he saw it happen.'

I nodded, jotted down the details. I'd wire them to Cobar and leave them to sort it out. They'd go out to Wilga Creek, nose around and put it in the too-hard basket. This shit happened everywhere, and we all looked the other way, even if we were staring right at it.

'Rightio,' I said, tucking my notebook away. 'Safe travels.'

'Where are you stationed?'

'Senior Constable Augustus Hawkins, Calpa.'

'Good day to you, sir, and God bless the new king.'

⁓

On return to the station, I was nearly felled by the stench of the dead sheep still rotting away in the river. I had a couple of strong coffees, stripped down to my shorts and pulled on my wellingtons, found a sack and a pitchfork and stuck a fag in my mouth, letting the smoke waft around as I waded around the carcass, fishing out bits here and there and tossing them onto the bank. There were a lot of beer bottles too. When Larne had a party, they tossed the empties in the river and sent them down to us.

I couldn't stop gagging despite the cigarette. My mind kept going to the three dead black kids floating in Wilga Creek. I filled the sack and dragged it part of the way back to the station. I'd get a trooper to dig a hole and bury it.

I put a kettle on to warm up water to wash in, then I heard footsteps. I emerged to find Denning and Baines in my kitchen.

'Been for a swim?' Baines said.

'We're going to interview you now,' Denning said.

'You'll have to wait while I wash and dress.'

I knew that the copper who discovered a victim had to be interviewed, but it should have been done by now. I dressed, heard Lonergan banging around in the front station, took a seat at my kitchen table, lit a cigarette and waited for the formalities to be over with.

Baines' plump face and disingenuous expression hid a crafty mind. Useful for a detective, I expected. Denning looked like a hanging judge. If he had the brains, I mused, that was where he'd be. I looked like a bush hermit and smelled of dead sheep.

'Heard Tom Fletcher killed a man with one punch last night,' Baines said. 'What does your *lingua franca* say about that?'

'Says that the dead man should have kept his trap shut.'

'Or it says Tom Fletcher's got a nasty temper and can do some damage when he wants. He had a go at you, and I reckon we should take a closer look at him.' Baines glanced at Denning, who was reading something in his file. 'Can I see the witness statements?'

'Gone to Bourke.'

'What set him off?' asked Baines.

'I don't think it has any bearing on your investigation, so can we get this over with? I have some chores to be getting on with.'

Denning opened his file and turned a page, appeared to read it, and then put it down with a short nod.

'You've been here since July 1908, three years – is that correct?'

'It is. Sir.'

'Says here you were a captain in the New South Wales Mounted Rifles, as we know. You served with distinction, rose through the ranks quickly, mentioned in despatches several times for gallantry under fire.' He nodded and raised his eyebrows as if he couldn't imagine me being gallant under any circumstances. As a matter of fact, neither could I, and I'd completely forgotten the where and why and how. 'Then badly wounded with a long convalescence.'

'Yes, sir.'

'You have been described as a heavy drinker, unstable, a loner who can be heard screaming at night.'

I took a deep breath and exhaled slowly.

'Constable?'

'Every man in the Western Division drinks heavily. I do my duty as a serving mounted trooper and I am on good terms with all the population.'

'Screaming?'

'Nightmares. I'm sure you have them too. Sir.'

'Impertinence will get you nowhere.'

I shoved the ashtray across at Baines to catch the ash he casually let fall on my kitchen table. Denning consulted his papers, cleared his throat, then glanced at me again. His pasty, sunburnt skin was covered in beads of sweat like smallpox blisters.

'It's been a long, slow decline since the glory days of South Africa, hasn't it, Hawkins?'

'What does this have to do with the deaths of the Kirkbrides?'

Denning closed the file, clasping his hands and placing them on the file. 'I understand you wanted to marry Miss Flora, but Mr Kirkbride refused, and you've been in a rage ever since, nursing a serious grudge against him and his family.'

I looked between the two of them, my skin prickling at unseen danger.

'What have you to say to that?'

'It's not true. I never spoke to him about Miss Flora, nor did she and I talk of marriage. We were friends, nothing more.'

'Are you saying Mr Kirkbride is a liar?'

'Yes, in this matter.'

'He says you were after his property and so wanted to marry his daughter.' He paused. My pulse was rising and getting a decent breath suddenly became hard.

'Miss Kitty Ryan says you were not visiting her after the dance. That you were not at her home that evening. That she doesn't know where you were. She says that, although friendly, there was nothing more to your relationship than that.'

12

The wretched noise of Lonergan heaving into a bucket in the laundry fractured the silence. The kitchen was tidy, all cracked and chipped crockery washed and lined up on the dresser, floor swept, the woodstove running on glowing coals. But my mind was in tatters. A buzzing sensation in both ears, the bees hurtling along my arteries, swarming in my chest. I gaped at the detectives, too surprised to speak. I noticed Baines looking at Denning in surprise, as if he hadn't known about this card up Denning's sleeve.

'Were you with Miss Ryan or not?' Denning asked.

'I was definitely there. Ask the punt man, he took me across around one am.'

'He says he doesn't remember.'

I sat back, shook my head. The punt man, Chips Grogan, was a bad-tempered bastard who couldn't lie straight in bed. Everyone knew it because he had it in for anyone who dared to cross his river.

'He's lying. Known for it.'

'I see. So Mr Grogan, Mr Kirkbride and Miss Ryan are all liars and you are not?'

'If I wasn't with Miss Ryan, where do you think I was?'

Denning raised an eyebrow. 'You saw them leave at eleven-thirty, you followed them, you made them leave the road, you shot Miss Grace Kirkbride, killed James Kirkbride and attacked Miss Nessie Kirkbride, then rode into town and reported their murders.'

'That's absurd ... I had no reason to kill them and you have no evidence that I did, otherwise you'd arrest me.'

Denning got to his feet, a smirk of triumph playing around his mouth. 'I think that's all for now. But you are not to leave the district without our permission, not until you are cleared – that is, if you are.'

Baines had his mask back on. They left me standing in the kitchen staring at the back of the door, the tremor in my hand suddenly reappearing. My first response was to reach for the bottle, but as my hand closed around that cool surface I saw Harry Greenleaf in his waterlogged tunic floating down the Darling.

Never mind, he was dead and didn't need the whisky, so I locked myself in my room and lay on the bed swigging from the bottle, then rolled over and took Flora's letters from the drawer. If she heard these accusations, she'd think I killed her siblings. She wanted me dead, and Kitty's betrayal hurt like the devil, and I drank ever more quickly until I passed out, clutching Flora's letters.

⁓

Lonergan woke me by banging on my bedroom door. Outside it was dark. I felt ill and drunk and lit a candle after yelling at him to stop, while I shoved Flora's letters back in the drawer. Swaying, I stumbled to the door and opened it. Joe Pryor stood there in his black suit as if he were making a formal call. I wondered for a moment if some nosy prick had called him to check on me, then I saw a bottle of whisky in his hand.

'Came over to see if you wanted a drink, but it smells like you're at the other end of a session,' he said.

'Hold on.' I shut the door, splashed my face, put on a fresh shirt and went into the kitchen. Lonergan had disappeared. A lantern sat on the table beside two tumblers and a bottle of whisky.

'Hit a rough patch, eh?' Joe said.

I had my head in my hands. It felt like all the sorrows of the world had dropped onto my chest and I couldn't breathe. Every lungful hurt my chest and I was sick of it, sick of myself.

'Those terrible dreams again?' he said.

'Nope, I'm good, mate. Any better and I couldn't stand it.'

He splashed the whisky into the glasses then raised his and drank. 'Glad to hear it. Had those nosy detectives in my surgery this morning. How do you find working with them?'

'A rare pleasure.'

'Have you read the autopsy reports yet?'

'Nope.'

'You still don't know anything more about time of death?'

I shook my head.

'You know, even if you'd left at midnight, you could not have got there in time.'

'A horse and rider is faster than a horse pulling a cart. If I'd left at midnight I could have been there at one-thirty. '

'On a wet night? No, you couldn't.'

'But it wasn't raining until about two-twenty.'

'Don't beat yourself up. Time of death is a very variable thing. I know you won't like this, but you've had a bloody great shock,' Joe said, in a gentle voice. 'You found them and I know you'll use that soldier swagger and say it was just your job, but finding the mutilated bodies of dead friends is different. It can catch up with you when you least expect it.'

Flying ants and moths whirled around the lantern, hitting the glass, falling and crawling back up, again and again, their drive towards death suddenly comprehensible.

'Nothing has caught up with me, I'm fine. Just overdid the grog, that's all.' I glanced over my shoulder at the closed door to Lonergan's room, then lowered my voice and said, 'Kirkbride asked me to kill the culprits, if and when we catch them.'

Joe's mouth dropped open.

'Does he think so little of me?'

'Or himself,' Joe said. 'I know he's in pain ... but still.'

'He's trying to trap me. Just say I did what he asked – which I wouldn't – he'd dob me in and dance at my hanging. Blames me for their deaths and then expects me to kill the killers.'

'He's not in his right mind. I'd ignore him, best thing to do. You need to eat something. Mrs Schreiber's made German sausage and cabbage stew, your favourite. And have a wash, you'll feel better, a cup of tea, bit of a stroll around, get some air.'

I picked up my whisky and, against my better judgement, drank it. When he left I went back and fell on my bed. Some days, like today, I thought it would have been better if I'd died in South Africa. A picture of me would be hung in the hallway of my father's home and visitors would pass by and stop to look at the young officer so heroically cut down in sacrifice to the Empire. Instead they get me, disfigured, drunk and mad. Nothing heroic about that.

~

At sunrise I did nothing, just turned over and sighed. Lonergan pounded on the door a bit later, waking me from a doze. I heard him open the door.

'What?'

'Denning and Baines are ready for you, sir.'

'They can get fucked.'

'You want me to tell them that?'

I rolled over and looked at his freshly shaven face, then rolled back, pulled the blankets up and sighed.

'I'll ... ah, tell 'em you're not well and escort them myself?'

Once he'd gone, I rolled out of bed, leaving my brain behind on the pillow, washed, dressed and reheated the sausage and cabbage stew from last night and ate it all, with great helpings of mustard. I could accept everything Denning said about me. But Kirkbride's lies, the shamelessness of them, made me wonder what else he was capable of saying.

I could not accept Kitty's faithless lies either, and although I was technically on duty, I left the police station to ride up to Larne and see her. It would be past four by the time I got there, and she'd be done with the school day. For once, I didn't give a shit who saw me.

~

Kitty Ryan was short, plump, plain as a pancake and in her late thirties. Not long after I arrived in the district, she made it clear to me that she would welcome a midnight visit. I was taken aback. But she wasn't married, and such invitations were not easy to come by, there being very few willing females around. I tested the waters and found that dumpy, dark-haired colleen was a charming wanton in possession of an arse like two globes of jelly. She was frisky and fun, and once we established what was what we settled into a pattern. We had been at it for two years now.

She lived in the teacher's cottage, a low, whitewashed, one-room cottage with a corrugated-iron roof and a slapdash stable out the back beside the inevitable peppercorn tree. I put my horse in her stable, as I was used to doing, and knocked on her back door, as I was used to doing. No answer, but I kept knocking and soon the door opened, and she stood there, wearing a dowdy brown schoolteacher's dress and a furious expression.

'What is it you're after, Gus, because I'll not be having you in my bed again.'

'That's good because I wouldn't get into bed with you, not after your treacherous betrayal, you lying little—'

124

She looked around the backyard and hissed, 'Get in here.'

I had to lower my head to get through the door, which she slammed behind me. A fire smouldered in the fireplace, a rack of lap blankets drying in front of it. My gaze rested on them for an instant as there was something about the purple blanket, but I couldn't pinpoint what exactly. An old, checked tablecloth, hanging from a sagging line of twine, divided the room. Kitty stood by it, scowling at me.

'What do you want?' she snapped.

'I never treated you badly or disrespected you. I did all I could to keep our liaisons a secret and succeeded pretty well.'

'Until you sent a couple of detectives here,' she yelled, her hands on her hips, wisps of black hair framing her freckled face. 'Asking me things that would make a sailor blush and drooling all the while. I've never been so humiliated in my life. I said no, you were not here – and to hell with you, you weren't.'

'What do you mean?' I said, incredulous.

'You gad about the district, womanising like—'

'Not anymore.'

'Yes, you do, you lying dog. But I don't care if I have you all to meself or not, it's your wilful blindness. You know why you go hunting after women? Because you want to be reassured women will still want you, despite all your scars, and when you're sure they do, you up and go, onto the next one. But there's always good old Kitty who'll have you in her bed if you can't find better. No, I won't lose me job over such a man.'

I stared at her, blinking. I thought she liked me, and this was what she was thinking all along? I never rushed things, never just thought about my own pleasure. And now she comes out with all this rubbish about scars and reassurance?

'I'm sorry, I don't understand what you're getting at. The detectives had to check my story.'

'I don't want policemen in my house,' she yelled, tears running down her cheeks. 'Not them and not you. Now, get out.'

'No, I won't get out. Not until you promise to tell them the truth.'

'And you know what will happen? The report goes to Sydney and the higher-ups read it and they say, dear me, a schoolteacher, entertaining men in her cottage like some tuppeny whore, and we'd better tell the Department of Education that she's not the sort that should be trusted with children. No, I have to look out for me, because nobody else ever has or ever will.'

'Kitty, they'll hang me.'

She shrugged. 'Life is hard for women like me. I'm sorry, Gus. I won't go to no factory or take up the life of a serving maid – not for you, not for nobody.'

'You don't think your life will be ruined if I hang for something I didn't do and you made it happen?'

'You'll find a way through it. Men like you always do.'

She wouldn't change her mind, and I wasn't going to marry her. There was nothing more to say.

~

The current, no matter how hard I swam, was bearing me backward, but I still wore my uniform. Work was the solution to life, I'd discovered.

126

Recalling the Jongs' distress at their son's escape, I decided to go and check on them, make sure they'd got away safely.

I rode away from Larne, east through the bonefields, past the creaking windmill and empty trough, until I came to the clearing where I'd first encountered Mrs Jong. In the distance I saw the corrugated roof of their cottage glinting in the sun. Dismounting, I took my rifle out and slowly approached, calling out, identifying myself, the hair on the back of my neck sticking up, all senses straining to detect danger.

There was a black shape in the dirt outside the cottage. Black crows took to the wing as I approached, leaving Albert Jong's body sprawled on the ground with half his head blown away. I sat on the cottage steps and looked at him. Poor bastard, trying to silence the voices in his head, probably. I had some sympathy for him, lying there outside his parents' home, wearing nothing but his mother's apron, a rifle in his hands. I'd seen too much of this sort of thing. I knew what it was doing to me, so I was relieved I could feel for this man who'd been dealt an awful card to play and couldn't do it anymore.

I looked around. I didn't know what I was hoping to see. An ambulance van? Another trooper, some senior officer who'd make the call so I wouldn't have to?

I went into the cottage and found his clothes in a heap on the floor. No wallet, but the name Kenmore printed on his shirt and trousers identified him. I took a bedsheet outside and, grunting and tugging, rolled his body in the sheet, then dragged him over to the biggest shed, opened the door and looked in. Dust motes rode the sunlight, which shafted through the holes in the roof. Racks of dried skins were stacked neatly against a wall, and a set of nicely sharpened and oiled knives hung on the wall next to some mummified emu claws. I dragged Albert in, laid him down and went back to get his rifle, then closed the door and began my ride back to Larne.

Trooper Parry had gone off somewhere and there was no one else around. I knocked on the local doctor's door. We had a doctor in Larne and a doctor in Calpa, which was possibly one doctor too many, as most people couldn't afford them, but there was no law against a doctor hanging up his shingle if he wanted to.

Dr Reg Tierney was a fat man with a face as red as a slapped arse. The good doctor was known not for his medical brilliance, but for his phenomenal capacity to suck down alcohol, which in a district of hard drinkers was quite some feat. He looked worried when he saw me.

'I need your help, in an official capacity,' I said.

He blinked a few times, then scrunched up his eyes. His breath smelled like a distillery. 'In what capacity?'

'I need a man certified as dead so I can bury him.'

'Oh – who?'

'Do you know the Jongs out by Curranyalpa?' I said.

He nodded. 'Albert?'

'Yes – how did you know?'

'Just a guess. Everyone's been jumpy knowing he's out and headed this way, but I always thought he was a greater danger to himself. How did he die?'

'Self-inflicted gunshot wound to the head. Specifically, the left eye.'

'Wait there, I'll write a certificate.'

'But aren't you going to—'

'Ride out there? No, you've told me all I need to know.'

'I'll have to box him up, send for a cart to take him to Bourke.'

'Oh, they'll have better things to do than traipse down here for a lunatic suicide,' he said.

I looked at him, waited.

Tierney sighed. 'Just stick him in the ground until Bourke get around to it.'

'Lend me a shovel?' I called after him as he retreated down the hall.

~

Shovel in hand, I nipped over to the post office, sent a telegram to Bourke with the details and rode back to Curranyalpa. The sun was going down and I had to hurry. Back at the Jongs', I lit a lantern and roamed around in the half-light looking for a graveyard. Came across a rough cross stuck in the ground under a peppercorn tree. I wondered who it was – an infant who never got to walk the earth, by the looks of it. I took off my tunic and started digging. The ground out here is sandy in parts, and after an hour I was maybe five feet deep. Good enough.

I fetched Albert from the shed and dragged him over the burrs and rabbit shit towards his grave. A couple of men appeared out of the shadows, giving me a hell of a start. Grimy, unkempt, menacing. Could have been Gog and Magog, barbarians from the wilder edges of the known. My rifle was in its holster on my horse and my hands were full of dead man. I dropped him, my hand going straight to my sidearm.

They had rifles in saddle holsters, but if they also had sidearms they weren't waving them about. My pulse galloped. I was in uniform – some protection at least. They rode closer, filthy, shaggy beards, ragged horses saddled with cracked tack, the half-light causing them to appear like some awful vision of my future. Then it occurred to me they could be the shooters from the other night.

'G'day,' I said. 'Looking for someone?'

'Heard you might need help,' one of them said, with a nod at Albert. He had a large gold signet ring on his finger.

'Who told you that?'

'Fella in Larne.'

'A couple of good Samaritans, eh?' I said. More likely they'd come to help themselves to the Jongs' possessions.

He shrugged. 'Who is he?'

'Albert Jong. Looks like he shot himself. D'you know him?'

Gog shook his head, sucked his teeth. He was a surly beast with an unnerving stare. No blinking. That's not natural. The other bloke, Magog, wasn't much better. He wore a filthy pink neckerchief with his shirt unbuttoned halfway, showing an undershirt that hadn't seen washday in several years. It did me good to see men like this – made me realise I still had a way to go.

'Thanks, but I have it all in hand,' I said.

These two made my hair stand on end. I was of a mind to question them about the Tindaree shooting, but not while they sized me up, and not near a freshly dug grave. Killing a mounted trooper brought swift and vicious reprisals but these two looked as if such deterrents were about as scary as a cup of cold water.

'Better get on with it,' I said, nodding at poor old Albert. 'What did you say your names were?'

No answer. They stared for a bit longer, then turned their horses and rode off. Albert rested in his soil, I backfilled, tamped it down and stuck a mulga wood branch on top of it. I left his rifle in the shed, locked the shed, made sure the cottage was secure and rode back to Larne as fast as I could.

~

Light spilled from the police station window onto the dirt road outside. Parry was back. When he opened the door to me, a stained cloth tucked into his collar and the smell of stew signalled I'd interrupted his supper. He stared at me, picking at his teeth with a filthy finger.

'Need to have a word with you,' I said.

He let me into the station, which was laid out the same as the Calpa station, but his was a mess.

'The Jongs – been to see them?' I asked.

'They've gone south to stay with their daughter. Why?'

'Found Albert Jong out there, bullet in his head.'

'Done himself in?'

'Looks like it. Have you had any reports of theft in the area? Come across any ransacked cottages, huts?'

'Yeah – why?'

'A couple of shady men rode up while I was burying Jong. Said they heard that I needed a hand and came to help. But the only person who knew was Tierney and he doesn't talk to men like that. They were bullshitting.'

'You reckon they were there to do the place?'

For God's sake, man, can you not put two fucking thoughts together?

'Word goes out the Jongs have gone to Wilcannia for a while,' I said, teeth gritted. 'Farm's unattended, the vultures take advantage.'

He opened the incident book. I took it and ran my eye down the list of dates and places.

'There,' he said, looking over my shoulder, belching and jabbing at the book. 'Clover Creek homestead – they reckon they had some stores stolen but I reckon that's just the blacks. And here, old couple at Mulya reckon their place was broken into while they were here to see Dr Tierney.'

'That's not far from the Jongs. Did you go out there?'

'Yeah, I did,' he said proudly, like I should recommend him for merit-based promotion. 'Skinning knife, whetstone, leather bag, iron pegs. Old Mr Brunt's a tinker, used to go up and down the river mending pots. I reckon he just put them somewhere and forgot. And these people here, the Chinese gardeners on Wilgaroon Downs, all their tools taken and the hut trashed. Now, that could be anyone with a dislike of the celestials. You just don't know.'

'Put all these in a report?'

'Yeah, yeah, I'm working on it.'

'Send a copy down to me. Actually, all the break-ins for the last two months – I want a list of where and when. And keep an eye out for two men, mounted, filthy, one wearing a gold signet ring.'

'Two dirty men on horseback?' he said and raised an eyebrow at me.

'Yes, turning up in places they have no business in being. You do ride your rounds every day, Trooper?'

'I do, sir,'

I knew he was erratic in his rounds but left him to it, emphasising I wanted those reports on the next mail coach.

I mounted up and rode back in the dark, jumpy as a cat, nursing my rifle the whole way.

13

It was a relief to get back to Calpa but as I approached I heard shouts. The sound was coming from inside the police station. I went through and found Baines, hands on hips, belly thrust forward, face all red and sweaty and Lonergan in his sights.

'Oh, you're here, not fucken laid up out the back with a bad case of the tremors, eh?'

I glanced at Lonergan, mystified by this attack.

'This little paddy gobshite trooper of yours got us lost this morning. Couldn't read his bloody map, didn't have a bloody compass on him either. Needs a kick up the arse.'

'I'll deal with him.'

'I'm dealin' with him now,' he shouted.

'Trooper Lonergan is under my command. I will deal with it.'

'Like you dealt with those fucken useless trackers of yours who are off

God knows where. You traps are useless, we've been mucked about, and if you hadn't gone on a bender – in the middle of a murder investigation – I wouldn't be riding about with the little tosser.'

'Let's step outside for a moment, Detective.'

The street was empty, as usual. Baines was all lathered up, huffing and puffing and poking his finger at me. 'Fucken useless, the lot of you.'

'You leave my men alone, d'you understand? They're not here for you to wipe your feet on just because you've had a shitty day. If Lonergan got you lost – and obviously he didn't, because you're back here—'

'No hope of sorting these murders with you lot around.'

'You've had everything laid on for you, mate, reams of carbon paper, pencil sharpeners, if you can't solve it don't turn to us to take the blame.'

He stared after me as I stomped back inside. Lonergan was rooted to the spot, eyes wide, like a rabbit feeling the wind of a bullet just before it hits. In the traps juniors went out with the more senior officers and were bossed about, set on the unpleasant tasks. They were never asked to guide a city bloke through the bush on their own. It was like taking a young city beat cop and asking him to raid an illegal Haymarket cockfight single-handed. If I hadn't got drunk ... but I had, so that was that.

But, drink or no drink, we were being set up. I could see that now – their failures were ours, or mine alone, and Bourke would be hung out to dry because we were out here and they weren't.

I fetched a map and navigation instruments and laid them on the table in front of Lonergan.

'Study this map. Mark where we are, then mark where Baines wants to go tomorrow. When you've done that, note all the possible landmarks between here and there, and at what longitude and latitude they lie, mileage and elevation, then work out the fastest way of reaching your destination. By the time we're done, you'll know it as well as you know the Lord's Prayer.'

He looked at me warily.

'You rock choppers do know the Lord's Prayer, don't you?'

He nodded, picked up the compass and gazed at the map like it was a gunpowder trail leading to a locked room.

'Put that down and start with a pencil and ruler. When you're finished, we'll go through it.'

I went to my room, closed the door and opened the drawer, needing to touch Flora's letters. They weren't there.

I pulled the drawer out, flung it across the room, yanked the cabinet away from the wall, looked under the bed, kicked the rug out of the way, tossed books onto the floor, opening them, then hurling them aside, searched the wardrobe, the chest of drawers.

'You been in my room?' I barked, slamming the door open and startling Lonergan.

'No, sir.'

My notebooks. My official police notebooks. I rushed out the front and found them still on the lower shelf, in perfect date order. I pulled the laundry apart, then went through the kitchen cupboards, taking out all the jars of sauerkraut and preserved quinces, tomatoes and pickled cucumbers, looking for God knows what.

If someone had been in here to steal those letters, they could have left something, a bloodstained rifle butt, a shell casing, a handwritten plan to kill and rape the Kirkbrides. The station was always locked but I never locked the private quarters, so that Mrs Schreiber could come and go.

I collapsed onto a chair, swallowed down the ramrod fury, let it dissolve back into amorphous shame. If Kirkbride had sent someone to steal those letters, then he'd know everything.

'Cup of tea, sir?'

I blinked a few times, surprised to see Lonergan in my kitchen in a way that made me question my sanity. He bustled around with the kettle and teapot while I made my way to the laundry and the half-full whisky bottle behind the mangle. I'd eased off the bottle for a while there, almost two years in fact, with the exception of keeping Joe company. But then last Christmas everything changed.

'There's a new order in,' Lonergan said, pouring boiling water into the teapot. 'It's from Corcoran. Saying I'm to keep doing escort while you man the station.'

I nodded. Of course there was – and soon there'd be a notice of dismissal.

'All right. Then you keep going on the map, we'll drill you on it until you can do it in your sleep. Not going to give those dicks any excuse to fit us up for what's coming. And I've heard you throwing up too many times – eat here with me, as my guest. Mrs Schreiber always makes too much anyway.'

'Thank you, sir, much appreciated.'

~

That night I lay in bed, smoking and fretting, the candle burning down, moths and insects trapped in the liquid wax like kindred spirits. Kirkbride and Denning could come up with anything, manufacture evidence, pay a witness. Plenty of poverty out here, plenty of people would lie for a quid. Denning could substitute his own findings. I didn't know how city detectives operated, if they could be bought, and I didn't know how to fight back if they came at me. I'd need a lawyer, and a good one. Have to go to my father cap in hand. I'd just about got myself standing in the dock with the judge putting the black cloth on his head when I must have conked out.

The terror woke me with a start, and then began the effort to drag myself back to my bed, my room, this life. The familiar rush and gurgle of the river nearby oriented me. I fumbled around, lit a candle, squinting in the light and checked my watch – two forty-five – and my thoughts returned to Flora, as they always did. I felt a desperate need to defend myself to her, to assure her I had not killed her siblings, no matter what people were saying.

I knew the longer I lay there fretting, the worse it would become. I got up, pulled on some old trousers, a shirt, boots and a sheepskin jacket, woke Felix, saddled him then rode up to Inveraray.

~

It was nearly three-thirty and Inveraray should be well and truly asleep. Even the cook who baked the bread wouldn't be up yet. I tethered Felix halfway up the long drive and walked the rest of the way, keeping to the shadows.

138

The night was clear, the moon making its way back down the sky, my breath misting in the cold, the frosty gravel crunching beneath my boots.

Flora's room was on the side of the house facing north and the fenced-off vegetable gardens. I crept along the homestead wall, waiting for some dog to go berserk, but it was silent. Just the ticking of the contracting iron roof and the yap-yap of a barking owl.

I picked her window and rolled a wood stump closer to it, then tossed a handful of soil at the glass. God help me if I'd got it wrong and it was Mr and Mrs Kirkbride's. I tried a small stone and another. She must be sedated, as I was getting no response. I was about to give up when her face loomed behind the glass like a wide-eyed wraith.

I stood on the stump, my head reaching the window. We stared at each other. I pointed to the sash, mouthed 'open'. She had a nightgown on, white with little frills, her hair like a choppy sea, dark and tousled.

She managed to get the window up a few inches, the noise making me wince. She leant down, her hands clutching the sill. We were face to face, her eyes wide. All that I wanted to say to her, all that I said to her in my daily thoughts, disappeared.

'How are you managing?' I whispered.

'I'm not.'

'Flora, I'm so sorry. It's my fault and I am going to fix it.'

'It wasn't your fault – it's my fault.'

'No, no, no, don't think like that.'

'I should be with them now, they'll be looking for me,' she said.

I grasped her hand, the stump wobbling beneath me. 'They wouldn't want that. I don't want that.'

'But I do.'

I held onto her. 'Flora, wait – I promise you, I will find the men who did this, I will hunt them down if it's the last thing I do. I'll make it right.'

'But they're gone.'

'I'll find them,' I whispered. 'I promise.'

'Can you? Can the living find the dead? Take me with you, then. I don't know how to be here without them. If you know a way ...'

We stared at each other, her dark-brown eyes wide and brimming with despair. Then she pulled her hand away, closed the window and faded back into the darkness.

I walked away from the house towards Felix. A single gunshot shattered the night. I was unarmed and there was no cover. I whirled around and saw a figure emerge from the shadows by the men's quarters. A light went on in the homestead, then another.

'Stand with your arms up.'

I saw a light flare in Flora's room and I put my hands up. A stockman I didn't recognise approached me, rifle pointed at my chest. Behind him I heard the Scots burr of McIntosh cursing and grumbling. A figure ran down the steps of the homestead, and in the bright starlight I recognised Robert Kirkbride.

The stockman lowered his rifle when he saw me, looked to McIntosh for instruction.

'Gus? What the hell are you doing?'

'It's you,' Kirkbride cried, his dressing-gown half-open. 'Creeping around in the darkness. What do you want?'

Before I could come up with a workable lie, I heard screams coming from the verandah. Flora struggling, trying to get free, screaming my name, frantic.

'I'll deal with this,' Kirkbride said to his men, and sent them away.

The front door slammed and then there was silence. A spray of stars glittering above, cool and indifferent.

'What are you doing on my property, Hawkins?'

'You sent someone to steal my personal property, my private correspondence—'

'I did nothing of the sort. You're mad and a drunk and you lie, and by God, I rue the day Flora set eyes on you.'

I'd punch the bastard if I listened to another word. Walked away to find Felix.

'Don't turn your back on me,' he shouted. 'You let my children die undefended and then you lied about it. Where were you? Lying drunk in a ditch? Or were you the one who killed them?'

Everybody on the station would hear him.

'I told the truth about where I was,' I swung around and shouted back. 'I'm not proud of it, but it's the truth, and don't think for a minute you can pin your children's deaths on me. And what's more, I don't want your property and I never spoke to Flora about marriage.'

'But you did – I have it on paper.'

'So you did steal my letters. Thieving and lying. Keep that up and, by God, I will come for you.'

'Are you threatening me?'

'Yes.'

I took to my bed with a bottle when I got back. Lonergan could manage without me. I could manage without me. Kirkbride must have found my letters to Flora, which I knew she kept, and realised her letters to me would be full of compromising material, words like 'love' and 'desire', things he'd know nothing about. The idea of him reading my letters to Flora made me ill. The humiliation of another man reading my most private expressions of sentiment – God in heaven, it was too much.

Left to my own devices, I simply drank until I passed out, my last thoughts before oblivion being to beg the universe to let me not wake to another day. I didn't recall Joe or anyone coming near me, but they might have.

I had no recall of how long this went on until I stumbled out of my bedroom into an empty kitchen. I checked the calendar. The funeral was tomorrow. I took a seat, put my elbows on the table and dropped my face into my hands. It had been ten days since the murders. It felt like weeks.

~

The day of the funerals was overcast, as if the sun had drawn a veil over itself in sorrow. Clouds, undersides a deep grey, piled up to the west. My thoughts were of Flora, dressing for her siblings' funeral, fastening the jet mourning jewellery, her face white, her mind unable to comprehend the silence. The absence.

Mrs Schreiber patted my shoulder as she passed. 'A terrible day, Herr Kapitän.'

'It is,' I replied, in a strangled voice. Tears threatened and I couldn't bear the thought, even in front of this decent, homely woman.

I was dressed in my only suit, as I was attending as friend and neighbour. Lonergan was doing guard duty at the funeral, organising the six lads into something resembling an honour guard. I ate some porridge, then reached for the plate of eggs. Corcoran came through the back door wearing his dress uniform. Lonergan and I got to our feet, and Mrs Schreiber wiped her hands and left, letting the screen door slam behind her.

'Ride through the night, sir?'

'Do I look as if I did? No, the Fletchers are putting me up for a few nights. Martin is staying over at Inveraray. Lonergan, you know what your duties are today?'

'Yes, sir. Senior Constable Hawkins has briefed me, sir.'

'Good, at ease, finish your breakfast.' He turned to me. 'Mr Kirkbride does not want you attending the funeral. You are to stay here until further notice.'

'What? Why?'

Lonergan looked up, a sliver of fried egg on his fork, dripping yellow yolk on the cracked plate.

'Lonergan, please leave us. Take your breakfast with you.'

When we were alone Corcoran said, 'Don't question my orders, and don't question them in front of junior officers.'

'Sir. But why does he not want me to attend? I've known the Kirkbrides for—'

'Because his children are dead, and you were not there to protect them. You were whoring in Larne.'

'Either I was in bed with Miss Ryan or I wasn't in bed with her and I lied. Which one is it going to be? You can't have it both ways ... sir.'

'I think either way is egregious, don't you? You are confined to the station until the meeting here at two o'clock. And while you are here you can complete the Tom Fletcher paperwork, which you failed to provide. The magistrate is asking for it and we haven't got it – why? Because you're drunk and indisposed? I don't want to hear another word from you, but by God we'll have words when this Kirkbride business is over.'

He turned and walked out. I was left with a plate of congealed eggs and the flies. Kev brought the mailbag in. I opened it, saw a letter from my father, tore it to pieces, then took it and dropped it down the long drop to shit on.

When I joined the Mounted Troopers I'd been drowning, and had grabbed at that uniform as it floated past. A uniform gives a man a place to hide, gives him routines and duties – or it did me. And if I didn't get a grip quickly, my uniform would be stripped away before I was ready to let it go.

14

I had completed the Fletcher paperwork but I'd forgotten to put it in the despatch bag and send it up with the mail coach. I raced over to Kev, who was suited up and ready for the funeral. He signed for it. Then I snatched it back. What was I doing? Corcoran and Martin were in town for the funeral and the meeting this afternoon – they could take it themselves.

I raced back to the station, locked the paperwork up, changed out of the suit and into old pair of work trousers and a shirt, saddled Felix and set off towards Inveraray Station, riding over the flat, stony plains to a low rise to the north of the station, where a tumbledown stone shepherd's hut stood.

It was the best vantage point for a view of the funeral. Jimmy had once brought me to this rise, and we'd looked down on the station and beyond to the Paroo River while he talked of tanks and bores, fences and feed.

I looked for the best terrain on which to engage the enemy and the best route for retreat, like I always did.

A scattering of bleached bones covered the ground beside the hut. I tethered Felix to a tree, took my binoculars out and clambered up the hut, hoping like hell that it wouldn't give way. I scanned the flat plain until I located the station and the crowd of mourners outside the homestead.

There were dozens of buggies and carts, and mourners in black milling around. As the coffins were carried out of the house and along the trail to the family graveyard, the troopers, mounted on their freshly groomed horses, saluted. Mrs Kirkbride, wearing a gossamer black veil, could barely walk and was supported by her two sisters, followed by Flora in a similar veil, a train of staff and friends behind her. Tom Fletcher, home on bail, walking behind Nessie's coffin, was obviously struggling. He'd courted Nessie so devotedly, and now he was trying to put one foot in front of the other as he walked his girl to her grave.

When I found their bodies, I'd done what my training said I must. But they'd been my friends, my neighbours, and as I watched them being laid to rest in the distance, tears filled my eyes. I climbed down from the stone wall and sat in the dirt, resting my head against my knees, the memory of the pitiful sight of their bodies, arms flung out, heads bowed or facedown in the suffocating mud, the icy rain trickling down my back beneath my shirt, the memory of it unrelenting.

Wiping tears away, I tried to farewell them on my own as the congregation sang 'Abide With Me' at the graveside, their voices carrying on the dry air. Nessie used to sing it – and I'd never heard anything as lovely as Nessie singing 'Londonderry Air'. Not an easy song, but she was pitch perfect and never resorted to fancy trills. Nessie was always happiest with a piano and a songbook and was known around the district for her beautiful voice. At picnics and dances she was always called on to sing, and she'd lead with 'The Keel Row', old people patting their knees keeping time, men tapping their feet, and by the third chorus we'd all be singing. Then Grace would be up dancing with the little kids and Flora would be laughing, her lovely face alive with happiness.

I had never realised how much fun girls could be, and following afternoons of hilarity with them I often thought of my two sisters, who both died as they were being born and now lay in the graveyard beside our mother.

Gangly Grace, all elbows and knees, was not a singer, but in her element with parlour games. Grace knew all the rules and enforced them with firmness and charm. She liked charades most of all, and without exception picked my charade. She could see clearly into my simple mind and felled me almost immediately, much to the others' amusement.

She loved to go for walks along the river, and she'd chatter away with her sisters, Jimmy and me. I taught her how to skim stones, and once, on one of these walks, she took my hand when we heard shots fired in the distance. Gunshot was pretty standard out there but scary all the same if you are only twelve years old. She took my hand, trusting I'd protect her, but nobody had protected Grace from what lurched through the gloom towards her.

I shook off the memories, clambered back up the stone wall and raised the binoculars to my eyes. Like most station graveyards, the three graves would be planted with rambling roses. Headstones would be raised and those left behind would visit, or not, depending on how much pain they could bear. But today I could pick out three wreathes of eucalypt entwined with pink mulla mulla, which had blossomed in response to the rain.

Once the last handful of dirt had been thrown onto the coffins, people returned to the house, where no doubt a spread of sandwiches and scones would be laid out for the mourners, with tea, or whisky for the men. Maybe some brave soul would make a speech. The whole town would know I did not attend, the whole district – my district, which I policed so diligently. Except for one hour when I hadn't.

~

I galloped back to the station, took off my coat, rolled up my sleeves and checked the blade on my axe. It glinted in the sunlight as if agreeing with me – *yes, heads do need to roll.* I stored firewood under a rough corrugated-iron shelter beside the water tank. I'd been impressed with the exactitude and symmetry of the Dutch woodheaps in South Africa. Calling them heaps was slander – they were precision constructions, with every stick of blackwattle split as evenly as matches in a box. My woodheap was homage to theirs. Redgum mostly, but whatever was around I dragged back to be chopped and stacked.

You see, chopping wood is medicinal. The Chinese bloke, the same one as sold me the face ointment, told me to chop wood whenever I could, as it would keep the scars from contracting, break up the tissue and keep everything hot and in balance. Chopping would also soak up the rage and bring harmony, or so he said, and he was right.

148

I often thought of the Boer who injured me when I chopped. If he'd been properly trained, he would have stuck the bayonet in my stomach. Much more efficient. Nobody survived a stomach wound. But it was personal for him, to repel the hated invader in a blind frenzy. So he went for the face.

I placed a log of redgum on my stump and brought the axe down hard. Creating two from one. I placed the half on the stump, considered where best to make the cut and slammed the blade down again. Raising the axe hurt like a bastard, taking the breath from my lungs. I knew I had to keep at it and the reward would come. In a couple of minutes, I had eight from one and found another short log, set it up, panting, squinting in the harsh light, the stable cats sitting on the iron roof of the heap staring at me with contempt.

It would have been more efficient to shoot all three Kirkbride siblings, so why hadn't they? The frenzied attack on Nessie spoke of rage. But not so Jimmy's wounds. Although brutal, the attacker had stopped once the job was done.

'Hey, Gus.'

I brought the axe down with a grunt, then looked around, panting from the pleasure and pain.

'Dr Pryor,' I said, wiping the sweat from my eyes. 'How was it?'

There were black shadows beneath his eyes, strain written all over his face. I drank from my waterbag, spilled half of it down my shirt.

'Awful,' he said, lighting up a cigarette and sitting on the old wooden chair that lived in the yard. 'Why didn't you go? Everyone was asking me.'

'Kirkbride didn't want me there.' I positioned a half, noted where to make the cut, picked up my axe and slammed it down with a grunt.

'Why?'

'Because I let his children die.'

'Ridiculous. I'll talk to him again. Nobody can get an accurate time of death unless they see the death take place. I told him that before. They probably died before you even left Larne.'

I took a quarter, placed it on the stump and examined it. Quarters were tricky. To get that beautiful symmetry in your woodheap, you had to pay attention – force required, angle of attack, likely resistance. I raised the axe.

'It's the look of the thing, not the facts,' I said, grunting as I brought the axe down. 'It looks like, and it was, a gross dereliction of duty.'

'I haven't heard anyone suggest this is your fault.'

'I have. Maybe you aren't gossiping with the right people.' I fetched another round, placed it on the stump and raised the axe.

'Yes, I mean, it was bad luck you went whoring when—'

'Kitty is not a whore,' I said, slamming the axe down and watching the two halves tumble aside. 'But she's dropped me in it by telling the dicks I was never there.'

'What do you expect from a woman like that? You know what they say about dogs and fleas.'

I shot him a glance. Joe had a puritanical streak in him, despite his fondness for the bottle. 'I need a beer,' I said. 'Fancy one?'

'Indeed I do.'

I wrapped the axe blade in an oilcloth and put it under the shelter, then took a couple of beers from the outside meat safe and we went inside. I peeled off my sweaty shirt, opened the bottles, handed him one and then raised mine and drank deeply. Nothing like a beer after chopping wood. Like a cigarette after sex. Pure satisfaction.

From outside in the street came the rumble of carts and the chatter of people as they streamed away from the funeral, sturdy workers, crammed into tight mourning suits and dresses, hurrying home to put on something more comfortable and get back to work. Few could afford a full day to mourn the Kirkbrides. I fetched a clean shirt and put it on.

'How was Flora?'

'I didn't see her after the interment. I suspect she went to her room. Mrs Kirkbride had to be led away to her room too, not long into the wake. I don't think anybody wanted to be there. It wasn't like a funeral for an elderly person. Maybe Kirkbride did you a favour.'

'Yeah, I can see that. Kirkbride decides he must spare Gus Hawkins the pain of his children's funeral, so forbids me to attend.' I lit a cigarette and we both drank deeply from our bottles.

'Gus—'

'What?'

'I heard you were found roaming around the Kirkbride property in the early hours a few days ago.'

I took a pull on my beer, eyed him suspiciously. 'Who told you that?'

'McIntosh. Said you and Kirkbride had a shouting match while Flora screamed from the homestead.'

'Is that why you're here?'

'If the murders are stirring up memories of the war ... maybe you should take some leave, get away from the investigation.'

'No. I am fit for active duty. I will not be drummed out of the force for madness.'

'Not saying you're mad, nobody is.'

I drained my beer and sighed, held the empty bottle up and raised my eyebrows. Joe nodded. I fetched two more bottles and opened them, sliding his across the table.

'Anyone ever tell you that you look like an undertaker in that black suit?' I said. 'Keeper of the dead house, mate, a bloody black goanna.'

He looked down at the vest with the watch chain tight over his softening belly. 'Plenty of black suits at the funeral and nobody mistook me for the undertaker.'

'That's a relief. Don't want to be pouring pills down a dead man's throat and getting nothing for your troubles.'

Joe tipped his beer down his throat with barely a swallow, wiped his mouth and laughed. 'Bloody smart-arse.'

Lonergan came through from the station, saw me all deshabille and empty beer bottles on the table. 'Wilson and Frosty are back, sir.'

~

The station kept spare horses for Frosty and Wilson but they mostly worked on foot, and I knew they'd have covered some serious ground in the last ten days. Wilson, in his fifties, looked knackered.

'You been home yet?' I asked him.

'No, need to speak to you first, boss,' he said. 'I sent Frosty home. I'll show you on the map where we been.'

'Leave that – come around the back and have a cup of tea first.' The detectives, Corcoran and Martin were due at two, so we had time.

I went into the living quarters and put the kettle on the fire, instructed Lonergan to make some mugs of tea and then joined Wilson in the yard, where he was perched on the chopping block, wiping his face with his neckerchief. 'You find anything useful?'

'Yeah, tracks of three men,' Wilson said.

'You found their tracks at the crime scene and followed them? A clear connection?' I said, pulling up one of the old chairs.

'Yes, we found tracks leading north-east, towards Tindaree Station, one man moving fast, he stumble then keep going for two mile, then he turn and zigzag all the way back, stopping maybe half-mile up from the crime scene.'

'Panicked, maybe?' Lonergan said, joining us with the mugs of tea.

'Yeah, he run like scared emu. He didn't try to cover his tracks or nuthin', not like a blackfella would.'

'And the other two?'

'Two more fellas on foot, heading towards the south and then stop at the river. They moving fast but they go straight to river. They must have crossed.'

'Did you go across and see if you could pick up their tracks?'

'Yeah, that's why we been so long. But all three fellas' tracks stop at the river. We go up to Kerrigundi and south to Nellyambo but no signs they go cross. But yeah, lotta sheep moving for crutching, ground all cut up.'

I fetched the tin full of Mrs Schreiber's oatmeal biscuits, shook them onto a plate and took it outside. Each was about the circumference of a cartwheel – she didn't muck about when she cooked. We slurped and crunched and speculated on the three suspects, but the fact that Wilson had clearly identified them as having been at the site and leaving it meant we had a hell of a lot more than we'd had before.

It wasn't long before Martin and Corcoran returned from the funeral aftermath, and I sent Lonergan to fetch the detectives from the Royal. When he was out of earshot, I asked Wilson if he thought the culprits were locals or blow-ins who'd shot through.

He looked into the middle distance, then at me. 'These two fellas, they know where they goin',' he said, then paused and shrugged. 'Hard to tell if they local.'

~

Denning, Baines, Corcoran, Martin, Lonergan, Wilson and I huddled around the map on the station counter, and Wilson pointed to where they'd followed the tracks. Denning nodded, looked down at the map, plainly ill at ease beside Wilson. I'd have expected better from a big-city detective, but as Baines said, Denning wasn't a star. We'd been through all the known blacks' camps in the district, asking questions, sorting out who was who and where they worked or didn't, which was a time-consuming job. Denning hung back, looking around with barely concealed contempt. Typical Pom.

'Covered a lot of ground,' Denning said. 'But slower than I'd hoped.'

'Tracking is an art, Inspector, and must be done in a painstaking manner,' Corcoran said, a glint of steel in his eye.

154

'No trace of these men once they hit the river?' Denning asked.

'Nothing, sir,' Wilson said.

'Just our luck,' Baines said gloomily. 'What's west of here?'

'The Paroo, then nothing. Or not for a while. There's White Cliffs to the south-west, a small opal-mining town,' I said. 'Or they could have gone north towards Wanaaring then on to the Queensland border. Or east, towards Cobar.'

'Coulda,' Wilson said, nodding. 'Or they could circle back and recross the river further upstream and come back here.'

'Where were their horses?' Denning said. 'You say they were on foot?'

'Yeah, they on foot and not leading horses neither.'

'So they couldn't have gone far,' Corcoran said. 'Most of the men who come to the district for work don't have horses, they ride bicycles.'

After more speculation, Corcoran dismissed Wilson, who looked thrilled to be out of there. They continued to examine the map and talk softly among themselves. Wilson's suggestion that the killers could have come back here was ignored. I lost interest, fading in and out, lost in a post-bender reverie of bad sleep, too many dreams and a falling sensation that had plagued me on and off for years.

'Right, this is what we know,' Denning said eventually. 'James and his sisters left their homestead at four-thirty and were expected to arrive in Cobar six hours later – they told the staff that was where they were headed. Miss Grace was said to be unwell, hence the delay in leaving. Normally she would have travelled with her parents and the older siblings would come in the cart. But Miss Flora travelled with her parents instead. The siblings took with them a bag containing two

155

ball gowns, a dinner suit, a sapphire necklace and toiletries. James had his fob watch and wallet, and Miss Grace wore a garnet ring. These are all missing.

'Nobody sees them again until James is spotted at the dance in Larne at approximately ten pm. He was seen by many people, dancing, drinking a beer, chatting and so on, but his sisters were not seen.

'The last sighting of James was at eleven, when he was seen leaving the hall and walking away along the main street in a southerly direction. Nobody saw them after that – no sightings on the punts or the road, no reported gunshot or screams.'

I jolted out of my apathy at the mention of eleven pm. I'd been through all the statements and I was sure nobody had said the last sighting of James had been at eleven pm. I would have remembered that.

'It would have taken them about two hours to get to where they were killed,' Denning went on. 'Let's say they leave Larne at maybe eleven-thirty and get to where they were killed at maybe one-thirty, and then the crime is committed.'

Denning glanced at me. If they had been killed at one-thirty, there was a chance I could have saved them, had I not, et cetera, et cetera.

'Next we have Trooper Hawkins coming across their bodies, he claims, at around three am. Autopsies say the approximate time of death was between ten and three. We can't get a fix on who died first, but it was probably Miss Grace.

'As we can see, the trackers have found three sets of tracks leading away from the crime scene, which fits with my belief that it was a premeditated act, but not well planned. My gut tells me the killers were the men dismissed by Inveraray at the start of the crutching season for agitating over labour conditions.

'Industrial unrest, there is your motive. Many of these men are from the criminal classes and therefore capable of committing such an outrage. These men were seen off the property only days before the murders and were set to cycle up to Bourke and return to their homes by train, as no other property in the district would hire them. They camped by the river – and there is a constantly shifting population of vagrants and blacks along the river – and were watching the Kirkbride homestead. They saw the youngsters leave and waited for them to return, knowing that as they went up the western road, there was no way back but the western road.'

'There's the eastern road, sir,' Lonergan said, clearly puzzled.

'We have their names and addresses, but I doubt they would return home after committing such a crime,' Denning said. 'They'll hang for this and my experience tells me they'll be on the run. North, to the Queensland border.'

'Nobody goes on the run out here on foot without maps and water,' Corcoran said. 'It isn't possible to survive. One miscalculation, you overshoot a bore or a tank, and that's it. The horse the Kirkbride siblings used on the night has not been seen since. Two horses from a property by the name of –' he checked his papers – 'Ellerslie are missing, and have been missing since the coronation weekend. I have no doubt the culprits are headed north and are camped in the bush around Toorale, and from there they'll go up to Queensland, where we can't go.'

It sounded like utter rubbish to me, but maybe Denning's long Geordie vowels, or that British ramrod-up-the-arseness of the man, was interfering with my judgement.

After half an hour of speculation, it was decided to send a manhunt. It was decided I'd lead it. We would head north along the western bank river to Toorale and Wanaaring, and then onto the border, stopping at stations on the way for provisions and to question everyone we met for possible sightings, then we'd work our way back down the eastern side of the river. Lonergan was to stay in Calpa on escort duty.

'I thought I was confined to the station, sir,' I said to Corcoran when I got him alone.

'Do you have a problem, Hawkins?'

Yes, I did. I was being got rid of. Sent on a useless expedition in the hope that I'd fuck up – or, even better, die.

'No, sir ... Yes, sir, I do. Denning just about accused me of killing the Kirkbrides, and now I'm leading a manhunt for the killers?'

'Just follow orders and shut the hell up.'

15

Lonergan cleared the tea things in the station. I stood out the front to get some air. Corcoran and Martin conferred. Baines strolled over, lit a fag. 'Saw your lip curl when Denning mentioned his gut.'

'Just a touch of indigestion.'

'Haven't you heard of the golden gut?' Baines said.

'Sounds like a sheep disease, black leg, pink eye, golden gut.'

'Nah, it's instinct, mate, a gut that's never wrong. Don't you soldiers follow your instincts?'

'If a soldier followed his instincts, the battlefield would be empty and the brothels full to capacity.'

He laughed but patted his stomach. 'Comes from further north.'

'Is that what Denning says to the magistrate? "I know they're guilty because me guts is gurgling?"'

'And then I take the stand and say, "More evidence is available if you'd care to sniff my fart, m'lud.'"

We batted this around, laughing like schoolboys, until I realised the six junior troopers were still in dress uniform and waiting to be told what to do. They hadn't even returned their weapons to the armoury, and God knew what state those were in.

Mounted troopers were issued with Martini–Henry Mk II carbines and Webley service revolvers. Failure to maintain your weapon was a serious offence in the army. Cleaning your rifle came after seeing to your horse and before seeing to yourself. Mounted troopers were taught this, but the discipline lapsed as the high stakes flattened out and fell asleep in the afternoon sun of endless paperwork.

'Set up the bench on trestles in the yard,' I ordered Lonergan to order them. 'Weapons are to be stripped and cleaned. They can do it there in twos – those not working on their weapons can prepare fodder bags, enough for each horse for at least two weeks. If they don't know how much that is, refer to the handbook. I want first-aid kits checked over, tent pegs counted and recounted, I want all tack checked and rechecked. Flour, tea, bully beef, all rations measured and checked. If we are going to hit disaster out there, it won't be because we didn't pack our toothbrushes.'

Lonergan snapped to it, shoulders a bit squarer with his newfound mapping skills. He was a quick learner and now guided the detectives without complaint. Came home a bit shaky from the effort of command in front of Denning and Baines, but he was on his way.

I hauled out what maps we had of the north and plotted, measured and noted. If we found a trace of these men – extremely unlikely – but if we did and fell into the chase, we had to know where the water was at all times.

Next morning, waking to an even greater sense of foreboding than was normal for me, I went through the usual morning routine while running through my plans for the manhunt. Miles to be covered, discipline, morale. The falling sensation, the unpleasant feeling that haunted me, passed through me again, accompanied by a strong sense of impending doom. Only this time it was a reasonable thing to feel. I put a hand on the wall and breathed, waiting for it to pass. Hadn't had these for a while, but now I'd had two in twenty-four hours.

Lonergan appeared and put the kettle on, and I quickly dropped my hand, straightened up. Then Mrs Schreiber came and did breakfast. I ate, gnashing my teeth on the toast, cutting my eggs savagely. This was my final meal before two weeks of tins, damper, listening to troopers' fart jokes and sleeping on stones, and I'd be fretting the entire time about my job, about Flora, about Denning and Kirkbride fitting me up.

Superintendent Corcoran appeared at the back door, scowling like a dyspeptic Titan. The scowl was, no doubt, for me. 'Leave us, Trooper Lonergan.'

Lonergan picked up his plate and cup of tea and, after glancing at me, went out the back.

'Martin will lead the manhunt,' Corcoran announced when we were alone. 'He told me you were found on Kirkbride's property in the middle of the night. Says you threatened Kirkbride, who claims you were after his daughter. You're not fit to lead a manhunt and I doubt you're even fit to wear the uniform.'

'Sir, if I may, this manhunt—'

'Sydney expects a manhunt, the Kirkbrides expect it, the detectives and the entire district expect a manhunt, and therefore there will be a manhunt.'

'Sir.'

'You have served your country, Hawkins, and I have taken note of it, giving you a long rope. But enough is enough. You and I will be having a discussion about your future as soon as this investigation is over. You are to stay sober until then and confine yourself to the station and other routine duties.'

'Sir.'

'I am returning to Bourke early tomorrow. Denning will go with me and return to Calpa the day after.'

'Sir.'

I watched him stride off to organise his horse. Ernest Martin couldn't lead an Easter egg hunt, and the whole thing was a waste of time anyway. There had been no reports of murders up and down the river, no reports of stolen horses, not even the Ellerslie horses had been stolen, it turned out. No boundary riders attacked, no reports of three men cycling frantically towards the Queensland border.

But an hour later Martin and the six troopers rode down to the punt, leading an extra two horses carrying supplies. They had enough combined weaponry and men to organise into volley fire, should it be necessary. The men who killed the Kirkbrides would no doubt attack them head-on in formation, using a similar countermarch tactic, which they would then return, and may the better men win.

The locals cheered like the troopers were going off to war. But anyone who knew anything expected nothing to come of it. It was a deflating moment. I'd been keyed up, making notes and lists of the thousand and one things needed to do a long manhunt successfully and bring your men home alive, whether or not you caught the culprit. Now I was confined to the station, left to count the flies on the wall.

~

That night I woke to the sound of a timid tapping on my window. I sat up, pushed the curtain aside and there was old Kev, holding up a lantern in one hand and a telegram in the other, his crinkled old face still full of sleep. I staggered out and found him in his nightshirt with a pair of wellingtons on his feet.

'Thanks, Kev,' I said, and signed his little book. 'You better get out of the cold, mate.'

He shuffled off across the street and I ripped open the telegram. It was from the Bourke station. A trooper was on his way with an urgent message for Corcoran and the detectives. They were to stay in Calpa until they received it.

I woke Lonergan and sent him to wake Corcoran, but he came back and said they'd already gone. I sent him riding as fast as he could up the western river road to recall them.

~

A couple of hours after sending Lonergan upriver, Denning and Corcoran were in my kitchen, sitting in uncomfortable silence. Then the trooper from Bourke galloped into town in a swirl of dust. He dismounted, sweaty and breathless, as if he'd seen the enemy massing over the next hill. Corcoran and Denning came outside.

'Trooper Copeland, Bourke, sir. I have a bag, from Enngonia on the stock route, an empty leather holdall handed in by some drover and sent down to Bourke on the mail coach, sir. They reckoned it could be Kirkbride's. It could have had the stolen gowns and jewellery in it.'

'And you have it with you?'

'I do, sir. Senior Constable Hurley reckoned the detectives needed to see it, sir.'

Denning and Corcoran looked at each other. The bag was in a hessian sack tied to the horse. The trooper untied it and handed the bag to Corcoran and they went inside.

'When did you leave Bourke?' I asked the trooper.

'Around four am.'

'Take your horse round the back, there's feed and water. Pub might do you a late breakfast.'

Lonergan was sent to get Baines, and then the four of them went up to Inveraray to see Kirkbride. Before he left, Lonergan took me aside and told me that when he went up the western road to fetch Denning and Corcoran, he rode past the Kirkbride buggy heading north, with two women in it and a man riding escort. As soon as he was gone with the others, I raced over to Joe's.

He was at his desk beneath the window that looked out onto the street, the inevitable skeleton hanging in the corner, the metal cabinets full of small jars and bottles. He grabbed the brandy, poured a couple of measures into two tumblers and handed me one, regardless of the early hour.

'Have you seen Flora? Is she all right?' I said, ignoring the brandy.

He drank his brandy quickly, then sighed and looked out the window at the street. 'No, she's not all right, so I advised Kirkbride to send her to a special sanatorium back east. She left this morning.'

'You sent Flora to a bloody madhouse? Why didn't you tell me?'

'Did I have to ask your permission?' Joe said, filling his glass again. 'She's a danger to herself, she needs care around the clock.'

'You sent her away?'

'Yes. Her father and her doctor are the best judges of what is best for her.'

'She can think for herself.'

'And has just suffered a terrible loss that drove her to want to take her life. And you turn up at her home in the middle of the night, stirring up trouble. You are part of the reason Flora is sick, according to Mr Kirkbride.'

'The hell I am.'

'Her family want her away from here so she can recover in peace and quiet, and the last thing she needs is you, sick yourself and in no fit state to do anything, trying to get at her.'

'I am not sick. Don't you take that fucking "doctor knows best" line with me. Bunch of charlatans, the lot of you, fakirs and conmen drumming your fucking opium like bloody roaming peddlers. Sedate the

165

population so they won't make a fuss, that's what you do, because you don't know what the fuck is wrong with them.'

'Finished?'

'Give me the address so I can write to her at least.'

'No.'

I threw the glass of brandy at the wall, where it shattered, splattering glass and brandy around, stomped out and went down to the river, wanting to hit someone.

Joe might say Kirkbride sent Flora away to get better, but for men like Kirkbride, there were always two reasons – one good, and then the real one.

~

That night I found Baines down at the hotel having a drink by himself, the usual drinkers giving him a wide berth, as though he were a leper on the run from a lazaret. I ordered a beer and took a seat next to him.

'Has it been confirmed that the men dismissed for disruption on Inveraray didn't return home?' I asked.

'They did go home,' Baines said, looking into his beer. 'Local cops confirmed it. One of them even had his train ticket stub from Bourke to Bathurst.'

'And the alleged stolen horses?'

He turned to me, bloodshot eyes, a sour look on his mug.

'But the empty bag is Kirkbride's?'

'He swears by it,' he said, flicking fag ash at the ashtray. 'So yeah, killers have gone to Queensland, taken the jewels and gowns with them.

But they just aren't the blokes we thought they were.'

Martin and the troopers would wander about, use up the allocated resources, get hot and filthy, wear out the horses and the budget would balance. I doubted Corcoran would send out more troopers to bring them back, because everyone expected a manhunt and by God they were going to get one.

The Queensland police would be notified but there was nothing the detectives could give them, no descriptions of the suspects, only a list of stolen property and the dates, times and nature of the crimes. Baines thought Bob Kirkbride had accepted that his three children had gone to the dance in Larne after all.

'Reckons young Grace was so excited about the ball, but by the time she felt better it was too late to get to Cobar, so they went to Larne instead for the dance as it was closer.'

'But they told the servants they were going to Cobar,' I said.

'Changed their mind once they was on the road,' he shrugged. 'Can't be proved but it sounds like a reasonable explanation.'

Not to me. If only James had been seen at the dance, then where were the two girls? Sitting in the cart all night?

'I know what you're thinking, mate, but investigations can't go hammer and tongs indefinitely. We'll put out a reward for any information. Get a load of shit back usually, but sometimes you get lucky.'

'And the inquest?'

'Yeah, well, they'll probably find that it was unlawful killing by person or persons unknown, restrict the evidence and put it in the pending tray. That's what usually happens, unless there's a fuss made, and there don't seem to be an appetite for fuss from Kirkbride. Leaves a nasty taste in your mouth but it's the way it goes sometimes.'

'Just between you and me, who do you think—'

Baines drained his beer and mashed his cigarette out. 'Somebody who knew them, that's what I reckon. And yeah, between you, me and the fencepost, I'd be looking a lot closer at Tom Fletcher.'

'No,' I said, shaking my head. 'No, Tom adored Nessie.'

'Exactly. A man who carries that around everyday can switch from hearts and flowers to knives and fists in an instant. It's the bread and butter of policing, the crime that puts money in our pay packet each week. Women and girls killed by husbands or sweethearts.'

I must have looked sceptical, because he nodded and went on.

'We done some digging on Tom Fletcher. His school reckons he had a hot temper, every bloke on Gowrie says the same.'

'But he was in Cobar at the ball – there are witnesses.'

'He left the ball early to go looking for them, took the Gully Tank stockroute. Reckons he never thought of looking on the western river road because that's not how you get to Cobar from Inveraray. But he could have.'

'He can't have killed them, the timing makes it impossible. I know that route, it's quicker, but—'

'He's on a fast horse and flogs it 'cause he's so stirred up because she didn't turn up as she'd promised.'

'Maybe, but why kill the other two?'

'Because they were there. You reckon Nessie wasn't a flirt, but that means she didn't flirt with you. But you don't know, she could have been

168

giving the come-on to all and sundry and Tom can't take it anymore. He's furious she's not at the ball, he finds them on the road, argues with Jimmy – and they didn't like each other – and smashes Jimmy's head in. Grace screams so he shoots her, Nessie's screaming, and she won't shut up so he hits her, and when she's down he takes her, takes what she's been holding out on but promising to other blokes.'

I stared at him, his baby face and hard eyes, the black bags under them, the sunburnt forehead. The things he'd seen etched in every line around his eyes.

Baines shrugged. 'She don't have to be a flirt for him to think she's a flirt. Just the idea of it can set some men off.'

'So why are you pulling out? If you think he did it, why not try to prove it?'

He got to his feet, picked his fags and matches up from the table and said, 'Sydney CIB runs on three things, mate: getting to the top, knifing the bloke who's already there, and then fending off challengers. We also run investigations.'

And with that enigmatic answer, he said goodnight and left. They packed up and left for Bourke the next day.

～

Lonergan had gone back to Bourke with Corcoran. Martin and the troopers were flogging a dead horse somewhere west of the black stump, and I had the place to myself again. Rather than hang around an empty station, I often found myself at the pub. One day, a bit too

169

early, I found Wally was polishing his glasses in the endless battle against dust. He measured out a double whisky and a beer and slid them over to me.

'How you going, Gus?'

'Good, yeah. Any better and I'd be dangerous.'

'Circus's left town, eh?' Wally said, fixing me with his kindly, bloodshot eyes. 'Listen, mate, you look after yourself.'

'Always do.'

'Nope, you were in a bad way when you first arrived, maybe you just didn't notice.'

'What do you mean, "a bad way"?'

'Queer in the head, you know. Kev and I laid bets on how long you'd last before someone found you hanging from a stable rafter. But you come good.'

'Did I?'

He laughed, slapped me on the shoulder and kept polishing his glasses with a damp rag.

The thing about coming good was you couldn't lie around drunk waiting for time to pass and goodness to return. You had to get up, go forward to meet it, then work your arse off to make it stay. Sliding into bitterness and cynicism felt like a relief at the time, but it was downward movement.

I busied myself around the station, dusting off the files, checking they were in order, sharpening pencils, auditing the tack room, writing it all up, putting in the effort to stay on the horizontal.

After days of this misery, Joe came hurrying into the station. We had avoided each other since Flora had been sent away, so I assumed this was not a social call.

'Bad accident at the mines in Cobar,' he said. 'I've been called in to help. Even Reg Tierney is going, that's how bad it is.'

'Any dead?'

'Three dead, seven badly injured.'

'What on earth do they want with Tierney?' I said. 'He'll kill 'em as soon as look at them.'

'Shunt the less urgent cases to us and get on with fixing the miners. Anyway, I'll be away for several days and so will Reg. Anybody hurt and you'll have to get them to Bourke or Cobar.'

'Yeah, all right. You're riding into Cobar?'

'How else do you expect me to get there?'

'Don't forget your waterbag, map and compass. And some oats for the horse.'

'You think I don't know how to do this?' he said, frowning.

'I know you don't. You should go with Reg, in his buggy. Safer with two of you. Tie your horse to the back of the buggy and swap them around halfway.'

'I'm perfectly able to get to Cobar.'

'Take a gun. You don't know who's out there now.'

He made an impatient noise and left. I returned to my book.

That night, Mrs Schreiber brought my dinner over and left it on the stove, picked up my washing and left. I waited until it was late and then went to Joe's and let myself in the back door. I quietly made my way up the hall to the surgery, picked the key to the filing cabinet from Joe's hiding spot, which I'd seen him use many times, and opened his files. I found his file on Flora, laid it on the desk and located a copy of a letter to a doctor at a sanatorium in Katoomba. I scribbled down the address, returned the file and let myself out into the dark night.

I put in for a week's leave, which was granted as soon as Lonergan returned to man the station.

16

Late July and Katoomba was cold. I was grateful for the fire in the room I'd taken at a guesthouse close to the sanatorium. A plain iron bedstead, painted white, and a white crochet bed cover, a heavy, dark polished wardrobe and dresser with a washstand, a floral porcelain washbasin and jug, all a far cry from my room at the Calpa police station, with its rusty tin ceiling, wobbly timber bed, grey police blankets and rag rug on the gritty floor.

I unpacked and dabbed my finger in a jar of ointment, and ran it over the scar, peering at my reflection, searching for improvement. I might have been looking at my reflection but I was seeing that day, Christmas Day in 1910, when everything between me and Flora changed. We'd seen each other often, never alone, but we'd always managed to sit or walk or ride together.

Then Joe and I joined the Kirkbride family for Christmas, which included lunch in the middle of a warm day. Not hot like it usually was, which, considering the amount of eating we had to do, was lucky. There were no turkeys out this way so we ate lamb, with all the rest of the festive sideshow, finishing with plum pudding and custard, then port and cigars for the men while the women withdrew.

After coffee, while everyone else was nodding off, Flora asked if I wanted to go for a walk.

'You're joking? A nap, more like it.'

'Oh, come on, we won't be missed,' she whispered.

A moment alone with her was hard to engineer, so off we went, following the river upstream, keeping to the bank. The day was still and clear, the flies phenomenal. After all the wine and port I was desperate for a drink of water but we kept going. The Darling isn't a straight line – few rivers are – but our stretch was particularly given to tight bends and offshoots. There'd been unseasonal rain recently, mentioned with gratitude in Robert Kirkbride's grace before lunch, which gave the water a fresh smell and a rare translucent depth.

'I have to sit down,' I said, collapsing onto a sandy bank in the shade. The river was up but even so it was a several feet down the bank to the edge of the water. Flora sat beside me and took off her hat.

I lay back and closed my eyes, desperate to just give in to the alcohol and heat. Flora was quiet beside me. At least I thought she was until I heard a splash in the water and sat bolt upright. She was in the middle of the river up to her neck. Her dress, shoes and stockings were neatly folded beside me. She was the most unpredictable female I'd ever met.

'Come in, it's deliciously cool.'

I smiled, shook my head. 'Nah, I'll just watch for bunyips.'

'Oh, go on, it's Christmas.'

'As if that means anything.' But I did strip off down to my shorts. She'd seen all my scars so we didn't have to go through all that again. I launched myself into the water and joined her in the middle of the river, where the water came up to my neck.

We wallowed and splashed, and it was, as she said, cool and delicious. After a while the glare of the sun on the water made us both squint and soon it was too uncomfortable. I got out first and Flora followed.

'Oh look, what's that?' she said.

'Your father, probably,' I said, turning to look with a thud of alarm.

She was there beside me in her silk chemise, which was now wet and clinging to every curve, every swelling, every hollow. Wet tendrils of hair hung around her smooth, white neck, drops of water glistening in the sunlight on her skin. She smiled at me, not embarrassed, not ashamed, just watching me with a question in her eyes.

I quickly turned away, fumbled for my cigarettes. I lit one, and as I inhaled, Flora said, 'Let's make love.'

It was some time before I recovered from my coughing fit.

'Gus?'

I swallowed hard. Standing there, the sunlight gleaming on the wet silk, she appeared as some sort of bush goddess in an Arcadian vale. The shambling, drooling incubus on my left shoulder, cock permanently in hand, said, *Go on, lad, get to it*, while the clean-shaven officer on my right said, *Bad idea, son*.

'Don't you find me attractive?'

I wiped my hand down my face, swallowed and said, 'Your father will shoot me.'

'How would he find out?'

'Please, get dressed.'

'Oh,' she said, looking down, a little sulky. 'I thought you were braver than that.'

Every cell in my body yearned towards her with a heat more intense than the air around us. 'Get dressed, please. Please.'

'I want to know what it's like, that's all.'

I snatched up her dress, shoved it at her. 'You'll find out on your wedding night.'

With a sigh she pulled on her clothes, then sat down to get her stockings and shoes on. I was way out of my depth. Finished dressing and started to walk back, not looking to see if she was following. Then I heard her singing to herself, relieved because I didn't want to carry her back to the homestead over my shoulder.

We hadn't been missed. We collapsed into wicker chairs on the verandah and took up glasses of cool lemonade. I felt a little shaky after that encounter and left soon after.

A week later, as if he'd suddenly glimpsed what was happening, Robert Kirkbride took me aside and said I would not be marrying his daughter. I had no land, for a start, and while I might have been born a gentleman, I was now a police trooper, of all things. Flora would marry a more suitable man of his choosing.

I was never invited to the homestead again.

Before the war I was in love several times, or so I fancied. After the war I had transactions. My feelings for Flora crept up on me, unfamiliar as they were. Like sticking a needle into scar tissue. Just because you couldn't feel it, that didn't mean it wasn't happening.

~

Small wooden cottages lined the streets of Katoomba, snowdrops and jonquils pushing up through the lawns in response to the winter sunshine. London plane trees were green and lush with their new growth, and the smell of grilling lamb chops filled the air. I wouldn't have been surprised to learn there was a great greasy cloud of mutton fat covering the entire continent. Visiting hours for the sanatorium were restricted and I had to wait until three before I could have half an hour with Flora, so I found a bookshop on the main street and bought a leather-bound copy of an illustrated book of birds in mythology, which I knew she'd like.

The large red-brick building housing the sanitorium was set on a ridge and surrounded by clipped box hedges and Japanese maple trees, and extensive lawns sprinkled with snowdrops. In the middle of the lawn stood a stone fountain, the sound of water endlessly splashing and mingling with birdsong. A long, wide balcony ran along the second floor, with wicker chairs and tables placed at discreet intervals. From the balcony the patients looked out over a forested gully, and far in the distance stood the sweeping escarpments that surrounded the Jamison Valley.

A nurse in a long, white-starched pinafore and cap stood by, her eyes raking the visitors, looking for tins of caramels or posies, anything that might produce a small moment of joy in the patient and thus dangerously upset their stability. Now and then I caught a whiff of carbolic and cabbage soup. The only feature that distinguished it from the military hospital in Cape Town was the absence of disfigured and dying men.

Flora suddenly appeared, a small figure, black mourning hanging loose from her fine bones, her cropped dark hair brushed down. I was taken aback by the thump in my chest as she appeared, that flare of joy she always kindled in me. She looked so young, giving me a shy smile that made me want to snatch her up and run.

The nurse watched impassively. I had thirty minutes.

'It's nice here,' I said, awkwardly staring over the railing at the grass below. 'Are you allowed to walk around?'

'They let me sit on that wooden seat down there where they can see me, and I feed the rosellas. It's like I'm bathing my eyes after a lifetime of dust.'

We sat in a couple of wicker chairs and looked out over the bushland. She told me she'd not had one visitor, not her parents or aunts and uncles. No one. Her hands lay in her lap, pale and perfectly formed, and on one finger was a single ring I'd never seen before. She noticed me staring and held up her hand so the gemstones caught the light.

'Garnet – it was Grace's.' Then she pulled a necklace up from beneath her dress. 'Nessie's sapphire necklace. It's all that's left of them.'

The stolen jewellery.

'I thought they'd shot you,' she said. 'Like they ... shot ... after you came to my window that night. I thought you were dead – nobody would tell me. You weren't at the funeral, and I thought it was because you were dead, and I'd wished you dead and it was wicked of me and then it happened. And then that night … Father wouldn't tell me but Dr Pryor said you weren't dead when he came to fetch me to send me here.'

Nice touch, Kirkbride, you bastard.

'Floss, it's all right, you can wish me dead, but I'm not, see?'

'Floss. Nobody calls me that but you,' she said, smiling at her hands as they twisted a handkerchief in her lap. Then she looked over at me. 'Nobody has told me anything. Said I didn't need to know but I do. How were they when you found them?'

I took a deep breath, exhaled, looked over to the distant escarpments and back at her. Rain, sodden dresses, the horror of their injuries, the bitter taste of my vomit.

'Nessie and Grace were lying down in the back of the cart. Nessie had her arms around Grace, and they were snuggled up under the blankets. They looked so peaceful, like they were just asleep, and James had the rifle in his hands – he was trying to protect them. It would have been very quick for all three.'

'They were shot?'

I nodded.

She blinked, tears welling in her eyes, then spilling down her pale cheek. I took her hand. We sat in silence for a while.

'I've never slept alone before I came here,' she said, holding tightly to my hand. 'Nessie and I always shared a bed, and in the mornings, sometimes too early, Grace would run in, climb up and wedge herself between us and we'd all go back to sleep.'

The three of them in the big bed, their glossy dark heads together, white coverlets and soft breath while sunrise coloured the world and the station kitchens baked bread rolls.

'At least they're together, all three of them.' She shook her head. 'I don't know how to be on my own.'

The sound of a man crying out split the still air. I could not bear this place – the smell of it, the walled-in misery, rattling down the corridor on wheels, dispensing doses of oblivion.

'I'll wait for you to come home,' I said. 'I'll cancel my transfer request.'

'I don't want to go home. Where is my home without my sisters and brother? I should have died with them. I told Father and Mother, Dr Pryor, I told them I should be dead too. It was all so unforgiveable, so utterly wrong, and God took them. He took them and they're in heaven and I'm left here alone to be punished.'

To take her mind elsewhere I gave her the book. She leafed through the pages while the nurse looked on, and stopped at a picture of a white swan wearing a small golden crown. She gazed at it for a long moment, then put her finger on the swan, as if she could feel the feathers through the paper.

'You told Father we never talked about marriage.'

'I needed to protect you.'

'He told me where you were when they died.'

My heart skidded to a halt. I looked around desperately. The nurse checked the watch pinned to her uniform.

'Do you love her?' Flora turned to look at me, a direct gaze that I could not escape from.

'No.'

I looked down at the wooden boards of the verandah floor, wishing they'd suddenly give way. Flora closed the book and placed it on the table between us. A cold gust blew up from the gully. I waited, hoping for forgiveness.

Once downstairs and in the grounds, I looked up at the balcony, hoping to see her watching for me. But she wasn't there, and I wished I hadn't looked back.

~

I walked the streets back to my room, the blue sky suddenly oppressive, the snowdrops looking like weeds. Telling his suicidal daughter that her sweetheart betrayed her. What sort of father did that? Leave aside for the moment the fact of my sexual incontinence – what sort of human inflicts pain on an already suffering and vulnerable girl?

The same man who humiliated Nessie's beloved by throwing a handful of dirt on the table, saying that's all he would ever have. The same man who lied about me wanting his damn sheep farm, wanted to fit me up for his children's murders – yes, that man. The man who dared say to my face that I was not fit for his daughter.

I found a pub and took a seat at the bar, joining my fellow men as they drank to the futility of it all. By my third double whisky I'd remembered the sapphire necklace and garnet ring Flora was wearing. Those items of jewellery that Kirkbride had reported stolen by the killers of his children. It could only mean that Kirkbride was mistaken, or that he had lied about what was stolen. In all probability the bag found at Enngonia was not Kirkbride's either.

Kirkbride was covering something up. That tallied with his out-of-character acceptance of the end of the investigation, and his request for me to kill the suspects without trial. If I could expose the reasons, I could get at him, bring him down with me, topple the great statue of the king. Not fit for his daughter, he said. We'd see about that.

I had to go to Sydney and see the detectives.

17

I settled into a seat on the train, gazing through the glass at the endless bushland, the small weatherboard cottages with smoke rising from their chimneys, horse and carts plodding on dirt roads and more bushland, endlessly replaying those minutes with Flora on the balcony, tormenting myself, a pastime I was very good at.

Finally the train pulled into Central and the memories rushed at me. Train trips between my home in Queanbeyan and Sydney had filled my teenage years as a boarder at King's, journeys filled with homesickness and worry of returning home, oppressed by nameless longing, boredom and the generalised anger of a young man at odds with the world he finds himself in.

Thirty-one and I hadn't changed, although now I recognised the nameless longing as lust. Easily slaked, but not so the anger. My war experiences appeared to have exacerbated that unappealing characteristic.

From Central I walked down Castlereagh Street, past the pubs and cheap shops, the streets busy with Clydesdales pulling drays laden with bales or barrels of beer, horse-drawn trams, people bustling here and there, more people than I'd seen in three years, all in one street. The noise, a tumultuous roar, caused a sudden tension in my shoulders, a gritting of teeth I had not felt since last in a city.

On the corner of Hunter and Phillip I found the Sydney Criminal Investigation Branch. I walked in and asked the duty officer if I could see Arthur Baines, then waited, watching men come and go in their cheap suits, laughing or grim, arrogant or shifty, the ubiquitous fag in their lips.

A door behind the counter opened and Baines appeared.

'Blimey, Trooper Hawkins – what brings you here?'

'Your sunny smile, Detective,' I said as we shook hands. He invited me into the detective offices. The large room was full of desks with men slouching, reading form guides, half-eaten sandwiches in front of them, or labouring over some bit of paperwork. Nobody looked up.

'The pit, where the juniors hack at the coalface,' he said, waving his hand dismissively.

He took me into a large room with a window onto the street, a blackboard and a large table and chairs.

'Have a seat. What can I do you for, eh?' he said, lighting up a fag.

'I wanted to talk about the Kirkbride case.'

He hesitated and looked out the window, then back at me. 'It's pretty clear what happened, since their empty bag was found up near the border,' he said, ashing his fag. 'We'll be putting out descriptions of the jewellery and gowns, see if they turn up in pawn shops. It was a robbery gone wrong. Murder and rape by persons unknown. We won't be going back, unless there's a full confession, and even then ...' He looked over at the door and said softly, 'I don't think we'd be undermining our own findings, now, would we?'

'What if you were wrong?'

'We aren't wrong.'

'But you suspect Tom Fletcher.'

'I never said that.'

'Have you told the Kirkbrides this?'

'Yep, the new inspector general himself wrote to them. They accept that it was robbery gone wrong.'

'I don't understand how the Kirkbrides can just give up.'

He gave me a look I couldn't decipher, something akin to a brick wall.

'I've seen the jewellery Kirkbride reported as stolen,' I said. 'It wasn't stolen at all.'

Baines didn't miss a beat. 'He's mistaken, that's all. Easy mistake to make when you're in shock.'

'Then he's an unreliable witness. He could have made a mistake about the leather bag too.'

He leant back in his chair and considered me. 'Just, ah, hold on for a minute. Back in a sec.'

I went to the window, looked out at the street, the busy pub across the road. I knew word of my visit would get back to Bourke, but I'd deal with that later. I was still a member of the Mounted Troopers, with a warrant card. One day, and it was getting closer by the minute, I'd have no access to anything, not even the police station outhouse.

Baines swept back into the room, all bluster. 'Come and have lunch over at the pub. The boss wants to meet you – Detective Superintendent Jack Tuttle.'

'Thank you, but I better get on.'

'Jack Tuttle,' he repeated. 'Wants to have lunch with you.'

~

The pub dining room was full of men in suits drinking, smoking, shouting, feeding and swearing. Once my eyes had accustomed to the dim light, I knew I was going to have difficulty with the crowd and the noise, and I set myself the grim task of tamping down my reactions.

Jack Tuttle was a man of appetites, pouring pints of beer down his throat and tackling a massive serve of roast pork with gusto. I had a beer and a mutton chop just to be sociable.

'Your boss speaks well of you,' Tuttle said, a sheen of perspiration on his red-veined face. 'Ted Buchanan, that is.'

'The Mounted Police super?'

'Yeah – says you were in the army, the New South Wales Mounted Rifles, in the Boer War.'

'I was, yes.'

Tuttle nodded as he chewed, sweaty jowls wobbling, his hooded eyes sharp as tacks. 'The new inspector general was a mounted trooper – solved the Tommy Moore case in Bourke. Heard about that?'

'No.'

'Ask Jim Corcoran, he served with him.' Tuttle paused as he sawed away at a chunk of glistening pork fat. 'Mounted troopers produce good officers – they can go a long way.'

I thought of Lonergan dithering about with his maps upside down, the six troopers breaking formation at the first sound of gunfire, me lying dead drunk on my bed while Calpa ticked over like a cheap watch.

He put down his knife and fork, drank some beer and dabbed at his mouth. 'As an army officer, you'd know that loyalty to your brother officers is the golden rule. It's the same in the police. Loyalty to your fellow officers and to the department is a rule us coppers live by.'

'Inspector Denning didn't show me any loyalty.'

Tuttle waved his hand as if Denning were merely an irritating fly. 'It's obvious to me that Miss Ryan was lying to save her reputation. A man of your background wouldn't lie. Your record will be amended so there's no trace of this misunderstanding.'

'Thank you, sir.'

'But you understand the Kirkbride case is closed?'

'I do, sir.'

He nodded with satisfaction. 'I'll have a quiet word to the Department of Education about Miss Ryan. We look after our own.'

He heaved himself up out of his chair, slapped me on the shoulder, said he'd see us later and left the pub, waving to the barman as he went.

Baines drained the remains of his beer, smacked his lips. 'Denning copped a serve over his treatment of you.'

'Good, glad to hear it.'

In South Africa, if another officer was discovered buggering a coolie or beating a whore, we never said anything. It was his business, unsavoury and you'd steer clear of him in the mess, but the rule was never cast a stone at a brother officer lest the stones come back at you one day, hard and vicious. It was the way the game was played: never mind that the Gatling's jammed and the colonel's dead, you step up and play the game as the rules are set.

Baines and I walked out into the street and shook hands.

'Listen,' I said, 'I don't want Miss Ryan to lose her job. Can you do something?'

Baines shook his head. 'You need a weapon with a bit of stopping power to bring Jack Tuttle down, mate.'

~

I returned to Katoomba to see Flora, taking my old room in the nearby guesthouse and breathing in the balmy air of the mountains redolent with spring flowers. I purchased a large bunch of daffodils, white jonquils and maidenhair fern for her.

I was told I couldn't see her.

'Who says so?'

'The doctor.'

'Ask her if she'd like to see me.'

They refused and I was shown the door.

I went back to my room and brooded. I could have chopped an entire redgum to kindling I was so angry, and I walked down to the Three Sisters, a bitter wind blowing. I read that legend had it the three rock formations were once three beautiful sisters who were coveted by men from a different tribe. In order to prevent the men from carrying the sisters away, the girls' tribal necromancer turned them into stone. Seemed a bit unfair to me. Had it not occurred to him to turn the men into stone instead?

~

The familiar dust clouds of Bourke greeted me as I stepped from the train. Topsoil from far away settled on my clothes, irritated my eyes, lodged in my beard. My brief absence in the east, with respite from the dust, made the assault even more uncomfortable. I went to fetch Felix, and as I paid the ostler he gave me an envelope. Inside was a note instructing me to report to Superintendent Corcoran upon my return.

I found my way to the police station. They were expecting me. I was made to wait. Like a boy outside the headmaster's office, I knew I was in for a bollocking and was impatient to get it over with.

~

Corcoran sat behind his desk, absorbed in writing something, as if I were not in the room standing to attention. The pictures of past superintendents, hanging along the wall, glared at all the miscreants who'd escaped their clutches. Corcoran's goldfish swam in circles.

'You've been visiting Flora Kirkbride and poking your nose into the Kirkbride case,' Corcoran snapped, replacing his pen in the stand. 'I never picked you for a fool, Hawkins. Many other things, but not that. Denning warned me – he told me.'

'Sir. Told you what?'

'That you are trouble on two legs.'

'I have never given the Mounted Troopers any trouble, sir. On the contrary—'

'No, you haven't. But you've been making up for it since the Kirkbrides were killed, starting that night and gathering apace. The case is closed until the Queensland police apprehend the offenders. That's it, done. Nobody from the Kirkbrides to the minister wants to hear about it again.'

'I saw Baines in Sydney, briefly, sir. Had lunch with DS Jack Tuttle.'

His eyebrows hit the roof. 'You had lunch with Jack Tuttle?'

'Roast pork, I think it was, sir. Denning's been put back on his chain and my record is to be amended.'

Corcoran blinked a few times. 'I expect Tuttle told you that the Kirkbride case is closed.'

'He did. But—'

'There is no but. Kirkbride is outraged that you visited his daughter without permission. He assumed Dr Pryor told you where Miss Flora was but Pryor denies it. He says the only way you could have known is if you'd looked in his confidential files, and to do that you would have to have broken into his home.'

I felt a bit queasy at that moment.

'What do you say to that?'

'Miss Kirkbride is a dear friend.'

'You are lucky your dear friend Dr Pryor does not want to press charges,' he said, and swung his chair around to look out the window for a moment, giving me time to reflect on either my own stupidity or Joe's lack of loyalty.

190

'When you first came out here, I knew immediately why you'd accepted a remote posting,' Corcoran said, swinging his chair back to face me. 'To drink yourself to death. And if you didn't, you'd be out of here after a few years, once you felt a bit better, and would go back to some privileged life in the east. But all of us in the Mounted Troopers have no other career than this, and no hope of one. Men like you, silvertails, come in and smash things and then leave the mess to us. You don't belong in the force, Hawkins.'

'I'm not resigning, sir, if that's what you want.'

'You are suspended without pay. You must leave the police station for Lonergan to man, return your horse, uniform and warrant card. You are to stay in the district until I say you can leave. Robert Kirkbride is a lot closer than Jack Tuttle. Now, fuck off and don't let me hear or see you again. For some time.'

I expect Corcoran would have sacked me if he could, but a plate of roast pork stood in his way.

I collected Felix and we headed south. Furious with myself and with Joe, I set Felix at a gallop, needing the exhilaration of speed and the power of the horse beneath me to excise the anger. It worked like a drug, one I knew I'd never tire of. But we had a long ride ahead and soon had to settle into a steady plod. I'd made this journey so many times before. But never with the sobering knowledge that I'd managed to get myself expelled from exile.

⁓

Lonergan was out the back in the stable brushing his horse and looked out at us as we arrived. I led Felix into the neighbouring stall, took all his kit off and watched him and Dancer have a smooch.

'I hope you weren't expecting the same from me,' Lonergan said.

I smiled, watching the stable cat join Felix and Dancer. It'd be nice to be missed by someone, greeted with pleasure when I returned, kissed and petted.

'So yeah, nothing happened and then ... nothing happened. Did patrols, cleaned out the stable, that's about it. A fella called Beavins from Gowrie wanted to speak to you, but he never came back.'

'Log it?'

He nodded. Back inside the station, I checked the filing trays, ran my eye down the incident book. Several spelling mistakes and an inkblot, but Lonergan was right, nothing had happened. Just the local business of producing wool, getting drunk, waking up the next day and doing it all again. I checked the mail. The personal letters from my father met their end in the stove fire, as usual.

'I got the order to man the station. They say you're suspended and to clear out,' Lonergan said, joining me.

'Yep.'

'You didn't kill them, for Christ's sake.'

'I did something else, so out I go.'

'Tell you what, I'm going to miss Mrs Schreiber. Lived like a king out here.'

'She stays. I'll keep eating here – I'll die if I have to eat at the Royal.'

I took Dancer and Felix on a ride south downriver, coolabahs and redgums lining the riverbanks and shading the road. The dappled sunlight hit the pitted dirt road. The water in the river was up. Grey herons waded along the shallows. Crested pigeons flew off in flurry of alarm as we approached. There'd be good fishing along here soon, for a brief moment, before the water dwindled and the mud hardened in the summer. Some days, after good rain, pelicans appeared, usually in threes, riding the updrafts above the river, scouting for fish, a long way from their coastal home and its certainties.

I found a low bank and let the horses have a splash in the water while I lit a fag and had a think about what to do next.

~

Back at the police station I threw some clothes into a bag, picked out a few books, looked around and left. Staying at the Royal was the only alternative. As I walked past Joe's house, he came out and invited me in for a drink. But once the door closed behind me, his expression changed to anger.

We stood in the dim hallway, barely able to see each other. Mrs Schreiber was working in the kitchen, frying liver, by the smell of it. She quietly closed the door and we were practically in the dark, just bright slits of light beneath both doors.

'You went to see Flora,' Joe said. 'You broke into my office and read her confidential notes.'

'I didn't break in – the place was unlocked, as were your files.'

'Kirkbride gave me a dressing-down when he should have saved it for you. You broke the law, several times.'

'I'm suspended without pay. Happy?'

'You're not sorry, are you?' he said.

'No, I'm not. She's had no visitors since she's been there. She's all alone and suffering.'

'And you think you can relieve that suffering?'

'You could have, and should have, told Kirkbride you didn't know how I found out,' I snapped. 'Shown a bit of loyalty.'

'I'm not going to be yelled at just to save your skin.'

'He yelled at you – so what? Are you so piss-weak that you caved in just because he raised his voice? Did he hit you, fire a gun at you, torture you? No, he told you off. And in the face of such overwhelming force, you threw me under the wheels.'

'You can't help but fuck things up, can you?'

'Spoken like a true friend.' I pulled the front door open, bright light blaring in, then let it slam behind me.

18

Sleeping in one of the cramped and stinking rooms at the Royal felt like punishment enough, and worry made for fitful sleep. Plenty of lucky souls don't remember their dreams but I do. Dreams and memories, and sometimes I don't know which is which. The dreams are so lucid they follow me all day, and I have to question my recall and remind myself that it didn't happen like that. Tossing and turning in a strange bed, mind racing and a muscle twitch just below my left eye. I lit a candle, checked the eye in the mirror hanging above the washstand. Couldn't see the twitching muscle but I felt it. Soon my hand would begin, almost in unison.

At school, if a master thrashed you with the cane, you bore it in silence, no matter how brutal. If you were beasted in the army, you bore it in silence. If you were lying in a tent on the veldt dying of typhoid, you did not cry out. To cry out was to be unmanned, because a man did not scream or lose control, nor did he apologise, explain himself or mistreat an inferior. Mastery of the self, at all times – for how could he rule over those below him if he could not rule himself?

I could manage by day. But at night the fear ran amok and I cried out, beginning each day with shame.

I opened the window to the sounds of the night, the frogs and crickets, sat on the bed trying to get a breath. The uniform, the station, the routines and duties – all of them contained me, and without those bindings I could feel myself disintegrating. I couldn't stay here and couldn't leave. Or I could – resignation offered a way out. Resign under a cloud and it would follow me for life. But this? Night after never-ending night?

~

At dawn I went down to the river, waded in and stood there watching the water as it slid around me, breathing in the scents of woodsmoke and frying bacon, my feet sinking into the mud. I heard a man call my name, turned and saw Henry Peyton, the overseer of Gowrie Station, heading towards the police station.

'Hawkins, I need to speak with ye.'

'I am suspended from duty and Mick Lonergan is in charge,' I said as I waded out.

'He's nowt but a stripling,' he said, a horrified look on his face.

'That's how it is. For now. Let's go and see him.' I wrapped a towel around my waist and he looked askance at me, barefoot, gingerly walking over the stony dirt.

Lonergan was bleary and buttoning his shirt as he stumbled into the station. 'Mr Peyton, can I help you?' He stared at me, blinking. I was half-naked, beard dripping water, the pulse under my eye almost frantic.

'One of my men, Archie Beavins, is missing. Gave no notice and didn't claim his wages. Men won't say why, or they don't know why. But a man works hard and then forgets to collect his pay?'

'He came in looking for me while I was away,' I said. 'Maybe he's come off his horse somewhere? Have you had a look around?'

'Didn't take his horse, and we can't spare men to go looking for the eejit, but you can, you and Wilson Garnet, or he can,' he said, nodding at Lonergan.

'All right, we'll get onto it today. Where's he most likely to have gone?'

'Chasing lassies, more than likely, and outstaying his welcome.'

'When was he last seen?'

'Wednesday. He didn't turn up for supper, wasn't at work on Thursday. So I'm ringing the alarm today.'

He nodded and left. Lonergan looked at me.

'You can manage this,' I said. 'Hunting for a missing bloke's a doddle. Wilson or Frosty know what to do.'

'Yeah, but just say I saw you and asked for help? Who's gunna know?'

Beavins was a nasty sort and could rot out there, as far as I was concerned. But Dancer needed a workout, and I needed something to do.

~

Mrs Schreiber was frying mutton chops in the kitchen, her sturdy bulk reassuring. She turned to look at me when I emerged from my room dressed in civilian clothes.

'Why do they make you leave your home, Herr Kapitän?' she asked.

'Oh, just a silly misunderstanding,' I said. 'I'll still eat here.'

She shook her head. 'Always the police are doing stupid things.'

'I hope you don't include me in that assessment.'

She smiled, her plump face lighting up. 'Oh, you do the drinking too much.'

'I shall cut back then,' I said, and sat down as she dished up a breakfast of mutton chops, grilled tomatoes and eggs. Afterwards, Lonergan and I got out the maps and studied the area around Gowrie, looking for smallholdings within walking distance of the station. How far would a man walk for sex? Depended on how much he'd been drinking – and he'd probably walk a lot further for love. We saddled up and rode off towards Gowrie with a half-formed plan as to where to look.

On the way to Gowrie we stopped to pick up Wilson. The usual mob of kids and dogs greeted us, laughing and kicking up dust. Wilson wasn't around, so we left a message for Frosty to meet us at Gowrie Station and headed there, riding two abreast through the cool morning air over the sparse plain.

We stopped on a low rise and looked out. Nobody and nothing for miles. A rabbit broke cover and ran in front of us. Lonergan whipped his rifle out and shot it within seconds, then we plodded on in silence.

We rode past several lambing paddocks, the tiny creatures staggering around in their new world, hawks and eagles circling above, foxes and wild dogs watching, waiting. At night the stockmen went around every few hours with lanterns, checking and rechecking the ewes, giving a hand if needed. Lambing could be a bloody business; sometimes neither ewe nor lamb survived.

First place to look was Beavins' bunk and trunk. Station hands lived cheek by jowl in quarters two to a room. Places like Gowrie, Tindaree and Inveraray had about twenty or so men in the living quarters. Beavins had shared with Pearson, but Pearson's belongings had been cleared out and sent off to his next of kin.

We searched the contents of Beavins' trunk, which had been stored under his bed. A change of clothes, another pair of boots, a winter jacket and hat, a crucifix on a gold chain and some coins. Beavins' bunk stank of unwashed feet and stale tobacco. While Lonergan watched, I felt around gingerly under the greasy pillow and then lifted the mattress and felt around between the bed board and the mattress and pulled out a brown paper bag.

I peered inside and found a wad of ten-pound notes, of all things. Didn't he know about banks? Peyton would have banked his wages for him if he'd asked. That was much safer than keeping cash under your bunk in the stockmen's quarters.

I counted a hundred pounds. He'd saved that much on a stockman's wages? He wouldn't have left such a sum behind if he'd run off. I tossed it in the trunk and carried the trunk over to the house and asked somebody to lock it up for me.

Before we left, I asked the housekeeper if I could speak to Miss Sally Gilmour. The housekeeper was Miss Fletcher, Will Fletcher's spinster sister, who'd grown up on Gowrie and run the homestead since Mrs Fletcher became an invalid. She was as tall as her nephew and brother, grey-haired with a matter-of-fact manner, dressed in serge and her hair tightly bound.

'I'll see if she has a moment. This is official business?'

'Yes.'

She nodded. 'You can speak to her on the verandah. I'll get her now.'

A few minutes later Sally Gilmour appeared, and what a vision she was. No wonder Jimmy Kirkbride had his tongue halfway down her throat. Buxom, with lips so plump and moist it was a shame to leave them unkissed. I suspect she was used to my reaction, for she looked at me like I was dirt on her shoe.

'Constable, I am very busy. What is it you want?'

'Mr Archie Beavins has gone missing. Did you know him well?'

Taken aback, she frowned. 'What makes you think I know him, of all people?'

'He mentioned you during an interview – he said you and James Kirkbride had been friendly at the coronation dance in Larne and he didn't like it.'

Sally Gilmour snorted. 'None of his business, or yours for that matter. But yes, I was friendly with Jimmy. No law against it.'

'Indeed.'

'I've spoken to those detectives already, told 'em what I saw, which wasn't much.'

'Do you know where Archie Beavins might have gone?'

'You seem to think he's a friend of mine. He's not. Ask Mr Peyton about him. Now, I have to get back to Mrs Fletcher.'

~

Frosty was waiting for us and we set off on the search for Beavins. The three of us roamed around on foot that day, circling Gowrie, following one trail then another, while flies buzzed and the day got warmer. The scrub down this way had been overgrazed, and it wouldn't have been too hard to find a man if he was out here. Would have been easier on horseback to see further. We came up with nothing by the time sunset rolled around and gave it up for the day. But I made Lonergan walk beside Frosty and pay attention to how he was reading the small signs and how to look for them, which was useful.

'We'll push the circle further out tomorrow,' I said, showing Frosty and Lonergan the map.

~

I rode back to town with Lonergan, mulling over the disappearance of Beavins. He was either dead or injured. Unless he'd walked into Calpa and taken a steamer down to Wilcannia. There was no other way out of the district.

Men disappeared out here, and we stumbled on their bones years later. Sometimes you could tell from the clothes how recently the person

201

died; other times the bones could be a thousand years old and we just wouldn't know. Coming to speak to me was interesting. If he wanted to renew a firearms licence Lonergan could have fixed that, but it was me he wanted to see. Not many blokes around here sought me out for my charming smile.

As if he was following my thoughts, Lonergan said, 'It's that money that gets me thinking. I've never seen that much in my life, and I reckon few blokes out here would have either, and he's got it stuck under his mattress?'

'Maybe he's had no time to go to town to bank it.'

'He came looking for you, remember?' Lonergan replied. 'When you went on leave. Could have banked it then.'

'Or he received it just before he disappeared. But whoever gave it to him would have had to make a very big withdrawal in Burke or Wilcannia. Or they've come in from somewhere else with the money.'

'Nothing to buy out here,' Lonergan said, waving flies away from his face. 'And you couldn't drink a hundred pounds with nobody noticing.'

'Gambling?'

'A hundred quid? If a man has a hundred quid to play with, he's not going to be out in the backblocks doing it.'

'Unless he's a crook,' I said. 'And is looking to fleece the men out here. Plenty of two-up games are rigged, and lots of people underestimate these stockmen, think they can flimflam and get away with it.'

'But no strangers seen in the district, or not that we've been told about.'

'Nobody who looked like a stranger. There could well have been strangers, men who were here for no good, who dressed as a bunch of shearers.'

Lonergan sighed. 'I couldn't be a detective. Too many ifs and buts. I like a nice clear order. Just do it and go home for supper.'

When we arrived back at the station, Lonergan went to put the kettle on but I hauled him back, made him write up the day in the incident book while it was still fresh in his mind. I was hanging over him, correcting his grammar, and through the window saw the Jongs, perched on their old cart, rolling slowly through the town.

I stepped outside and hailed them. 'Mr and Mrs Jong, heading back home?'

'We are, but not to live,' Mrs Jong said, bringing the cart to a halt. 'But first, I'll thank you for your help with Albert. We're grateful to you for digging him a final resting place.'

'Not final. I did wire Bourke for a coffin and a van to take him to Bourke. Parry should have followed that up.'

'He got in touch with us and said Albert's still buried on our property, and he's sent a reminder to Bourke,' Mrs Jong said.

'I am sorry it ended like this.'

'Was never going to end any other way.'

'If you wait a moment, I'll fetch my horse and escort you up there, show you where he's buried.'

~

They hadn't been back since I warned them away from the place. I hated to see the pain in Mrs Jong's eyes when she came out of the cottage, seeing her neat little home ransacked.

'We'll not be staying here any longer,' she said as she and I went through the shed, noting down what had been taken.

'Where will you go?'

'Back to live with Dulcie and Howie at Wilcannia. It's a nice little town and Eddie loves the girls. Howie gets me to help with maintaining his kit, so I don't feel like I'm a burden.'

'What about this place?'

'Oh, I'll leave it to the boys,' she said. 'I'm too old to be selling it, and what with Albert buried here, Eddie would not be happy to see others living here.'

'And your granddaughters – how are they getting on? You said one of them was a little unruly.'

The old woman took off her hat, rubbed her sparse hair, whisked some flies away.

'Rosie, she's a good girl, but people will tell you otherwise. People will say she's wild and got the madness like her uncle, but she wouldn't be that way if a man she trusted hadn't interfered with her. That sort of thing does bad things to a child. It hurts them in a place that is not made for hurt but for love – that's what makes it evil.'

'Do you know who did it?' I asked.

'I do indeed, but no use telling anyone now. Howie took a whip to him, ran him out of town, but our Rosie, she's left with the worst of it.'

'May I ask, did it happen around here?'

She shook her head. 'No. It's best forgotten.'

'A bad business, and I'm sorry, Mrs Jong.' I shook her hand and mounted up. 'When you're ready, if you'd like an escort down to

Wilcannia I can take you part of the way. Just tell Parry to wire me.'

'Thank you, for all you've done for us.'

I stopped by Larne police station to give Parry a boot up the arse over the failure to fetch Albert Jong. This was the twentieth century – we didn't leave men in bush graves anymore. Parry wasn't there. I left a note, but as I was suspended, he could simply ignore it.

~

When I returned to the Calpa station I found Lonergan leaning against the kitchen sink grinning at the letter in his hand. He saw me and quickly folded the letter and tucked it in his pocket. A bowl of crimson quandongs sat on the wood chopping board waiting to be boiled down for jam. Quandongs needed a fair whack of sugar.

'Letter from your girl?'

'Yeah,' he said, all blushes and shuffles.

'What's her name?'

'Ada. We're going to get married.'

'Congratulations. She in Balranald?'

'Near. Her parents are in wheat too, not far from my parents' farm.'

'Pretty?'

He lit up like the sun. 'Yeah, real pretty.'

'Then what are you doing here?'

'Her father thought it was a good idea, go and get the itchies out before settling down. He reckons the farm will be ours one day, and he wants me to be serious about it.'

'Wise man.'

'I miss her, but.'

Envy smeared itself across my heart. I picked up the coffee pot, opened the cannister. 'Want a coffee?'

'Yeah, thanks. I've never had coffee like yours before.'

'Get it shipped from South Africa. The Dutch know their coffee.' I placed the pot on the stove and took down two cups.

'You got someone special?' he asked.

I put the cups on the table, found the sugar, put it on the table, picked up a cloth, wiped the table. 'Not anymore.' A lump in my throat was building.

The coffee boiled up, drops of water escaping the seal and hitting the stovetop, hissing as they evaporated.

'Ada called it off once,' he said as I poured the coffee. 'I wanted to die. Wanted to go out to the shed and bury my head in the arsenic sack.'

I nodded, sipped my coffee.

'My mum said, "Stop moping around like a wet chook, boy, just get back out there and change her mind."'

'And your dad?'

'Said, "Do what your mother tells you," like he always does. And I got Ada back. Had to work at it but I just didn't give up. I reckon I'm the luckiest man in Australia now.'

'Well done.'

We didn't keep sacks of arsenic at the station, but there was always the river.

~

Will Fletcher had asked me to come back that evening and dine with the family. Since Mrs Fletcher's accident she dined in her rooms, and old Miss Fletcher, Will's sister, ran the house. She kept a mean table, maybe as revenge for being asked to keep house.

Tom and Will and I had a beer on the verandah before dinner and watched the sky as it changed from orange to pink to mauve then dark blue, a sight few people tired of. Will Fletcher talked about fencing wire and Tom said nothing. I glanced at him now and again, thinking of Baines' suspicions. Will was very protective of his son, as you'd imagine, and would lie to save him, for all his Christian principles. And if Tom was the killer, his clothes would have been covered in blood. Easily got rid of on this vast property. He was quick to anger, Baines was right about that. Maybe I was just too used to him to see what Baines could see.

Dinner was boiled mutton, boiled sprouts and mashed pumpkin, followed by suet pudding with a couple of stray raisins and a thin trickle of cocky's joy. Tom picked at his food and stared into the middle distance much of the time. He wasn't who he used to be, and never would be again. His massive shoulders were shrinking, all of him was. It might have been the guilt eating him. Will cast worried glances at him now and then. Once Miss Fletcher withdrew and the port and cigars came out, he encouraged me to tell old war stories, probably in the hope Tom would show some interest.

'Tell us again about Elands River, Gus. Three thousand Boer and only a handful of colonials – what a fight it must have been.'

'It was a battle and a siege, and there were five hundred of us, not a handful.'

'What did that British Colonel Hore say? "I cannot surrender. I am in charge of Australians who would cut my throat if I did." And you would have too, eh?'

Hore did say that, and Will loved this story, chuckled into his whisky each time he heard it. I was just a lad of twenty at the time of the siege, a spotty subaltern busy shitting myself and pretty keen on the idea of surrender. It was the older, tougher enlisted men who knew what they were doing, who would not consider bowing to the Boer – or anyone else, for that matter. They were men like Beavins, Pearson and the rest, men who could turn their hand to anything, drove ten thousand sheep, knock up a couple of miles of fencing, skin a kangaroo, win at two-up, hold their own in a brawl, bed the barmaid and be home in time for tea.

I excused myself and went down the hall to the indoors lavatory, and passed Sally Gilmour on the way in the dim light of the hallway. Her eyes were lowered, but just as she passed, she flicked me a glance and kept walking, leaving an indefinable female scent in the air. She let me know that she knew I was aware of her. I was more than aware of her, and for an overheated moment that drooling incubus on my left shoulder whispered, *Go on, mate, she's ripe for the plucking, and you know how you love a good pluck …*

It was quite a job gathering my wits once she'd passed. I found Tom drinking port by the fire alone. Will had gone to bed.

'How long has Miss Gilmour been with you?' I asked, settling back into my armchair.

'Couple of years, I reckon,' Tom said. 'The first nurse Mother had left as she couldn't tolerate the climate. Mother is very attached to Miss

Gilmour. She's very good at the practical side of things and she is devoted to Mother. Had a hard life before she came here, apparently.'

'Jimmy Kirkbride was keen on her.'

'Jimmy was keen on all the girls,' he said, and drained his glass of port. 'Like his father.'

That comment hung in the air. The fire roared like a small, caged beast. Tom threw another log on it, feeding its fury.

'Your mother and ...' I said, treading carefully. Bringing up a man's mother's adultery was asking for trouble.

'Kirkbride?' Tom said, looking daggers at me.

'He's going to find it hard to manage without Jimmy,' I replied, remembering the force of Tom's fist in my face and changing tack.

'I reckon Kirkbride finds that hardest of all, harder than losing Nessie and Grace. No legacy, family farm passing into a stranger's hands.'

'It'll be Flora's, surely?'

Tom gave me a sharp look. 'Flora has to marry a wool man, someone who can take over Inveraray, so at least there'll be grandsons to inherit.'

'Who told you that?'

'Kirkbride. Father and I went to pay our respects. Despite everything that bastard has done to our family, Father said we had to be Christian. After all, he was – is – Nessie's father. And that's what Kirkbride talked about. His legacy.'

'And Janet Kirkbride? How's she holding up?'

He shook his head, slowly. 'Stays in her room.'

I remembered her keening, the unearthly despair.

'I blame Jimmy for Nessie's death. I told you that, didn't I?' Tom went on. 'He had some bit of jam he wanted at the dance and dragged his sisters along with him. He was shameless, thought he could get away with it, and he did, what's more. And now Kirkbride has given up we'll never know.'

Tom tossed his port down and refilled his glass and mine.

'What father in their right mind gives up on finding the killers of his children? What sort of man is Kirkbride? Talking about Flora's marriage while Nessie is barely in her grave. He had a lot of sympathy at first, but now?' He shook his head. 'He's weak, he's pathetic, a man without honour.'

We both gazed at the fire, the flames consuming the log with glee. Tom had always expected that one day it would be Nessie sitting across from him, and they'd talk about something funny one of their children had said or done, or when the rains would come. The world he thought was coming vanished on that winter road.

'Did Nessie mention anything to you about the governess leaving to get married?' I asked.

Tom's head jerked up, surprised by my voice, or perhaps by the question.

'No, she was dismissed. It upset Nessie and Flora too.'

'Why was she dismissed?'

'Because of all those rich young men Kirkbride was always having to stay, dangling Nessie and Flora like bloody breeding stock. Trying to arrange their marriages to suit his bloody purposes.'

'What's a governess got to do with that?'

'Kirkbride overheard her sympathising with the girls. Wouldn't tolerate being undermined in his own home, so out she went.'

We continued to drink in silence and I considered what he'd told me. Either I was an extremely poor judge of character or Tom had a particularly cold-blooded form of moral insanity. Or Baines was just wrong. But then Tom brought up another possibility.

'Remember that rich meathead from up north came visiting at Inveraray? Or maybe you were on the nose then. He couldn't stop the drool running down his chin when he looked at my Nessie, and she served him tea and smiled while her father ...' He stopped and shook his head, buried his face in his hands.

'In cattle, was he?'

'Bindagabba Downs, big holdings. Right on the border with Queensland and beyond. Kirkbride would have sold my girl for that land.'

'Is that near the Yantabulla stock route?'

He nodded, eyes closed, a tear swiped away.

The Yantabulla stock route was where the alleged Kirkbride bag was found. None of this was making sense, except that I did know of all those wretched suitors who trailed through Inveraray hated it, as did Tom. But marriage to a Kirkbride girl was a ticket to wealth and influence, so there was no shortage of these flabby fops, laughing loudly at Mr Kirkbride's jokes and leering at the girls.

I couldn't be sure but I'd always felt Kirkbride wanted me and Tom to know when these creatures were around, riding out with them or just letting the gossip run. It was a surprise Tom hadn't thrashed one of them.

19

I slept at the Royal again that night, a bad night. A wall of flame, a roaring, angry beast, rose before me, towering into the darkness, and then the scream, high-pitched, cut short. Nessie's shattered face and a bayonet cutting my chest to ribbons, and I jolted awake, confused as to where I was and if I'd actually screamed or just dreamed it. But the dream that came at me again and again, charred wings beating my face, was when I tried to scream but struggled to part my lips, and would wake sweating as if I'd been in front of that wall of flame.

I couldn't stay at the Royal another night. No matter what anyone said, I knew waking to the sound of a screaming man was not pleasant, so early next morning I rummaged about in the stable loft and found the station tent. I wandered along the riverbank north of the station until I found a reasonably secluded space where I could sling a rope between two trees and drape the canvas over and peg it to the ground. I laid another roll of canvas out inside the shelter and placed a bedroll in the middle, then added matches, a lantern and a waterbag and I was set. The end of July and another month of winter to go, but I'd be warm enough.

~

After breakfast, Lonergan and I met up with Frosty and continued our search for Beavins. With no tracks and no idea where he was likely to go, all we could do was circle Gowrie, making the search area wider and wider until we found something. It was the way we usually searched for lost people. Most we found, some we didn't.

Flies were up and about, crawling all over our faces, infuriating the horses. The sky had a brassy look to it, which often heralded a dust storm on the way, and with a westerly I reckoned we were for it. Not good during lambing.

On we plodded through the decimated scrub. Rabbits were bad out this way, and instead of looking for a man Lonergan and I were both watching the ground ahead for rabbit holes which our horses could step in and damage themselves.

'Smell that,' Frosty said, turning to the south-west.

'Death.'

'Too much for rabbit.'

We dismounted and secured our horses, then I smelled it too. It was bad, retching bad.

'Lonergan?'

'Sir?'

'Don't just stand there spewing your guts up, walk towards the direction of the smell. Dead man's not going to hold up a sign for you.'

'Sir.'

He took a handkerchief out of his pocket, clamped it over his face and marched towards the source of the smell as if he were facing the Russians in the Valley of Death. Frosty and I followed at a distance.

We saw a man lying facedown on the ground, dressed in a filthy stockman's shirt. His hands had clawed the ground and it looked like he'd pulled himself out of a shallow grave, as his legs were still covered in soil. He'd been beaten, as his head was bloody, flies all over the wounds.

Lonergan stood looking down at him.

'Feel for a pulse, for fuck's sake,' I yelled at him.

He crouched down and lifted the man's wrists. 'Still alive, sir.'

I rushed over and we pulled at him gently, freeing him from what looked like a shallow grave.

'Lonergan, go to Gowrie and get help. Frosty, get me some water, quick, then go with Lonergan, make sure he doesn't get lost.'

I managed to turn Beavins onto his back. His face was a mess of clotted blood, pus and black rotting flesh. I dribbled the water over his bloodied, split lips while helping him sit, then tried to get some down his throat. His eyes fluttered so I kept pouring, not too much, but enough to wet his mouth and cool him a little. That Beavins was still alive said a lot for his toughness.

To stop him drifting off I kept talking. Every time I felt him slacken in my arms, I'd shake him and raise my voice, dribble some water on his face.

'Who did this to you, mate? Who was it? You owe them some money? Touch their girl?'

The stench of him was sticking in my throat, the blood and pus. By the looks of it, from what I'd seen in South Africa, he had blood poisoning. A raven watched from a nearby mulga tree, waiting for its chance. If Beavins had lain on his back, they would have taken his eyes by now, as they did with injured sheep.

'Come on, Archie, stay with me. Tell me who bashed you.'

His lips moved, but no sound. I told him a few stories of Africa in an effort to keep him tethered to my voice, shaking him every so often and rambling on, getting the odd curl of his lip, blink of his eye. He was holding on, tough as nails, so I kept it coming: racing our horses along the beaches near Cape Town and taking them in the surf afterwards, the Zulu warriors dancing in leopard skin and drinking blood, the whorehouses of Port Elizabeth with women of every colour and shape to be bought for a pittance.

The sun bore down and the raven watched. When I stopped talking, a great silence surrounded us.

I began to think Lonergan and Frosty had met with an accident, but I kept dredging up the stories I'd told in pubs for years on my return. Soon the wind picked up. If I was right, we were in for a dust storm too. That'd be nice, holding a dying man while choking on bulldust.

After an eternity, I heard horses coming towards us. The raven gave up and took off.

'Hear that, Archie? Help is on its way, mate, just hang on.'

I laid him down in the dirt, got to my feet and saw riders coming through the scrub, a stretcher strapped to a horse.

When we got him back to Gowrie several hours later, I was in need of a stiff drink. I think everyone was. The station was unnaturally quiet as the dust hung on the horizon, a looming wave of towering red dust. Sally Gilmour was on the verandah with, I assume, Mrs Fletcher, who was in a bath chair, covered up in a bright crocheted rug and watching the activity.

I'd never seen Mrs Fletcher before and couldn't help but stare, curious to see the woman who'd had a long and scandalous affair with Bob Kirkbride. She was thin-faced with thick grey hair brushed and tied to the side in a pale-pink bow, her black eyes sharp beneath a furrowed forehead, watching everything.

I went up to pay my respects. 'Good afternoon, Mrs Fletcher, I am—'

'I know who you are.'

Sally Gilmour stood behind her, expressionless.

Tom Fletcher came out and joined us. 'Found Beavins?'

'Yes, he was beaten and managed to survive for days out there until we found him. Tough man.'

'He got what was coming to him,' Tom said.

Dark tendrils of hair framed Sally Gilmour's face and blew in the breeze, but she stood as still as a pillar of salt.

'What for?'

'For repeating what Pearson said about Nessie to me.'

I nodded to the end of the verandah and Tom came with me, away from the women. 'He's been savagely beaten. Did you—'

216

'I'm on bail, remember? As much as I'd have enjoyed beating him, no, I didn't.'

Henry Peyton approached us. 'Beavins has just passed away.'

'Damn it – he survives until we get there and then carks it?' I said, wildly annoyed by his poor timing.

'Often the way,' Peyton said, hands on hips.

'May he rot in hell,' Tom said, with unnerving vigour.

Beavins could well belong in hell, but I'd wanted to know why he'd come to speak to me. And if Tom had beaten him to death, only Beavins would have known.

~

Henry Peyton told me Archie Beavins was paid the same as all the others, and in cash. What he did with it was his business, but most of the men banked what they didn't drink or send home at the post office in town.

'I can't explain why he had a hundred pounds in his trunk. Two-up games, cards? They gamble heavily in quiet times, but Beavins wasn't known for being any more stupid than the others. Now, Tindaree, they have a problem with men gambling all their wages in one night.'

'He had the money wrapped in brown paper.'

Peyton shook his head. 'Can't help you, Gus. I'll send it on to his mother. I think she's in Nyngan.'

I was going around in circles. If Tindaree Station had a gambling problem, then gamblers had to get the money from someone. If Beavins was running a book, we hadn't found it in his possessions. If he was cheating men out of their winnings it might have earned him a bashing. Questioning these blokes again wasn't going to lead anywhere, but it had to be done.

I knew Beavins had a liking for Sally Gilmour and a hundred quid stuffed under his bed. I reckoned he was bashed for one of those two things, and it was my dreary duty to help Lonergan find out why, because no Sydney detective would come out here for the likes of Archibald Beavins.

~

Lonergan and I lined up the Gowrie Station men and questioned them together, but I made him ask the questions as it was good practice for him. But the men weren't talking. They told us when they last saw Beavins and that was it. If he was in trouble with a gambling ring, they didn't know about it.

'Tits on a bull,' Lonergan muttered when we were done.

Joe rode in and made a cursory examination of the body, then staggered away and retched.

'Officially dead,' he gasped. 'Blood poisoning and blows to the head. Box him up and send him to Bourke. I'll sign the paperwork when you're ready, Mr Peyton.'

Peyton nodded, and as he walked off I pulled him aside. 'Can you check your books and see when Beavins reported for work on the Sunday after the dance in Larne?'

'He gave a statement.'

'I know, I'm just cross-checking. The troopers who took the statements were inexperienced.'

'He weren't a pleasant fellow, but he weren't a killer.'

'Just have a look for me as soon as you can.'

He nodded and went off to get men to bang up a coffin as the first gusts of dust came through. Joe was in the shade of the peppercorn tree having a puke. I took my waterbag from my horse and walked over to give it to him.

'I reckon Beavins' wounds look mighty similar to the Kirkbrides', I said.

He swallowed, wiped his face and nodded. 'They do, insofar as it's blunt force trauma. But I reckon he's been punched, not bashed with a stick or a rifle butt. I mean, the skull hasn't been breached, unlike ...'

'Three people in the district dead of head wounds within weeks of each other?'

'Classic brawl injuries. Left eye is a mess, contusions and lacerations, cheek, mouth, all delivered with a right-handed fist. Leave it to the coroner, mate.'

And Corcoran reckoned I was a know-it-all.

'About the other day, Gus – I'm sorry.'

'No worries. It was wrong of me.'

'Bad times bring out the worst in us,' Joe said. 'Nothing to do but sit around and brood or drink and then here we are, another tragedy. Seems we're lurching from one to another.'

'Yeah, but it's going to be a bumper clip this year. Cheery news, eh?'

He managed a weak smile. 'It's an ill wind. Speaking of which, I want to get back before the dust hits. You finished here?'

'Can you just wait a moment?' I said, looking down the road to the Gowrie laundries. 'I need a quick word with someone.'

I hurried down and found the maids bringing in the wash before the dust storm. I saw a girl I knew battling a billowing sheet, Sheila Stewart, daughter of Hector Stewart, the station blacksmith. She had mousy hair and a stocky figure, wore steel-rimmed glasses and a stained apron over a grey skirt.

'Sorry to bother you, Miss Stewart – a quick word?'

'What about?' she said, glancing at me as she wrestled the sheet.

'Were you working the day after the dance?'

'I was on in the afternoon, but I can tell you now, we was all too stunned to get much done.'

'Do you wash young Mr Fletcher's shirts and trousers regularly?'

A fat old wash drab like a walking barrel came to the door of the laundry. 'Get a move on, Miss Stewart,' she screeched. 'Dust won't wait for you to be done gossiping.'

'Yes, I do, and no, there wasn't,' Sheila muttered to me.

I wasn't on official police business, so I walked away before I got her in trouble.

~

Joe and I rode back along the river under the only tree canopy in the area, the redgums and coolabahs.

'Where did you find Beavins?' Joe asked.

'Crawling out of a shallow grave over by Peery Bore.'

'Nasty. Why would they bash him?'

'Joe, have you ever had a good gander at this district? A bunch of exhausted men working six days a week on isolated properties on the edge of the godforsaken. They've got nothing to do but drink, gamble and lust after the few women who work out here, and they settle their differences with their fists. That's why it happened.'

The wind picked up, the treetops thrashed about and visibility dropped as red dust swirled. I pulled my bandana over my nose, tugged my hat down and squinted. Felix was shaking his head, uncomfortable in the gritty wind. I stopped and dismounted, shouting at Joe to keep going. I took my bandana off and tied it around Felix's head to protect his eyes. Then we kept moving, head down against the wind, filthy and coughing. I took Felix to the station stables to brush him down and wipe out his ears and nose, all the while cursing Beavins for giving up.

People were stabling horses, stuffing cloth in gaps, shutting windows. It was going to be suffocating. Birds flitted about, frantically looking for shelter. Soon visibility would be zero. We were stuck inside, and after we'd completed the paperwork for Beavins, I spent the time stripping and reassembling all the guns in the armoury, cleaning and polishing belt buckles, boots, buttons, brass lamp bases and candlesticks. I was suspended but it was still my station.

Lonergan patched a tear in his shirt, gazed out the window, sighed, sewed on buttons, gazed out the window, sighed, polished his boots, gazed out the window at the red swirling dust. Lunch was followed by a nap and then, desperate to get out, I held a neckerchief to my mouth and nose, grabbed some whisky and went over to Joe's, leaning into the wind, fine grit hitting me like buckshot.

I found Joe in his surgery with his own bottle of whisky already on the way down.

'Nothing else to do,' he slurred.

He looked the worse for wear, bloodshot eyes, puffy face. I didn't know why Mrs Schreiber put up with us. But I supposed she'd seen a few things in her time.

Joe and I were old hands at oblivion, passing the bottle back and forth. The lower the level in the bottle, the looser the tongue. The past revealed itself in dribs and drabs, but was never spoken of in the sober light of the next day. Sometimes one or both of us passed out. We acted like it had never happened. Men didn't talk about such incidents. We accepted it as our right, because being a man was unendurable sometimes.

Joe slumped across his desk as he handed me a tumbler, then with a trembling hand splashed some whisky into it. Outside, the wind howled, roofs rattled, the ochre-red air, thick as fog, raged about in a fury.

'There's your precious empire at work,' I said, nodding at the window. 'Every drop of sweat is blown away or shipped to England for their mills. What are we left with?'

'There are some very rich men out here.'

'Some very poor ones too.'

'Who get paid because there is an empire. Without those woollen mills in Yorkshire, we'd still be in huts at Botany Bay.'

I followed the Wallabies. Joe was a British Isles man. That was just how we were.

'Feels like I'm always down at Gowrie inspecting the dead or dying,' he sighed.

'You mean Beavins this morning?'

'The overseer before Peyton took a marking knife to his throat, then Mrs Fletcher had her accident, then Pearson, now Beavins.'

'You were here when Mrs Fletcher broke her back?' I said, lighting up a fag. 'How did it happen?'

'Yes, it happened only days after I arrived from Echuca and I was still in shock from the look of this place. I didn't know anyone, but I was put to good use. She just said she fell against a tree stump, had sharp pain and then numb. I knew when I got there she'd never walk again,' he said, and downed a good inch of whisky at a quick gulp. 'Getting her onto the stretcher and getting her back to town was a ... job. Thing is, she was as naked as the day she was born.'

'Naked? Out here?'

'As the day she was born,' he hiccupped.

'She was with Kirkbride, though. Why didn't he cover her before he went for help?'

'He reckoned he panicked and shot off to get help. When we got her back to town, we brought her into my surgery and wired for an ambulance. She never cried, never complained. Well, she couldn't really, given what she was up to.'

'You reckon God smote her down in disgust?'

'A grown woman her age carrying on with a man like that? God smote her down all right,' he said, and refilled his glass. 'Ended up in a private hospital in Sydney near her daughters.'

'Mrs Fletcher?'

'No, God,' he said, and laughed so hard I thought he'd be sick. I wasn't a pretty drunk, morose then asleep, but Joe was often a complete mess.

'Nice girls, Maude and Anne. Statuesque, I'd call 'em. Married wool brokers.'

'You met them?'

'Mmm, they came for a visit once, arrived when I was busy doctoring away at their mother.'

I glanced out the window at the red haze hanging in the air.

'Hester Fletcher didn't want to live with her daughters, did you know?' He lit a cigarette and shook the flame from the match. 'Nope, she wanted to be back out here, to torment her husband, probably. He fixed up part of the homestead so she could come back. Has nothing to do with her, but he looks after her, doing his duty.'

'Hell of a story.'

'Will's a good man, a good man. I know many people who say it's more than she deserves for what she did.'

'And Kirkbride?'

'Pinched another man's wife,' he said, squinting at me and shaking his head at the enormity of the sin. 'S'like stealing his sheep or his home. Just not done.'

I refreshed our glasses and we sat in silence for a bit, watching the sky and the closed doors of the store across the road.

'You'd know about that,' he said eventually.

'I've never been with a married woman, or not knowingly.'

'And Flora?'

I stared at him for a long moment. 'Flora is not married, and nor have I had connections with her.'

He shrugged, swaying, eyes shut.

'And you? You could have seven dead wives hanging on meat hooks somewhere.'

'A bluebeard, eh?' That set him off, laughing and rocking back and forth, then slowly he calmed down, wiped his eyes. 'I am a bachelor, old man, and I don't mean I bat for the other side.'

'Perhaps you prefer sheep.'

And the conversation descended into filth, a particular brand of it often found in wool-growing districts. Sheep were basically unlovable beasts. Not like horses, dogs or even cows, so it was the sheep that carried our sins for us, all of our sins, while we rode on their back to a prosperous future.

The wind dropped. We peered out the window at a different world, a silent, eerie ochre-coated one. Without a word, we got up and went to the front door, opened it and went outside. Everything, Kev's geraniums, the windows of the store, the walls of the houses, the cluster of mulga at the edge of town, all of it was caked in sticky dust.

I left Joe and walked over the powdery deposits to the police station. Even the river was a dirty orange. No sound – the birds' throats were probably clogged with dust. I went straight to the stables and found the horses in reasonable shape, bit of a wash and an eye and ear clean and they'd be all right.

Kev brought the mail over while I was with the horses. A letter from my father, which was quickly despatched unread. A letter I'd written to Flora, unopened and returned, and a letter from Robert Kirkbride. He wanted to inform me that his daughter, Miss Flora Kirkbride, no longer resided at Katoomba. I would never see her nor hear from her again. And as I was a bounder of the worst order, I should simply shoot myself and be done with it.

20

I slept in the station that night. The riverbank, the entire town, was a mess of dirt and dust. Next morning, I retrieved my camping kit from the riverbank and spent the day cleaning it while Lonergan went off to do the rounds. I checked my eye twitch several times and rubbed the Chinese ointment over my scar, noting the date and time I applied it.

I couldn't get Beavins out of my mind. He was murdered, plain and simple. Not manslaughter but murder, despite what Joe said about punch-up wounds. Beavins had come to the station looking for me. Not any old trooper, but me. I barely knew him, apart from the interview after Pearson's death, and there was nothing more to be said about that. Except he was angry about Sally Gilmour and Jimmy. Now he was dead. Maybe Miss Gilmour knew more than she was saying.

I wasn't sure if there'd be an inquest into Beavins' death, but if there was it'd be Lonergan who'd have to front up at court, because I wasn't supposed to be doing anything beyond reflecting on my character flaws. Lonergan came back in the late afternoon and saw me scrabbling through the files, but said nothing. I knew I was never going to be reinstated and had no right to be here, and certainly no right to be nosing through old files. They'd kick me out once the dust had settled, so I had to complete my mission before that day arrived.

Mrs Schreiber had brought some Lancashire hotpot over, which took our minds off files and futures. We made short work of it, then moved on to the evening lesson in navigation.

Lonergan had taken to maps and navigation like he was born to it. Mounted trooper training wasn't terribly rigorous, and as men were more likely to find good work in a factory, anyone who could spell their own name was quickly snapped up, shoved into a uniform and deployed on the fringes of settlement.

We were now up to celestial navigation with a sextant, standing outside the station in our thick coats and scarves, gazing at the stars, charts and notebooks resting on an old kerosene tin, beside an almanac and my precious marine chronometer. The odd passer-by on the way to the pub gave us a wide berth. If I did anything of use out here, it was teaching Lonergan to navigate.

As we scribbled and squinted, the passers-by multiplied and soon the roar of a pub in full swing filled the silent night. Shouts of laughter, shrill mockery, more laughter, getting louder the more they drank, and more reckless.

'There'll be tears before bedtime,' Lonergan said, shaking his head like an old hand.

The ruckus did have an end-of-days edge to it. Steam escaping a valve at a high velocity. Exhausted men drinking off the muscle ache and resentment.

'Hear that?' Lonergan said, glancing nervously down the street as something was hurled outside amid gusts of laughter. It could turn at any moment. We packed up and went inside the station to wait.

'I won't be able to stop 'em.'

'Course you can.'

'Oh yeah, right, like I'll put the fear of God into them. I'm a wheat farmer and they know it – the bastards know it as soon as they look at me.'

'It's the uniform that does the work for you. You're not Micky Lonergan from Pakapoo Creek.'

'Balranald.'

'Whatever. You're Johnny Law, the coercive arm of the mighty state of New South Wales, reaching into their stinking daks and twisting their balls until they see the error of their ways.'

But it was a full moon, and any copper would tell you that the full moon brought trouble.

~

There was a lot of lightning on the horizon earlier on, and only now did the thunder come rolling in with great crashes and booms above us. In between the thunder, the sound from the pub seemed to swell. We put the kettle on and by the time it had boiled there was a knock at the back door – Wally was sending for some reinforcement.

'You coming?' Lonergan said to me as he went to the armoury.

'I'm suspended, remember.'

'Yeah but ...'

'Don't go there armed, that'll just wind them up.'

'What if they go for me?'

'At least one of them will still be thinking straight and will stop their mate from taking a swing. And if they do, Wally has a rifle behind the counter.'

He took a deep breath, put the rifle away. 'You coming?'

Walking into a bush pub when every bastard in it was shitfaced and kicking up was the job, and a big part of the job. I had made it clear from my first days in the post that I would administer some corrective violence should I meet with unreasonable resistance, and out here that sort of policing works. Never had any more problems, but Lonergan mustered about as much menace as a tea cosy.

'I'll wait outside. If they get stupid, I'll lend a hand.'

We marched down the road, thunder rolling above in the bleak skies, and arrived at the pub. We peeked through the window at the rabble surging around the bar, the thick fug of fag smoke, the upturned tables and spilled beer, men staggering and shoving.

'Cometh the man, Micky, lad,' I murmured, slapping him on his shoulder.

He straightened himself up and marched in. 'Closing time, gentlemen.'

I peered through the window. Nobody heard him at first and he shouted it again. All heads turned towards him, incredulous laughter and jeers, insults and shoving. It was on the turn – any second now. Time to tighten the screw.

'Closing time,' Lonergan repeated, standing still as a rock and giving every man who glanced at him a stony glare. Wally quietly placed his rifle on the bar, his oily white hair glowing in the lamplight.

There were a few refractory ones, making threats and squaring up. Lonergan shifted his weight, shoulders back, arms held apart from his body, and gave them all a look that said, *don't give me any grief*. The troublemakers straggled out, laughing and jeering, but they went. I walked inside, nodded at Lonergan. He'd done well.

'What's up with them tonight?' Wally said, stowing his rifle under the bar.

'Full moon,' I said. 'Lightning. Moon in Scorpio. All of the above, plus we had to ask questions at Gowrie yesterday. Archie Beavins found dead in a shallow grave.'

Wally sighed, shook his head. 'Always Gowrie.'

'I reckon Inveraray is coming up on the outside in the trouble stakes.'

'Yeah, but Gowrie does something to a bloke. Dunno what's in their water.'

As we walked out, Wally said, 'Better check your horses, Gus.'

Out in the dark street, men milled about, laughing or falling over. There were whoops and a bit of carry-on from down by the police station, and the sound of a horse kicking up. We hurried down there to see a horse galloping away and a gang of men laughing fit to burst. They saw us and disappeared. The stable door was wide open.

'Those bloody shitheads,' Lonergan cried. 'They've stampeded Dancer.'

We saddled up and galloped up the road. Dancer would be mad with fear, and I had a deep urge to kill the bastards who'd done this. We followed his tracks down the road, and then he seemed to have careened off the road and into the scrub. I'd hoped to find him standing on the dusty road, flanks heaving and wondering what to do next.

I hopped off Felix and was able to see where Dancer had crashed through the scrub, breaking twigs along the way, his hoofprints clear in the moonlight.

Then I saw him. He was down in a gully, reins tangled in a bit of mulga, struggling to get up, panting, frothing at the mouth. Felix went to him, nosing his face, blowing through his nostrils, whickering as if to soothe his friend.

'Oh, mate,' I murmured as I approached him slowly.

He'd come down hard when the bridle snagged and his front leg was bent and broken. I took my pistol out, walked away, then clicked the safety off. Lonergan took his horse and Felix several yards away. I went back and sat in the dust, resting Dancer's head on my knees. His eyes were rolling from the terrible pain and fear. I stroked his nose and his neck, smooth, soothing strokes.

'That's it, lad, you did well. Served with honour, dear friend. A police horse without peer.'

He stopped struggling at the sound of my voice. His breath was coming fast, but he trusted me – after three years he trusted me.

I put a bullet in his head and he was free.

I sat there with Dancer's great head on my lap and wept. The wind whistled through the mulga. My tears fell onto his soft, gleaming coat and I wanted to stretch out beside him, bury my face in his mane and shoot myself too.

'Gus,' Lonergan said eventually. 'We gotta leave him, mate.'

He was right – we had to keep going. I laid Dancer's head down gently in the dirt and took the bridle off. Then I undid the girth and pulled at the saddle. Getting a saddle off a dead horse is not an easy task. But with a bit of heaving, pulling and grunting, we got there. I took the saddle blanket, with its New South Wales Mounted Police badge, and covered his head. Mick and I saluted him, then left him to the darkness.

Dancer had been with me since day one out here, and for him to die at the hands of these drunken fools filled me with rage. If they'd taken Felix, he would have galloped off, had a bit of a snack, then come back. But not Dancer. The devil was after him, and this time it was real.

He had a bloody great government brand on his arse, so he could never be stolen. That was the theory, anyway. And he wasn't stolen, as he'd been saddled with his police kit first. This wasn't about nicking a good horse, it was about us asking questions at Gowrie Station.

~

I slept over in the police station. More accurately, I lay in my old bed overnight. I couldn't sleep. My dancing partner was dead and I could hardly stand it. If Corcoran came around sniffing sheets, he could go to hell. I was leaving as soon as I'd punished the men who killed my horse.

Next morning, I went to the Royal and found Wally in his cellar, shifting barrels.

'Gus, what can I do you for?'

'Last night you told me to check the horses. Why was that?'

He wiped his face with a grimy handkerchief, put his fleshy hands on his hips. 'Don't remember.'

'Yes, you do.'

He pressed his lips into a grim line, shook his head. 'Nup.'

'Then I'll get Lonergan to question you and you can repeat that, and then I'll get him to charge you with obstructing a police officer in the course of his duty.'

His jaw dropped. 'You wouldn't do that.'

'I will do it if you don't tell me what happened.'

'Just those bastards from Gowrie. Most of them were from Gowrie last night. They were drinking and shouting, calling Tom Fletcher this and that, calling you this and that, and then some bright spark decided it would be a good idea to teach you to mind your own business, that Pearson was dead and Beavins was dead because of you.'

'How'd they figure that?'

He threw up his hands. 'Fucked if I know. And I don't want to know.'

'Maroney? Kelly?'

'Coulda been them, and some others.'

'Thank you. Now, that wasn't so hard, was it?'

He snorted and turned back to his barrels. 'You didn't hear it from me.'

I worked my way down the street, knocking on the few doors that constituted Calpa's main street and asking if anybody had seen men in the street that night, close to the police station stables. As I thought, nobody had seen a thing, even if they had. But then the maid from the Royal, the very sweet Maryanne, popped into the station when I was gazing at the calendar with my mind at a standstill.

'Hello, Miss Lea,' I said.

'Wally told me you were looking for witnesses to your horse theft. I saw them and I don't mind telling you who they were. I heard you had to put the horse down, and I can't abide cruelty to animals.'

'Prepared to go to court and stand as a witness?'

'I am, and then I'll hand in my notice.'

'Brave of you,' I said.

'Not really. I've had enough of this place. Women aren't safe. The men who killed the Kirkbrides is still out there, and nobody seems bothered about it anymore. I know Polly from the Larne Royal is terrified, but the men tell us girls we're hysterical and to be quiet. All very well for them.'

'So who do you reckon you saw?'

'Liam Maroney and Patrick Kelly. Plain as day. I was watching from my room over in Kev's place. I look out onto your stables. I see you and the other fella come and go all the time. I watched these blokes, and they couldn't see me 'cause I blew my candle out.'

'So they won't know you're a witness – not until they come to trial.'

'Not unless you tell them,' she said.

'I'm not going to do that. Thanks for telling me,' I said.

Maryanne gathered herself and left. I walked outside and looked at Kev's house. There was a small window in the whitewashed wall facing onto the dirt road and opposite the police station stables. She would have had a clear view.

With Wally and Maryanne as witnesses, I had enough to make arrests. I got Lonergan to telegram Bourke asking for a police wagon to take the offenders back once the arrests were made. Lonergan was to make the arrests first thing the next day, as we didn't have a lock-up big enough to keep two men overnight. Nothing happened quickly out here.

~

Lonergan and I rode over to Gowrie Station at dawn and rehearsed exactly what he was to say and do. As we rode up the drive I could hear him muttering to himself, going over it, as if it were some complicated mathematical formula.

'Just think of your badge, that's who's talking,' I said.

'Yeah, but—'

'No. No buts. You take that crown and you smash these bastards over the head with it. The King's behind you.'

'Mad,' he murmured.

The galahs and corellas greeted the new day with their usual screeches of pleasure. Dogs barked, and men were up and about at Gowrie, watching us with interest. I went up to the house and knocked. Will Fletcher came to the door and I told him what we were here for.

'We've had enough disruption around here lately what with Pearson and Beavins.'

'Two of your men were seen stealing a police horse.'

'Oh, for god's sake, two of them? We're already two down, and the rest won't work if Tom's around. Now you want to take another two?'

'Yes, Maroney and Kelly.'

His mouth tightened and he shut the door. I rejoined Lonergan as Henry Peyton came over.

'Mr Peyton, good morning,' Lonergan said, while I stood beside him. 'I'm here to arrest Mr Maroney and Mr Kelly. Can you please fetch them?'

'What? What in the hell for?' he said, looking at me.

'Horse theft,' Lonergan said.

'Wait right here, I'm going to speak to Mr Fletcher – this is ridiculous.'

'He knows,' I said.

'Theft of government property is a serious matter,' Lonergan said, squaring his shoulders.

Peyton looked to the house, expecting reinforcement from his boss, but got nothing.

'Mr Peyton,' I said, sensing Lonergan's resolve sag. 'If you kill a mounted trooper's horse and get away with it, next thing you'll be killing a mounted trooper, and that cannot stand.'

He fumed, hands on hips. There was nothing he could say to that. The two men cursed and carried on, as was to be expected.

'It was just a joke,' Maroney said as his arms were yanked back by Lonergan. 'We was just fooling around.'

All the remaining staff watched from the verandah of their mess quarters. Lonergan cuffed the two men and then linked them to a long chain. Then looked at me. I mounted up and rode with him but the two prisoners had to walk back to town like convicts as we didn't have the wagon yet. We rode slowly, with them dragging their feet until Lonergan gave them a tug. The sun had a bite to it and it would be a good hour until we reached Calpa.

'What are we charged with?' Maroney said. 'Making arses of ourselves?'

'You will be formally charged with theft of government property and animal cruelty.'

'Oh, fair go, animal cruelty? We wasn't cruel, that the horse fell wasn't our fault.'

'He wouldn't have been out there if you hadn't stampeded him, an act of cruelty in itself.'

Maroney and Kelly exchanged sullen, disbelieving looks. I knew we did worse things to animals every day out here. But I wanted to make that charge stick. They chose the wrong horse that night.

'Just a fucken horse,' Kelly muttered.

I stopped and glared at him. 'Just a fucken police horse, Mr Kelly. That one word is a distinction you'll have plenty of time to think on while in gaol.'

21

The wagon hadn't arrived so we tossed them into the lock-up, gave them a waterbag and some pannikins and shut the door. Mrs Schreiber was in the kitchen frying up bacon and kidneys. She put the kettle on as we clattered into the kitchen. I was amused when Lonergan went out the back and washed his face and hands. She wouldn't feed dirty men. We sat quietly like two kids in the nursery waiting for Nanny to bring us milky pudding.

'I cannot abide cruelty to horses,' I said, cutting myself some bread and buttering it. 'The British treated their horses badly during the Boer War. Most of them died six weeks after they arrived – they overloaded them, didn't give them time to acclimatise. Their cavalry troopers were stupid and their officers even more so. I've seen too many horses killed for no good reason.'

Lonergan stared at me, as if I'd blurted out some secret. I suppose I had.

Mrs Schreiber dished up the bacon and kidneys, added some eggs and left us to it.

'My horse was called ... he was eighteen hands, big bastard, bravest warhorse you could imagine. We worked together for three years. After this,' I said, pointing to my face, 'I never saw him again.'

Shouts emanated from the lock-up. I put down my knife and fork, went and opened the door. 'What?'

'Bit of bacon wouldn't go astray.'

I shut the door. They wouldn't be eating my bacon, horse killers that they were. We made another pot of coffee and Lonergan did the dishes.

'Mrs Schreiber will do that.'

'Nah, me mum always made me do the dishes, now I can't help myself.'

My horse was called Gordon of Khartoum. Known in the horse lines as Gordy. Sold to the British, who sold him off to an abattoir after three years of brave and loyal service. Calling us savages and pointing their finger, yet the British finger somehow always dripped blood.

~

After taking my time with the coffee, I opened the door to the station, went to the lock-up and leant against the wall. I lit a cigarette and offered them a smoke, which they took gladly.

'You two were rostered off the Sunday after the coronation dance, right?'

They both nodded. 'But you ain't no trooper now so we don't have to tell you anything.'

'That's right, you don't. But it's in your interests to tell me what you know, because if you don't I'll just assume you have something to hide, and Trooper Lonergan, he won't like that. You'll be sorrier than a steer in a stockyard if you lie to him.'

They exchanged glances. Micky wouldn't have known a lie if it ran up his arse and rang a bell. But they didn't know that.

'So you came home to your quarters on Gowrie as soon as the hall was locked up?'

'Yeah. Already told another trooper this.'

'Did you come down the Larne to Calpa road?'

'Yeah.'

'Who do you reckon bashed Beavins?'

They fell silent, shadows on their faces.

'Dunno,' Kelly said.

'Did he ride home with you the night of the coronation dance?'

'He went with Jack Hirst and Toby Shawcross from Tindaree Station. They left early, real early. Jack had a bottle of whisky. He said they were going to drink it down by the river and that the dance was a waste of time as all the girls were dogs.'

'Except Sally Gilmour.'

'Yeah, and she had Beavins by the short and curlies, but she wouldn't dance with him that night, said he stank. Thought she was too good for a working man. Beavins was mad as a bull ant, so Hirst and Shawcross said did he want to go with them an' he said yes.'

Lonergan came in. 'Wagon's coming.'

I hurried into my bedroom, picked up the thruppence and showed it to Maroney and Kelly. 'Seen this before? Got an A and an E inscribed on it.'

'Yeah, that's Beavins' – Archibald and Elizabeth.'

'He's got a wife?'

'Nah, she died not long after they married, poor bastard. He always kept that coin on him, but, on a string around his neck. Where'd you find it?'

'They're here,' Lonergan said.

I grabbed the paperwork and shoved it in a folder while Lonergan took the handcuffed prisoners out the front.

'We'll be back on Gowrie soon enough,' Maroney said. 'Fletcher needs us.'

I doubted that very much. A conviction of animal cruelty and stealing government property ended their chances of employment on any stock property. They should have thought of that before they picked on a police horse.

~

We handed them over to the troopers, along with the paperwork. The sun was high and it was hot, not as hot as it was going to get over the next few months, but it would be a long ride to Bourke for these two.

I went inside and dug out my notes and read Beavins' statement again. He had to have lost the engraved thruppence at the murder scene. Or somebody had pinched it and lost it there. Kelly claimed Hirst and Shawcross left early with Beavins to go drinking. But in the statements they gave to the junior troopers, all three men claimed they left the dance when it finished and returned to their quarters on Tindaree and Gowrie respectively, arriving between two and three. Now I knew from Henry Peyton that Beavins had not been seen on Gowrie until suppertime on the Sunday night, and as the men lived cheek by jowl there could be no mistake.

The detectives couldn't have cross-checked the men's statements with the overseer's records. I had a *Detective Handbook*, which I sent away for a couple of years ago, and I flicked through it to the section on taking statements.

In the field, sometimes the book went walkabout. But when in doubt, you returned to the book and followed the book. Every junior officer knew that, because when things went pear-shaped and the book was lying back somewhere in the dust, pages riffling in the wind, you could be in serious trouble.

The *Detective Handbook* confirmed what I knew from observation. Denning and Baines were running a sloppy investigation, either because they were told to or because they were sloppy detectives. If I were a gambling man I'd put two bob each way.

My reading of the evidence said Beavins had a motive for attacking Jimmy. Sally Gilmour was playing up with the hated greenskin Jimmy Kirkbride, ignoring the working man who had his heart set on her. But Jack Hirst and Toby Shawcross? I couldn't picture them, just an indistinct composite of filth-covered beasts. But my ears pricked forward and I found myself settling low like a kelpie, into the stalking position.

Early morning saw me riding up the western road to Tindaree Station. Broad paddocks stretched away to the west, where sheep moved across the earth like a dun-coloured, amorphous mass, eating grass and trailing dust, shit and money.

At Tindaree I found the overseer getting ready to go off for the day. Men milled around or got on with saddling horses.

'Mr Crowther, a word if I may?'

'Make it quick. We've a lot to do.'

'Jack Hirst and Tobias Shawcross – do they work for you?' I asked.

'Yeah, they're our doggers. Good at it too.'

'They around?'

'Shouldn't be. They come in for supplies but sleep out most nights, get more at dawn and dusk, and they fix the fences, lay the baits and burn the carcasses.'

Doggers were usually solitary men, a bit touched. But if they were fixing fences and throwing poison around, that would be a two-man job. It was a sad business to be in. Shooting a dog was one thing, but a nest of puppies went against the grain. Unless they had no grain. Worn away by years of brutal work in a brutal environment.

'Do you remember if they were expected to sleep over here on the night of the dance?'

'Oh, for Christ's sake,' Crowther said. 'I thought that business was over with. You lot have been through this already.'

'I'm just following up.'

'Yes, from what I recall, they came in for a wash and brush up on Saturday and were going to take on more supplies on the Sunday and head off again, but I'd have to check the books to be sure.'

'If you can just check on that, I'd appreciate it.'

He gave me a curt nod and headed off. The stockmen kept up their stares until I rode off.

~

I had to return the saddle and the rest of Dancer's kit to Bourke and sign off on them. I would not be issued with another police horse, as suspended troopers don't need horses. Another long ride into Bourke on Felix, but it couldn't be helped.

Hours later, I saw the low buildings and general squalor of Bourke, sitting on the banks of the Darling like a raddled old slattern dangling her feet in the muddy water, glass of gin in one hand, fag in the other, and always up for a kiss and a party. It was around one. I dropped the saddle with the quartermaster and hastened to the usual pub to see what was on for lunch. A couple of troopers were there, seated at the usual table, shovelling mounds of liver and onion in before heading back out into the heat and dust. They nodded when I joined them, accepting my pariah status as unremarkable.

We swapped a bit of banter and one of them, Hirsch, said he'd been at an autopsy that morning.

'Strong stomach, mate,' the other trooper said.

'Yeah, drew the short straw with that one,' Hirsch replied, and forked a chunk of seared liver into his mouth. 'Coupla blokes crushed by a wool bale, poor bastards. Never seen injuries like it. Never want to again.'

We both nodded, murmured.

'You musta seen a bit of blood and guts as a soldier,' Hirsch said.

'A bit, yeah. Most soldiers died of disease, though.'

'You discovered the Kirkbride bodies, right?'

I nodded, thanked the girl who put a plate of steak in front of me.

'The doctor who did their autopsies come over from Dubbo today to do these wharfies.'

'What's his name?'

'Gardiner. Didn't say much.'

I put down my knife and fork, got to my feet and excused myself.

'But you haven't eaten your lunch,' Hirsch said in horror.

'You have it.'

He was pulling the plate of steak and potatoes towards him, drool running down his chin, as I hurried out. It wasn't far to the hospital – nowhere was far away in a town like Bourke. I left a message for Dr Gardiner and waited, but a clerk informed me that Dr Gardiner had no time and if I wanted to speak to a doctor I'd have to look elsewhere.

I had no leverage, no warrant card to coerce him with, no official business to intimidate him with, so I decided to wait and speak to him face to face. I didn't know how long autopsies took but Dr Gardiner didn't appear until nearly six o'clock, by which time I was ready to eat my boots. Finally he appeared, a tall, skinny fellow, probably around forty, with a cap of curly red hair and drinker's bags under his eyes.

I approached him and he brushed me off. 'I have a train to catch.

Now, if you don't mind.' Gardiner was a picture of weariness and had the irritability of a put-upon man.

'I won't take up much of your time,' I said. 'Perhaps I can walk you to the station?'

'What is it you want? I don't see patients just willy-nilly on the pavement.'

'Dr Gardiner ...'

He faced me for the first time and I detected a flicker of professional interest. I knew that look – doctors who dabbled in surgery couldn't help themselves.

'Bayonet, Boer War.'

'I thought the Boer loathed blades and spears.'

'Captured weapon. Were you there?'

'Yes, a captain in the medical corps, with the New South Wales Third Imperial Bushmen.'

'Came back on the *Drayton Grange*?'

He raised his chin, a hint of combativeness. 'My name familiar, eh?'

'No, but I knew some TIBs who came back on the *Drayton*. A death ship, so I heard. I served as a captain in the Mounted Rifles.'

Gardiner relaxed, looked at his watch. 'Let's have a quick drink. It's not often I run into another ex-officer.'

'The Riverview Hotel?'

He agreed and we walked back to the hotel, and after a whisky and quick exchange of regimental particulars, we agreed to dine. The dining room of the Riverview was crowded with paddle-steamer crews but we secured a table and ordered the day's special, a rabbit and mushroom pudding.

'The *Drayton Grange* was an appalling experience. The army should be ashamed of themselves. I know the Royal Commission blamed the embarkation authorities in South Africa, Colonel White and me equally, but I can assure you it was all White's fault. Talking out of his fundament, no medical knowledge whatsoever, but he was my senior officer. You know how it is.'

'Yes, I spent a lot of time running around fixing the mess the COs made too.'

After our meal we kept drinking and swapping tales of army fuck-ups. It wasn't long before I felt like I was sitting in a tent under a brilliant starlit African night, passing a bottle around with the other junior officers, roaring with laughter as the conversation got filthier and filthier. Other diners looked over occasionally, but this was Bourke.

'Missed my train,' Gardiner said eventually, wiping tears of laughter from his eyes. 'Never mind. Now I'm here, we may as well make a night of it. There's a billiards hall down the road – fancy a game?'

My father said billiards was a fast way for a young man to ruin himself. His comment was a fast way to get a young man interested, and I'd taken to the game with enthusiasm.

~

Gardiner leant over, squinting through his cigarette smoke, angled his cue and took a shot. I watched the cue ball roll across the green baize and gently tap the red and then the white ball.

'Nice shot.'

A few players clustered around other tables, intent on their games. The table was lit by suspended oil lamps, which illuminated the baize. Smoke from our cigarettes hung like mist in the lamplight, and the hard wooden floor was pockmarked with cigarette burns. We'd brought a bottle of whisky with us and swigged from it now and then. No crystal cut glasses and cigars.

Gardiner was living and working in Dubbo because of the findings of the Royal Commission into the conditions on the troopship returning soldiers to Australia.

'Ruined my career,' he said moodily.

'Wars tend to do that. Unless you're at the top.'

'I expect that's why you're a mounted trooper.'

'It is,' I said as I positioned my cue. 'I was expected to go up to the university like my father but chose to go soldiering instead. And now I'm a police trooper out in the middle of nowhere. Bad chest and arm injuries.'

'But you survived.'

'Only because my father called in some favours and got me into a private hospital in Cape Town.'

'If you survived long enough to get to hospital, you must be made of stern stuff. Those field hospitals were next to useless for chest injuries. Who's your father?'

'Dr Thomas Hawkins, Medical Superintendent of Queanbeyan Hospital. Does his own autopsies, surgery, maternity, the lot.'

I took the shot. The cue ball knocked the red.

'Autopsies, eh? I put my hand up to act as a coronial surgeon for the Western Division because I thought it would improve my career. But

I resent every single one of them. I can do more for the living in my own hospital in Dubbo, instead of labouring away over the dead only to have my work rubber-stamped, filed away and forgotten.' Hanging off his cue, he leant forward unsteadily and fixed me with a bloodshot eye. 'I like my patients to thank me, Captain, and no corpse is going to shake my hand and praise me for pulling out their intestines.'

He took his shot, a bit wobbly. It was time for me to thrash him.

'You've got two doctors down your way,' he said. 'I don't see why one of them doesn't put his hand up to do autopsies. I mean, it's standard work. Two doctors in the wastelands are an extravagance, after all.'

'I know one of them – I'll see what he says about it.'

'Thank you. And what is it I can do for you, old cock?' he said, bleary and swaying. 'What did you want to talk to me about so urgently, for heaven's sake?'

'The Kirkbride autopsies.'

His face paled and he leant back, moving into the shadows.

'I was on duty that night,' I said. 'I found the bodies, and as I'd delayed leaving for an hour, the time of their death is a matter of personal significance.'

'I see.'

'The autopsy report says death between ten and when they were found. Is that as accurate as you can be?'

'Given the current state of knowledge, yes. Why – do you have evidence that contradicts this?'

'No, nobody has firm evidence of any sighting. Nobody carries a watch but police and doctors.'

'It is highly likely that if you had got there in time, you would be dead too. And I would err on an earlier time of death, given the lividity of the corpses.'

He offered me another fag and we lit up again.

'Stupid habit, but hey-ho,' he said, and gulped from the whisky bottle. 'Make your peace with it, Captain. It was a difficult case for all concerned. I spent hours on the youngest female, only to be told the coroner had agreed to the family's request not to do an autopsy on her.'

'You weren't informed beforehand?'

'No. The police officer who was to supervise, chap called Martin, was running late, so I went ahead and started. As far as I knew, I had three bodies to autopsy – I wasn't going to wait around for him. Called in at late notice and in Cobar for one day.'

'So the family doesn't know that Miss Grace was autopsied?'

He looked over his shoulder and lowered his voice, the billiards game forgotten. 'No, they don't. Nobody but my assistants and I knew – and Martin, and of course the funeral home, but they wouldn't say anything. Martin insisted that my report be replaced with the one that now lies in the file, stating that only an external examination took place.'

'He asked you to falsify coronial documents?' I said, gaping.

'Of course I refused. After the *Drayton Grange* affair, I have to keep my nose clean, even though that was not my fault. Royal Commissions can ruin a man. But where was I? Yes, Martin assured me Mr Kirkbride would be furious if he knew the autopsy had gone ahead.'

'You replaced the full autopsy report with the one that says an external examination only took place?'

'Oh, please, don't tell me police files never magically disappear,' Gardiner said with a raised eyebrow. 'I didn't come down in the last shower, and I've been dealing with autopsies and the police for seven years now. You've heard of the Farmers' and Settlers' Association? Robert Kirkbride is a prominent member, and very active on the Western Lands Board, and he's also a great friend of Sam McCartney, with even more friends in Macquarie Street. Men like him ask for something, they usually get it. And if they don't get it, they make trouble. Both Martin and I are public employees, and I have a wife and five children.'

Colour returned to his face and he took a deep breath, as if telling the truth had released him.

'I can tell you this, though, it wasn't because she was their youngest that they wanted her spared. It was because young Miss Grace Kirkbride was in the family way.'

I stared at him, the words incomprehensible for several seconds. 'That can't be right. She'd just turned thirteen the week before she died.'

He snorted. 'I'm afraid it is right. I see this sort of thing very often – most weeks, in fact. Desperate girls will do anything to cover their sins. And by the time they get to me, all I can do is assist their passing.'

'I'm sorry, I'm not following you.'

'Due to a botched ... procedure, young Miss Grace was dying when she was shot. Bleeding out. Wouldn't have survived much longer.'

The bullet hole in her back, the rain smacking into her lifeless corpse, the lantern throwing a golden ring around her, the taste of vomit in my mouth.

They killed a dying girl.

'It is a most grievous business,' Gardiner murmured as he gazed at the billiards table.

'And their clothes? What happened to them?'

'Martin took them all. It was a police matter so I didn't pay much attention, although I can tell you Grace's undergarments were soaked in blood, as you'd expect.'

The stain on the bed of the cart.

Neither of us wanted to play on, and we returned to the pub for a nightcap and drank in silence. We both took rooms in the hotel and I lay on the bed, waiting for sleep. I looked up at the pressed-tin ceiling, the egg and dart pattern, the repeat, the dots of mould and rust, the rabbit pudding sitting in my stomach like a stone that needed throwing.

I didn't know how long I lay there, trying to make sense of what Gardiner had told me. No wonder Kirkbride wanted a cover-up. He must have known Grace was pregnant, Gardiner was right, and acted quickly to prevent it becoming widely known. Had to be why the governess was dismissed. And if Grace had the procedure that night, it would explain why neither she nor Nessie were seen at the dance.

Who was so debauched they'd interfere with a child? And, what's more, be so careless as to get her pregnant? Now, to me, that said the man who did it was either unaware Grace was able to get pregnant or felt so safe he could be reckless, as his identity would never be uncovered.

My father never explained the facts of life to me. The talk among the lads at school was sex, girls, how to do it, what not to do, and on and on until we were overwrought and overheated with lust. But just to finesse my knowledge, so to speak, I asked my father's manservant a few questions. He told me a gentleman always leaves the church before the choir sings, unless they are married. So that's what I did, even in South Africa, even in a country brothel. Not because I was all that considerate or caring, but because it was what a gentleman did, and I was a gentleman.

But if a man was set on raping a twelve-year-old girl, he'd already lost any standards he might have set himself, so to hell with it. It beggared belief that such a man had got near enough to Robert Kirkbride's youngest child to do what he did.

22

On the long ride back to Calpa I stopped in Larne to see Kitty. She'd be at work but I knew she went home for lunch, so I hung around outside the schoolhouse until I heard the bell ring and then rode down to her house on the edge of town. I put Felix around the back and waited on an old bench, watching her sheets on the clothesline blowing in the breeze.

She came around the back, wearing a blue gingham dress with her black hair rolled up.

'Home for lunch, Miss Ryan?'

'Get out of here,' she said, going to the back door and unlocking it.

'Heard from the department?'

'What do you think? Out at the end of the term, no reference.'

'I'm sorry – I really am.'

'Sure you are, Gus,' she said, and glanced at me. 'Why aren't you in uniform?'

'Suspended without pay.'

'Good.'

'Fair go, Kitty.'

'Fair go – oh, that's rich, that's a good one. A fair go for me who's done nothing wrong except having a bit of male company now and then.'

'What are you going to do?'

'Have my lunch.'

I followed her into the tiny house, lowering my head to get through the doorway. She tied an apron around her and swung the kettle onto the stovetop, then picked up a loaf of damper and a knife and let out a deep sigh.

'You remember I found the Kirkbride bodies?' I said.

'Mmm?' she said, sawing away at the old loaf. 'And?'

'Grace had a blanket tangled around her feet when I found her. It was identical to that purple lap blanket you use. You had two of them.'

Kitty startled and dropped the bread knife. 'Plenty of blankets around like that.'

'You think?'

'Are you a bloody expert on blankets now, eh? Along with everything else, bloody know-it-all.'

'They were in a cart travelling south from Larne to their homestead. Grace had that blanket and she got it from you. I think I know, partly, why you lied about me visiting that night. You were frightened because I sent detectives here, and you felt guilty as hell because Grace and Nessie had been here.'

I saw a flicker of fear in Kitty's eyes.

'Grace had an abortion performed on her that night.'

'And you think I did it? How dare you? How bloody dare you?'

'Then who did?'

'I'm a schoolteacher – or I was until this wretched business.' She burst into tears, burying her face in her hands.

I fetched a glass of water but she slapped it from my hands. It hit the ground and shattered.

'You just bring trouble,' she cried. 'That was me best glass, too.'

'I'm sorry, I'll get you another.' The kettle boiled up and over onto the stove. I took it off the hob, poured the water into the pot and got a couple of mugs. Then I finished cutting the damper, spread some golden syrup onto it and put it in front of her.

'Eat. You have to go back to work with something in you.'

'Reg Tierney does them,' she said, and blew her nose. 'There, I've said it. I told Jimmy, I said, "Don't let Dr Tierney do it at night, it's best to come first thing in the morning," but Jimmy wanted it done then.'

'You were worried Tierney'd be drunk and make a bad job of it?'

'But it didn't matter, did it, because somebody shot the poor little love.'

'They came here afterwards?'

'Yep. Jimmy went off to the dance and Nessie and I covered Gracie up with blankets and made her sweet tea and Nessie cuddled her, poor wee girl. So young, both of them. Grace with her trusting eyes … she … didn't know what had hit her.'

Kitty looked down at the table, wiped away a tear with her apron.

'Who do you think got at Grace?'

She gave me a look.

'Not …'

'Happens more than you could ever imagine.'

'But surely not in the home of a—'

'Gus, sometimes you're just three penn'orth of God help us,' she snapped, brushing crumbs off the table. 'In any case, can you imagine Robert Kirkbride sending his daughter to Reg Tierney?'

'No – so what happened?'

'It was Jimmy.'

'Not Jimmy's baby?'

'I don't know, but it was Jimmy's idea to get rid of it,' she said. 'Nessie told me. She said her parents wanted to send Grace away to a home for fallen women in Sydney to have the baby. On her own. Jimmy and Flora jacked up about it. Flora wanted the baby to be raised at Inveraray and just say it was an orphan, but Jimmy reckoned it was better if it was just got rid of.'

'And Nessie?'

'Poor love, she agreed with Flora, but old man Kirkbride wouldn't have it, said it was a disgrace, that Grace was a slut and was to be sent away to Sydney. Jimmy decided to bring her to Tierney in secret, then say she suffered a miscarriage.'

We stared at each other, shared incredulity.

'That's how he was,' Kitty sighed. 'No doubt Jimmy had shown many a young girl to that man's surgery.'

'And then they come here to recover?'

'If I'm here, yes. The stories ... break your heart.'

'Not worried about the law?'

'I was when those detectives turned up. Thought they'd come for me. Are you going to dob me in?'

'Of course not. Just putting the puzzle together as to why they were on that road when they were.'

'Just bad luck,' she said, shaking her head. 'Just terrible bad luck.'

'Why didn't you tell me?'

Kitty gave a snort. 'None of your business. Don't mind telling you now, though. Been awful keeping it all to meself.'

I spooned sugar into the tea while she ate the damper, then cut a slice for myself, dipping it in the tea to soften it.

'But I'm not sorry to be leaving this place,' Kitty said. 'I helped Tierney once and then he ends up sending all the girls here. Like I'm running a hospital ward, unpaid and all. Only did it because I felt sorry for them. Maids, laundresses, barmaids. The working girls who have no male protectors, girls who are young, naive – girls like me who were orphaned and looking to be loved, girls who have nothing to offer a man but their bodies. No land, no dowry, no connections.

'And I'm sure you'd know all of this, being an heir to the throne yourself. You'll go back east when you've finished and marry a good girl who has family and money. And the girls you leave behind? Marry a stockman or a publican who'll beat them, have umpteen pregnancies and die early from exhaustion. Don't you know it, Gus? Haven't you ever been curious about them and their lives?'

As she talked, I looked up at the mantelpiece, where Kitty had an old mantel clock, one that I'd constantly had to fix and fiddle with to keep it going.

'What is it?' she said, turning around to see what I was staring at.

'What time did they leave here?'

259

'Who? Oh, the Kirkbrides – they left at twenty past ten. I remember because I looked at the clock as they left, because I knew it was a long journey for wee Grace in the state she was in.'

'What state?'

'She had a sore tummy and a bit of bleeding, but Tierney told Jimmy that she would bleed for a bit afterwards. So they left.'

Even if I'd done the right thing and left Larne on time, they would have died long before I'd have got there. It was some comfort, for me at least. But secret comfort wasn't enough – would never be enough.

Now I knew why the Kirkbrides were on that road and why Kirkbride had orchestrated a cover-up. But their murder didn't appear to have any connection to those two facts. It had come from a completely different direction, I was sure of it. Like two comets on dreadful trajectories, smashing into each other in a random moment of horror. Unless the man who impregnated Grace wanted no trace left of his crime and killed her. Killed her on the road that night because he couldn't get at her any other way.

~

The ride back to Calpa, meandering alongside the river while the sun sank over in the west, was a ride I couldn't afterwards recall, so lost was I in putting what I'd discovered from Dr Gardiner and Kitty into the story I thought I knew.

In the months before the murders, Flora and I were meeting in secret and risking Kirkbride's wrath; we couldn't keep away from each other. I knew something was troubling her, but in my usual self-absorbed way, I thought it was our subterfuge. I had no idea Grace was pregnant and being sent away, because Flora didn't tell me. If she had, it could all have been so different.

After Kirkbride warned me off Flora at Christmas, I lost myself for a while, too upset to care about much. There was a lot of woodchopping in that period, a lot of drinking. And then Jimmy dropped by and gave me a letter from Flora, said he'd come by tomorrow and pick up the return if I wanted to reply. From that blistering January day we wrote to each other every week, and Jimmy faithfully smuggled the letters back and forth under his father's nose.

Our letters went from shy and tentative to longer and more personal, until we were pouring ourselves onto the paper. I lived from letter to letter, every moment filled with longing for her. We met in secret, Jimmy covering for us. Then, in late June, when the talk was all about the coronation of King George and the celebrations, Flora and I arranged to meet at an isolated shepherd's hut I knew of.

I waited on the bank of the river, mouth dry, impatient. I sighted Jimmy and Flora riding abreast in the distance. Jimmy saw me and waved. I cantered over, Flora beaming at me, a smile so delicious I just wanted to drag her off that horse and eat her up.

I'd ridden up to the shepherd's hut a few days previously, dusted it down and checked it over. Stone walls and a slab bark roof, fallen in here and there, a beaten-earth floor and the remains of a bush cot, made of saplings and flour bags. It'd have to be the floor for us, so I left a roll of canvas there.

Once Jimmy shot off to do whatever he was going to do, we rode along in silence. Soon we arrived at the hut, standing alone on top of a rise not far from the waterholes. The air was still, just the low buzz of insects, budgerigars like twittering emeralds swooping over the ochre soil. We hobbled the horses, I took my rifle and put it by the door, then I laid a big sheepskin coat out on the floor. Flora saw it and blushed.

'We don't have to,' I said.

What might be a passing tumble with another girl was deadly serious in Flora's world, and only took place once a ring was on her finger. But we would marry, she knew it and I knew it. She unpinned her dark hair and tiptoed over, stretched up and kissed me, and when she was naked she lay back on the woolly fleece, her arms outstretched to me.

Afterwards, she laid her head on my shoulder and I wrapped my arms around her, and nothing had ever felt so right. For a brief moment, in Flora's arms, the rush of desire subsided to a long moment I cannot find words to describe, sublime and rendering me as helpless as a lamb.

'What would happen if we made a baby, here, today?' she said.

My nerves jolted, a thud of alarm in my chest. I raised my head and looked at her. 'We won't, because I made sure we won't ... And if we did, we'd marry and have the baby.'

'You know we can't marry.'

I blinked a few times, rolled onto my side. 'Because of your father, you mean? Because he's the only obstacle as far as I can see.' I stroked her hair, the fine, dark hair at her temple, glossy against her white skin, touched her lips and kissed her, but she pulled away and looked at me.

'Is that what you want?' I said, my mouth suddenly dry, my pulse rising at the thought of fighting Kirkbride after impregnating his unmarried daughter. 'A baby, so we force his hand?'

'No, because I don't think we'd win. He'd find another way to stop us.'

'What other way is there?' I couldn't help thinking that she wanted a baby, for all the hell that would break loose around us.

Flora sat up.

I touched her smooth back until she shivered. 'What other way?' I repeated.

'What happens to unwanted babies?'

'But it wouldn't be unwanted – it would be our baby.'

She looked over her shoulder at me. I pulled her back down and put my arms around her. There was an undertow but I couldn't get a grip on it. We only had a few hours and I didn't want to fill them with talk of her father. We made love again, slowly, trying to find each other, but Flora had turned inward, to thoughts of babies and her father, and I had a fleeting sense of foreboding. I knew I'd taken all due care not to get her pregnant but it wasn't impossible.

As I dressed, I said, 'Your father won't give permission, but we can just leave.'

'Don't say any more,' Flora said, still naked on the sheepskin, a sight to raise the pulse and gladden the heart. Except for the clouds settling over her. 'It doesn't matter if he doesn't give his permission because I can't run away with you.'

'Then why are we here?' I said, feeling an unfamiliar pain spreading across my chest. 'Doing what we've just done?'

263

She bowed her head and I saw a tear fall onto her hand. Outside, the flies buzzed, a crow called, its cry ending on a dying note, a note that said *everything you undertake will die away*. I got down next to her, took her face in both hands.

'I'm not worth much, Flora, but I could be. Retrace my steps, get back on the right path.'

'Please don't,' she said, pulling away.

'Is it one of those blokes he's been throwing at you? Are you marrying someone else? Is that why we're here? A farewell before life as a rich pastoralist's wife?'

'You know that's not fair,' she said, swiping at her tears. 'I'm not marrying anyone if it's not you, but I can't leave. Grace needs me.'

'You want me to wait until Grace is grown up? She's only a child, for goodness sake,' I said, getting to my feet. It was so clear to me what we had to do. 'Look, we'll leave, get married and soon your father will accept it and then we'll come back and you'll see them whenever you want.'

'No, I can't leave her, I just can't.'

We packed up and rode away in silence. On the east side of the river, James came over the horizon galloping and yelling. We watched him raise the dust until he caught up with us, panting and laughing. There was no chance for Flora and me to say anything else to each other. The three of us plodded on, Jimmy chattering away. He didn't notice my grim silence or how Flora's head was lowered, how she wiped her eyes, how she was trying to keep it at bay until she reached the safety of her pillow.

As we neared Calpa, Jimmy rode on ahead and I rode closer to Flora.

264

'It's all right,' I said, 'you don't have to choose me or your family.' The lump in my throat was so big I could hardly speak. 'I won't write again and I'll apply for a transfer.'

I didn't know who ruined who that day. Flora put her sister's needs above me. Asked me to wait. She wouldn't have asked me to wait if she felt what I felt, I was sure. She'd have known that to wait while such feelings propelled one forward was impossible. I was crippled by the pain, uncomprehending, desperate to speak to her just once more.

Two weeks later, Jimmy, Nessie and Grace were dead.

At the time, I thought Flora was making excuses not to marry me – that she'd sampled the goods and found them not to her taste, and all that talk of babies was a distraction. But it was her love and loyalty to her little sister that prevented her from leaving. Maybe she felt she couldn't tell me because she was tainted by Grace's state, and that I'd run a mile if I knew. I'd have been shocked, as I was now, as her family had been, and if I'd known of Jimmy's appalling plan, I would have tried to talk him out of it. But it would not have changed my feelings for her and what we hoped for.

23

Late August and the marking of the lambs had begun. A brutal process that was hard for me to watch, involving knives and tails and balls everywhere. It was also time to dip the rams, so all the stations were busy. The ewes had their time of trial at crutching; now it was the rams' turn to be mustered by barking dogs, forced into pens and then put through a narrow chute, from where they plunged into a long trough full of sheep dip, a mix of arsenic and other chemicals that killed lice and ticks.

A man stood by the trough with a long pole, pushing each ram under the surface of the water twice, to make sure the poor bastard got the full measure. The rams emerged into another pen, shook themselves off and looked for ways to escape. The arsenic mix splashed on the stockmen, on the working dogs and seeped into the ground around the trough.

Some blokes reckoned after the dipping they suffered from headaches and confusion, but it was considered a weakness to pay attention to such minor ailments. I reckoned they were slowly being poisoned. We used arsenic to poison every other living creature, so it made sense. But a man had to have a job so they just got on with it.

I was on my way to see Tom and stopped to watch, from a distance, the bustle and noise of the dipping. A wide, powder-blue sky, warm sun and clear, still air made for perfect conditions.

Will Fletcher nodded towards me, then walked over. 'Come to watch the circus, eh?'

'Thought I'd look in on Tom, see how he's getting on.'

A shadow crossed Will's face. 'Nothing to do for him. Has to do it himself.'

'Is he about?'

'Not here, as you can see.' He turned away from the men and the dipping and said, 'He's got it in his head that one of those young bucks who Kirkbride was always entertaining had something to do with it. He's promised me he won't do anything stupid, but he's not himself.'

I'd never heard so many words come from Will's mouth in one go.

'Kirkbride won't act, even if he too has his suspicions,' he added. 'But my boy will act, given half a chance.'

'I'll talk to him.'

He nodded and turned back to the young rams, bunched up, tussling and jostling, out to kill one another. Seeing mature rams run full force into each other's skulls while vying for a lady sheep is quite a sight. In a pen they couldn't do it, but that didn't mean they didn't want to do it.

I suspected Tom was on the right track and I wanted to feel him out, see what he knew. Maybe, after Nessie or Flora or both rejected the culprit, his pride dented, he managed to get at Grace, and then, not satisfied with that, he planned and carried out the Kirkbride murders. Now, that was a long bow to draw, but rich young men didn't like being told no and they often suffered from a sense of invincibility – a combination that worked well in a battle setting. But add a touch of moral insanity, put the man in the joining paddock and you had a dangerous beast.

Up at the Gowrie homestead I tethered my horse under the peppercorn tree, strolled over to the front door and knocked. Miss Fletcher answered the door, her face drawn and blotchy. She told me Tom wasn't home. I was just about to mount up when Miss Fletcher called me back. She said Mrs Fletcher wanted to speak to me, and she'd fetch Miss Gilmour to take me to her.

Sally Gilmour suddenly appeared, neat and fresh in her blue nurse's pinafore, white-starched collar and cuffs. 'Come with me, Constable,' she said, in a crisp, no-nonsense manner.

I feasted my eyes on her charming behind as she led me around the verandah. Uncanny how I felt my wits desert me around this girl. Any moment I'd be headbutting the nearest male.

The Gowrie homestead verandahs were wide and shady and had optimistic garden beds running alongside filled with fleshy plants, the sort of plant that was built for arid life, slow-growing and jealously hoarding any moisture that came its way.

Mrs Fletcher was sitting in a wicker chair, a pink ribbon in her thick grey hair and a colourful crochet rug over her knees. She was seated outside what I presume was her room which had a set of French doors opening onto the verandah, obviously added when she withdrew from the world. From this position one looked out to the north-east and the station's flower and vegetable gardens, with their pipes and tanks and brilliant greens set against the dusty background. Beyond them, the paddocks stretched away into infinity.

'Good morning, Captain Hawkins.'

'Good morning, Mrs Fletcher.'

'You were at King's with Thomas, he tells me,' Mrs Fletcher said.

'Three years ahead. I do remember him though, always bashing around the sporting fields.'

'Bashing,' she laughed. 'Yes, that's my Tom. His sisters are big girls too, you know. Big-boned and strong. Great hockey players, both of them.'

I thought of Robert Kirkbride, leaving her naked with a broken back in the sun for hours.

'Tom tells me you were a cavalry officer in the Boer War.'

'Yes, I was.'

'I had a cousin in the Bechuanaland Rifles, under Lord Methuen. He was killed at Klerksdorp.'

'I'm sorry to hear that.'

'And you?'

'New South Wales Mounted Rifles, 1st Regiment, Le Gallais' Brigade, then the 2nd Regiment.'

'Stayed for the whole thing, eh? Good for you. Have to see things through to the end.' Mrs Fletcher gave me a thoughtful look. 'Perhaps you would take tea with me.'

Not an invitation, more a directive.

'Thank you, I'd like that.'

Sally Gilmour was despatched to fetch the tea. As she walked away I found my gaze pulled towards her luscious figure.

'She's a very pretty girl, isn't she, Captain?'

'Er ... yes, very,' I blustered, caught out by Mrs Fletcher's sharp eyes.

'Did you know that beauty, for a young girl, can be a curse? If her family has rank and position, she'll catch a good husband with it, but if she's from the lower orders, she's pursued, harassed and abused, and is often in danger from the men around her.'

She smiled but there was a razor's edge to it. A very uncomfortable moment passed as I did a quick moral accounting of my past dealings with pretty young girls with no family.

'Miss Gilmour, as my employee,' Mrs Fletcher continued, 'indeed, as my companion, is under my protection, Captain. She's had a difficult life and I would see that changed from here on in.'

'Of course, Mrs Fletcher, I can assure you—'

'Why did you stay for the whole of the war?' she asked, putting a merciful end to my blather. 'I would have thought one tour to be enough, given the stories.'

'I found I had an aptitude for soldiering and was rising up through the ranks. Saw no reason to stop.'

'You must have seen some marvellous sights.'

'I did.'

'Worth your injuries?'

'I think so, yes. The injuries are pure bad luck. I signed on for a third tour, thinking I was invulnerable. Turns out I'm not.'

'The curse of all men,' she said with a smile. 'And some women. Tom tells me you were raised by your widowed father. What does he think of you being out here?'

'We are estranged.'

'Siblings?'

'No.'

Sally Gilmour returned with a tray of tea things, and behind her was a maid with another tray. A linen cloth was placed over the small table beside Mrs Fletcher. Cups and saucers were laid out beside mesh cake covers over plates of seed cake and small cucumber sandwiches. Sally Gilmour poured the tea and handed a cup and saucer to Mrs Fletcher and then one to me, which I fumbled as I was trying to look anywhere but at her.

'Seed cake, Captain? It's very good. Sally, put a slice on a plate for Captain Hawkins ... Yes, that's right.'

I juggled tea and plate, putting one down so I could deal with the other, relieved that my hand didn't shake. I wished Sally Gilmour would remove her pretty self from the vicinity lest my boorish instincts betray me again.

'Leave us, please, Miss Gilmour,' Mrs Fletcher said. When we were alone, she said, 'Don't let the estrangement from your father go on for too long. Such silences do nobody any good, and then suddenly life is over.'

The seed cake was very good, and I made short work of it as she watched, satisfied with my appetite.

'I expect you know how I sustained my injuries, never to walk or ride again,' she said.

Another sip of tea.

'You and I, we marched towards our injuries, knowing they could happen. But Tom ... a young man doesn't fall in love with anything but forever in his heart. He's been terribly injured by the death of Nessie. He stares into the abyss every day and weeps every night. Overcoming tragedy takes years, and I worry he's not patient enough.'

I must have appeared startled, because she said, 'I speak frankly because I've no use for anything but frankness these days. I can't ask you to help Tom if he doesn't want help, but if he does ...'

'If I can help him in any way, I will, of course.'

'He may speak more openly to another young man than to his mother. Knowing how Nessie died, the torment she endured at the hands of those beasts ... I think it's more than he can bear.'

We talked of other things, and I left after promising I would keep an eye out for Tom. As I walked back to my horse, I couldn't help but dwell on Mrs Fletcher's words. How did she know the circumstances of Nessie's death, when even Nessie's own mother didn't know?

~

While I was taking tea the wind had blown up, and when I left it chased me down the long drive, past the penned rams and shouting men. Much further along were the Gowrie laundries, the long rows of clotheslines, held up by forked saplings, with white sheets and tablecloths flapping in the wind. I saw Sheila Stewart again and waved to her. She beckoned me over.

'Miss Stewart.'

'Look, I couldn't stop to talk the other day,' she said, pushing her spectacles back up her nose, the wind teasing her hair from its bindings. 'But I remembered something about Sally Gilmour and Jimmy Kirkbride. You still interested?'

'Yes, of course.'

'I change Mrs Fletcher's bedding, you know – I go in there and take the dirty sheets away. Sally's gathering up the other linen for the bag and sometimes we chat. She used to laugh about Archie Beavins, but said he was useful.'

'For what?'

'I couldn't see the use of him meself, beyond fixing fences and droving sheep, but that's me. And Sal has no time for any bloke, not really – said they was all filthy dogs. Had to agree with her there, so when she said, a few days before the dance, that she'd see Jimmy Kirkbride there, I was curious. 'Course, Jimmy has money, and a rich dog's better than a poor dog, but I said he'd go to the ball in Cobar, surely. And she said no, he'd be coming for her. All confident and glowing she was, because she'd promised him he'd get what he deserved. I thought she meant a kiss or summat more. But maybe she knew something else?'

'Thank you for coming forward with this, Miss Stewart.'

'I'm just sorry it didn't occur to me earlier ... The house was in an uproar and old Miss Fletcher was riding us maids something cruel, so I forgot.'

Back at the Calpa police station, a head full of questions, I rushed in the back and rummaged around for my private files. Something wasn't right and I had to know the how and why of it. But I couldn't find it in the loose file of notes. I took my coat off and went out the back, found my axe, unwrapped the oilcloth, then set a short log on the stump.

I raised the axe, wincing at the sensation as my scars stretched, then brought the axe down hard, watching the two halves fall aside. It was the signal to the stable cats to stop what they were doing and come and watch. They took to their positions on the roof of the woodpile, flicked their tails and waited. What for, I did not know.

I set a half on the stump. Thought of Jimmy going to the dance and organising the procedure for Grace for the same night. Brought the axe down hard, watching splinters fly. Put a quarter on the stump. By God, Jimmy was a cocky so-and-so, but that was outrageous, even for a Kirkbride.

With a combination of force and precision I whacked the quarters into eighths. The cats yawned, *so what?* Lonergan appeared, put his horse in the stable and eventually joined me.

'Found Mrs Jordan and her kids stuck on the eastern road with a broken cartwheel.'

'You fix her up?'

'Yeah, enough for her to get home.'

I fetched another short log set it up on the block and looked at Lonergan.

'Yeah, right, I know, go and write it up.'

As he walked off I brought the axe down hard, watched the halves fall aside like two heads under a guillotine.

Lonergan came back outside, leant against the water tank and watched. Without looking up, I said, 'You heard Corcoran give the order that no one was to know how the Kirkbrides died. That they died of gunshot wounds.'

Set a half on the log. Raised the axe, feeling the pain shoot down my side.

'Yeah, and Denning said the same thing,' he said. 'But people talk.'

'Have you heard anyone anywhere speak of bashing and rape?' I said, and brought the axe down hard.

'No ... but then, I don't let people question me. I says it's police business. Shuts 'em up.'

'Bob Kirkbride, you, me, Joe, Corcoran, Parry, Denning, Martin and Baines, plus the autopsy doctor and his assistants, are the only ones who should know.'

I set a quarter on the stump, raised the axe.

'Why?' he asked.

'Because a person who shouldn't know what actually happened to Nessie does know. Somebody talked.'

I brought the axe down and saw the two pieces fall, only I hadn't made perfect eighths.

'The coroner's assistants, maybe?' Lonergan said, and started picking up the chopped wood and stacking it. Watching him jam the eighths into the pile tested me, but I held my tongue.

'They'd be under strict, legally enforceable instructions not to discuss their coronial work. And as Mrs Kirkbride and probably Miss Flora Kirkbride were not to be told, it would be egregious to speak of it.'

'Who knows?' he asked.

'Mrs Fletcher.'

He nodded, scratched his chin slowly. The screen door at the back opened and closed. One of the stable cats, a manky piebald I named Kleptes for his relentless kitchen pilfering, crept out.

'What's he doing in there?' I snapped.

Lonergan turned to look, stamped his foot and the cat shot off to the stable. His two mates on the woodpile blinked at me. They were decoys, had to be. I put the axe down, found my cigarettes, lit one and shook the match flame out.

'Sally Gilmour knew Jimmy was going to the dance,' I said. 'She knew it days before.'

'Wasn't a last-minute change of plans, then? Because that's what Baines reckoned it was.'

'Nope, Jimmy was planning to go.'

And planning to get Sally Gilmour in the joining yard at some later stage. The coldness of the plan beggared belief. A bit of carnal refreshment with Sally while his little sister was undergoing an illegal, dangerous procedure at the hands of a drunkard.

'And it wasn't just Jimmy who was going after Sally, it was also Archie Beavins,' I said.

'How do you know that?'

'Those pigs who stampeded Dancer, Maroney and Kelly, said Beavins was stuck on her. They said Beavins left the dance early with two men called Hirst and Shawcross because Sally was making him jealous with Jimmy Kirkbride. And all three men lied in their statements about when they returned to their quarters.'

The thruppence I'd found at the crime scene belonged to Beavins, so I had to assume he was there. Maybe paid to be there. Paid to be there and kill the Kirkbrides by some rich young man with a grudge who melts away when the deed is done.

Beavins could be the man who ran south, zigzagging through the scrub, horrified by what he'd witnessed. Or done. He tells his girl, Sally, swears her to secrecy, and she, who brings news of the outside world to Mrs Fletcher, relates the details of the killings. That had to be how it had worked. Which meant that Sally Gilmour – if Hirst and Shawcross were the murderers – was in serious danger. I had to find those two quickly.

24

It was spring and the district rang with bleats as ewes and lambs called to each other. Entering a lambing paddock was bad form out here as it upset the ewes, but I had to speak with Jim Crowther, and I had to do it now.

The sun was coming up, that time of day when the noise level rises and the world takes on its colours for the day. At Tindaree I'd been told where Crowther was: he'd fetched up to the lambing an hour ago with some bad news. As I rode in closer, I saw dun-coloured mounds dotted about and heard the flies, loud and thick.

I rode over to a cluster of men, who barely registered my arrival. Dingos had been at work overnight and Crowther was dark, the men on watch almost in shock. Dead lambs were scattered about, throats torn out, gashes in their sides where the dingo had gone for their kidneys, leaving their guts strewn around in the dirt. The ewes were bunched up in a terrified mob. The smell of blood and death put me in mind of the murders.

Another horse and rider was coming and fast. Crowther looked up. The boss, on his way to see the damage.

'Mr Crowther, a quick word?'

'Can't you see, man? Whatever it is it can wait.'

I glanced at the men whose job it was to check the ewes and lambs every few hours to make sure none of the birthing ewes were in trouble. Their faces had a green tinge to them. If a worker killed a sheep, broke a bone while shearing, smothered it or cut the jugular, they had to buy it and then it would go to the kitchens. There were a lot of dead lambs and ewes here, so these blokes were in strife, with a lot of mutton and lamb to be chewed through.

'Hirst and Shawcross – where are they?'

'Not doing their bloody job, that's for sure,' one man murmured.

True enough, but dingos were dingos, and cunning bastards at that.

Forsythe was getting closer, slowing his horse down to a trot while he looked around at the carnage. There were eagles and hawks circling already, ants marching in formation towards their targets. Doesn't take long for one creature to profit from the death of another.

'They're up in the scrub to the north-east, where all these bastards live,' Crowther said. 'Should have cleared it long ago.'

'Did you check their whereabouts on the Sunday after the dance?'

Crowther slowly raised his eyes to mine.

'Right, I'll leave you to it.'

Forsythe hailed me and I rode over. He looked devastated, as you would at the loss of hundreds of pounds' worth of stock.

'Look at this, Gus. What do I pay these worthless feckers for? To kill vermin and to protect the sheep.'

'Dingos are a mighty foe.'

'Shouldn't be here. Blasted dingo fence, we put that in and still they get over it? Useless doggers.'

'That'd be Hirst and Shawcross?' I said.

He nodded, surveying the carnage. 'I pay them to shoot the dogs, I feed them, I supply them with ammunition and they shoot the roos instead.'

'I'm on my way to speak to them now. Want me to tell them to come in?'

'What do you want with them?'

'Police matter.'

'Tell them to get down here, at once.'

~

It was a long ride to the scrub in the north-east of Tindaree but it had to be done. I knew the patch of scrub Crowther was referring to, quite a substantial piece of the original vegetation, kept because they hadn't got around to clearing it yet. If it was harbouring vermin, then its days were numbered. I set off, hat pulled low, a Colt pistol on my hip and a bad case of indigestion from Mrs Schreiber's blood sausage.

The land out here had been hammered by the hooves of millions of sheep over the decades and now the soil was tightly packed. Saw this everywhere in the district. Hard-packed soil that turned to mud in the rain, then dried as clay, then blew away in the strong winds. No grasses to anchor it anymore. Great gullies caused by this erosion were scattered around the land like cracks in an old man's heel. Winter rains made it worse. No matter, they just drove the sheep further west.

I saw the low grey-green of the scrubland ahead of me lying beyond a creek which ran through steep cliffs of eroded red soil. A couple of redgums clung on, half their root mass hanging free, stripped of dirt. White cockatoos fluttered and fussed high in the branches. Just a matter of time before these mighty trees crashed down into the gully.

It was getting close to midday when I heard gunshot and set Felix towards it. Sounded regular, not the random gunshot of a roo shooter, more like shooting a corralled herd of goats or camel. Methodical. Beasts that couldn't get away. I moved towards it, getting a fix on it every time a shot rang out. As we got closer, I took out my sidearm and fired into the air so they'd know there was someone else around and not shoot me. The shooting stopped.

We pushed through a stand of mulga and saltbush, the smell of fresh blood and shit and cordite reminding me of the Transvaal. My senses straining at full alert, pulse racing, scanning every shadow, every movement for a lurking Boer. Felix held his nerve, going forward willingly, trusting that I knew what I was doing. We rounded a curve in the creek bed and came across a couple of hobbled horses, scrawny beasts with sad eyes, a scattering of fodder on the ground beside a cart. There was a campfire nearby with a billy, a couple of bedrolls and what looked like a full whisky bottle.

The cart was neatly piled high with dead dogs, their scalps and tails removed. Another cart stood nearby, with a load of fencing wire and posts. Two men came out of the scrub, rifles pointing at me, then they lowered them when they saw me. The same two men as on the Jong land, Gog and Magog from the edge of the unknown.

'Good morning.' I dismounted, to their surprise. I'd holstered my pistol but was aware of its weight on my hip.

'You looking for us?'

'Nope, just heard the shots and thought I'd take a look,' I said. 'Is it just dogs you're shooting?'

They looked at me, then walked away through the straggly scrub. I followed and found two massive mounds of dead kangaroos, the air thick with flies. In a fenced-in area lay the freshly bleeding corpses of a couple more dozen roos that'd been chased in there. Some of the dead animals had been skinned and then the skins pegged out to dry on the dirt. Both men were covered in stubble, with blood-smeared, sweat-stained shirts and weathered, bloodied faces.

There was a sudden movement in one of the piles of kangaroos. A joey emerged from its dead mother's pouch. One of the men climbed the pile of carcasses, grabbed the joey by the tail and then climbed back down, boots crushing skulls and paws. He held the struggling joey on the ground and with his other hand smashed the butt of his rifle into its head a couple of times until it stopped moving. Then he flung it back onto the pile.

The blood in my veins ran cold. It was them who'd killed the Kirkbrides, I knew it. Probably paid to kill them, along with Beavins. And then they killed Beavins to stop him talking.

'You was the trooper in Calpa,' one of them said softly, looking at me.

'I am the trooper from Calpa, currently suspended.'

'Fucked up, did yer?'

A brace of kookaburras burst out laughing, their merriment dying away on a bleak note. I sensed these two knew I was looking for them. Perhaps one of the men on Tindaree told them I'd asked Jim Crowther a while back.

'I'll be getting on, then,' I said, and walked back to my horse, expecting to get a bullet in the back at any moment. Felix and I got out of there as fast as we could. I was not going to tell them about the lamb and ewe killings, or that their employer wanted to see them, because I wanted them to stay put while I went for reinforcements. I had no handcuffs, no rope, no warrant and – without the element of surprise – no chance of subduing the pair of them.

Not much later, as I rode alongside the creek gully, I heard horses galloping. Turned in the saddle – Hirst and Shawcross riding at me. For a second I debated waiting to see what they wanted, but my body was telling me I already knew. I was out of uniform and an easy take. I spurred Felix on to a gallop. Heard a shotgun blast behind me. There was nothing and no one to come and help me.

We galloped for what seemed an eternity, the crack and thump of the odd bullet propelling me on. They were serious. Felix was grunting now, the effort causing him to foam up, but he'd do it, I knew he would, so I urged him on. Then a wallaby ran out on our left flank. Felix was up and I was down, falling, expecting to hit the soil of the veldt, waiting for the bayonet as I writhed breathless in the dust. They were closing in on me. My rifle was with my saddle and Felix was gone.

My only hope was to roll into the gully, let them get close and shoot them with my pistol. They'd seen where I came off and they'd see if I made a run for it. The gully was it. I rolled over the edge and fell further than I had estimated, landing badly on my thigh, which screamed in pain along with every other part of my body. I scrabbled to a crouch, heart pounding, hearing the rhythmic thud of horses getting closer and closer.

I saw a movement to my right, upstream. A naked man, old with a white beard. God come for me? Me in the future? What the hell? He gestured for me to join him. I scrambled, still crouching, towards him, keeping as low as I could, panting and on fire. He pointed to the bank. He'd lost his mind but I soon saw a dugout, a precarious cave hollowed out of the stony creek bed and redgum roots, and crawled in. A blanket, neatly folded, a billy, a few tins, a battered old Bible and a rifle. The God-bothering swaggie with one eye.

He took the rifle, put his finger to his lips and I heard him scrabble up the bank. The hooves got closer, until I heard panting horses, the jingle of bridles, the foul-mouthed bastards asking for me.

'Satan is behind ye, boys,' the old man said in a calm, cracked voice. 'Best to ride on before he gets to thee, for down ye will go into the spitting sulphur lakes of hell.'

Hirst and Shawcross laughed, told him to get out of the way or they'd shoot him.

'The sinners in Zion are afraid; trembling has seized the godless,' he pronounced. 'Who among us can dwell with the consuming fire? Who among us can dwell with everlasting burnings?'

I had my revolver in both hands, squatting at the mouth of the dugout, eyes on the bank above me, ready to shoot if they so much as dangled a filthy boot over the side.

'Why don't ya put some clothes on, you stinking old maggot?'

'Why don't thee repent? Go in peace and take the Lord's hand.'

They spoke in mumbles to one another, then one called out, 'Just wanted a word with you, Trooper.'

I heard them cock their rifles.

The old hermit started singing, 'O God, to whom revenge belongs, Thy vengeance now disclose.' A hymn I remembered droning at school. Plenty of smiting and cutting down. Hirst and Shawcross could just shoot him for a bit of peace. I had no idea why they didn't.

There was nothing more, the ever-present buzz of flies, then the sound of hooves moving away into the silence. The hermit slithered down the bank and joined me at the mouth to the dugout, waving the rifle. 'No bullets in it, but they don't know that.'

'Thank you, sir, you are very brave.'

''Tis the Lord, standing with me,' he said, shaking his old head. 'They'll come back. Satan likes to win. You get on through the scrub and follow the creek east down to the river. You'll come out a couple of miles south of the Larne punt. No more'n a half a day's journey.'

'You should come with me – they could come back and kill you.'

He raised both his arms. 'For he is the minister of God to thee for good. But if thou do that which is evil, be afraid; for he beareth not the sword in vain: for he is the minister of God, a revenger to execute wrath upon him that doeth evil.'

'Rightio ... thanks again.' I nodded and scrambled up the bank on the scrubby side, then looked back at the old man. He still had his arms raised.

285

I couldn't afford half a day. But to arrest them I needed more than just a revolver and harsh words. More pressing was the need to get the hell away from them quickly. It wasn't hot, but nor was it weather for walking over stony, hard ground with no compass and no water and no bloody horse.

~

I set off, keeping the gully to my left. The scrub tore at my clothes, my hands. The sun bored holes in my eyes and the grinding throb of a thousand insects drilled into my brain. The ground was littered with bleached bones and singed twigs, blackened leaves. A haze hung in the air, a smell of burning timber and something deeper, greasier, decaying.

Coming off Felix had dislodged something in my mind and I found myself looping around and around the memory of falling in South Africa, that long, slow instant between unseating and impact. The shock of the landing, air jolted from my lungs, the sudden fight to the death. I didn't like going back to that moment and yet was dragged there by the scruff of my neck, day and night. Then a bullet hit a tree trunk right next to me with a sudden thwack.

I dropped to the ground. They hadn't given up. Panicky, I checked my position. Back in the gulch was the only shelter. I slithered over, tearing my trousers and rolling over the edge, landing on my scarred shoulder, breathless at the pain, then I was up and crouching and running at the same time, tripping over bones and scree. Another bullet, the crack and whizz of it overhead. I heard their horses coming right at me.

I checked my revolver. Six shots. Maybe a hundred yards' range, but if they got that close it would be because I was dead.

I kept running, trying to keep my head low. No sound from them, just my own harsh panting, and the crows bickering over my soon-to-be corpse. After a while I peered over the top of the gully. Just flat plain and a shimmer in the distance. I scrabbled up, scanned the bleak plain. Nothing happened. Kept walking.

~

Thirst was a problem. When you get thirsty you're already drying up, and it took mental effort to keep from dwelling on it. I longed to lie down and soon just gave in to it, stretching out on the stony red soil with a grunt of relief.

At twenty I could shoulder my spear and shield and, like a hoplite running across the dark Homeric plain, go all day. At thirty-one, with the constant pain of injury sapping my stamina, plus years of drink under my belt, I was struggling. The shame of it. An officer drags his broken carcass forward into the enfilade, a joke on his lips, his last thoughts of his country as he lays himself on the altar.

I blocked the sun from my eyes with my arm. Any moment the call would come, '*Stand to your horses.*' Except I didn't have my horse. Sharp stones dug into my spine, flies clustered at my eyes, my nostrils. Ants appeared from all directions, small lizards twitched over the soil to see the spectacle. I sat up, swept them off me and noticed, lying nearby, a scattering of dead galahs, their vibrant pink breasts faded in death. So many it had to be a poisoning. The sky was bright and hard, no tears.

I got to my feet, wincing at the pain shooting down my side, squinting in the harsh light. A glass of beer, frothing at the rim, condensation on the glass. A waterbag of tepid tank water. I wouldn't lie down again. Fall, maybe, but not lie down. I'd submit to the sword of an implacable, cold-eyed Trojan warrior, but not a couple of scum-crusted doggers from Bugger Me North.

~

Towards dusk I had to stop. My headache was so bad it felt like someone was firing a Maxim gun into my skull. I couldn't see the creek gully in any direction and had no clue as to where I was. My watch was chained to a button on my tunic, which was hanging in the wardrobe at home, so I'd no hope of even the most rudimentary form of navigation. All I knew was west, and once the sun went I could go off course and end in a very tight spot. There was no shelter to be had and the air temperature was rapidly dropping. If the wind started up I'd be in for an unpleasant time.

In the dying light I saw, ahead of me, a half-stump of some dead tree. It was as welcome as a sturdy tent and I flopped down, leant against it, pulled my coat close and tried to doze. A smell of decay, greasy and foul, gusted past me now and then, noxious fumes of death almost making me gag. Got to my feet and looked around, and in the distance, on the starlit plain, I saw a haystack, a conical haystack like I'd once seen in a book of French paintings. Except the hay was black against the frosty, silver starlight.

I walked towards it, confused yet half-believing I had fallen into a painting. All around me lay blackened puddles and splatters on the pale, compacted clay. Paint splatters, surely. The painting book lay in my lap as I sat by the fire, and in the kitchen Mrs Baker was roasting lamb. The fireplace was smoking, clouds of grey smoke and singed hair and cooking meat.

The black hay took wing as I approached, sundering the smoke with harsh warning cries. The picture shifted to a pile of guts and skulls, bones, fur, intestines. In the grey flesh shredded by a thousand beaks I saw the lumpen bodies of wombats, of all things. Wallabies, paddymelons, emus, grey kangaroos, dingos, dogs, rictus mouths, open jaws, starlight glinting on teeth, empty eye sockets, viscera, tendons, all piled on a pyre of half-burnt mulga and belah. Wisps of smoke heavy with the stench of putrefaction floated around and rose above to the heavens, where God, accepting this sacrifice, would send back rain.

I turned and ran, slipping and slithering over the stones, an unnamed terror riding my shoulders, maddened by the smell of the grave, my throat and tongue coated with death, the grimacing creatures in pursuit. Stopping only when I felt the horror recede, I dropped down to the ground, exhausted. I must have fallen into a doze as the spectres of the dead danced in a starlit circle, Grace in the middle clapping her hands, the floppy white bow in her hair shining and bouncing to the rhythm, while the galahs, pink breasts modestly glowing, danced strip-the-willow with their partners, the bush ravens, those sober, solemn gentlemen of death.

~

I was woken by the usual dawn chorus, and a more reassuring sound I had yet to hear. My body ached, the scars cutting and scraping my flesh as if I were being skinned, my tongue and mouth dry and sandpapery. I got up and walked. Never saw the gully again but I kept walking away from the sun, because that way lay the Darling and I couldn't miss it.

By midday I was stumbling again, but I kept the sun behind me and towards dusk I saw a hut in the distance and made straight for it. Rusty galvanised iron and bark slabs fixed to rickety, unfinished timber and a metal door. In the wind, the bark slabs on the roof lifted and settled, whistling in the cracks like a mouth organ with only two notes.

A couple of scrappy acacias nearby, bent in the wind, a rope slung between the house and a forked sapling stuck in the ground and anchored by more rope. An infant's stained and yellow nappies flapped in the wind. Outside the shed, on a rough slab bench, stood a galvanised iron washtub with a wooden washboard sitting in the grey, greasy water. I wavered – drinkable? Washed nappies. No.

I called out, identifying myself. Never knew what mad bastard was in these huts. Had my hand on my sidearm. A thin child, possibly a boy, maybe around seven and wearing nothing but torn and filthy grey short pants and brandishing a sharpened stick, came to the doorway and told me to go away.

'Your mother or father home?'

He nodded, his lips cracked, dry snot caked around his nostrils, nose burnt bright red along with his cheeks. From inside the hut came the sound of small children grizzling. The boy lowered his sharp stick and I peered in, waiting for my eyes to adjust to the dim light. The air inside the shed was hot and fetid, sour milk, shit and dust.

A young woman sat at a rickety table, bodice open, nursing what looked like a skinned rabbit but was in fact a naked baby. No nappy, just its bony buttocks cradled in her hand. The mother's clothes were stained with what could have been blood from her split lip. Her golden hair, matted and knotted, had been scraped back from her weathered face and tied into some sort of knot. She looked up without interest. Two more infants, filthy faces, wild, matted fair hair, and both wearing cut-down flour bags as smocks, looked up at me. One of the children was cross-eyed. Each of them had one of their mother's knees and clung on for dear life.

'I'm sorry to disturb you ... I'm Constable Hawkins from Calpa.'

She nodded as she rocked back and forth. On the table stood an open tin of IXL blackberry jam, flies crawling around the jagged edge of the rim.

'May I have a drink of water?'

'Round the back.' She looked past me and out the door to nowhere.

I stepped outside. Two little girls, around four or five, both wearing cut-off flour bags, came pelting around the side of the shed, laughing and panting. Stopped dead when they saw me. Eyes wide, sunburnt, flaky skin.

'Don't be frightened, I'm just after a drink. Can you show me? Is there a tank?'

The taller one sniffed and wiped her hand across her nose. The smaller one clutched her sister, half-hiding behind her.

'Where's your father?'

'Pushin' the cart.'

I followed them around the back to a water tank up on stumps. Turned on the tap. A thin trickle of brown water fell in the dust. The water smelled of death. Some animal dead in the tank. There had to be another source of water.

'Is there a creek or something?'

The little girls stared at me. They looked like they had scurvy, not an uncommon disease out here. I dipped south and pulled out a sixpence and a few pennies and handed them to the eldest.

I left them and kept going in the direction they assured me the river lay in. Eventually I saw a human figure, a lone man in the distance where the scrub thinned out to paddocks, and made my way towards him. He was pushing a poison cart, a device that cut the ground into furrows and deposited poisoned grain into the soil. The rabbits would grub for the grain but the sheep wouldn't. The Romans sowed the fields of the conquered with salt. We used poisoned grain.

He looked at me, took his hat off, wiped his bald head with a handkerchief and then replaced his hat.

'G'day. I'm trying to get to Larne,' I said. 'Am I close?'

'That way, mebbe an hour,' he said, pointing east.

'Spare a drink?'

He handed me a waterbag and I sniffed at it, then drank as deep as was polite and handed it back, thanked him.

'You got a wife and six kids back that way?'

'Yeah – what about them?'

'I stopped there for a drink. Something in your tank.'

He sniffed, wiped his hand over his nose like his kid. All day pushing a poison cart for a hut, a pound of mutton and some cocky's joy.

The water made a hell of a difference and I hurried away. I kept going until I could smell the mighty, muddy Darling, and never has a smell been so welcomed. The last few miles were full of thoughts of a beer, cold and bitter, lots of beer gulped down with scarcely a swallow.

I saw the tree line and made for the punt. There was no paddle-steamer around and I had to rouse the punt man, the delightful Chips Grogan, from his comfortable seat, where he sat, arms folded, scowling at the river.

'Spose youse want to cross?'

'Yes, I do.'

'Don't spose you ride a young chestnut?' he said. 'Came running about with no master yesterday.'

'Yes, that's my horse. Where is he?'

'I took him across and give him to Trooper Parry. You'll have to pay for his crossing. I don't cross for nowt.'

'You'll have to send the account to the Bourke police.'

'The hell I will. You pay for yourself and your horse or you can't cross.'

'Listen, you miserable, lying bastard, you know who I am,' I said, taking a menacing step towards him. 'You take me across and send to Bourke for the money or I will do you for hindering a mounted trooper in the course of his work. And I'll take great pleasure in it.'

He glared at me, hesitated for a minute and then decided better of it. I got on the punt and he clambered into his boat and rowed across the river, towing the punt. Would have been less fuss to just take me in his little boat. But he was the punt man, and by crikey he'd pull his bloody punt across the Styx if he had to.

I hurried into town to the station, found the water tank out the back and filled my stomach fit to burst, then washed my face, splashing the water about, reluctant to leave the stream of clear bliss. I went inside and found Parry.

'Couple of blokes shooting roos to the west, Jack Hirst and Toby Shawcross, doggers on Tindaree, they shot at me,' I said. 'We need to bring them in.'

'Thought something had happened to you. Got your horse out the back, the chestnut.'

'And you didn't think to ride out and look for me?'

'Yeah, I would have, but now you've turned up.'

'Some old swaggie who lives in the creek bed stopped them with religion.'

'Yeah, that'd be Digby Doolan. Naked? Yeah, that's him. Uses the scriptures like a fucking mallet.'

'I can't order you, but I think apprehending these two is an urgent matter.'

'I'd like to be of assistance, mate, but as you say, you're suspended. And they done nothing wrong. Shooters shooting on the property they're licensed to shoot on.'

'They aren't licensed to shoot me, for fuck's sake.'

'Yeah, but you don't know for sure they were shooting at you, do yer.'

Parry was the perfect trooper for out here – not much between the goalposts and lazy to boot. I had no money for food or beer and the Larne publican didn't do credit, no matter who you were. Nothing for it but the long ride back to Calpa.

25

It was around eleven when I got back. I had to cool Felix down, brush him, feed and water him, but what I really wanted to do was eat and then fall on my bed. Lonergan was still up, the light glowing from the kitchen. I pulled a bottle of beer from the meat safe, flipped the lid and drank. No beer ever tasted so good.

'Gus, mate, where you been?' Lonergan said, coming to the back door. 'Thought you was dead.'

I pushed past him, went to the stove, lifted the lid on the pan – congealed mutton stew – found a spoon and just shovelled it in. The other pot had some rice and I ripped into that as well.

'Tom Fletcher's gone missing,' Lonergan said.

I mumbled, mouth full of food.

'His father came here, wants us to search for him. But I waited for you.'

'I've found them,' I said, swallowing.

'Who?'

'Shawcross and Hirst. Doggers from Tindaree. The men who left the dance early with Beavins – the men who killed him, killed the Kirkbrides and killed Albert Jong too, probably.'

'I know 'em, filthy pigs, both of them. Came in here while you were away with a brace of dog scalps wanting their money. I paid 'em and they left but you couldn't get the stink out of the station for another day.'

'I have to arrest them,' I said, scraping at the rice. 'Or you do, you and Parry.'

'No way am I going near those two. Anyway, an order's come through for me. There's a boxing troupe setting up their tent in Larne. First night tomorrow. Jackie Mack and his Muscle Men. Me and Parry have been ordered up there to keep the peace.'

I sighed with relief as the food hit the spot and just kept shovelling it in until I was sated. Then I wiped my mouth and sat down for a cigarette and another beer, feeling like a new man.

'No man around will miss a boxing troupe,' I said. 'Hirst and Shawcross will turn up and we'll be waiting.'

'And Tom Fletcher?'

'First thing in the morning, we'll go out and look around.'

I made straight for my bed, took off my filthy clothes and crawled under the blankets with a groan.

~

All hands on Gowrie Station were off marking lambs. A maid showed us around the corner of the homestead to the verandah, where Mrs Fletcher sat with her view of the verdant station vegetable and flower gardens, bees and butterflies busy with spring blooms. She was knitting – a baby's jacket, by the look of it. Sally Gilmour sat with her, stitching what looked like buttercups onto a piece of pale-blue linen.

'Oh, Captain Hawkins, thank goodness you've come,' Mrs Fletcher said, putting her knitting aside. 'Tom's gone.'

'When did you see him last?'

While she spoke, I noted it all down in my notebook. 'Tom's tough,' I said. 'He knows this land like the back of his hand. And I assume he's taken water with him?'

'I think so. But I suspect he's not lost ... I fear ...'

'Hard not to, but chances are he'll turn up right as rain. Just gone off to get his thoughts in order, most likely. We'll set Trooper Garnet on it today. Tom's on his usual horse?'

'Yes, the big black. But nobody saw him leave, it's just that his horse is gone too.'

'Right, we'll get back to you when we have something.'

'What if he's gone to Queensland?'

'We'll wire Quilpie and Cunnamulla, tell them to keep a look out for him,' Lonergan said. 'They'll pass it up the line.'

Sally Gilmour turned her languid gaze on Lonergan.

Mrs Fletcher, worry written all over her face, looked away at the stands of deep green, crinkled silverbeet, bamboo tripods covered in vines heavy with yellow blossom, rows of cucumber plants, all of it neat and regular. 'He's all I have,' she murmured.

Miss Gilmour, her face impassive, eyes downcast, startled when I said I wanted a word with her in private. We went to the end of the verandah. She smoothed her skirt, tucked some hair behind her ear.

'Miss Gilmour, the men who killed Archie Beavins have not been apprehended, and until they are I advise you to stay close to the homestead. Don't go to the laundries, the stables, anywhere.'

For once she lost that knowing look and fear crept into those pretty eyes.

'But what would they want with me? I haven't done anything.'

'Neither had the Kirkbride sisters.'

She nodded, swallowed and looked around, then went back to Mrs Fletcher. I hated to think what Hirst and Shawcross would do to her. I left a scribbled note to Henry Peyton and Will Fletcher saying that until further notice they should challenge anyone who was on their land or near the homestead who was not a Gowrie employee, even if they knew them. Left it with Miss Fletcher and told her the same thing. Hirst and Shawcross were cunning, like the wild dogs they killed, and they couldn't afford to have both me and Sally Gilmour alive.

~

We left the homestead and continued on to the Garnet camp. 'You go out with Wilson,' I said to Lonergan. 'Do you good to take charge. Got your maps sorted, now you can put it to practice.'

'What are you gunna do?'

'I'm suspended, remember.'

'I thought Tom Fletcher was a mate?'

The truth was I was worn out by my traipse through the Tindaree badlands. I wanted to be anywhere but here. I wanted to be back in the gentle, green pastures of the Monaro, where I grew up, snow gums in blossom, towns with well-fed and cheerful occupants, rose arbours and orchestras in pavilions on a Sunday afternoon and girls in pretty dresses and parasols, the dead swiftly whisked away, bakeries and daily papers, fruit barrows and dogs, just for the sake of their joyful eyes and comforting presence.

'And we got the boxing tonight,' Lonergan said, dragging me back to the brutal moment.

'That's the mounted trooper's job – months of talking to yourself and then days of frantic activity. You'll be right with Wilson, may even find Tom. Just do what we did for Beavins. I'll ask around town, the punt man, Kev and the rest. Knock off in time to eat and we'll go up to Larne together.'

~

A drumbeat, deep and dangerous, announced the appearance of the boxers. The area was lit by flickering torches, men shoved to get close to the front, boys stood open-mouthed as the boxers clad in bright satin shorts swaggered onto the stage in front of the crowd and looked out with menace. They flexed their arms and puffed their chests out, giving off an aura of power and dominance. Jackie Mack stood to the side, shouting at the crowd, listing each fighter's virtues, his ability to go six rounds and never falter. Half the fighters were black, the other half just the usual mongrel white. Every man who could walk was here. When entertainment like this came to town, you didn't yawn and stay home with a book.

'Who'll have a go?' Mack shouted. 'Five pounds to the man who can go three rounds with one of these gentlemen. Come on, who'll take a glove? You, sir, you've got the right look in your eye.'

He was addressing me. Men turned and looked. I was tall but not brawny, despite my woodchopper's shoulders, but I could make up for that with attitude. It'd be a fight worth seeing, a disgraced trooper taking on some disgruntled local he'd roughed up. But I'd made a spectacle of myself many times before, outside pubs and brothels, before I went back into uniform, and had nothing to prove.

Mack was good, I had to give him that. He was stirring the men up, playing on rivalries, playing on fear of the blacks, playing on hatred of whites. Shows like this never put two blacks together – you got more aggression with white versus black, and more aggression meant a better show. Then a man shouted he'd have a go. Mack invited him onto the stage and it was Tom Fletcher. We'd spent hours looking for him and the fool turned up here.

A roar went up from the crowd, like a wild beast. Men shouted, punched the air, screamed insults, spittle flying. They surged and pushed against each other, jostling to get a better view. I had to stop Tom and tried to push my way through to the front. A giant fat bloke with his trousers held up by ragged roo-skin suspenders blocked the way. His bald head shone with sweat.

'Let me through – that's my mate,' I yelled.

'Fuck off,' he snarled, shoving me until I fell back against another man, who pushed me forward again. The giant turned and bared what was left of his teeth. I felt myself pulled back by some unseen hand and a voice hissed in my ear: 'Don't fuck with him, mate.' The giant now had his back to the stage and glared at me, his massive arms held apart from his body. I melted back into the crowd, my place filling by stinking eager punters.

I raced around the back of the tent and found my way barred by a burly slab of a man. His fist was a round of solid wood, somehow attached to his arm. He held it up and I stepped back.

'I must speak to Mr Mack, immediately,' I panted.

'Fuck off, or I'll fuck you off meself, and you'll be spittin' yer teeth out for a week if I do that, matey.'

I was fond of my teeth, and Lonergan and Parry were sitting on their horses somewhere, minds idling, so I took a step back.

'Mack will be breaking the law if he lets that man fight. Just let me warn him.'

The muscle blinked as the thought battled its way through the thickets, then he lumbered off and returned with Mr Mack. He was a small, nuggety man, like an Irish bookie, all scarlet waistcoat, green satin coat and a nose that had been smeared across his face a few times.

'State your business.'

'That man, Tom Fletcher, is on bail. He fights, he'll go to prison.'

'What did he do?' Mack asked, eyes lighting up with professional curiosity.

'Killed a man with one punch. You don't want to be getting involved in what could be a nasty court case, one that goes looking for licences and the like, do you?'

'Who the fuck are you?'

'Mounted trooper. Senior Constable Augustus Hawkins, Calpa, currently suspended.'

Mack threw back his head and laughed loud and long.

'I may be suspended but I arrested Fletcher,' I went on, 'and I will be called to give evidence. And trust me, I will blacken your name whenever and wherever I can.'

He gave me a sly look. 'You don't sound like a trap – sound like a man with a few quid, more 'n likely. Tell you what, you pay me what his fight will earn, and you can have him. Thirty quid. Now. In cash.'

'As if anyone would come to this cesspit with thirty quid on them. No, you tell him he can't fight, and his father will pay you tomorrow.'

Mack shook his nuggety head. 'My sources tell me Tom Fletcher is on the nose with the workers on his old man's farm. Lotta them here tonight, see? The crowd is building.'

He was right. Gowrie men were coming out of the flickering shadows, trying to get into the tent or standing around the bookie.

'I'll fight, instead of him,' I said. 'Defrocked local trooper, a greenskin who's put a few noses out of joint over the years. I can put on a good show.'

'I'll bet you can, but he's angrier than you are and he's ready. Watch the show from the wings if you like. Maybe you'll decide you want to go on next.'

I tried to argue but he stepped away. The crowd was roaring now, angry and unpredictable. Soon they'd be swinging punches at the man beside them if the show didn't start. I went back inside the tent. Tom emerged in a black satin pair of boxing shorts, gloves on and a hard look on his face. His opponent was a blackfella, tall and lean and almost pure muscle. What he didn't have in weight he'd make up for in speed and fury.

When the fighting started, the crowd roared, and when the blood splattered on them they roared even louder. They screamed and shook, spittle flying through the thickened air, the sweaty stench, the shadows on the tent wall. It was electrifying.

But I couldn't watch anymore. It was almost like watching myself, blinded by fury and pain, like Tom, ready to strike out at life, at all the failed promises, disappointments and horrors of existence. Fight them until you were knocked senseless and didn't have to feel anymore.

Outside, in the flickering flame light, it felt like we could be anywhere and it would be the same, men bashing men in the light of a fire, women in the shadows, waiting to mate with the victor. *Cupiditas aeterna*, or so it seemed.

Parry and Lonergan were on horseback, just giving that hint to the punters that while this may feel like a wild barbarian rite, the sober-minded New South Wales government was never far away, and was more than ready to slam the first unruly man to the ground and put a boot on his neck.

I knew it would just be a matter of time before some resentful stockman from Gowrie dobbed Tom in, and then Lonergan and Parry would have no choice but to put him in the cells. I wanted no part in it and went looking for a drink.

I could see the lights of Larne in the west, small buildings crouched low and huddled against the river. As I looked around for a tent selling beer, I noticed how most men were drunk and argumentative, their girls trying to pull them away from the usual flare-ups. It was pretty much like the dance, except there was no dancing, no supper – nothing at all for the women except a break in the routine.

In the outer rings orbiting the main attraction were two-up rings, cockfighting rings, women selling homemade gidgee that would strip the lining of your stomach, blacks drunk, whites drunk, abusing one another, the black women stumbling and falling, too drunk to move. Plenty of opportunity for exercising the law, but Parry and Lonergan stayed mounted, overseeing it all as the shadows of the dancing flames flickered across their impassive faces.

I felt something against my back and realised it was a gun.

'See them trees over there? Walk straight and steady or I'll shoot you.'

The breath that carried the voice smelled of burning corpses. I had a feeling it was Hirst or Shawcross. Lonergan was looking the other way. I had to do what this man wanted. This was going to end badly.

26

Waiting in the darkness by the clump of mulga was the other one, Hirst or Shawcross, both of them interchangeable brutes. Then one of them called softly to the other. Hirst was the one with the gun in my back. Fear swarmed through me, furious bees, sending my pulse racing and nausea surging around my guts. I felt a hand reach around and take my revolver from its holster.

'Kill me and you'll be in trouble,' I said with a conviction I didn't have.

I got a thump across the ear. The three of us walked east under the brilliant stars, crunching across the dirt, snapping twigs, heading into nowhere. Bones shone in the starlight. Small animals scuttled away, sensing predators on the move. The gun poking in my back nudged me along. They were going to do me like they'd done Beavins. Bash my skull in then drop me into a shallow grave. I'd walked in the valley of the shadow before – I didn't like it then and I didn't like it now.

'Got some whisky?' I asked.

Hirst grunted.

'Give a man his last drink and a fag. Only fair.'

Another grunt. We stumbled on. I had no idea where we were as the landscape between Larne and Cobar was pretty featureless. At some signal I failed to see, they both stopped. Shawcross pulled a bottle of whisky out of a pocket in his coat, took the cork out and handed it to me. The time had come.

I took a sip and we shared the bottle around like participants in some ancient ritual, preparing to cross the border from life to death. A sweat broke out beneath my clothes despite the cold night.

Shawcross took a length of rope and tied my hands behind me. At this point I was keen to see Lonergan galloping in all guns blazing, but he probably had no idea where I was.

'Why?' I asked to prolong the moment.

Hirst shrugged. ''Cause you ask too many questions.'

'Did you kill Albert Jong?'

They both picked up their rifles. I clenched my tied fists. Heart pounding like a piston. The laughter and ruckus of the boxing carried through the still night, along with the howls of wild dogs and dingoes. Nothing around us but stony plains.

'Why didn't you bash Jong like Beavins and the Kirkbrides?'

'He were a mad fucker.'

So they had killed him, killed all of them. A useful snippet of information to glean as I headed towards infinity, put it in the eternal in-tray for God to sort out.

'On your knees.'

That I would not do.

'On your knees, I said,' Hirst snarled.

I held back the urge to vomit, to shit myself, to run, but said, with all the sangfroid I could muster, 'Are you aware of how bad you smell?'

He smashed at me with the rifle butt, straight into my gut, and I doubled over, trying to breathe. Shawcross hit my head, and as I hit the dirt I kicked out at Hirst's shins and brought him down with me. Cursing like a bullocky, he tried to get to his feet, but I kept kicking him. Shawcross fell about laughing, the stupid bastard.

I rolled about in the dirt and got to a standing position, panting and backing away as fast as I could. Hirst was cursing Shawcross for laughing and so Shawcross bashed him with his rifle butt in the face, again and again. I ran at Shawcross, giving him the full force of a rugby tackle, still with arms tied, and we both hit the ground. His rifle went flying. I had him pinned beneath me and brought my knee up into his balls as hard as I could. He screamed and flailed at me with his fists, but I managed to get myself upright. Ignoring his blows, I sat on his guts and stamped the heel of my boot into his face until he was as still as Hirst.

Panting and a bit wild, I looked around for the next bastard to come at me. But they were both out to it. I stayed by them, trying to work my hands free, rubbing the rope against a sharp rock. By the time I got the ropes off, Hirst was coming to. I had my fists now, so I straddled him and gave him a few punches until he was out.

It was tempting to beat the two of them to death. But that wasn't the job. I'd caught them and coerced them, so now I was to hand them on to a judge who'd place a black cloth on his head and refer them to the hangman. Weeks or months to contemplate the flames of hell. It was unlikely they were believers, but one could hope.

There was no more rope, so I kept an eye on Hirst. I got their rifles, emptied the ammunition, emptied their pistols, stashed them in a pile and looked around. Nothing and nobody for miles.

I went through their pockets and found their fags and some matches, so I sat in the bright starlight smoking, waiting, trying to think through the whisky and knocks. My head pounded like a miner's bell and I could have drunk the river dry. I closed my eyes.

I was falling from my horse, hitting the veldt, too winded to keep a tight hold of my rifle with its fixed bayonet. It happened so quickly, the transfer from my hands to the Boer. I had to get it back and yet I couldn't see through the blood. I remembered I had a pistol on my hip and quickly used it, firing into his guts at close range, his blood spattering over me as he fell, dead, onto his precious veldt. It happened so quickly and so slowly, and when the medics came for me I kept going on about the rifle. I wanted them to find it and give it back to me, insisted on it, flailing around until they knocked me out with morphine.

Next thing I knew, I was being kicked awake.

A rifle butt was held aloft over me, the man silhouetted against the brilliant stars. A shuddering thump of alarm hit my chest. *Here it comes.* In that long moment, I thought of my father. I would never see him again and he would never know what became of me.

Before I could even raise my arms to protect myself, I heard shouts, rifle shots, horses pounding the ground as they galloped out of the darkness. Shawcross and Hirst ran, when their best defence would have been to stay calm, take a knee and shoot the oncoming horses.

Lonergan, howling like some otherworldly Irish banshee, was leading. He hurtled past me, followed by Parry thundering through clouds of dust, and then Felix, going for his life, trailing a lead rein. Lonergan and Parry rode their horses parallel at the two men, tripping them with a rope suspended between them.

I got to my feet and watched as the troopers jumped off their horses, wrangled Hirst and Shawcross to the ground and cuffed them. I whistled to Felix, who trotted over, relieved to find me in the middle of what must have seemed yet another incomprehensible human debacle.

'Gus, mate,' Lonergan cried, running over to me, panting and shining with sweat. 'You all right?'

'Yes, thankfully,' I said, relieved. 'That was a nice bit of work there, Trooper. You too, Parry.'

'Thank you, sir.'

'Bit of fun, eh?'

'Yeah, it was,' Lonergan said, panting, hands on hips.

We both laughed. That hairy little paddy was a bloody hero.

'Listen, did you pick up Tom Fletcher?'

Parry and Lonergan glanced at each other.

'Yeah, poor bugger,' Lonergan said. 'Did some damage to the other fella, all right, and good thing we stopped the fight when we did. But yeah, broke his bail so he's in the Larne cells.'

'Who told you?'

'Some fella called Clarence Hooker,' Lonergan said. 'Tom'll have these two for company now.'

'No. They can't be together. Parry, you go back and wire Bourke urgently for a police van and extra troopers, and bring them out here to take charge of these two. Ask for another pair of troopers to escort Tom into town.'

'Why not put them in the same van?'

'Because these two killed Tom's girl, and I wouldn't put it past them to tell him while they're rumbling up the river, and then more than likely there'll be nobody left alive in the van by the time they get to Bourke.'

~

Lonergan stayed with me while Parry rode back to town to make the arrangements. We stood and looked down at the two men as they stirred and then we gave them some water, and Lonergan formally arrested them. They were bloodied and knocked about and none too happy.

'You did well to take on both of them,' Lonergan said.

'Look at their blotchy skin and teeth – they've got scurvy,' I said. 'Live on flour, roo meat and whisky. Not hard to take down a man with scurvy. Just like I told you, a well-fed trooper is an effective trooper.'

We took the saddles off our horses and used them to rest against while we waited for the van to come, smoking and staring at the stars as the wild dogs and dingos circled, smelling blood and looking for opportunity. We had to shoot over their heads a couple of times when they got too close.

'Tempting to let the dogs do their worst, get their own back,' Lonergan said.

'Tempting, but it's the worst thing a trooper could do. You just can't make it personal, no matter what.'

I'd have enjoyed smashing their faces to pieces in the name of Nessie Kirkbride. I'd do it and not give it a second thought. But the uniform – even though I was suspended, the uniform had its code.

'How did you know where to look for me?' I asked.

'Polly, the barmaid from Larne, came running up and said she was real frightened for you. Said she saw Jack Hirst marching you away into the bush. Took her bloody time telling us, but.'

'Good old Polly, eh?'

'When I realised they'd got you, I couldn't think straight. Parry just stood there useless. Polly started on, screaming at us to do something, so I got Felix and we just galloped in the direction she said and then we saw them. I knew Parry had a rope and I told him, I said, "This is what we're gunna do – give me one end of the rope and keep the horses parallel, or it'll be arse over tit," then I started yelling to make 'em run and we got the bastards.'

'Got them before they killed me, and nicely done too.'

'When Martin stationed me at Calpa with you,' Lonergan said, 'jeez, I was windy about it. But I've learnt more from you about being a trooper since I've been here than in my training or two years in Bourke.'

'Good coffee, mate, that's what a trooper runs on,' I said.

'Decent food,' he replied.

'Routine.'

'Good spelling.'

I laughed at that one. 'Grammar too, don't forget.'

We continued compiling our list until he nodded off. I looked over at him, dead to the world, mouth open, sleeping the deep sleep of an uncomplicated man. The chill of the ground rose through my bones, and even the knowledge that I could have been in that ground couldn't stop the envy igniting in my chest as I thought of the life Mick looked forward to with his Ada, a life straight and true.

~

A van arrived in the early morning and took Hirst and Shawcross off to Bourke. I straggled into Larne. Lonergan turned south and went back to Calpa to mind the shop, and Parry parked himself back behind the counter of his station to count the flies. I sent the van ahead to Bourke and said I'd be along as soon as I'd seen the doctor. I kept finding fresh blood on my face and had to have somebody look at it.

Joe was the only doctor I had any time for, after years of being prodded and poked and seen as a medical oddity. That I survived the bayonet attack was down to youth and luck – no secret there. But white coats sometimes brought out the shakes in me, and now I had to work hard at controlling myself, particularly as I'd been up most of the night, been bashed and my nerves were still in repel-the-threat formation.

Fortunately, Dr Tierney couldn't give a shit and was only interested in looking at a laceration on my forehead and how many stitches it needed. He reeked of brandy, his breath almost making my head spin as he hummed and hawed. I was not happy having stitches in my head; my pulse raced and I wanted to throw up. Couldn't even stand haircuts usually.

the Kirkbrides and they replied because he was mad. Thereby confessing to the Beavins and Kirkbride murders.'

'That won't hold up in court as a confession,' Corcoran said. 'We need more.'

'Why did you assume Albert Jong killed himself?' Martin asked.

'He was naked except for his mum's apron and with a rifle in his hands. It looked like he'd shot himself but that's what I was expecting to find so I didn't pursue it. Now we question them about Beavins and the Kirkbrides.'

'But the Kirkbride killers are in Queensland,' Martin said. 'We know that – they found the Kirkbride leather holdall.'

'We don't know it, we assume it,' Corcoran said. 'Kirkbride could have been mistaken about the bag.'

A clerk knocked on the door, then opened it and said, 'You're needed downstairs, sir.'

'Important?'

'The mayor, sir, asking about the arrests.'

'I'll be back in a minute,' Corcoran said, leaving Martin and me staring at each other. The stench of mutual loathing filled the office; at some random signal it could quickly turn into a right old collie shangles.

'There is evidence that the killers went to Queensland,' Martin began. 'That gets up your nose, I know, and so you've constructed this whole mad tale and inserted yourself in the centre of it to cover for your failings.'

'I know you burnt the victims' clothes when you were supposed to retain them as evidence,' I countered.

'Ever the know-it-all, aren't you, Hawkins,' he said. 'Let me ask you this: do you have children?'

'Is that a rhetorical question?'

'I don't know how many bastards you've sired, and I daresay you don't either,' he smirked. 'But let me tell you, to lose three of your children to murder is one of the cruellest blows a parent can suffer. I have four children and—'

'I know, the Kirkbrides have suffered, but—'

'I did what Kirkbride asked because he and Mrs Kirkbride have been – and still are – in hell. I know it was wrong, but it was for the right reasons. You go stirring this up again and it goes to trial, they will have to relive the whole thing, including Miss Flora, who is in no state to cope with it. All the terrible details of the way they died will come out.'

'You can't just pervert the course of justice because people are hurting,' I said, thinking of the thruppence love token I'd held back because I'd wanted to solve the crime. 'You can't let these killers get away with it.'

'But we aren't,' Martin said. 'They have confessed to Jong's murder. Gaol for life or a hangman's noose, and the Kirkbrides are left alone. There's justice done.'

I realised he didn't know Grace had been pregnant, or that she'd had an abortion and was dying when she was shot. Flora must have told her parents on the Sunday morning, while they were still in Cobar – told them where Jimmy, Nessie and Grace had gone and why. It would have been horror heaped on horror for Janet and Robert Kirkbride. They, somewhere in that nightmare of pain, found the strength to try to cover up the pregnancy and abortion. Kirkbride told Martin to burn the clothes and apply for a stay of autopsy on Grace due to her age. And Martin did it because he felt sorry for them.

A trial would bring out all these details. If Kirkbride felt he was grist for the gawpers now, wait until they got the details of Grace's rape and pregnancy, the illegal botched abortion, the rape and mutilation of Nessie. The population would be transfixed, and King Kirkbride would topple into the dust, his family a byword for immorality and shame, an Ozymandias left broken in the sands.

Unfortunate? Yes. But I needed everyone to know I had atoned for my sin. I had found the Kirkbride killers and caught them, and they would be put to trial, sentenced and hanged, and I would be exonerated, my honour redeemed.

Corcoran came back into the room and settled behind his desk. 'Where were we?'

'The Kirkbride case is closed, and we charge them with the only murder we have evidence for, and that is of Albert Jong,' Martin said.

Corcoran slammed the desk with his fist. 'No. Hawkins has made a good case. We'll bring in Sally Gilmour for questioning and then we have our witness.'

I took a deep breath and thought of Flora, struggling with grief, her grip on life tenuous. She'd been through enough and would never recover if a scandal blew up.

'We got the killers and we can lock them up. Best result for the district,' I said, avoiding Corcoran's eyes. 'And we don't have to recall the detectives.'

Fed up, Corcoran shook his head, sighed. 'All right, the shooting death of Albert Jong it is. Is he still where you buried him?'

'I expect so.'

'Right, you'll need to talk to the Jong family about an exhumation before we send the official request.'

~

Shawcross and Hirst had been in solitary cells all night, fed and briefed by the lawyer so they knew what the charge was, but had not seen each other since being locked up. We all crowded into the stuffy interview room, Martin and me, one suspect, the solicitor and a stenographer. They perched on rickety chairs, as did we. There was a scarred and worn pine table between us and a high-barred window above, and all of us were armed with notebooks and files, except for the prisoner, cocky and defiant, but handcuffed.

We began with Hirst, the one with the gold signet ring and the stubble like a burnt wheatfield. Up close, the deep lines around his eyes were visible, the whites of his eyes yellowing already from a life in the sun. The breath on him could fell a dog at twenty paces. To be in a small, airless room with him was a feat of endurance.

'Shawcross done it,' he said as soon as we were settled.

Martin looked at me. The solicitor whispered something in Hirst's ear and Hirst shoved him away with his shoulder.

'Done what, exactly?' I asked.

'Beavins. Beavins, Jong and the three Kirkbrides too.'

The stenographer wrote it down word for word. Martin, the solicitor and I all exchanged looks. But I pressed on, because who was I to prevent these charming fellows from confessing their sins?

'You had nothing to do with it?'

'Nope. Tried to stop him.'

'Tell us exactly what happened with the Kirkbrides,' Martin said.

'We was at the dance and there wasn't much going on. Beavins is all angry when Jimmy Kirkbride turns up, says he wants to teach him a lesson. We say, "Come drinking with us instead." So we rode back towards Calpa, found a place by the river and shared a bottle. Beavins kept checking the road—'

I looked up from my notebook. 'Your horses?'

'With us.'

'Go on.'

'He comes running back through the scrub saying, "It's him, Jimmy Kirkbride, are you with me?" Shawcross'll be in anything violent, so they run off. Next thing I hear a gunshot and I run after 'em and I see the young girl's dead, so's Jimmy Kirkbride, and they're taking turns with Nessie Kirkbride. Then when they're done Shawcross kills her with his rifle butt.'

'Did you try to stop him?' Martin asked.

'Shawcross is a mean bastard, you don't want to stop him when he's got the taste of blood. I panicked, ran off into the bush, and then I ran back to them because I knew I was a dead man if I didn't stick with Toby. Spent the next day arguing about what to do, then we agreed to act like nothing happened, or that we didn't know.'

I took a deep breath, exhaled slowly, put down my pen. Fucking animals.

'You could have come to the police with this information,' Martin said.

'And you would have protected me from them two?'

'You'd have been in a cell, Mr Hirst, where they couldn't get you.'

'What about the money Beavins had?' I asked.

Hirst came over all sly. 'He was paid to get at Jimmy. Paid to knock him around. Told us this the next day, the bastard. Shawcross wanted half the money, but Beavins said nope. So Shawcross killed him.'

'Buried him alive?'

Hirst shrugged.

'Who paid to have Jimmy beaten?' Martin asked.

'Not saying – not unless you can make this go away for me. I done nothing.'

Martin and I left the room to confer. I was way out of my depth. I was catch and coerce, not plea bargains. Corcoran was called down and we conferred in the narrow hallway.

'We need to recall the detectives to do this properly,' I said.

'Do you believe him?' Martin asked me.

'We'll have to question Shawcross. He'll probably say it was Hirst who did it, but it's on the record now so let's move forward with it.'

Martin ummed and ahhed. 'The case is closed.'

'You heard their confessions,' Corcoran said. 'I say the case is open again. I'll deal with Sydney and whatever tripe they want to bung on. Go and interview the other man, see what he says.'

Corcoran went to wire the detectives and Martin and I looked at each other.

'They'll go through all the evidence again, and the statements,' he said, the colour draining from his face.

'You better pray that they plead guilty so there's no trial.'

'I was just helping a friend, that's all.' The consequences of Martin's actions filtered through that calcified brain of his like groundwater into a dark cave, poor bastard. 'I'll lose my job. I've got four kids. I just did as he asked. I thought there was no chance of catching the killers.'

'Come on,' I sighed. 'Let's go back in, see what Shawcross has to say.'

28

As expected, Shawcross blamed Hirst and both blamed Beavins, but my job was done. I went out the back to the cells to see Tom. He was sitting on the rough wooden bench, arms folded, rough grey wool blanket in a heap on the floor. Above him, set high in the whitewashed wall, was a small, barred window through which the bright blue sky could be glimpsed. The cell was hot and stuffy, and it would only get worse as the day wore on, but he seemed oblivious to all discomfort, even the swollen bruises and lacerations on his face.

'Your father been out to see you?'

He shook his head. 'Sent word not to bother.'

'We've caught two of the three men responsible for the murders of Nessie, Grace and James.'

His sullen expression dissolved and he looked up at me, almost the old Tom. 'Two? Where's the third?'

'Archie Beavins. He's dead.'

He jumped up from the bench and slapped the wall. 'That fucker! Walking around like butter wouldn't melt in his mouth, and all the time he knew what he'd done. Told me straight to my face what Pearson said about Nessie all the while knowing he'd killed her. Who are the others?'

'Jack Hirst and Tobias Shawcross, doggers from Tindaree.'

His legs suddenly gave way and he sat heavily on the bench again.

'I'll send for your father,' I said. 'You need to see him.'

'No,' he said, shaking his head slowly, tears trickling unchecked.

'He's had a great loss too, mate. He knows what it's like,' I said.

'He's going to have to forfeit the bail money. Half the value of one year's clip, at least.'

I rubbed my beard, shifted my weight. 'He'll get over it.' Did fathers get over their sons' misdemeanours and ill fortune?

Tom snorted. 'Why didn't you let me at them? I'd rather go to prison for killing them than Pearson.'

'Because this way they'll hang and you'll keep living,' I said.

'That's what you call this?'

I waited, hoping to find some words of comfort in my addled brain, but none came, except the underwhelming, 'You'll more than likely go on remand to Bathurst Gaol.'

He raised his head and stared at me, then shrugged.

~

327

It was noted that I had done the legwork and that Lonergan and Parry had assisted in the arrest. Handshakes and good cheer all round for the mounted troopers of the Bourke District, drinks on the house at the local for any member of the traps, local scribblers breathless with excitement, pictures in the paper.

We were shabby and underfunded, but we'd done what those city dicks could not or would not, and Corcoran, despite the pressure to leave the case well alone, was a happy man. I was commended, as well as recommended for promotion. I thought promotion was going a bit far, but naturally did not object, humility not being one of my strengths.

As to who paid to have Jimmy Kirkbride beaten up – that was a seam to be mined by someone else. It could have been any man in the district who'd lost his girl to Jimmy's smile and swagger.

Beavins, Hirst and Shawcross had killed the three Kirkbrides, but a question still gnawed at me, despite the cheers and clinking glasses, the backslapping and laughter: who the hell had raped Grace Kirkbride and started the awful train of events?

~

A couple of days later, Arthur Baines came back to Calpa, without Denning, and parked himself in the Royal again. I bought him a beer once he'd settled in.

'You ride down?'

'Nah, got the train to Bourke and a paddle-steamer was going down here. A bloke from the police prosecutor came with me to make sure we don't stuff it up. He stayed in Bourke.'

'You interviewed Hirst and Shawcross?'

'Yeah. Couple of mangy mongrels they are too. Doesn't matter which one of them did the killings, because they were both complicit and they'll both hang. Not that I told them that.'

'Did they tell you who paid Beavins to kill Jimmy?'

'You're not going to believe this, but they reckon Sally Gilmour did,' he said. 'But where does a nurse get a hundred pounds, and why would she spend it on having a man killed?'

'Sally Gilmour? Bloody hell. I suspected she knew more than she was saying – at least, I think I did.'

'Going out to Gowrie Station tomorrow to ask her a few questions,' Baines said, and slapped an order on the table. 'You're to come as my second.'

~

Will Fletcher didn't want any part of it. He wouldn't let us interview his wife as she was a bedridden invalid and knew nothing about affairs outside the house. Miss Gilmour was no longer in their employ.

'I'm sorry, Mr Fletcher,' I said. 'But your wife spent her days with Sally Gilmour and she may well know something important.'

'My sister, Miss Fletcher,' he said gruffly, 'will sit in on the interview. It's not proper to have two strange men in my wife's room alone with her.'

Mrs Fletcher's room was large, light and airy, with open French doors and sheer lace curtains billowing softly in the breeze. Vases of sweet-smelling lavender were placed around the room and the side wall was covered in a floor-to-ceiling bookshelf stacked with leather-bound volumes. It was one of the nicest rooms I'd seen out west. Mrs Fletcher sat in a well-upholstered armchair beside her bed, a pale-blue and grey rug over her lap. Her small, dark eyes sparkled, and there was high colour in her cheeks and a red ribbon in her thick hair.

Beyond the French doors lay the green vegetable gardens, alive with bees and butterflies, and beyond them in the far distance was a mob of sheep, their bleating carried on the breeze. Miss Fletcher had a maid find chairs for us and the three of us seated ourselves.

'What can you tell us about Sally Gilmour, Mrs Fletcher?' Baines asked, in a respectful tone, pencil poised.

'Very little, but I can tell you about me.'

He scribbled something down. 'All right, let's start there.'

'When I married William and came out here, this was a thriving district and Gowrie was at the peak of its wool production. I had my children and they had nurses and a governess, and then Tom went to King's, and the girls married. I was bored and still young. Bob Kirkbride had always made eyes at me. Men flirt – it passes the time and reassures them they still have their virility.'

Miss Fletcher lowered her head and blushed. I could see the disgust on her face. I might have been mistaken but I think Mrs Fletcher enjoyed baiting the bloodless Miss Fletcher.

'But he never stopped, and we went further and further and I found myself in love with him. He was, back then, a very charismatic man and lots of fun, like Jimmy. For a while I thought he loved me, and I think he pretended to do so. We used to meet in a shepherd's hut to have ... relations. But what really excited him was that I was Mrs Fletcher, daughter-in-law of old Bill Fletcher, who used to enjoy stealing Kirkbride sheep. I realised what he wanted was not me but revenge.'

I was taking notes at a furious speed but had to look up at that point.

'The last time I saw him, I accused him of wanting me because he felt he was taking something away from Will each time we met,' she said. 'We fought, screaming at each other. He hit me and I ran away, out of the shepherd's hut. He chased me and grabbed me by my hair and hit me again and I fell back on a tree stump ... That was that.'

She watched our faces carefully. The gossamer curtains rippled as the soft breeze carried the distant sounds of the sheep. I realised that she'd spent the last three years in this room, going over and over the events that had ruined her life, losing that daily intercourse with others that keep a human anchored to what's real and what isn't. There were plenty of us out here.

'He didn't even have the decency to protect me while he went for help,' she continued. 'I think he wanted me to die. I lay there in agony, knowing what a fool I'd been and how the disgrace would hit Will and my children. I wanted to die and the doctors were afraid I would. But Will, damn him, never said anything, never reproached me, just hired the best nurses, and got his sister in to run the house.

'I never saw Bob again. No letter, no card. I expect he had his wife to deal with and it was best forgotten. But then he refused to give Nessie a proper marriage settlement when Tom wanted to marry her. I decided

I'd had enough. I paid Archie Beavins to kill James Kirkbride. Then Bob would have nothing, like I have nothing.'

Miss Fletcher gasped, a high-pitched cry of shock and horror. Her hands went to her face and I wondered if she should have been spared this. I wished I had been. I took a breath, waiting for Baines to respond, but he was too stunned and just stared at Mrs Fletcher. I swallowed, and managed to say, 'But Jimmy was innocent and never did you any harm. Why kill him? Why not Bob Kirkbride himself?'

'Jimmy is as far from innocent as his father – you know that, Captain, surely. And he was his father's heir. Nothing would hurt Bob Kirkbride as much as losing the future. Without Jimmy to take over Inveraray, the whole Kirkbride empire falls to dust and blows away,' she said, waving her hand through the air. 'It's in the Bible. The sins of the father are paid for by his children.'

I gazed at her, a little uncertain about her sanity. 'But didn't you say,' I said, flipping the pages of my notebook back, 'that all this started because your father-in-law, Bill Fletcher, stole sheep from Kirkbride? So who's paying for his sins?'

'Me. I am,' she said, gesturing to her legs beneath the blanket. 'And Will.'

'And Tom's paying for yours by losing Nessie,' I said.

'I never meant that to happen,' she said, dropping her gaze to her lap and plucking at the wool of the blanket. 'I had no idea the Kirkbride girls were going to a stockmen's dance. I don't know what Janet was thinking, letting them traipse off like a couple of laundry maids. I kept a firmer hand on my daughters. Because you have to out here.'

'You wicked, wicked woman,' Miss Fletcher shouted, jumping to her feet, fists clenched.

I quickly put myself between her and her sister-in-law's bed, but Miss Fletcher stumbled out of the room. A wail of pain rose up from outside in the hallway, thin and high-pitched. Thumping footsteps and sobbing fading away. Baines was a sickly shade of pale and appeared struck dumb. The worldly detective who thought he'd seen it all.

'And ... ah ... Miss Gilmour? How did she figure in all of this?' I asked, closing the door and taking my chair again.

'Sally lured Jimmy to the dance, and Archie was to kill him on his way back home. That way nobody would know who'd done it.'

'Archie got a couple of men from Tindaree to help him. A couple of animals with no—'

'Sally told me.' She raised her eyes to mine, jerked her chin up, defiant. 'I can't help that. Men drink and get violent, that's what they do. As I said, Janet Kirkbride should never have let the girls go to the dance.'

'Did Sally Gilmour tell you what happened ... to Miss Nessie?' Baines said. 'How she suffered?'

'Yes, she did. Mr Beavins told her. Sally said he wanted her to know he hadn't touched Nessie – that he would never. How she laughed. Sally saw straight through men, not like me.'

Baines and I bent over our notebooks, scribbling, re-reading, buying time to digest it all.

'You paid Archie Beavins a hundred pounds to have James Kirkbride killed and he didn't bat an eyelid?' Baines asked.

'He did, and Sally had to coax him. She said they could use that money to get married. Men can be such fools. As if a pretty, clever girl like Sally would shackle herself to a stockman who could barely spell his own name. She's been fleeing men like him all her life. But he thought so much of himself that he accepted it as his right. Then, at the dance, she was to make him so jealous of Jimmy that he'd be in a rage and less likely to fail or run away.'

Baines and I exchanged a glance, as if neither of us could quite grasp what these two women had cooked up in the cold light of day, over their sewing.

'Where is Sally Gilmour now?' I asked.

'I sent her away to protect her. She only did what I asked of her. You can arrest me if you like. In fact, I'd like you to. I don't care what happens to me – my life has been over for a while now. I'm glad I lived long enough to get back at him. All I ask is that you tell Robert Kirkbride it was me who killed his children.'

Out in the hallway, Baines and I looked at each other. Baines was now a light shade of green, like algae bleached by the sun. I dare say I looked similar – I certainly felt like I'd been fed something rotten. Men getting drunk and beating a woman to death? Common as muck. Women ordering and paying for the death of a young man? It was like the tide going out and refusing to come back.

'What happens now?'

'You tell me,' Baines said, wiping his face with a large handkerchief. 'I'll speak to the husband and wire Sydney tonight for instructions.'

'Do you want me to stay here overnight, make sure she doesn't—'

'I reckon her husband will nail her door shut and be done with her, more than likely.'

Walking down the dim hallway towards the drawing room, I felt ill with shock at what I'd heard in that comfortable bedroom. Memories of what was left of Nessie's face, the horror of it, the cold night and the taste of vomit, all dismissed with the wave of Mrs Fletcher's hand. I had to stop and steady myself against the wall. I could hear Baines' voice echoing down the hallway from the drawing room and spared a thought for Will. He'd have to tell Tom, and his daughters in Sydney. I wanted a drink like I'd never wanted one before, whisky, swigged from the bottle.

As I continued on my way, I passed Tom's room. The door was open and I glanced inside. On a table beside his bed, I noticed a picture of Nessie, as sweet and lovely as a spring morning. Beside it he'd placed a small vase of wildflowers and a candle. I swallowed down the lump in my throat and stepped back into the hall, suddenly wishing I was far away from here.

~

The next day Baines was in and out, wiring Bourke and Sydney, smoking like a train, sweating and infuriated with the heat, shirtsleeves rolled up, swiping at flies until he lost it, shouting about shitholes and Calpa. I got him a cold beer from the river and we took a break in the kitchen.

'I got the feeling Tuttle was warning me off the Kirkbride case when we had lunch,' I said. 'He's not going to be happy about this, is he.'

'He reckons you shouldn't have stirred things up. But you did the right thing by cutting us in on the kill.'

'And Kirkbride?'

'I've been to see him and his wife. Told them the killers have been apprehended. Dunno if I fancy going back and telling them it was Mrs Fletcher who organised it.'

'She didn't organise Hirst and Shawcross, just Beavins, and I reckon if it hadn't been for those two, Beavins wouldn't have done it – not with the girls there.'

'True enough, but that don't help the Kirkbrides. They aren't relieved – in fact, they said they couldn't bear any more. So, ah … yeah, Mrs Fletcher's confession will be tough to hear. I'll go and see them this afternoon. Can you come?'

'Rather not.'

Baines let out a great sigh. 'Me too. But the good news is all persons involved, apart from the nurse, have pleaded guilty. Therefore, no trial, just sentencing. Kirkbride's solicitors give value for money, and I reckon they are beavering away as we speak on keeping the whole thing under wraps. I expect Will Fletcher wants it kept quiet too.'

He lifted the bottle of beer and poured it down his throat with barely a swallow, then wiped his mouth and sighed. 'Dunno how you can bear working in this heat. And it's not even summer.'

'You get used to it.'

'Tuttle reckons if you want to apply for a transfer to the Detective Branch in Sydney, the gods will smile on your application.'

'Yeah?'

'Got a nose for it. Some blokes don't. Gotta be able to think sideways,' he said, slicing his hand along a horizontal.

'Have to keep my rank. I won't go down.'

'I bet you won't,' he said sourly.

He went back to the front desk and his papers. Tuttle's offer surprised me, but the prospect of a future among those surly, hard-faced detectives was not appealing. But most of all, finding people dead from stupidity and brutality toughens a man. I could already feel a bony carapace inching across my body. Soon it would close over and that would be it: I'd be nothing but a walking rock.

~

Baines and I rode up to Inveraray, tethered our horses and walked across the dirt to the house, the old date palms standing sentry.

'Comin' in?' he said, half-pleading.

'Better I wait outside. Kirkbride won't appreciate my presence, in any capacity.'

But I hung around, half-inclined to go up to the graveyard to pay my respects. They'd been my friends, and the beloved siblings of the girl I loved. But I didn't want to see their graves, see those dates bookending their short lives, see the night I found them, their blood washing away in the rain.

One day, long down the years, I might be able to picture them, the girls singing, me pounding away at the piano and Jimmy conducting, pulling faces as he made us all helpless with laughter. Or walking in single file through the long grasses in a good season, hands trailing the tips of the grass, marvelling at the miracle as bright rosellas sped past twittering. The grasses would come back if we left the land alone, and then their graves would be sheltered and protected, and they'd be left to return to the earth in peace.

~

Baines reappeared and we silently made our way back to town. I met him in the pub later, where we nursed our double whiskies and talked of cricket and John Denning.

'He's got a promotion and transferred to Phillip Street. He's the coming man, so they say.'

'You said he was in trouble for his disloyalty to me.'

'Yeah, he was. But he was also loyal to the top, and they don't overlook a man who does what he's told. Like I said, always on the up or down, with an eye on your back for the knife that's coming.'

'Well, congratulations, I hope you enjoy working with him.'

Baines gave a short laugh. 'How's that lazy little paddy going, eh? Couldn't pull a greasy stick from a dog's arse, and then he bloody well saves the day.'

'Not many younger troopers could have managed it.'

'Yep, he'll go a long way if he keeps it up.'

'Doesn't want to. He's got a wheat farm waiting for him and a pretty girl to marry.'

'Yeah? Lucky little bastard.'

'Fancy your hand at farming?'

'Grew up on a dairy farm. Dad left it to me older brother, who's busy running it into the ground. Nah, I like a pay packet, nice and steady.

Come out here and see how hard these blokes work ... yeah, I reckon I'm grateful to the old man, finally.'

'Did you a favour?'

'Yep, reckon he did. Listen, mate, what I need you to do now is get on with the exhumation of Albert Jong. Gotta pull the strings on the bag tight so those bastards can't crawl out.'

29

I escorted Baines back to Bourke, a long and painful ride for him, and picked up the official replacement for Dancer, a young and fit bay called Viscount Wolseley, or Vic, as I named him. He was a frisky lad, all the newness of life coursing through him, tossing his head and up for anything. He settled in for the long haul back to Calpa and I was left to my thoughts.

An hour out of town, I saw Joe coming down the Tindaree Station drive.

'Good timing,' he said as we fell in side by side.

'What's up at Tindaree?'

'Doug Forsythe – his heart's a bit dicky,' Joe said. 'Have you seen the papers?'

'The Bourke paper?'

'No, the Sydney papers. Came in on the last steamer – Mrs Forsythe was showing me. A big headline, "War Hero Captures Kirkbride Killers".'

'Me?'

'Yes, you, you dozy bugger,' he laughed. 'You should see if you can get a copy. Cut it out and save it for your grandchildren.'

I felt ill at the thought of being in the papers. The idea of strangers reading about me made my flesh creep. It wasn't even me they were reading about, just some illusory war hero made of a puff of smoke and a magic wand.

'I didn't do it on my own, for God's sake,' I said. 'I'd be dead if it weren't for the others.'

'It's a better story. Anyway, you tracked them down. You'll be transferred anywhere you want now, although I expect Corcoran wants to hold on to you.'

I wondered if Kirkbride would see the same newspaper. Now, that I would enjoy. It wasn't a very charitable thought, but I didn't let that stop me thinking it. Kirkbride opens the paper with his morning coffee and reads about the glorious me, the man unfit for his daughter, who avenged his dead children.

'I'll send a copy to Flora,' Joe said. 'I'm sure she'd want to know they've been caught, and that you caught them. I think she'll be impressed.'

'How would you bloody well know what she'll think? You barely know her in any capacity except as some pill-pushing—'

'Oh, just drop it, Gus, I'm sorry I mentioned her.'

'Where is she? If you know where she is, you have to tell me.'

He gave me an exasperated look. I held my tongue. He would never tell me and that was that.

I stabled Vic next to Felix. Lonergan's horse had gone back to Bourke with him. The kitchen was as I left it, and Lonergan's room empty. No empty tea mugs anywhere. I could drink freely, fall wherever I liked, scream all night long and keep my incident book pure in look, if not content.

I walked through to the station. The lithograph of long-dead Queen Victoria caught my eye, a shaft of sunlight illuminating her. She gazed to the left, away across the vast dusty or jungled expanse of her empire, a small crown balanced on her regal skull, a blue sash draped across her maternal bosom. In the patina of dust covering the monarch's picture, some joker had traced the outline of a cock and balls.

I remembered being told the news of her death while out on a dusty, grimy manoeuvre on the veldt, exhaustion deep in my bones and hunger eating me alive. A hush fell over the men, wind whipping around us. We were soldiers of the Queen, our allegiance pledged to her alone. I was young and felt her death as a shocking break with the sacred.

After wiping the picture clean, I ate my supper in silence, staring at the mail that had come in last night. The usual gazettes and another letter from my father. The days stretched ahead to the horizon, empty and drear. I made a coffee, took a few sips, letting the sweet, bitter fluid slap me around, then I reached for my father's letter, opened it and read.

He was sorry.

I slapped the letter down. Jumped to my feet. Through the back door, letting it slam behind me. I didn't know which way to turn – down to the pub, down to the river, get on Felix and go for a gallop, or all of the above.

In the Mounted Rifles, when a man died we said he'd thrown a seven. But I'd thrown a six and a half that day on the veldt, and had questioned the nature of luck ever since. In the military convalescent home in Cape Town, I'd been surrounded by other wounded officers in bathchairs – heads trembling, hands shaky, fags burning their fingers – who at the end of each day would be wheeled away and drugged up for the night. I felt better than some and worse than others. But we were all bound together by the risks we'd taken and the way those risks had played out.

Back home, in my old bedroom, the tin soldiers on the bookshelf mocked me, a nurse hovered over me day and night, the house constantly smelled of beef tea brewed for the invalid, people spoke in whispers outside my door, and the fevers came and went, leaving me shaking and delirious or limp.

My father, a doctor who emerged from his mother's womb in a white coat, would come home and check on me, bark at the nurses and go off and have a stiff whisky or three. I wanted to get better for him, as he had never wanted me to go soldiering. But force of will can only go so far. I cried out in my sleep, night after night, blood-curdling screams. How could anyone live with that and not snap? And he did snap. Accused me of wilful instability – why couldn't I be a man and just pull myself together?

I remembered that day so well. The shame, the awful, burning wave of shame.

That night I packed a bag and left while the house was asleep. I caught a train north to a place called Yamba, took a shack, lay on the beach and drank. From there I took off and brawled my way around New South

Wales. I was angry and would fight all-comers. A weary copper told me, after he let me out of the lock-up one morning, that seeing as I'd been in the Light Horse, I should join the Mounted Troopers. So I did. Once I settled in at Calpa, my father must have tracked me down because the letters came regularly.

I had destroyed every single one unread. Until now.

I had not seen him since that day in 1905 and now he said he was sorry. As a father, and as a doctor, his helplessness in the face of my injuries had terrified him, he said, and it had come out as anger – he'd only realised this since I left. He thought I was going to die, he said, thought I wanted to die. He must have written this in every one of those letters I so blithely burnt. Remorse, shame, despair – how easily they spread, like typhus in an army camp. He had doggedly apologised every few weeks for three years, and a man like my father rarely explained himself or apologised for anything.

The river gurgled and rushed. A grey heron stood perfectly still on the opposite bank, beak like a small spear. The clouds on the horizon, bright, white, tufty tops. They could bring rain or they could float right by. I remembered the night of the boxing, when Hirst held the rifle above my head, how in that moment, certain it was my end, my thoughts had flown east across the plains, over the Great Dividing Range, to where my father sat alone in his drawing room.

We used to sit together in that drawing room, reading by the fire in the evenings. We'd work in the garden together, train dogs together as we rambled around the countryside, visit relatives together, breathing sighs of relief when the visits were over, exchanging a smile that bound us together in mutual understanding.

I rubbed my face and sighed, walked back to the yard, in through the back door, through the laundry and into the kitchen, where his letter lay on the table. Through all these years, a dull ache had lodged itself deep inside me, one I'd done my best to ignore. But now I couldn't ignore it – not anymore.

~

I hadn't been to speak to the Jongs about exhuming Albert's body, which Corcoran wanted done in person. I was avoiding it. And I wanted to track down the man who raped Grace Kirkbride. Reg Tierney reckoned she was eighteen or nineteen weeks along, which meant the culprit had got at her in March or April.

That was around the time they'd have been getting the rams away from the ewes, so not a terribly busy time and good for entertaining horny coxcombs with vicious tendencies and eyes for a fortune. In Kirkbride's house. Got at her under his host's roof. It boggled my sensibilities but not my understanding. I had been at boarding school, after all.

Flora had written to me about these young men in her secret letters, very clever sketches too. But Kirkbride had her letters now so there was no way of knowing who had been staying there in those months.

I put the quest to one side and returned to the Jongs. I thought they'd been through enough, but Baines was right – we had to keep banging nails into the Hirst and Shawcross coffin.

~

345

The Jongs were now living in Wilcannia, which was about a two-day ride. It was late September and unseasonably warm, a bad sign for the coming summer. I put in for a couple of days to conduct police business at Wilcannia and leave was immediately granted. I left Felix with Wally and set off on Vic in the early hours of the morning, following the river road. A blanket of heat lay over the land and the only breath of air was to be found by the river.

In the early afternoon we stopped and I took my bedroll down to the riverbank, found some shade, rolled my canvas out, stripped down to my shorts and lay down and lit a fag. It was a day when every living creature found a scrap of shade and lay still and drowsing, waiting with sublime patience for it all to pass.

We set off again around eleven pm and arrived in Wilcannia midmorning. Like most towns in the west, Wilcannia had broad streets, wide enough to drive a mob of sheep through. It was flat as a tack but had some sturdy stone buildings like the post office, the courthouse, the municipal hall and the hospital.

I called in at the cop shop and introduced myself, and asked the duty officer if he knew where the Blackwoods lived. I told him about the Jongs and what I was there for. He stabled Vic for me and gave him a feed, and I went away with an address and a rough pencil map.

The Blackwoods' house, on the edge of town, had a bullnose verandah and a collection of sheds clustered out the back, a horse paddock, a tree with a rope swing and a clothesline held up with forked saplings. A black dog chained up beside a half-barrel went berserk as I approached, and a young woman, thin and worn and wearing a stained apron over an equally stained dress, came out to investigate.

'Can I help you?' she said, in a tone that indicated she didn't want to help anyone.

'Mrs Dulcie Blackwood?'

'Who wants to know?' she asked, waving at the flies.

A little boy about four years old burst out of the house and tangled himself in his mother's dress, a piece of bread in his fist and a gobbet of green snot hanging from his nose. Dulcie put her hand on his head as he hid in her skirts and watched me.

'My name's Augustus Hawkins, senior constable, Calpa.'

'Oh, you're the man who buried our Albert,' she said, breaking into a pretty smile. 'Mum will be pleased to see you. Come in and have a cuppa – she's out the back. You got time?'

Mrs Jong was sitting out the back of the house under a vine that had been trained to cover some sort of trellis. She had several rifles on a table, all taken apart and the pieces resting on old newspaper.

'Trooper Hawkins, how nice of you to call,' she said, getting to her feet.

Dulcie went to put the kettle on with the small boy still attached to her skirts by one hand.

'A grandchild?' I asked.

'Howie's brother's boy, Sam. His mum's poorly so he's here with us for a bit. What brings you to Wilcannia? Just passing through?'

'No – that is, I came here to ask you something. It's about Albert.'

'Mmm?' she said, nodding her head and continuing to rub the gun barrel.

'I am sorry to tell you this, but Albert didn't take his own life. He was

347

killed by the same men who killed the Kirkbrides. They have confessed to killing him.'

She looked up, surprised, and held my gaze for a long moment.

'My poor boy. Well, Eddie will be relieved to know. And now we can give him a good Christian burial.'

'Which will be a great comfort, I'm sure. However, despite the confession, we need hard evidence, which means an autopsy. If you are minded to rebury him, then we could expedite the process – at police expense, of course—'

Dulcie came out with the tea things. 'What is it, Mum?'

'It's Albert. He was murdered, he didn't kill himself.'

Dulcie placed the tea tray on the table and sat down heavily, a stunned look on her face. 'Who? Who would kill him?'

'A couple of doggers from Tindaree,' I said. 'They killed him and robbed your place. It's best you know the truth.'

Dulcie wiped her eyes on her apron. The little boy stood in the doorway, wide-eyed and watching.

'My brother was never mad growing up – he was the sweetest boy. He went mad when they put him in the asylum. And then he gets murdered? Where's God? What's he doing?'

'Now, love,' her mother said. 'Albert's safe with God and we know the truth. As the constable says, it's best to know the truth.'

'Is it? Their truth, not ours. My Rosie told the truth – she told them about the man putting his thing in her, told them it hurt her, and they said she was lying, said she was a slut, said she lured him. So when is it best to know the truth, Mum?'

348

'Dulcie, don't—'

'Rosie's running wild now and they said she'll be taken away from us if she don't settle down, get put in a home for bad girls. What's going to happen to that man who did it to her, but? What's his truth? That she was a minx who asked for it because a man like him would never lie?'

'I am sorry, Mrs Blackwood,' I said.

'Yeah, sorry because you coppers do nothing,' Dulcie shot. 'You just shut us up and tell us it didn't happen.'

'That's enough, Dulcie.'

Dulcie got to her feet. The little boy ran over and tugged on her dress. She was crying, her fists clenched. 'No, I'm not keeping it a secret anymore.'

Her mother looked away, shaking her head. Dulcie started talking and the terrible truth tumbled out into the harsh light of day.

30

By late afternoon, Vic and I were on the western river road to the north and kept going through the dusk. The occasional campfire on the riverbank pricked the darkness. In the moonlit night, the river looked as if it were made of silver, snaking through the darkness, starlight filtering through the fringe of trees.

Close to dawn and Vic had had enough. I wanted to sleep but no amount of tossing and turning helped. Sat up, lit a fag, watched the river flowing past. Nameless beasts crawled around in the dark shadows on the opposite bank and slithered away into the mud. A tangle of branches, limbs brown and shining like the Wilga Creek children, drifted with the current. I flicked my cigarette at the river; its glowing tip arced away, hit the water and was gone.

When I woke it was late afternoon and I'd overslept. I fed Vic, found some damper in my saddlebags, washed it down with the rank water from my waterbag and set off. We'd make Calpa by nightfall.

As I rode into town, laughter and thumps floated out from the pub in the still night air. I made sure Vic was cool, fed and watered. I took off my boots and left them by the back door. Went to my room, took my tunic off, brushed it down, hung it up, took off the filthy sweaty shirt and breeches and placed them neatly in the laundry for Mrs Schreiber. Then I took a bottle of beer and drank it, almost in one go.

When I shut my eyes the flames were still there, so I opened them and dressed in a fresh shirt and a clean pair of trousers. Washed my face, combed my hair, rubbed my ointment along the scar. The flames were all around me now, leaping up in my chest, funnelling up my neck until they burnt the backs of my eyes.

I grabbed a bottle of whisky and walked over to Joe's, going around the back as I usually did. I walked past his bean trellis, the vines struggling in the early heat. Through the kitchen window, I saw Joe sitting at the table in a pool of golden light from his lantern beside a pile of papers and unopened mail. Light glowed around the side of the house. Mrs Schreiber's room, where she had a fireplace and a chair where she liked to sit and knit for her dozens of grandchildren. I opened the screen door and walked in.

'Gus, good to see you,' Joe said. 'Been down at Wilcannia, so I hear. Long ride.' He fetched the tumblers, placed them on the table. 'Take a seat, mate.'

'I have to tell you something.'

He sat down, poured the whisky and leant back in his chair. 'Well, sit down while you tell me.'

I swilled the whisky he offered around my mouth, then swallowed and slammed the glass back on the table. He exhaled a cloud of blue smoke and watched it rise to the ceiling, eyes on me, waiting. Two whisky glasses, spirits racing each other to the bottom, only to go around again and again. I had the words but they wouldn't come.

Joe put his head to the side, gave me a quizzical look.

'At a place called Ventersberg, in South Africa—'

'Ah. The war,' he said.

'Just what were you expecting?'

'Go on.'

I couldn't go on. My chest was on fire. No breath to be had.

'Kitchener ordered the British to burn the farms over the heads of women and children, like the good Christian man he was. We Australians, like the good lickspittles we are, escorted the women to railheads, where they were shunted off to camps. I know many of them died in those camps, but nobody talks of it.'

'Sit down, mate. Have another drink. It's over, been over for years.'

'Look out the window. It's never over. Mate.'

He half-smiled, as if to humour me.

'That was our job – not to burn, but to escort the women to the railheads. One night, in Ventersburg, there was a delay. My men were impatient, hungry, we wanted to eat, sleep. I rode over to see what was taking the Brits so damn long. I saw a barn and a house in flames, two women being roughly pulled along, screaming infants. I watched. I watched as a servant, a young black girl, no more than twelve, darted out of this burning house. A British soldier caught her, threw her on the ground, raped her. And when he was done, he tossed her back into the flames.'

Joe didn't blink, didn't look away.

'I could have saved the girl – I could have ridden down there, pulled him off her. But I just watched. I was twenty-one and I thought our job as soldiers was to protect the women and children, and it wasn't. It never is. Not there, not here, not now, not then.'

'Did you—'

'I reported him. I knew who he was, but the British did nothing. Not a damn thing. But not because he was an outstanding soldier and they needed him.'

'Then why?'

'Because she was black.'

He shook his head, murmured something, sipped his whisky.

'She was black, Joe – do you understand me?' I said, putting my hands on the table, leaning over, my face close to his. 'Your precious empire of Christian decency.'

'Oh, come on, one bad egg.'

'And what of the fucking evil chicken that keeps laying these bad eggs?'

'I've always wondered if you'd feel so angry at the empire if you hadn't been injured.'

'Have you wondered that?' My eye twitch pulsed like the heart of a terrified rabbit. 'And this girl died because it was war and bad things can happen in war, but at home we're all upright, decent people?'

'If you want a fight, you may as well leave. I'm not interested tonight,' he said, sensing I was close to losing it.

'That girl was black. Rosie Blackwood was poor. But Grace Kirkbride? You took a fucking risk there. Or maybe it was the risk that got you all hot and bothered, eh? Nothing like danger to arouse a man.'

I lunged across the table at him, grabbing his shirt collar, dragging him over the table as if I were hauling a drowning man from the sea. All his papers, the bottle and glasses, the lantern, crashed to the floor. I smashed my fist into his face, feeling a ferocious rush of blood and vengeance as I did. Joe spun around, hit the table and fell to the ground.

'Get up,' I panted.

'You're mad,' he cried, cringing against the wall, his blood spattered all over his shirt.

'Get up.'

He clung onto a chair and pulled himself upright. When he was on his feet, I struck him again. I held him by the throat and punched him again and again, thrilling to the feel of bone on bone and flesh, feeling tears spurt from my eyes. I didn't know if it was Joe or myself I was beating.

'Enough, Herr Hawkins,' I heard Mrs Schreiber shriek. 'Stop it!'

Joe, his face bloodied, head lolling. I took my hand from his neck and let him drop.

'You raped Grace Kirkbride. She was twelve when you did it. Twelve years old, you fucking mongrel, twelve,' I shouted. 'The last town you were in was Menindee, not Echuca, and you raped Rose Blackwood there – they told me. How many girls? How many towns?'

I heard Mrs Schreiber gasp, heard her bedroom door slam. I yanked him up and wrapped my arm around his neck. He gagged, clawed at my arm.

'Grace is dead because of you,' I hissed in his ear. 'Pregnant because of you. All of them are dead – Jimmy, Nessie – because of you.'

Joe couldn't breathe, let alone admit his guilt, so I loosened my grip, grabbed his arm and twisted it behind his back. Blood pounded in my ears. I wasn't sure if I could stop.

'I can't be blamed for their murder,' he gasped.

'Oh, but I do blame you.'

'I'm sorry,' Joe grunted, trying to stay upright. 'I've tried to stop, it's … why I came here.'

'You're sorry I have your arm halfway up your back, you mean,' I snarled, twisting harder. Then I threw him down. He writhed on the floor, crying and repeating how sorry he was, over and over until I wanted to kick the life out of him.

'You sent Flora to a madhouse so she couldn't tell anyone about Grace's pregnancy, about what they were forced into doing because of your fucking perversions. You sent my girl to be with strangers, you filthy, lying cunt.'

He coughed, grunted each time I kicked him. 'Mrs Schreiber,' I bellowed. 'Pack your bag, all your things, and go to the station now.'

She emerged into the hallway, took one look at the chaos in the kitchen and retreated into her room again.

'You should get out, leave this district,' Joe said, tears streaming down his face, mixing with the blood and mucus. 'Search for Flora.'

I lunged at him, grabbed his throat in two hands, pulled him up and smashed his head against the wall again and again. 'Don't you presume to tell me how to live, you fucking dog.' Then I threw him down. He hit the lantern and a spill of flame spread among the piles of letters and journals on the floor. Mrs Schreiber ran past, holding her bag like it was a babe in her arms. I walked out after her. Within a minute the house was on fire.

'He's still in there,' she cried.

'Let the fucker burn, see how he likes it.' Hands clenched into fists, panting like a dog.

'Get him out,' Mrs Schreiber cried again, pulling at my arm.

I hesitated, then pulled a handkerchief from my pocket, clamped it over my mouth and raced into the kitchen. He was still lying on the floor. I grabbed his collar and dragged him out, dumping him on his dying beans.

'Go to the station, Mrs Schreiber. Now.'

She hurried away and I stood over Joe, panting as the flames roared, kicked him in the guts, kicked him again, then pulled him up and made him walk back to the station. Nobody was around, the pub still resonating with howls of laughter.

I threw Joe into the lock-up, tossed a blanket in and locked the barred door. Mrs Schreiber was sitting at the kitchen table, wiping her eyes and sobbing.

I splashed a bit of whisky into a glass and gave it to her, then put the kettle on.

'I'm so sorry, so very sorry ...'

'It's not your fault,' I said, closing my eyes, gripping the back of a chair, trying to be calm.

'I see it and I wonder, but I think it isn't my business.'

'You saw him do it?'

She shook her head. 'When he has a lame horse, the patients come to the surgery. I am cooking or cleaning. I don't pay attention. But Fraulein Grace always smiled at me so I am fond of her. Her mother goes in with her and he examines the girl on a table behind a long screen, but she is sleepy afterwards. We always carry her to the buggy for Mrs Kirkbride.' She blew her nose, shook her head. 'Why had he given her the laudanum? I should have said something, but he is the doctor and ... her mother was in the room. He is the doctor.'

'It's not your fault. I trusted him too.'

'What will I do? I cannot go to Cobar tonight.'

'Make yourself comfortable in the second bedroom and I'll wire your daughter in Cobar to come and get you. No hurry.'

I left her to settle down and went into the station. From the side window I could see the enormous orange glow of the fire, hear the shouts. Kev ran into the station, his eyes streaming from the smoke, wrinkled face all sooty.

'Gus, what are you doing? Fucken surgery is on fire.'

I peered out the window of the station. 'So it is. You better go and put it out.'

~

In the morning I got up, worked the coals and put some kindling in the stove, then put a kettle of water on to boil. Soon Mrs Schreiber was up. I put on a clean pair of breeches, a clean shirt, took my tunic out and gave it another brush, rubbed the brass buttons until they shone, put it on, found a pair of boots and cleaned them, and all the while Dr Tierney's words were echoing through my head: *There are other doctors out west who should be struck off.* He was telling me but I wasn't listening. I thought he meant the drunken bigamist at White Cliffs, or the opium addict in Cobar, not the bloody rock spider sitting in the middle of my own town.

I left the station, rode up to Inveraray and found Kirkbride in his study, standing by the fireplace looking down at the empty grate. Above the mantelpiece, his grandfather glared at his descendants, daring them to destroy what he had made out of a wasteland. Kirkbride looked like he hadn't shaved for days.

'You know?' I asked.

He nodded, didn't look at me.

'I know why James, Nessie and Grace went to Larne, and I know who got Grace pregnant,' I said.

His head jerked up, eyes wide, just for a moment, then he turned away, took a seat at his desk. 'Grace was only thirteen – of course she wasn't pregnant. I don't know where you got that idea from. Maybe one of your drunken delusions.'

'She had an abortion in Larne, which James organised for her.'

He took a deep breath and sighed. 'They went to the dance, that's all.'

'Don't you want to know who interfered with your daughter? Don't you want to tear him apart with your bare hands?'

He clenched his eyes shut.

'Joe Pryor did it. In his surgery. Doped her up with laudanum and did it while she was asleep. With her mother on the other side of the screen.

In the same room, the utter coolness of it, the sheer brazen ... thinking he could get away with raping your daughter.'

Kirkbride slapped the table, hard, shouted, 'No!'

'He dined with your family, tended to them in their most vulnerable moments.' I picked up a pen, tried to shove it in his hand. 'Write to every powerful man, every medical man, every minister for health and tell them that Dr Joe Pryor raped your daughter. Get him struck off, get him gaoled. Use your influence for some good.'

I waited, panting with fury, wanting him to match it, willing him to flare into a tower of rage that would sweep everything and everyone before it.

He let the pen fall, dropped his face into his hands.

'You're happy to let him do it again? To another trusting little girl?'

'Tell these men what?' he said. 'That my daughters were killed after procuring an abortion like a couple of cheap streetwalkers?'

I reared back, and after a few deep breaths left him to the gloom of his study. I walked out down the hallway, past Flora and Nessie's empty room, the silence of the homestead almost too much to bear. Outside, the sun dazzled and the air was still. The sound of a mob of sheep beyond the horizon carried through the air. There were three dead dogs hanging from a fence, a warning to others watching from the scrub.

31

The pungent stench of the burnt-out surgery hung over the town. Smoke drifted around the ruins. Nobody was around, nobody asking where Joe was. Back at the station, I found a note from Mrs Schreiber. Her daughter had arrived and she couldn't wait any longer. She left an address for me to send her wages.

I took off my tunic, brushed the dust from it and hung it up, changed out of the official breeches into a pair of old trousers, took off my official Mounted Trooper shirt and hung it over the back of the chair, good for another wear.

I found another bottle of whisky, a pack of cigarettes and some matches, and placed them on the table. I went to the armoury, unlocked it, found my Colt revolver, checked it and loaded some ammunition into it. Through the cell bars I saw Joe slumped on the floor, his face swollen and bloody, his shirt stained. He looked up; one eye had closed over completely.

When I came off my horse and copped a bayonet in the face, it was only days after Ventersburg. My concentration had lapsed for a second and then I was just a bloodied bag of meat being carried off the field and put in a corner to die. Some part of me felt I deserved it, because I hadn't saved that girl, because I was fighting on the side that looked away. Maybe getting injured was a just punishment.

The memory of her death came at me, over and over, and I still didn't know how to think of it, so I tried not to think of it at all. Every time I saw her slight body flying through the air in that infinitesimal moment, a wall of roaring flame behind her, I'd quickly turn my thoughts away, block them, refuse them daylight. But they came to me at night and would not be denied, and I'd wake in terror. But rage was what I really felt. It sang through me, black and murderous.

I fetched the whisky and cigarettes, opened the cell door and placed them beside Joe, then held the revolver out. Our gazes held for a few seconds, then he took it. I locked the door and went out the back to the stables.

~

I found my own saddlebags, covered in dust, checked them for spiders and laid them over a rail. There was Felix's saddle, his blanket, bridle and the rest of his kit. All of it needed endless upkeep in the dry air. I found a tin of neatsfoot oil and a rag from the back of the tack room cupboard and started rubbing the oil into the saddlebags, getting into every fold, under and over, rubbing, smearing and rubbing some more.

I put it aside and took the bridle, undid the buckles, moistened the rag in oil and smeared and rubbed. Kept rubbing.

The smoke from last night's fire hung like a fog in the still air. There was no one about. No one asking questions. Just a white cockatoo on the telegraph pole, gnawing at the wood, and he'd keep gnawing until the pole fell and we were, at last, cut off from civilisation.

32

I signed the despatch papers for Joe's coffin at the Bourke Railway Station and watched as the undertakers loaded him into a goods car. Waited until the train pulled out of the station in clouds of coal smoke and steam, and watched it head east until it vanished into the horizon, curious at my calm detachment. One day, maybe I'd feel sadness – but then again, maybe I wouldn't.

As a boy I'd pored over the *Iliad* and admired Hector, that morally strong, unselfish warrior, a man devoted to wife and family, a man whose terrible death and desecration did nothing to besmirch his essential honour. I wanted to be like him. But it seemed that I was Achilles, spurred to destroy by a need for vengeance and ever prey to the violence roiling in my breast.

As I entered the police station, I saw a familiar figure at the end of the hall. 'Well, if it isn't Michael Patrick Lonergan himself, as I live and breathe.'

'Gus, what are you doing here?'

'Didn't Corcoran tell you? I've resigned.'

'Is that right? They should be begging you to stay.'

'Thank you, but I've had enough. Going east.'

'To do what?'

'Something different. And you?'

'Transfer to Balranald and a commendation,' he said, grinning like a kid on Christmas morning.

'Well done. That'll impress your future father-in-law.'

'Yeah, and Ada too. She wants to know all about how we brought down the Kirkbride murderers.'

'Milk it for everything it's worth,' I laughed, and slapped him on the shoulder.

I gave him my father's address in Queanbeyan. He wanted to send me a wedding invitation, and I couldn't help getting a bit choked up at that. Apart from my father, Mick Lonergan was the only other person I'd lived with for any amount of time. I felt honoured he still thought enough of me to ask me to his wedding.

I didn't want farewell drinks and all that malarkey, but Jim Corcoran and I had a quiet whisky or three in his office.

'Sorry to see you go, Gus,' he said, 'although there've been a few times when I could have happily kicked your arse into the next county.'

'I apologise for my, er ...'

He waved his hand. 'You wouldn't be the first trooper to have a problem with drink, nor the first to dally with women at the wrong time. This is a hardship posting and normally we'd overlook it, unless the trooper really fumbled, as you did. Not possible in a city posting.'

'Got someone lined up for Calpa?'

'Nobody lines up for Calpa. The word's gone out, so we'll see who sticks his hand up. Going to be a sad and sorry district for a while to come, I'd say.'

'Has Tom gone to Bathurst?'

'Been a delay. I've been sitting, having a chat with him at the end of the day. Hell of a thing his mother did. He told me about his grandfather, how it all seems to have started. Old Bill Fletcher had some sort of feud going with Old Rob Kirkbride, but that was so long ago no one can remember what it was about. Something to do with sheep, as you'd expect.

'Long after the old bugger was stopped from riding, he'd go and cut Kirkbride fences for something to do, take a dog and a waterbag,' Corcoran continued. 'He was found dead by a cut fence, eaten by crows, apparently. I reckon he'd have been happy with that.'

'You knew him?'

'Met him a couple of times. Mean streak in him wide as the Darling in flood.'

'Why wasn't he caught and stopped?'

Corcoran shrugged.

'A plague on the house of a man who steals another man's stock, eh?' I said.

He took a deep breath and sighed. 'I don't think anyone can top Mrs Fletcher's revenge. She's pleading guilty, so no trial, straight to sentencing. At least she spared her family that.'

It was some small comfort. We chatted on about his plans for the district, such as they were.

'I meant to tell you,' I said, 'Jack Tuttle mentioned the Tommy Moore murder. Said you and the new IG worked on it together.'

He looked up, surprised. 'Together? Hmph. It'll be a cold day in hell before Col Edwards does anything with anyone other than his wife, and even she probably gives a sigh of blessed relief when it's over. I solved the Tommy Moore case, and I caught the bastard too ... but that's history now.'

After a moment's silence, I got up to leave. I had a train to catch and wanted to see Tom. Corcoran and I shook hands. He'd been a good CO and I told him so.

'A word from the wise before you go, Gus,' he said. 'Don't be thinking glory will get you anywhere. It's the politics. I don't play and you sure as hell don't, so take that with you and think on it in all your future endeavours.'

On that surprising note, I left.

~

I went down to the cells to say goodbye to Tom. He looked as if he had not moved since I last saw him. The grey blanket bunched up on the timber bench, the whitewashed walls of the cell scarred with scratched names, curses, dates, the piss bucket stinking in the corner, and Tom, unshaven, hollow eyes.

'Still here, eh.'

'Cobar or Bathurst,' he shrugged. 'Why would I care?'

'Don't give up. You can still plead guilty to manslaughter with gross provocation – a good solicitor will sort it out. You'll be back on Gowrie before you know it.'

'I heard the surgery burnt down and Dr Pryor killed himself. What happened?'

'Men snap.'

'Like that bloke on Goonda.'

Goonda was a smallholding bought by a stringybark settler. Bloke couldn't make a fist of it so he shot his six children, then his wife and then all his stock. A couple of workers managed to get away, but then he burnt down his house, while he sat inside it.

'I'll come and see you in Bathurst, mate. Look after yourself.'

'Stop with your fucking pity, Gus. You of all people. Nessie is dead because of you. Because you had to go tomcatting. And all the while Flora was crying her eyes out. Nessie told me. Nessie told me everything. I know all about your secret meeting with Flora. I know that you ruined her and then called it off.'

He was sitting on the bench, hunched forward, hands dangling between his knees, and by God I wished there were no bars between us.

'You know nothing about me and Flora.'

'I know you can't have her. And why should you, eh? You were the one who let Nessie die.'

367

I backed away and then turned to walk out, but he shouted after me, his voice echoing through the lock-up.

'Flora wrote to me, asking about you. She wanted to know why you never came back to see her – why you never sent a message to her through me. You could have tried but you didn't.'

'You kept that from me?' I said, wheeling around.

He nodded slowly, giving me a sly look. Then he came over to the bars, the gaol cell stench following him, piss, vomit and fury.

'Yeah, I did,' he laughed. 'Told her you'd been dismissed and left Calpa, that you'd ridden off, almost too drunk to stay on your horse.'

'Where is she?' I said, stepping back.

'Fuck off,' he spat.

'You can blame me if it makes you feel better, mate,' I said, wiping his spittle from my coat. 'Take care of yourself now. Have a good cry – they might have prison hankies you can use, if you ask nicely. Might want to watch your arse too.'

He slammed the cell bars like a captured ape as I walked away.

~

I settled onto the train heading east, staring out the window at the dry plains, seeing my reflection in the glass, the scar etched across my face like I'd taken a knife to myself after a night on the turps. The landscape slowly shifted just before Dubbo, and then we were in the Central Tablelands, green and gentle, and I detected a flicker of excitement in my chest, a good sign. Then the train started to climb, Bell, Mount Victoria, Blackheath, the neat cottages and well-fed people, gardening or just strolling along as the train hurtled past, kids running along footpaths, waving at the train, their fresh faces like small flowers. Incredible, all of it.

I felt my father's letter in my coat pocket, the folded paper between my shirt and the lining of my coat. I was eager to see him and full of hope.

The train pulled in at Katoomba and people got off and on. There was time to buy and drink a cup of tea at the station kiosk, so I wandered along the platform, inhaling the mountain air, until the guard blew his whistle and people bustled around, returning cups and saucers, laughing, talking. The engine started up, clouds of steam and smoke whirling around, and when it left I watched it head east, standing on the platform, heart in my mouth. Flora had probably been moved but I needed to see for myself.

~

I took the same room in the boarding house as I had back in July. I'd been blacklisted at the sanatorium on my last visit so walking in and asking where Flora had been sent wasn't going to work. And if she was there, they wouldn't tell me.

Later in the afternoon I walked to the sanitorium, through the open gates and followed a gravel drive leading past the main entrance and around to the service entrance. I was a hard man to disguise, but pulled my hat down walked with purpose. Then I lit a cigarette and dallied under a tree as if I were waiting for someone. Nobody told me to leave.

A young man came out to have a cigarette. He wore an orderly's smock which marked him as my man.

'Nice evening,' he said with a nod.

'It is indeed. On your break?'

'Just about to finish.'

I walked over. He looked disconcerted.

'Want to earn a florin?'

'Piss off, you fucking homo,' he spat, dropping his smoke on the ground.

'Not after that. I need to know if a patient is still here. She was here back in July.'

'I can't give out that sort of information.'

'Two florins.'

'What's her name?'

'Miss Flora Kirkbride.'

'Yeah, she's here,' he said, his eyes on the coins in my hand.

'Describe her.'

'Dark-brown hair, brown eyes, thin, quiet, always wears mourning.'

I paid him, left the property and found my way to the bushland near the cliff edge, the bush Flora overlooked from her verandah.

I pushed my way through the thick scrub of acacia and tree ferns and found the paling fence that enclosed the sanitorium. It was a bit rotten from the mists and dampness so not hard to kick a hole in it. Except I had to do it very stealthily. Breaking a paling with a deafening snap, waiting a moment, then doing it again.

I struggled through the gap I'd made and found myself in the dense bush on the sanatorium property. I crept closer to the back lawn, stealthily, moving as if my life depended on evading detection. I discovered some bushy shrubs which gave me perfect cover, and through which I could watch the grounds, looking for routines, working out blind spots and gaps, like scouting in the Transvaal. I spent hours crouched behind these shrubs, legs almost numb from lack of circulation. In July, Flora told me she liked to sit on the bench and feed the birds, so she would come, I just had to wait.

Late the next day she appeared, clad in a bulky coat, her dear face so pale. She sat on a bench, then took a crust from her pocket, tore it up and tossed the crumbs on the ground. The crimson rosellas flew down and gathered at her feet, twittering and feeding. She smiled at them and elation coursed through me.

Kirkbride and Tom Fletcher must have conspired to tell me the same story, that she'd been spirited away far out of my reach. But here she was, my girl. Did they really think they could shut her in the tower and I would not scale it? That I would not swim the Hellespont to get to her?

I could get a note to her, smuggle her out of this awful place, spirit her away on the train. We could be together finally, as we had wanted. It wouldn't be hard, but it would have to be well planned, because if I was caught I'd go to prison and she'd be back in the madhouse.

~

In my room that night I wrote a letter to Flora, telling her that if Tom had told me the truth, I would have come for her long before. I explained my plan, telling her of my observations of the nightwatchmen, when to be in the shadows and when to run across the lawn to me, waiting amid the tree ferns. We'd step through the hole in the fence and hurry through the sleeping streets and catch the first train to Sydney.

My plan rested on her coming back to that bench by the tree ferns, where I had my vantage point. From there I could not be seen but I could speak to her without raising my voice. I'd tell her where I'd stashed my letter with the instructions. She could collect it later from under a brick by the side path. Flora had spirit; she would not falter.

I folded the letter, put it in an envelope, put a coat on and walked down the road towards the sanatorium, planning to slip into the grounds and place the letter where she would find it. It was a cold mountain night, shadows on the footpath. I passed great mansions lit from within, golden light spilling out onto perfect lawns, and small weatherboard cottages with no lights and dogs chained and barking.

I kept to the shadows on the corner opposite the entrance to the sanatorium, big wrought-iron gates that held patients in and intruders out. But I knew how to get in. The building loomed large against the night sky, dark and forbidding. There were lamps on here and there, and I wondered if one was Flora's, burning bright to help me find my way to her. A fox, set on his nightly rounds, crossed my path and stopped to take my measure. No fear, just cool appraisal of possible threat. Then he went on his way – but it seemed as if, on those stealthy paws, he'd snatched my resolve and padded away into the dark.

What if Tom had been lying? What if his confession was a parting shot, to wound me as he had been wounded? Or what if he hadn't been lying, but she didn't want to run away with me?

I thought of all I'd seen and done, or not done. Of the nights still drenched in sweat and terror, the sudden plummeting sensations that plagued me. The drinking. Flora always met the upright army officer, sober, courteous, able to hold a conversation, a man who knew the customs of his class and could practise them in his sleep.

She didn't know the man who went back to his cave and drank himself senseless to blot out the shame, then woke screaming in terror to find himself passed out on the kitchen floor. The man who had watched a girl raped and killed and had not acted to save her. The man who had womanised around the place, discarding the girls and then reverently holding her hand and making promises. The man who had held Joe Pryor prisoner for days, listening to his pleas in grim silence, until he finally gave in and put a bullet in his head.

It was better for Flora that she never know that man. Better for him, too, because he could never bear the shame of seeing pity in her eyes.

The lamps burning in the sanatorium went out, one by one, until the building was in darkness. I tore the letter in half, turned and walked away.

33

The train pulled in at Queanbeyan around four. My heart pounded as I looked out onto the familiar platform. Father had sent his coachman to collect me in a buggy. I'd already sent my trunk and Felix down on an earlier train, so I walked to the buggy with nothing but a dry mouth and hope.

As we clopped down the familiar streets, breathing in the cool air, memories rushed at me. We turned the corner and the shingled roof of my father's house was visible above the trees. Soon I'd see its ornate balustrades, turrets and other Victorian features. The late-afternoon light would make the blue of the plumbago vivid, the horses would be grazing in the home paddock, tails swishing, the red brick of the house blazing, a thin, peaceful line of smoke rising from the chimney pots.

He must have heard the buggy arrive as he suddenly appeared on the verandah, two unfamiliar servants behind him and dear old Mrs Baker, housekeeper and the nearest to a mother I'd had. Father was still stern and upright, his iron-grey hair thick, a few more lines around his eyes. He blinked away tears as we shook hands then embraced for a long moment. I felt my own tears as well, but no shame as I finally laid down my sword, just gratitude that I wasn't in a far-flung war cemetery or a shallow grave out west.

After supper, Father and I settled into our chairs by the fire in the drawing room. The room was exactly as I remembered it, except there was a new dog in front of the hearth, and above the fireplace, in an ornate silver frame, stood a photograph of me as a young officer, clear-eyed and square-shouldered.

We talked late into the night as, outside, a blossom tree danced in the wind and the crickets clicked in the darkness. I told him of discovering the murders and how it all unfolded. As I spoke, the stony plains of the west appeared, divided by the shimmering brown river winding its way south, turtles suspended in the shallows, wallabies drinking as shafts of afternoon sunlight fell through the trees. White cockatoos screeched and fussed as they settled down for the night. Over by the fence a flock of sheep huddled, nibbling the grasses as through their skin, silently pushing out to the light, grew the golden fleece that bound us all.

Acknowledgements

This story takes place on the traditional lands of the Barkandji people, and I pay my respects to Elders past and present.

This is a work of fiction. However, the location is not, and it was the site of some of the harshest wool-growing practices in Australia during the nineteenth and early twentieth centuries. I have changed the names of the two main towns in the story, but – for now – the Darling River still flows. Augustus Hawkins is a fictional character, as is his war record. He is no Flashman. Rather, his experiences in the Boer War are an amalgamation of the many battles and skirmishes Australian soldiers were involved in.

Some Australians did sign on again and again, some fought under direct British command and some even fought on the side of the Boer. Many of these men were traumatised by their experiences and returned to a world that saw manifestations of trauma as moral weakness and failure of will. They suffered terribly, and I pay my respects to those men, and the women who cared for them.

Writing is mostly a solitary pursuit, but publishing a book is a collaborative venture, and so I'd like to thank Ruby Ashby-Orr, Elizabeth Robinson-Griffith and the team at Affirm Press. Also thank you to Julian Welch for his thoughtful editing and to Bill Bennell Kooyar Wongi for his reading.

Thanks to Penelope Edwell, curator at the Justice and Police Museum, Museums of History NSW, for her generous help. Also, a huge thank you to the indefatigable librarians at the Northern Beaches Council Library for their patience, professionalism and courtesy when dealing with my endless requests for obscure material through the Interlibrary Loans Service. Thank you, also, to the librarians at the State Library of NSW and the archivists at the NSW State Archives.

Thanks to the Sydney Faber Academy, Margo Lanagan and Gretchen Shirm and to my fellow participants in WAN 22 who have been so generous with their support.

Thanks also to my family and dear friends, both in Adelaide and Sydney, without whom I would not have lasted the distance.